NORTHBROOK PUBLIC
1201 CEDAR LA
NORTHBROOK, IL

P9-DNP-662

DISCARDED
Northbrook Public Library

3 1123 00808 2094

Praise for the Novels
of Karen White

"Heartwarming and intense . . . a tale that resonates with the meaning of unconditional love."   —*Romantic Times BOOKclub* (4 stars)

"A terrific insightful character study."   —*Midwest Book Review*

"A wonderful, touching story that will touch the heart of everyone who reads it."   —Writers Unlimited

"An amazingly emotional read!"   —The Best Reviews

"Kudos to Karen White for penning a wonderful, heartfelt novel that will be thoroughly enjoyed by fans of women's fiction."
—BookLoons

"*Pieces of the Heart* touches the heart and does not let go even after the last page has been turned. Karen White is an author on the rise."
—Book Cover Reviews

continued . . .

Written by today's freshest new talents and selected by New American Library, NAL Accent novels touch on subjects close to a woman's heart, from friendship to family to finding our place in the world. The Conversation Guides included in each book are intended to enrich the individual reading experience, as well as encourage us to explore these topics together—because books, and life, are meant for sharing.

Visit us online at www.penguin.com.

The Color of Light

"[White's] prose is lyrical, and she weaves in elements of mysticism and romance without being heavy-handed. This is an accomplished novel about loss and renewal, and readers will be taken with the people and stories of Pawleys Island." —*Booklist*

"The reader will hear the ocean roar and the seagulls scream as the past reluctantly gives up its ghosts in this beautiful, enticing, and engrossing novel." —*Romantic Times BOOKClub* (4½ stars)

"A story as rich as a coastal summer . . . dark secrets, heartache, a magnificent South Carolina setting, and a great love story."
—*New York Times* bestselling author Deborah Smith

"An engaging read with a delicious taste of the mysterious."
—*New York Times* bestselling author Haywood Smith

"Karen White's novel is as lush as the Lowcountry, where the characters' wounded souls come home to mend in unexpected and magical ways."
—Patti Callahan Henry, award-winning author of *When Light Breaks*

Praise for
Karen White

"The fresh voice of Karen White intrigues and delights."
—Sandra Chastain, contributor to *Blessings at Mossy Creek*

"Warmly Southern and deeply moving."
—Deborah Smith, author of *The Crossroads Café*

"Karen White writes with passion and poignancy."
—Deb Stover, award-winning author of *Mulligan Magic*

"[A] sweet book . . . highly recommended."   —*Booklist*

"Karen White is one author you won't forget. . . . This is a masterpiece in the study of relationships. Brava!"   —Reader to Reader Reviews

"This is not only romance at its best—this is a fully realized view of life at its fullest."   —Readers & Writers Ink Reviews

"*After the Rain* is an elegantly enchanting southern novel. . . . Fans will recognize the beauty of White's evocative prose."
—WordWeaving

"In the tradition of Catherine Anderson and Deborah Smith, Karen White's *After the Rain* is an incredibly poignant contemporary bursting with Southern charm."
—Patricia Rouse, Rouse's Romance Readers Groups

"Don't miss this book!"   —*Rendezvous*

"Character-driven and strongly written . . . *After the Rain* . . . marks Karen White as a rising star and an author to watch."
—*Romantic Times BOOKClub*

LEARNING

to

BREATHE

K A R E N   W H I T E

NAL
ACCENT   NEW AMERICAN LIBRARY

NAL Accent
Published by New American Library, a division of
Penguin Group (USA) Inc., 375 Hudson Street,
New York, New York 10014, USA
Penguin Group (Canada), 90 Eglinton Avenue East, Suite 700, Toronto,
Ontario M4P 2Y3, Canada (a division of Pearson Penguin Canada Inc.)
Penguin Books Ltd., 80 Strand, London WC2R 0RL, England
Penguin Ireland, 25 St. Stephen's Green, Dublin 2,
Ireland (a division of Penguin Books Ltd.)
Penguin Group (Australia), 250 Camberwell Road, Camberwell, Victoria 3124,
Australia (a division of Pearson Australia Group Pty. Ltd.)
Penguin Books India Pvt. Ltd., 11 Community Centre, Panchsheel Park,
New Delhi – 110 017, India
Penguin Group (NZ), 67 Apollo Drive, Mairangi Bay,
Auckland 1310, New Zealand (a division of Pearson New Zealand Ltd.)
Penguin Books (South Africa) (Pty.) Ltd., 24 Sturdee Avenue,
Rosebank, Johannesburg 2196, South Africa

Penguin Books Ltd., Registered Offices:
80 Strand, London WC2R 0RL, England

First published by NAL Accent, an imprint of New American Library,
a division of Penguin Group (USA) Inc.

First Printing, March 2007
1   3   5   7   9   10   8   6   2   4

Copyright © Karen White, 2007
Conversation Guide copyright © Penguin Group (USA) Inc., 2007
All rights reserved

ACCENT REGISTERED TRADEMARK—MARCA REGISTRADA

LIBRARY OF CONGRESS CATALOGING-IN-PUBLICATION DATA:
White, Karen (Karen S.)
Learning to breath/Karen White.
p. cm.
ISBN 978-0-451-22034-9
1. Single women—Fiction. 2. Life change events—Fiction. I. Title.
PS3623.H5776L43 2007
813'.6—dc22   2006032476

Set in Adobe Garamond
Designed by Ginger Legato

Printed in the United States of America

Without limiting the rights under copyright reserved above, no part of this publication may be reproduced, stored in or introduced into a retrieval system, or transmitted, in any form, or by any means (electronic, mechanical, photocopying, recording, or otherwise), without the prior written permission of both the copyright owner and the above publisher of this book.

PUBLISHER'S NOTE

This a work of fiction. Names, characters, places, and incidents either are the product of the author's imagination or are used fictitiously, and any resemblance to actual persons, living or dead, business establishments, events, or locales is entirely coincidental.

The publisher does not have any control over and does not assume any responsibility for author or third-party Web sites or their content.

The scanning, uploading, and distribution of this book via the Internet or via any other means without the permission of the publisher is illegal and punishable by law. Please purchase only authorized electronic editions, and do not participate in or encourage electronic piracy of copyrighted materials. Your support of the author's rights is appreciated.

With love to Tim,
for all that you do.

Acknowledgments

Writing a book is never easy, nor is it ever entirely a solitary process. Not only do I rely on the love and encouragement of my family, but also on the expertise and moral support of two talented authors who have the task of reading and critiquing my work before anybody else sees it.

So, as always, I'd like to thank the usual suspects: Tim, Meghan and Connor and also Susan Crandall and Wendy Wax. This would be a very lonely road without you!

Thanks also to my mother, Catherine Anne, and her sisters, Aunts Lulu, Janie, Gloria and Charlene, who have always been a great example of what a sister should be like. Your connection to each other was the basis for the strong ties between the O'Brien sisters in this book. And I promise that any other similarities are completely fictional!

CHAPTER I

The brittle, yellowed paper of the sealed envelope felt light and inconsequential in Brenna O'Brien's hand. Her fingers brushed the elegant, faded script on the front, and she marveled at how something so full of possibility could seem so fragile. Closing her eyes, she considered her thirty-three years for a moment, and realized how much her life resembled the unopened letter: unfulfilled possibilities and potential disappointments kept safe inside the heart of a woman who dared not lift the seal.

Slowly slipping the antique letter back inside the acid-free sleeve of her scrapbook, she closed the cover and turned toward her dresser. She slid open the top drawer, listening to the rustle of forty-two silver chains, shimmying against each other. Recalling her date the previous evening, she fingered through the pile of chains, then pulled out her Saint Jude medal and hung it around her neck. After last night, the patron saint of hopeless causes would be her constant companion.

Blotting perspiration from her forehead with a tissue, she grabbed her purse and headed for the door of her small apartment inside the large, antebellum home she shared with her landlady and two other tenants. Downstairs, she taped a note to Mrs. Grodin on her apartment door about her nonfunctioning air-conditioning unit, then continued out the main door of the old house. She blasted the air conditioner in her bright yellow VW Bug as soon as she started the engine, halfheartedly wondering if there was a way to fit in the backseat to sleep.

Pulling out onto Magnolia Drive, she drove the four blocks to her sister's store, passing the neat shotgun cottages and pastel-colored houses lined up like little old ladies dressed for church that defined the town of Indianola, Louisiana. Fat bundles of pink and red blossoms hung heavily from the crape myrtles that filled the median on Main Street, creating a backdrop to the old shops and restaurants that lined the sidewalks on either side. She waved to people she had known all her life as she drove past the library, Indianola Elementary, and the house she had grown up in and where her eldest sister, Kathleen, now lived with her family.

It was unremarkable in its familiarity, a pleasing frame around the picture of Brenna's life of nothing special. Except for those two brief years after she'd turned sixteen and her world had shimmered with possibility, her life had become as simple and uncomplicated as a slice of white bread. Perhaps this was her penance for a sin committed by her birth, but weighing it over in her mind, as she did so frequently, she always came to the conclusion that this was the life she was meant to live. She had learned well the lessons of Catholic guilt and atonement at her father's knee, and it was now as much a part of her as breathing.

Easily parallel parking her car in front of Mary Margaret's Motivations and Grocery Emporium, she stepped out, paused for a moment to garner emotional strength, then entered her sister's shop.

The bell above the door tinkled as Brenna breathed in the rich aromas of brewing coffee and heavy incense. Mary Margaret spent a month in India on missionary trips with her husband each year, bringing back all sorts of scents, spices, and general gewgaws to sell in her store. Not that there was much business in Indianola for statues of Shiva or miniature carvings of people posed in positions from the Kama Sutra. These last, Brenna knew, were kept in a drawer behind the counter, as it wouldn't do for the Baptist minister's wife to be displaying such things on the shelves in her shop.

"Hey, Mary Margaret—it's just me." Brenna eased her way down a crowded aisle toward the front counter, past the chewing tobacco and insect repellent and an eight-armed goddess from whose outstretched fingers hung Mardi Gras beads and a sack of beef jerky sticks.

"Hey, yourself, baby sister," Mary Margaret said as Brenna emerged from the jungle of retail offerings. "Grab a seat and I'll get you some caffeine."

Gratefully, Brenna perched on the vinyl stool directly under the air-conditioning vent, and watched her sister sprinkle a dark powder into her cup before pouring the coffee. Although ten years older than Brenna, Mary Margaret appeared much younger than her forty-three years. With her light brown hair in a single braid down her back, and wearing a bright purple-and-gold sari, she could be a high schooler ripped out of the sixties and dumped in the new millennium. Although she wore a white T-shirt underneath to hide her stomach, it never ceased to amaze Brenna that the minister's wife could be allowed to roam around town in such a getup.

Without turning around, Mary Margaret asked, "Did you go to confession this morning? I hear you and Chester Anderson were out late last night."

Brenna rolled her eyes. "Did Mrs. Grodin call you this morning?"

Mary Margaret turned around to face her sister, a steaming cup in her hands. "Nope. Mr. Northcutt from across the street called me to report that he had seen Chester kissing you on the front porch of Mrs. Grodin's boardinghouse at around twelve o'clock in the morning."

"Mr. Northcutt needs to get a life. I refuse to be his only source of entertainment. Luckily Chester only slobbered on my ear, because I turned my head. And, no, I will not be going out with him again."

Leaning forward, Mary Margaret lifted the chain from Brenna's neck and raised an eyebrow. "Hopeless causes, hmm?"

Brenna raised her own eyebrow in response. Taking the proffered cup, she raised it to her nose, sniffed deeply, and changed the subject. "Is Richard still fending off the church ladies?"

Mary Margaret leaned her elbows on the counter, clasping her beringed fingers under her chin. "Well, they finally stopped telling him that he was going to hell since he married a Catholic. Now they just take issue with my brews and potions. Not that they've never taken advantage of any of them, of course." She winked. "I'd starve without their business."

Brenna took a sip of her coffee and studied her sister carefully—the way her skin glowed and her hair shone and her soft, willowy body reflected joy and contentment. Slowly Brenna put her cup down, feeling the old familiar heartburn that had nothing to do with food.

"Was it all worth it? From Daddy's disowning you to all the anonymous hate mail—have you ever regretted marrying Richard?"

Mary Margaret stayed where she was, but her bright blue eyes darkened. "Not for a moment. Not even once in the last ten years." Reaching over, as if Brenna were still a little girl, she pushed her sister's hair out of her eyes. "You take the good with the bad—for that's the stuff that life's made of." Pausing, she squinted closely at her youngest sister, like a surgeon before cutting. "Your date must really have been bad. I'll pass the message along to Kathleen that she's been fired from the blind-date business." She gave Brenna a discerning look. "Your hair needs cutting—you're hiding those gorgeous green eyes. And what have you been using to clean your face? Looks like you could use a good exfoliator."

"Soap, water, and a rag," Brenna answered. "I seem to be at the age when I'm getting pimples and wrinkles at the same time. Do I put the zit cream on top of the wrinkle cream or is it the other way around?"

The bell over the door chimed and they both turned toward it, but whoever had entered the store had already disappeared down one of the aisles.

Mary Margaret turned back to her younger sister. "I have something that I just brought back from India that I think would be perfect. It neutralizes the oils in your skin while deep-cleansing the pores and moisturizing the places where your skin needs it most."

Brenna smoothed the floral chiffon of her nearly transparent blouse, a gift from another sister that neither suited her body nor her taste, and tried to act more animated than she felt. "If it's free, I'll try it."

An innocent smile crossed Mary Margaret's face. "Hang on just a minute while I go in the back to get it. It's kind of rare, so I don't keep it out. But I swear you'll love it."

She disappeared behind a beaded curtain, the long ropes gyrating in her wake. Brenna took another sip of coffee as she waited, then casually turned on her stool to see who else was in the store with them. She could hear whoever it was rustling about in one of the shelves, so she knew they hadn't left. But it was unusual for a customer not to call a greeting when they walked in.

Her attention was distracted by Mary Margaret's reappearance.

"Got it! It's a mask, so we need to smear it on and then let it sit for about ten minutes."

Brenna eyed the squat, unlabeled glass jar filled with what seemed to be a white petroleum jelly. "I've got to be at the theater by ten to place my concessions order. Can you have me cleaned up in time?"

Mary Margaret's smile didn't dim. "Not a problem. I've been told by more than one person that I'm a miracle worker." She twisted the lid open.

Brenna screwed up her nose. "What is it?"

Mary Margaret stuck a finger in the jar. "To be honest, I'm not really sure—mainly flower extracts and distilled seeds, I guess. I did try it on my own skin and it didn't turn me the color of a chili pepper, so I figure it's okay."

"Wonderful. That's very encouraging. I guess if nobody comes to my theater to watch the movie, they can at least come to see the human chili pepper." Instead of moving away, Brenna stayed where she was, ready for yet another onslaught of a sister's mission to change her. As the youngest of five girls, she had long since grown used to it.

Mary Margaret reached over to spread the white cream across Brenna's cheeks and nose. It was cold and slimy and smelled surprisingly like marigolds. Her sister smiled. "I wouldn't worry about that, Brenn—I've got something for rashes, too."

Brenna sat frozen, unable to retreat any farther without falling off the stool. "How comforting." Her sister pulled back Brenna's hair and began spreading the cream on her forehead. Closing her eyes in resignation, Brenna said, "I can't believe I'm letting you do this to me. You'd think I'd learned my lesson after Claire's vitamin incident." She tried not to shudder as she recalled another sister's run-in with one of Mary Margaret's vitamin concoctions. It had made Claire so energetic and refreshed that it had led to late-in-life twins.

Mary Margaret's warm breath brushed the top of Brenna's head as she leaned forward to make sure the cream was spread evenly. "And Claire thanks me every day for Mary Sanford and Peyton Charles. It just took her a while to get used to the idea, that's all."

Brenna smothered a laugh as she felt a cold glob of the cream on the end of her nose, threatening to drip. "Just don't ever do that to me. If I ever wake up in bed next to Chester Anderson, I might have to kill you."

They both started laughing and stopped only when they heard a soft cough behind them. A deep voice, with only remnants of a Southern accent still clinging to it, said, "Excuse me. Can you tell me where I can pay for these?"

The two sisters turned in unison to face a tall man with a day's worth of dark beard stubble on his cheeks. He held a bag of disposable razors and a can of shaving cream, the current edition of the *Indianola Post* crunched under an arm.

Brenna blinked twice, feeling the air leave her lungs like a rapidly deflating balloon. *Oh, Lord.* It really was him. She blinked again just to make sure, staring at the once-familiar features and feeling the heartburn congeal in her chest again.

He hadn't changed at all. His dark brown hair carried a few gray strands around the temples, and laugh lines framed blue eyes in a deeply tanned face, but he was still the same. He had lost any hint of boyhood in those narrow cheeks, and his eyes most certainly didn't stare out at the world with unbridled enthusiasm as they once had. They were guarded now, and darker, as if a curtain had been drawn down over them.

He gave her a reluctant smile. "Hello, Brenna."

Mary Margaret tilted her head as she looked at the man. "Do we know you?"

He turned to Mary Margaret. "Brenna and I went to high school together." He juggled the items in his arms and stretched a hand out to her. "I'm Pierce McGovern."

Mary Margaret's eyes widened in recognition as she pumped his hand up and down. "Oh! Of course I remember you! You and Brenna, well . . ." She looked at Brenna, then stopped. "You're Dr. McGovern's son, then. I heard you were coming back in town to move him into the nursing home. He's a dear man—delivered my two oldest."

"Yes, well. It's good to see you. Both of you." He indicated the items in his hand. "I just took the red-eye from San Francisco and drove in from Houston, so I'm a bit bushed. If I could just pay for these . . ."

"Of course! The cash register's over here." Mary Margaret led the way to the far end of the counter.

Brenna stared after them, trying to find her breath before she passed out and slid off the vinyl stool. She concentrated on the back of his shirt, rumpled and travel-weary like its wearer, and suddenly smelled Polo cologne and the crushed velvet upholstery of the backseat of Dr. McGovern's Buick.

Mary Margaret placed Pierce's purchases in a small brown paper bag and slid it across the counter with a wide smile. "It sure is good to see you, Pierce. Please tell your daddy I said hey—and we'd love to have you both over for Sunday dinner. The whole family gathers every Sunday after eleven-o'clock Mass at Kathleen's house—that's our oldest sister—and we'd love to have you join us." She gave her youngest sister a pointed look. "And Brenna will be there, too, so you can catch up on old times. They're at six-fifteen Shelby Street, right next to the fire station." She waved at the air. "But you probably already know that. We'd love to see you." She winked. "Just bring your sneakers. The fellows always end up playing a game of touch football in the front yard, so I want you to be prepared."

Pierce cleared his throat and lifted the sack. "As much as I'd love to catch up with Brenna, I really don't know what my schedule's going to be. . . ."

Brenna wondered if her sister could hear the desperation in his voice.

Mary Margaret stopped him by putting a hand on his forearm. "Nothing's ever going on around here on Sunday, I promise. We'll just set out a couple extra plates, no problem. So y'all come on by, you hear?"

With a weak smile, he nodded, offered his thanks again, and then turned away. He caught sight of Brenna and stopped. As if of its own accord, the corner of his mouth twitched. He pointed to his own nose and said, "You're dripping."

A large clump of mask chose that moment to loosen its hold on her nose and fall to her lap. A full-fledged smile spread over his lips as he turned away. Brenna sat, unmoving, until she heard the tinkle of the bell over the door. In horror, she reached her hands to her face, belatedly realizing what she must look like.

Slowly but deliberately, she leaned forward until her masked forehead touched the cool laminate. Her Saint Jude medal slipped out of her collar, clinking against the counter as Brenna began to laugh until she cried.

CHAPTER 2

As soon as the door shut behind him, Pierce reluctantly allowed a laugh to escape. He didn't want to, but there had always been something about Brenna O'Brien that made his ears tingle in a completely involuntary reaction to her smile. But that had been when he was young and stupid and still believed the best of people—especially women. Cynicism had come early and cheap for him, brought to him on the smooth, trim heels of a younger Brenna O'Brien.

He tossed his package onto the empty passenger seat of the rental car, then slid behind the wheel. After starting the engine, he looked back at the large plate-glass window of the store. He should have left the second he recognized her voice. But like quicksand, it had pulled at him, sucking him into an encounter he had studiously avoided for almost sixteen years. Steering away from the curb, he gunned the engine, eager to put it all behind him, almost glad it was finally over. That done, he wouldn't have to think about her or see her until his dad's affairs were settled and he was completely immersed in the plans for his company's new multiplex theater.

Slowly, he drove around Indianola, passing the World War II memorial in the main square, then pausing in front of the house where he'd grown up. Because he was an only child, the neighborhood children had been his siblings, their mothers his surrogates in the absence of his own, who had left him and his father when he was eight. He stared at the fat oak tree in the corner of the property, grown taller and wider since he had last seen it, the thick roots pushing through the grass toward the sidewalk. He felt a special affinity with the old tree. They had both grown, shifting their roots to accommodate a new maturity. But seeing the roots meet the unyielding cement of the sidewalk, Pierce wondered if he, too, had found an insurmountable barrier in his life.

Pierce moved his gaze to the house. Despite new owners and a new shade of paint on the shutters, the house was the same. If he closed his eyes he could almost see a cluster of children playing kickball on the sparse grass of the front yard, and a younger, barefoot Brenna O'Brien fleeing across the grass, terrorized by a butterfly.

Shaking his head to clear it, he pressed down on the accelerator and drove to the nearby town of Greenwood, where his father had moved shortly after Pierce had left for college. It had been closer to the hospital, making the commute less of a burden on the aging doctor. Pierce hadn't imagined that leaving the house where the only memories of his mother lived would hurt as much as it had. But at least the move also meant that he wouldn't have to spend any time in Indianola on his rare visits home.

Pulling into the covered carport of his dad's house, he shut the engine off and paused, listening to the high-pitched screech of the cicadas growing in intensity with the steady rise of the day's heat. This was a hard trip. Moving his father into a nursing home was an admission of the old doctor's growing frailty and inevitable mortality. His father was the last hold on his youth, and one that Pierce had thought he'd never have to let go.

When nobody answered his knock on the front door, Pierce opened it himself and walked into the foyer. He had hired a full-time housekeeper, but she wasn't expected until eleven. Following the sound of the TV, Pierce found his father asleep in his recliner, his head tilted back and his breathing coming in intermittent snores.

Pierce walked over to the television and flipped it off. His father stirred and opened his eyes, his face warming into a smile as he recognized his son. With shaking arms, he lowered the foot of the recliner and struggled to stand before embracing Pierce.

Pierce towered over his father, shocked at how small and brittle the once powerful man with a soldier's build had become. For the first time, Pierce noticed the walker on the other side of the recliner and the lamp table covered with pill bottles. A wave of guilt and anxiety washed over him when he realized how long it had really been since his last visit.

"It's good to see you, Dad."

The old man sat back gratefully in his chair. "Good to see you, too, son. Sorry I didn't get the door, but I sat down to catch the news and I guess I fell asleep."

Pierce looked at his father with concern. "Have you had breakfast?"

He squinted for a moment as if thinking hard, then said, "I'm not sure. I don't think so."

Moving the walker in front of the chair, Pierce said, "I'll go make us something to eat and then we can talk."

The old man nodded as Pierce retreated into the surprisingly well-stocked kitchen and began making grits and bacon. The smell reminded him of Saturdays when his father would get up early to make him breakfast, and Pierce would lie in bed letting the aroma pull him out from under the covers.

They sat down at the small kitchen table that still bore the marks of his childhood—dents from falling blocks, number two pencils, and skateboard wheels.

Pierce tried his best to inject a cheerful tone. "Dr. Fitz told me Liberty Village is a great place. Lots of activities and excursions. And a library. I knew you'd like that."

His father nodded and put a forkful of grits in his mouth.

"They have shuttle services to the mall and a movie theater, too."

Again, his father nodded and continued to chew without saying anything.

Pierce took a few bites and they ate in silence for a few moments. Finally, his father said, "I'm sorry to hear about you and Diana."

Pierce looked closer at the older man, wondering if he'd see any "I told you so" in his eyes. Instead, all he saw was true compassion. "Yeah, well, thanks. I guess I'm not very good with relationships."

"What happened?"

Pierce shrugged. "Just . . . nothing. Everything." He looked at his father and didn't think either one of them really had the energy to listen to the truth. Shaking his head, he said, "It didn't work out."

"Maybe she wasn't the one for you."

Pierce took a bite and took his time chewing and avoiding his father's gaze. "Maybe."

The doctor leaned back in his chair, his eyes discerning but kind. "Did you make it easy for her to go?"

Pushing back from the table, Pierce avoided looking at the older man, knowing they both recognized the truth. "I don't think I'd end a marriage just to prove a point, Dad. I don't think that was it at all. We were just . . . incompatible."

His father looked at him with steely eyes, and Pierce knew he hadn't fooled him a bit. "I see."

Standing, Pierce began to clear the table. "I guess our first order of business is to visit your apartment at the Village to determine how much space you'll have. Then we'll know better what we can keep and what we'll need to get rid of."

The old doctor sat back in his chair with a mug of coffee and continued watching his son, the gray eyes missing nothing and making Pierce feel five years old again.

Brenna unlocked the sliding gate in front of the Royal Majestic Theater and tugged hard to open it. It was getting rusty and needed painting, and she made a mental note to add it to the growing list of things she couldn't afford to fix.

Still, when she had slid the wrought-iron gate and chained it open, she couldn't help but smile. The gleaming mahogany of the ticket office and the wainscoting in the foyer smelled of fresh polish, and the black-and-white tiled floor, though chipped in places, gave the small theater a decidedly elegant air. She touched the large brick on the wall with reverence, as she had done every day for the last five years she'd been the manager and owner. It read 1939, the year the first film shown in the theater had been released. Glancing around at the towering ceilings and brass chandeliers, Brenna knew that her little theater had been grand enough to host even Vivien Leigh and Clark Gable.

"Good morning, Miss O'Brien."

Startled, Brenna swung around and spotted Beau Ward, the tall, skinny teenager who worked as her assistant manager whenever he wasn't in school. "I thought we'd agreed that you'd call me Brenna." She continued on inside, unlocking the double glass doors that led into the carpeted lobby and concession area.

She faced him again in time to see his cheeks coloring, accentuating the patches of acne on his high cheekbones. "Well, on account of you being unmarried and kinda old, my mama said I needed to be more formal and call you Miss O'Brien. I hope that's okay with you."

Staring at him a moment, she decided against the long speech she'd whipped up about how she wasn't so old or how being unmarried in no way meant that she was ready for the glue factory. With a sigh, she said, "That's fine, Beau. I'm sure your mama is right."

Brenna stepped behind the counter and grabbed two Nestlé Crunch bars and handed one to Beau. "Want one?"

The boy's face brightened as he reached for it. "Thanks." He ripped open the candy bar and took a bite, lopping it nearly in half. "If it's any help, Miss O'Brien, my mama can't understand why you're not married. She says you're real pretty." He held up the candy bar. "And you're nice, too. You know, my mama was talking about maybe setting up a date with you and my uncle. . . ."

Brenna held up her hand, trying to keep the look of horror out of her eyes. "I'm only nice while I'm here. At home I collect heads and shrink them in a big pot on my stove."

Beau looked startled for a moment, then gave her a tentative smile. "You're joking, right?"

"Sure," Brenna said, throwing a meaningful look over her shoulder. "I've got a bunch of boxes that need to be opened, and this counter restocked. When you're done, bring me a list of things we'll need to order. We've been pretty busy, and they cleaned us out of Junior Mints last weekend."

Plopping the rest of the candy bar in his mouth, Beau nodded and disappeared into the storeroom behind the counter. As Brenna began to walk across the lobby to her office, she heard a car pull up outside and recognized her sister Claire's white Cadillac. Claire stepped out and waved, her white nurse's shoes padding quietly across the marble floor. The second oldest in the O'Brien clan, Claire stood about a head shorter than Brenna's five-five and wore her hair in a perfect French twist. Even though her ash blond hair came from a bottle, she still referred to herself as the only blonde in the family.

Claire kissed her younger sister on both cheeks, European-style. "I can't chat. I'm on my way to the hospital." She stared closely at Brenna, squinting at something on her forehead near her hairline. "You've got something in your hair."

Brenna's hand went up and she felt the crustiness of the dry facial mask. "That would be Mary Margaret's mask. Does my skin at least look better?"

Claire scrutinized her younger sister again. Finally she said, "I think so. Maybe your crusty hair is just throwing my judgment a bit."

Scraping her hair with her fingernails, Brenna said, "I need to get to work. Is there anything you need?"

"Yes—I wanted to remind you that the scrapbooking party is at my house on Monday at seven, and I wanted to ask if you could bring a salty snack. I know it's early, but Buzz and I are going away this weekend while Kathleen takes the kids, and I'm just crossing things off my to-do list. We'll be back in time for Sunday supper."

Still watching flakes floating down from her hair, Brenna said, "Sure, not a problem. I'll be there."

Claire started to walk away but Brenna called her back. "Would you mind sending Buzz over later? My Roach Motels are full and need changing. Tell him I'll have beer in the fridge."

"Sure. I'll tell him. I'd do it myself, but I have to take Mary Sanford for her fitting for the Little Miss Crawfish Pageant costumes." She stopped. "Oh, I think I have another date potential for you. Do you remember Buddy Halbert?"

Brenna scrunched up her nose, trying to recall a face. "Sort of. He had cousins in town, didn't he? And they sometimes used to visit in the summers."

Claire brightened. "That's right. Well, he's started to work as a salesman for Buzz's company, and I think he's just darling. I'll give him your number." With a quick step she walked toward her car before Brenna could protest.

A sudden recollection came to mind, and Brenna called out to her sister's retreating back, "Wasn't he the one involved in some kind of a hunting accident a while back?" Claire just waved and disappeared behind the tinted glass of her windshield.

Feeling something clench in the pit of her stomach, Brenna turned

away and retreated to her office. First, she'd wash the front of her hair
to get the rest of the dried mask out; second, she'd find the poster for
The Lake House to place in the large glass display box out front; third,
she'd make a note to not answer her phone for the rest of the week in
case Buddy Halbert decided to call.

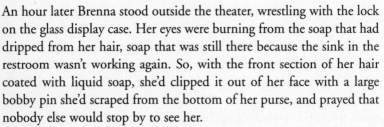

An hour later Brenna stood outside the theater, wrestling with the lock
on the glass display case. Her eyes were burning from the soap that had
dripped from her hair, soap that was still there because the sink in the
restroom wasn't working again. So, with the front section of her hair
coated with liquid soap, she'd clipped it out of her face with a large
bobby pin she'd scraped from the bottom of her purse, and prayed that
nobody else would stop by to see her.

"Hello?"

For the second time that day, Brenna felt her mouth go dry and her
toes curl at the sound of Pierce McGovern's voice.

He seemed as startled to see her as she was to see him. "You work
here?"

She nodded before finding her voice. "Yes. I do." She spied the older
man in the wheelchair next to his son. "Dr. McGovern, it's good to see
you again. I haven't seen you in Indianola for a very long time."

The doctor's eyes warmed as he nodded. "No, but it's good to be
back. Pierce is here to settle me into Liberty Village, and I'm using him
to help me take a walk down memory lane. If I'd known I'd bump into
you, I would have done it much sooner."

Brenna took his wrinkled hand in her own and then gave him a peck
on the cheek. He held tightly to her fingers, not allowing her to step
back.

Color infused her cheeks. "That's sweet of you to say. I can't believe
you remember me."

He smiled up at her, his hand surprisingly strong around hers.
"You're as pretty as your mama, you know. And that's certainly not a
face anybody could forget." He still clung tightly, not allowing her to
step back. "Isn't she pretty, Pierce?"

"Prettiest girl in town." He even sounded as if he meant it.

His words made her want to cry. *Prettiest girl in town.* How many times had he said that to her a million years ago? She was saved from saying anything when Dr. McGovern spoke.

"Your father and I never saw eye-to-eye, but your mother and I were good friends. I delivered you, remember. I'd never seen such bright red hair or heard such squawking." He squinted at her strawberry blond locks, wrinkling his forehead a bit when his gaze settled on the soapy spot. "I see the color's calmed down some. Do you still squawk when you're angry at the world?"

Concentrating on the old doctor and ignoring his son by his side, she said, "Only sometimes." She squeezed his hand and he finally released her.

The doctor wheeled his chair around to face his son. "Pierce—it's Brenna. I know you remember her."

Pierce gave a quick, succinct nod. "Yes, I do. Haven't stayed in touch, though." Brenna avoided looking at him by staring at the poster in her hand, and thought the tortured expression of Keanu Reeves might match her own.

When he didn't say anything else, Brenna forced herself to look up into Pierce's cool blue eyes. "We had a few classes together." *Only home-room, chemistry, and film club. And we ate lunch together every day at eleven forty-five.*

Pierce stared back, unblinking. "Actually, I ran into Brenna earlier. She had something on her face." His gaze traveled up to her forehead and to the soapy hair, and his mouth quirked.

Brenna felt herself coloring again and quickly looked away. Dr. McGovern wheeled himself in between them. "Your sister Kathleen called me and invited us to Sunday supper at her house. We'll be there and then we can catch up. I'm sure Pierce would like that, too."

As Pierce nodded, his gaze settled on her hair again, and he opened his mouth to say something. Instead he closed it for a moment, then said, "Never mind. I know better than to ask."

She watched as he tilted his head back to study her theater, taking in the huge marquee with the broken lights, and the iron lions sitting sentry at the entranceway, their black paint peeling, and seemed to consider it for a while. Then he looked back at her and said, "I guess this means we'll see you Sunday." He made a sudden move with his hand, as if he wanted to brush the hair out of her face that had fallen from the bobby pin, but he stopped in midair, as if just realizing he had almost touched her. Instead he gestured for the key in her hand that she let him have.

He inserted it into the lock on the poster case and pushed hard on the frame with his other hand, jostling the key until the case popped open. He handed back the key with a boyish grin. "I used to work here during the summers, remember? Guess I haven't lost my touch."

"Thanks," she said, trying not to recall summer nights sitting in the back row of the darkened theater, aware of everything and nothing except for Pierce McGovern sitting beside her.

"You're welcome." He stared at her for a long moment, as if waiting for her to say something else. When she didn't, he turned from her and put his hands on his father's wheelchair.

She nodded and somehow managed a smile as they both said their good-byes, then watched Pierce walk away pushing his father's chair. She would be fine. As long as she could force herself not to look at Pierce and remember.

If only she could.

Wearing only her functional cotton underwear and a long T-shirt, Brenna lay in bed, unable to sleep. She could almost taste the heat pressing down on her, nearly obliterating the sound of the tap-tapping of some huge insect as it pounded against her closed window.

With resignation, she got out of bed, pulling the shirt away from her chest where the sweat made it stick. Mrs. Grodin hadn't answered her door or repeated phone calls from Brenna asking for mercy. She pictured the woman now, a large bulk curled under the covers of her bed with her air-conditioning unit blowing crisp, cool air over her sleeping form. Out of sheer frustration and orneriness, Brenna let her apartment door slam behind her, hoping she'd awakened every single air-conditioned resident in the house.

Stomping downstairs to the kitchen, she grabbed a glass, filled it with ice from the freezer, and then poured water from a pitcher in the fridge. Lifting her T-shirt in the darkened kitchen, she placed the cold glass on her stomach, sighing with relief.

Letting herself out of the main door, she crossed the front porch and stood in front of the large swing to check for bugs. Satisfied, she sat down, pulled her legs up, and rested her head on her knees. A sticky breeze blew through the large mimosa tree that brushed against the side of the house, rustling the leaves like a hushed conversation that Brenna couldn't quite hear.

She took a long sip of water, feeling the iciness drip down her throat, while her other hand fiddled with the Saint Jude medal that still hung from her neck. There was some relief in knowing that Pierce would be gone soon. Then she could resume her life as a calm, efficient theater manager, and of horrific dates that left her too scarred to feel numb.

Staring out into the warm summer sky, she waited for a single star to take shape and pulsate, to enlarge itself and move closer and let Brenna know it was okay to wish. But the stars remained cold and remote, tiny specks tucked under the dark cover of the night sky. If she could wish, she'd wish for life's instruction booklet. Something to tell her whether this was what her life was meant to be. Whether life was supposed to be lived for one shining moment, a single chance that would alter the course of your life forever. And if after that moment, one was relegated to sit and wait for life's final breath that signaled all the joy, pain, and penance were over.

Slowly she took the Saint Jude necklace off and let the chain slip through her fingers before landing with a soft clatter on the floorboards beneath. She pressed her damp eyes into her knees, ignoring the empty space on her chest where the medal had been, and wondered how many prayers she had sent up into the night sky in the last sixteen years, and why the saints never seemed to hear her.

CHAPTER 3

Brenna slid the ice cube from one ear to the other, letting the chill water drip down her neck onto her chest. It might actually have been a sensual moment if the dousing had been done by someone else and if it hadn't been so damned hot.

A quick rap on the door made the ice cube slip from her fingers and slide down her chest, neatly wedging itself into the top of her black lace bra. She pulled her blouse away from her chest and peered down at the delicate wisps of black lace. Her visits to victoriassecret.com were her only extravagance, and one that was unlikely ever to be discovered. This particular extravagance was the Desire model and had set her back forty-four dollars plus shipping. It had been worth every penny.

She tried to flick out the cube of ice as she stood and approached the door. "Who is it?" Her fingers managed to push it farther down into the slip of black lace that dipped into her cleavage.

"It's Dooley, Brenna. Colleen said you were having some trouble with your air conditioner, so Bill sent me over to take a look."

Maybe having so many sisters wasn't such a bad thing after all— especially a sister who was married to the man who owned the local hardware store. With a shout that closely resembled glee, she unlocked the dead bolt and pulled open the door.

Dooley's eyes immediately went to her chest, where one hand was still entrenched trying to fish out the ice cube. The blouse was drenched from the melting ice, clinging to places it had no business clinging.

She gave him a bright smile. "Come on in—the unit's over there by the bed. I need to go change."

Making a hasty retreat, she grabbed a shirt off the stack of folded laundry still sitting in a basket waiting to be put away, and disappeared into the bathroom.

When she emerged, Dooley Gambrel had already removed the unit from the window and had pried off the back. Not for the first time, Brenna marveled at how very little he had changed since kindergarten. He still wore his medium brown hair cut short above his ears and parted on one side. His nose carried a smattering of freckles, and his light brown eyes still lit up whenever he saw her. He was one of those few people who could be recognized by their baby pictures. Growing up had consisted of growing bigger and older, but not necessarily different.

Squatting down, Dooley shook his head. "It doesn't look good. I'll take it into the shop, but I think this dog is dead."

Brenna sat down heavily in her desk chair. "And if I need a new one, it'll take Mrs. Grodin about a decade to get around to it." She pressed her forehead against the chair's tall back. "Just shoot me now and put me out of my misery."

Dooley stood, a sweet smile on his face. "I could never do that, Brenn. How 'bout I just bring up the loaner from my truck and you can use it free of charge until Mrs. Grodin gets you a new AC?"

Feeling more joy and excitement than she'd felt in a lifetime of Christmas mornings, she leaped up and swung her arms around Dooley's neck, then kissed him on the cheek. "You are my knight in shining armor! How can I ever thank you?"

Dooley's face darkened about three shades as he searched for a suitable place to put his hands. With a shaky smile, he said, "You could marry me."

Brenna hugged him again, then stepped back. "Yeah, yeah, yeah. Stop leading me on. You know we could never get married. Our children would be too good-looking and too smart and all the other parents would be jealous. It just wouldn't be fair."

"Yeah, I guess you're right." He reached over and tugged on her ponytail like he'd been doing since the first day of kindergarten. Shoving his hands into the pockets of his jeans, he said, "Oh, I almost forgot. I found this under the swing on the front porch. Thought it might be yours."

He held out his callused hand and showed her the Saint Jude medal on its silver chain.

With fingernails that had been bitten down to the quick, she picked it up, letting it dangle in front of her. "Yeah. It's mine. Guess I forgot I'd taken it off."

Dooley squinted at it to get a closer look. "Which one is that?"

Sliding it over her head, she said, "It's Saint Jude. Patron saint of hopeless causes."

He tilted his head, looking at her closely. "Looks like I could use one of those, too."

Brenna nudged him gently with the flat of her hand. "Aw, come on, Dooley. There's never been a piece of machinery you couldn't make better. I have every faith that you'll be able to fix my air conditioner. And if you can't fix it, then nobody can."

He stared at her with his gentle brown eyes for a long moment before speaking. "Well, I'd best get this one loaded into the truck and I'll bring the other one up."

"I'll help." Brenna grabbed a pair of sneakers and slipped them on her feet.

With lots of grunts and groaning, they managed to take the broken air-conditioning unit out the front door and into the driveway, where his pickup was parked. Brenna had wanted to leave it in front of Mrs. Grodin's apartment for her to trip over, but Dooley had talked her out of it.

As he unhooked the tailgate, Dooley said, "I ran into Pierce McGovern at the gas station yesterday. I don't think I've seen him since his daddy moved away after his high school graduation."

Brenna concentrated on loading the old unit into the truck and then grasping the new air conditioner and sliding it forward on the truck bed. "Yeah. I saw him yesterday. He's here to get his father settled into Liberty Village."

"Were you glad to see him again?"

Brenna stopped and stared at him. "Why would I be? It's not like we've kept in touch."

Dooley kept quiet.

"What?"

"Nothing. Just that I remember how you two were in high school, that's all."

"That was a long time ago, Doo. I hardly remember anything from back then."

He grunted as he shifted the weight of the unit before backing up the front steps. "You know he's divorced now."

She focused on her feet in studied nonchalance as she struggled up the stairs. "No, I didn't know. Like I said, we haven't kept in touch."

Dooley let out a grunt. "It was in all the tabloids. Irreconcilable differences. That's what that talk-show host he married said. So she left him." He blinked, trying to keep the sweat from dripping in his eyes.

Brenna stumbled and Dooley stopped, giving them both a rest. Brenna could no longer feign disinterest. "Really? That was the only reason she gave?"

Dooley waited to answer until they were up in the apartment and the new unit was safely installed in the window. He took out a bandanna from his back pocket and wiped his forehead. "Yep. As far as I can tell, though you never can believe everything you read." He shoved the bandanna back into his jeans. "I don't know if you've ever seen her show, but she seems nice enough."

Brenna turned her back on him as she went to the bathroom sink and filled two glasses with tap water. She waited until she was sure her expression was in control before turning around again and handing Dooley his glass. "I might have seen it once or twice. I thought she was trying too hard to be like Oprah—which doesn't make sense, because everybody knows that women don't want to take advice from a skinny woman."

"I thought she was kinda pretty." Dooley took a long sip, his eyes never leaving Brenna's face.

"I guess—if you like that petite, blond type." She turned around to refill her glass, glad to be able to hide her face.

"She's not blond, Brenn. She's got the same color hair you do—reddish blond—and she's about your size, too."

Brenna emptied out her glass in the sink, watching the water spiral down into the drain. "Whatever. I guess I never paid that much attention."

He handed her his glass. "Yeah, well. I gotta go. You need to be rescued from Kathleen's on Sunday again? I could be there by two."

"Make it two thirty. Aunt Dottie's going to be there, and I want to make sure we have a chance to chat. That will give me plenty of time to eat, talk, and skedaddle before whatever Romeo my sisters have invited can make the moves on me." *And before I find myself in the same room with Pierce McGovern.*

Dooley regarded her silently for a moment, as if he had heard her unspoken words. Then he winked before he turned toward the door. "I'll be there. Maybe we could go watch *The Lake House* or something. I haven't seen it yet."

She held the door open for him. "Sure. Anything's better than being hit on by some guy at a family gathering while everybody watches like they're at some freak show."

Dooley paused for a moment at the door, his soft brown eyes measuring. Without a word he turned and left. Calling over his shoulder, he said, "See ya Sunday."

Smiling, she closed her door, thankful for his unfailing friendship and wondering what in the world she'd do without him if he ever got married.

Brenna drove from St. Andrew's Catholic Church to Kathleen's house with her nephew Timmy, Colleen's eldest, riding shotgun. Although she'd never admit it to anyone, because she really did love all her nieces and nephews, eight-year-old Timmy was her favorite. He had hair the color of Halloween pumpkins and freckles that dotted his face from forehead to chin, and if the Olympics had a category for worrying, Timmy would be a three-time gold medalist.

His parents had taken him to a child psychologist to find out why his personality bordered on the glass-half-empty side of the fence, and to teach him how to cope with life, but nothing had seemed to stick.

But, to Brenna, Timmy was amazingly introspective for a child, and his biting sense of humor always made her seek him out. She claimed that because she was his godmother, it was her duty to spend more time with him than the others, and everybody seemed accepting.

Timmy was so much like herself, it was obvious to Brenna that his personality was a genetic thing and unlikely to change. Watching Timmy clutch the door handle of the car as he stared wide-eyed out the windshield, she said a prayer of thanks once more that her father was not around anymore to browbeat a grandchild into being the type of boy Patrick O'Brien deemed worthy of being his grandson.

As she pulled her Volkswagen up to the curb in front of Kathleen's house, she narrowly missed being sideswiped by a careening red Lincoln with whitewall tires. The Lincoln flew up the curb and into the yard, landing squarely with two wheels in the grass and the vintage car neatly pinning the mailbox under the front bumper.

Leaping from her car, Brenna called back to a white-faced Timmy, "Don't worry—it's only Aunt Dottie."

Before she even reached the driver's side, Aunt Dottie was pulling herself, her large straw hat, and her oversize purse out of the car. Smoothing her navy blue polka-dotted dress, she peered up at Brenna through Coke-bottle glasses, the magnifying effect of the lenses making her green eyes look like lime lollipops.

"Hello, dear. I suppose Kathleen moved her mailbox, because I always park here and I never recall it being in that location before." She squinted toward the front of her car. "Well, I thought I saw a mailbox." With gloved hands, Aunt Dottie took the large hat off her head and stared at it closely. Giggling to herself, she placed it back over her white bun. "When I forget where I'm going, I always check my hat. This is my Sunday hat, and I'm either going to church or Kathleen's." She squinted her eyes at Brenna. "Since you don't look like Father Joe, I guess I must be at Kathleen's." The old lady looked around. "But I wish she hadn't moved that mailbox. Now I won't know where to park anymore."

Brenna took her arm and guided her up the front walk, followed closely behind by Timmy. "Aunt Dottie, I thought we already had a talk about your driving. I think it's time you allowed yourself to be chauffeured. You know that I'm just a phone call away."

The old woman waved a hand through the air. "I can drive just fine—as long as I only need to see straight ahead, since I can't seem to see anything on the side anymore. And I don't drive at night at all. Too much reflection in my glasses." She stopped suddenly, looking frantically on the cement of the walkway behind and in front of her. "Where are my glasses? I can't see, and I can't drive home if I don't have them!"

Calmly, Brenna said, "They're on your nose. I think maybe we should have another heart-to-heart."

Peering closely into Brenna's face and blinking her magnified eyes, Aunt Dottie replied, "Are you married yet?"

Timmy chuckled behind her as she pulled on the old woman's arm a little more forcefully than necessary, and led her aunt up the stairs toward the front door. Ignoring her aunt's last question, Brenna said, "Let's go get you some sweet tea and get you settled, and then we're going to have our little chat."

The door opened and Kathleen stood in the doorway, smiling at them. As her gaze strayed over their heads toward the Lincoln and the remains of her mailbox, the smile dimmed but remained bravely in place. With kisses all around, Kathleen ushered them into the entrance hall, the smell of roasted chicken and simmering gumbo wafting from the kitchen.

Kathleen's middle daughter, Marie, a miniature version of her mother and a near mirror image of Brenna, appeared and took possession of Aunt Dottie, leading her into the front parlor, where a televised baseball game could be heard in stereo.

Brenna wiped a smudge of flour from her sister's nose and rubbed it on the bold red apron Kathleen wore that proclaimed her "Queen of the Kitchen." It had been a gift from Brenna when Brenna was still in high school, acknowledging her oldest sister's Martha Stewart–esque abilities. Kathleen hadn't managed yet to line their inground swimming pool with cut-up credit cards, but Brenna felt sure it was on the agenda.

"Thanks, sweetie." Kathleen put her arm around her sister and led her into the huge gourmet kitchen, a gift from her husband, John, on their twenty-fifth anniversary. Although sixteen years separated Brenna and her oldest sister, their build and bearing were identical and, except for the extra lines at Kathleen's eyes and forehead, they could have passed for twins.

Brenna paused on the threshold, staring at her sister's neck. She reached up to finger the sparkling necklace that Kathleen wore, whistling softly. "Whoo-eee. I didn't know this had become a formal occasion. That sure is a fancy piece of jewelry you're wearing."

"Shh, Colleen might hear you. She got a quantity discount on eBay on these genuine Diamonelle necklaces, so she bought one for all of us. You'll have to put yours on, too, or her feelings will be hurt."

"Great. I really need a necklace like that." She popped a cheese straw in her mouth, her eyes closing in pleasure. "Do you think Colleen is only ordering that stuff to hide an affair with the UPS man? I mean, he's there every day making deliveries."

Kathleen didn't smile. "That's not funny, Brenn. And talking like that is a great way to start ugly rumors about your sister."

Brenna was spared from responding by the opening of the kitchen door. Claire and her husband, Buzz, breezed into the kitchen, followed by a flash of color and noise that Brenna recognized as the twins PC and Mary Sanford as they ran though the kitchen and into the hallway to find their cousins.

Buzz offered a brief greeting before heading out in the direction of the TV and the company of his brothers-in-law. Claire eyed a crab-stuffed pastry but didn't touch it, instead reaching for a raw carrot sitting on a vegetable tray. "How was your date last night with Buddy Halbert?"

Brenna stared at Claire for a long moment, wondering again if the four women she called her sisters were really on her side. "You could have mentioned that he was missing a leg."

Claire dug around the vegetable tray with a long red fingernail. "I thought you'd figure that out yourself when I told you that the guys at work nicknamed him Stumpy."

"It never occurred to me. Otherwise I never would have suggested that we go roller-skating."

Kathleen seemed to be choking and quickly covered her mouth with her hand.

Claire crossed her arms over her ample chest, her whole demeanor that of someone completely affronted. "I didn't think it would matter to you."

"It doesn't! It was his annoying habit of chewing tobacco and spitting it wherever he deemed fit that I found so objectionable. I'll never get the juice off my white slacks—and they were my favorite." She popped another cheese straw in her mouth. "I should send you the dry-cleaning bill."

Kathleen came over and put an oven-mitted hand around Brenna's shoulder, her smile not completely hidden. "I'm sorry. I'm sorry about Chester Anderson and I'm sorry about last night. You know we only want you to be happy." She glanced up at Claire, who had slipped a cheese straw from the platter and was now shoving both it and a carrot stick into her mouth.

Brenna kissed her oldest sister on the cheek before pulling away. "Thanks—really. But maybe it's just not meant to be. And maybe you all should just take a break from matchmaking. I know how exhausting I'm finding it, and I can only imagine what it's doing to y'all."

With a hand covering her full mouth, Claire said, "Um, you might want to wait on that. Colleen and Bill met some guy in Biloxi last weekend who has family in the area, and they invited him to come today and meet you. I think she said his name was Elvis."

Brenna rolled her eyes. "Thanks for the warning. I'll go make myself a plate of food and lie low for a while."

She exited through the swinging door and made her way to the dining room, the table stacked high with food, and family members slowly marching around the perimeter with plates, like vultures over a battlefield. She relaxed when she noted that Pierce and his father hadn't arrived yet.

Spying Timmy wedged between the pedestal legs under the table, his nose stuck in a Harry Potter book, she whispered his name and tossed him one of Kathleen's homemade buttermilk biscuits. He caught it and grinned, then returned to his reading.

Kathleen entered and placed a large platter of fried chicken in the middle of the table as Brenna began to fill her plate with food.

She grinned and made chitchat with the same family members and friends who had been congregating in this house ever since Brenna could remember. When her mother had died when Brenna was six, Kathleen had taken over the cooking and hostessing duties long before she'd inherited the house at the death of their father, almost seven years before. Now she reigned over the weekly family gathering, filling in as seamlessly as the fading out of older faces around the table and the introductions of new.

Reaching over the corn soufflé and sweet potatoes for the biscuits, Brenna grabbed two with the intention of throwing another one under the table for Timmy. She found herself frozen with the biscuits in her hand as Pierce entered the dining room, assisting his father.

Giving a warm greeting to Dr. McGovern, and a cursory nod in Pierce's direction, she turned to Marie next to her and began to ask her niece about school. The entire time she was chatting and piling food on her plate, she was acutely aware of Pierce McGovern on the other side of the table. With great effort, she kept her eyes focused on the food and her niece, and was silently congratulating herself on her own nonchalance when she realized she still held Timmy's biscuit. With a quick underhand motion, she tossed it under the table.

"Ouch."

The voice was a lot deeper than her nephew's. Squatting, she peered under the table. Pierce McGovern's blue eye stared over at her as he held his hand over his other. A fork, which he had apparently bent to retrieve, rested near his foot. Timmy was nowhere in sight.

"I'm so sorry! I didn't know you were there." Her heart immediately dive-bombed her stomach, making her insides jump and roll in a queasy dance. She jerked her head up, soundly smacking it against the underside of the table. When she managed to stand, she found herself staring across the table into the amused face of Pierce McGovern.

The old doctor's face was lined with concern. "Are you all right, Brenna? That was a pretty sound bump, or you have the hardest head I've ever seen."

Rubbing her head, she said, "Probably a little of both. I'll be okay."

Kathleen's husband, John, entered the dining room, his face warming when he spied Brenna. In his quiet voice, he said, "Hey, girl. I've been looking for you. When Kathleen and I were antiquing last week in New Orleans I found this, and I knew you'd want it."

Glad for the distraction, Brenna placed her brimming plate on the sideboard and took the small wax envelope from her brother-in-law. Inside lay a brittle and brown envelope, the dark ink hardly faded in the nearly ninety years since it had been written. With mounting excitement, she said, "It's World War One, isn't it?"

John grinned shyly. "Yep. And it's never been opened; can you imagine?"

She shook her head. "No. I wonder why." Her excitement dimmed considerably as she felt Pierce move around to her side of the table. Turning her back to him, she looked at the Atlanta address, noting the woman's name at the top. "Could have been to a mother, wife, or sister. But never opened."

"I knew you'd like it. It might not be a wartime love letter, but there's a chance it is, which is why I immediately thought of you and your collection. Do you think you'll open this one?"

Brenna felt Pierce's presence behind her, and she forced herself to focus on the letter. "I'll put it with the others."

John shoved his hands into his pockets. "I read in the paper this morning that the city council has given their okay to raze your father's old post office and build a new one. You know, they did that several years ago in Greenwood, and found an old mailbag filled with letters that had never been delivered."

"Yeah—I read that, too. Although I doubt they'll find anything like that here in Indianola. My father was pretty much a hands-on postmaster. Don't think anything like that could have slipped by him."

Kathleen walked by with a bowl of steaming gumbo, and Brenna saw the way John watched his wife, his eyes glowing like a newlywed's. He reached out to brush her arm with his hand as she walked back to the kitchen, eliciting a smile and a glance from his wife. It had never ceased to amaze Brenna that the only time John did not appear to be quiet and shy was when he was around Kathleen. It seemed her presence alone gave him the strength he needed to face the world outside his accounting office.

She shifted her gaze and saw Pierce standing closely behind her and watching.

Brenna carefully picked up her plate from the sideboard with her other hand. "I owe you big-time for this—thank you." She leaned forward and gave John a peck on the cheek.

Blushing, John shoved his hands in his pockets. "Just enjoy it—and let me know what it says if you open it."

John caught sight of Pierce, and stuck out his hand. "I'm John Evans, Kathleen's husband. Are you the same Pierce McGovern who's been in the paper recently talking about building a multiscreen theater at the new mall?"

Brenna's plate of food began to wobble as she pivoted to look at Pierce. "No, John. This is Dr. McGovern's son. He's here to settle his dad into Liberty Village."

Not looking at her, Pierce shook John's hand. "I didn't realize it had made it into the papers. It's still in the preliminary stages of planning."

Brenna stared at him and blinked. "But we don't need a new theater. We have one right here in town."

Pierce at least had the decency to look uncomfortable. "I know that. But, like I said, nothing's definite. We're just doing market surveys and that kind of thing right now. There's a good chance that they'll change their minds."

She felt the breath rush from her lungs as if she'd been punched. "Oh. I see. That's good news then." With a wobbling smile, she excused herself, trying not to think of her Majestic having competition from anywhere. She was already struggling for moviegoers and couldn't afford to lose a single one.

Crossing the foyer, she stopped, her attention distracted by the group approaching the front door. Walking up the stairs with Bill and Colleen was a man with dark hair and a white leisure suit, apparently the date potential Claire had mentioned earlier. Turning as quickly as she could with a full plate of food, Brenna fled toward the back of the house and out the utility room door to the backyard and the sanctuary of her childhood.

As she clomped through the grass in her high heels toward the child-sized playhouse her father had built for a younger Kathleen, she could think of nothing but the smell of polish that surrounded the Royal Majestic, and the frayed yet soft red velvet seats in the theater. They were *hers,* and they were beautiful and not part of a horrible, huge impersonal multiplex cinema that smelled of plastic and new carpet and cheese nachos. He had said nothing was definite. That it probably wouldn't happen. But what if it did?

Sticking her head into the doorway, she was relieved to find it empty.

Ducking inside, she positioned herself at the miniature table and in a chair that seemed made for Thumbelina and tried to find her appetite. With a heavy sigh, she cut a piece of chicken and stuck it in her mouth, chewing thoughtfully.

At the same moment that she realized she'd forgotten to get something to drink, the small door opened and Pierce stuck his head inside.

"Are you all right?"

No. As long as you're in town I will never be all right. "I'm fine. You can go back to your father now." When he didn't make a move to leave, she said, "Did you know that I owned the Royal Majestic?"

He entered, then pulled up another Lilliputian chair and sat down across from her. "Not until yesterday."

"Would it have made any difference if you'd known?"

He paused. "I don't know. But it's not necessarily bad news, you know. Historic theaters all around the country are being retrofitted for different uses once they're no longer profitable movie theaters. They're not all being mothballed."

She stared up into the face that had once held all the answers for her, and she knew, without a doubt, that the way she felt had not changed in all those long years. Even if he had broken her heart once. And even if he was in town now to take away the one thing that made it worth getting up for each morning; the one thing that had filled her life with purpose and kept her from dwelling too long on all the paths not taken.

Brenna's head swam with old memories, new worries, and the distinct aroma of shrimp gumbo. "Go away," she somehow managed to mutter.

His eyes narrowed in the old familiar way. "You've always been real good at telling people to go away, haven't you? Give me one good reason why I should leave."

Because if you don't, my heart's going to break all over again, and I'm thirty-three years old, which makes me too old to put back all the pieces. Not knowing anything else to say that would make him leave, she threw a hand over her mouth and clenched her eyes shut. "I think I'm going to be sick."

CHAPTER 4

Pierce immediately jumped up and went to Brenna and slid her chair away from the table. "Put your head between your knees."

Sticking his fingers inside his nearly empty glass of tea, he pulled out three ice cubes and wrapped them in a napkin. Pulling her hair away, he placed the chilled napkin on her neck, noticing how pale and delicate her skin appeared.

He shouldn't have touched her. He had intended only to move more of her hair out of the way, but his fingers had lingered on her neck. Her hair, though cut shorter now, was still the same, rich texture bouncing in delicate waves around her face and had the same weighty feel beneath his fingers. He could smell her shampoo, something fruity, making him remember her soft head against his shoulder in the back of a darkened theater.

He made his voice sound flat. "Breathe deeply, but don't hyperventilate, and keep your head down until the queasiness stops." A sharp, jarring thought stilled his heart for a moment. "Are you pregnant?"

His question was met with a quick bark of laughter and a shake of her head, and he felt stupid for feeling so relieved. She mumbled something into her knees, so he squatted down next to her to hear her better. "What?"

She lifted her head slightly. "Are you still here?"

"Yes. I'm here. And I'm not leaving until I know you're all right."

Slowly she sat up, her head nearly eye level with his. Her eyes were still the color of the ocean at sunset. All through the years of his marriage to Diana, he'd never been able to see a sunset at the beach without thinking of Brenna O'Brien.

She pushed the hair off her forehead, her hands clenched into fists. "Why do you care? There is absolutely nothing good about you coming back here, and I'm trying to pretend that it's all just some never-ending nightmare. But every time I open my eyes, there you are." She closed her eyes, her shoulders slumping. "So just hurry up and pillage my life and move on as fast as you can so I can get busy putting it all back together again."

He surprised himself by grinning a half smile. "After all, tomorrow is another day, right?"

She opened her eyes and looked at him but didn't smile. "Please don't make fun of me. Leave me some self-respect."

"I wasn't making fun of you. Some people think it's a compliment to be compared to Scarlett O'Hara. She was strong and resilient, and rebuilt her life after everything was taken away from her."

"But you always said she was a bitch."

He stood abruptly. He wasn't getting into it with her now. "If you're okay, I'm going to go back to the house. But just so you know, I'm not back in Indianola to—what did you call it—'pillage your life.' This area could use a multiplex cinema. How your theater reacts to it is completely up to you. Business owners across the country have been in the same position as you, and the ones who survive are simply those who learned how to reinvent themselves."

He watched as a soft pulse throbbed at the base of her throat. He knew what it tasted like there. *Like salt and gardenias accompanied by the sound track of a Hollywood blockbuster.* He looked back at her eyes.

In a low voice, she said, "I've already done that once, Pierce. I'd rather not have to do it again."

"That was your choice, not mine."

"That's not true." The spot at the base of her throat pulsed once more.

He turned his head and picked up his plate and glass. "You're right—it takes two people to miscommunicate. Let's acknowledge that and move forward, okay?" He juggled with his glass to try to turn the doorknob.

"Oh, to hell with it." Giving up, he returned to the table and put his plate and glass down again and sat. "I'm hungry. You're just going to have to put up with me for a little while longer, I guess."

She didn't say anything but pushed the food around on her plate, arranging it in different piles but never lifting a forkful to her mouth. "I'm sorry to hear about your divorce."

He paused and looked at her, but her eyes remained focused on her plate. "It happens. I didn't think you'd kept track of my life, though."

She looked up, meeting his eyes, the green of hers darkening like a storm over the ocean. "I haven't. Dooley Gambrel told me about it."

Leaning back in his chair, Pierce let the front legs lift off the ground. "So, Dooley's still in town. He always followed you around like a puppy."

Brenna's eyes narrowed. "He's my best friend. He's stayed with me through thick and thin and is always there when I need him."

Pierce watched the slow progress of a spider on the wall behind Brenna, its goal the web in the corner, its path blocked by a framed drawing of a crayon stick girl standing next to a small house. Placing his fork on his plate, he said, "I guess we all need at least one person like that in our lives."

She leaned forward, her arms wrapped around herself. "Do you?"

Their eyes met again, and he couldn't look away. "I used to. A long time ago."

She sat back in her chair, those green eyes never leaving his. "I didn't think you'd come today."

"I didn't want to. But your sister Kathleen called to invite me and my dad, and it was an offer I couldn't refuse."

Brenna raised an eyebrow.

"That apron of hers is a good disguise, but I could have sworn I'd wake up with a horse head in my bed if I'd said no."

Brenna laughed, the color returning to her face, and he found himself reluctantly smiling in response. "She's nothing if not persistent. Trust me. I should know. She's trying to play matchmaker." A shadow fell over her eyes. She looked down at her hands, and he recognized the gnawed fingernails, could nearly feel them in his own hand as he clutched her fingers tightly while watching one of the old black-and-white horror movies she used to love.

"And you don't want her to?"

"No. Not really. I'm . . . content with my life. I don't really see the need to change it."

"Content—not happy? And that's good enough for you?" He wished that he hadn't said that.

Looking down at her chewed fingernails, she said quietly, "Yeah. It is. I'm familiar with the alternative—remember?"

He felt anger and shame hit him at the same time as a memory of the way her skin tasted against his lips. "I remember." He watched as her hands fluttered, then came to rest at the base of her throat, blocking it from his view. He looked away, wanting to ask questions, but not sure he wanted to hear the answers. It was all so long ago, and none of it should matter to him anymore. *I missed you for a long, long time.*

"I'm content," she said again, as if by repeating it they both could understand it better.

His eyes strayed to the table and the clear plastic sleeve containing the antique letter, hoping something about it could explain to him why she would choose contentment over happiness. "Why do you collect old letters?"

Reluctantly, she turned back to him and gave a little shrug. "I got started on it right . . . right after you went away to college, and it's sort of taken off. I've collected about three dozen or so letters—from different wars. All of them are letters either sent home from soldiers or from those left behind to the men at the front."

He picked up the letter, holding the plastic sleeve gently. She took it from him and looked at it reverently, as if she held not just the ink and paper, but the words and the heart of the person who wrote it. He stared at her long, pale fingers, the gnawed fingernails devoid of polish, and thought how vulnerable they made her look. "Don't you find it kind of depressing?"

She looked at him, her eyes bright. "No—just the opposite, actually." She paused for a moment, her expression thoughtful. "These letters are from people at a moment in their lives where the only thing that mattered was how they felt about each other. And that's the only thing I need to know, or want to know. I don't open them because then I can wonder what happened to their lives afterward. Because knowing the truth . . ." She stopped talking and shrugged.

Pierce slowly let his chair down so all four legs touched the floor. "Then you can't be disappointed."

He stared hard at her, torn between wanting to shake her or hug her.

She had somehow become the woman her father had wanted her to become, and for a brief instant, Pierce mourned the girl he'd known who could have been so much more. He began picking up the plates and straightening the chairs with his foot. "I'll go take these back."

She stared down at her hands folded in her lap and acted as if she hadn't heard him. "Please don't do this, Pierce."

He didn't pretend to think she was referring to the dishes or even her precious theater. "I'll make my stay as brief as possible. There shouldn't be any reason why we have to see each other again."

Brenna nodded, and he thought she wouldn't say anything else. He opened the door.

"I remember a time when you loved the Majestic as much as I did."

He stared at her for a long moment until her eyes met his. "I did. I probably still do. I'd hate for it to go. But that's not really up to me, is it?" He nodded good-bye, then let himself out to go find his father.

Brenna squatted down on a chair near the window so she could see the back door of the house, and made herself breathe. As she forced air into her lungs, she thought how much easier it would have been if he had insisted they talk about what had happened between them, or at least been indifferent toward her.

Instead, he had looked at her with his familiar eyes, and she knew he was remembering, too. And not just the bad parts. But the bad parts were like oceans: too far to swim across, with the threat of drowning should she even try.

Resisting the urge to stay where she was, Brenna stood and made her way back to the house and her sisters and the parts of her life that had sustained her all these years.

As she cautiously approached the dining room, Mary Margaret emerged from the parlor.

Glancing around as if to ensure nobody could hear her, she said, "Elvis has left the building."

"Really? I can't imagine my sisters allowing a single, straight male to leave my presence without making a date."

Mary Margaret brushed Brenna's cheek with the back of her hand. "It's been a hard day for you, hasn't it? I could tell there was something between you and Dr. McGovern's son that day he came into my store."

"There's nothing there. There was once, but it's gone."

Mary Margaret studied her for a long time in the penetrating way that she had that made Brenna think of a priest on the other side of the confessional. "Oh, sweetie, I'm sorry. It's that bad, is it?"

Brenna took a deep breath. Mary Margaret had been twenty-six years old and living in Berkeley, California, when Brenna met Pierce. The only person who had known about their relationship had been Brenna's disapproving father. But that had been so long ago, it didn't matter anymore. And she certainly didn't want to put Pierce on her sisters' collective radar.

She forced her shoulders back and smiled bravely at Mary Margaret. "Why did Elvis leave?"

Mary Margaret took Brenna's arm and began to lead her toward the kitchen. "His weekend replacement at the casino didn't show up, so he had to head back to Biloxi and slip on his blue suede shoes." She pushed the kitchen door open. "Even though he has to return to sender, he sends his deepest regrets. But I told him it would be a blue Christmas before you'd ever go out with him."

Brenna laughed, surprising herself. "Thanks, M. You were always my biggest defender."

Mary Margaret's eyes softened. "And your other sisters. Don't ever think that we didn't know what it was like for you after I left home and there was just Daddy."

Brenna nodded, wanting nothing more at that moment than to sit down with her sister and tell her everything: all the hurts and disappointments that nobody knew about except herself. But her penance was a long road, made to travel alone. She turned away.

"Brenna, there you are."

They both turned around to see Dr. McGovern leaning on his walker, with Pierce behind him. "I think all the biscuits and gravy have put me in a stupor and I need to go lie down. I wanted to say good-bye to you before I left."

Brenna kissed the old man's cheek as Dr. McGovern held her hand. "*The Lake House* is a great movie—I've already seen it twice. Maybe I can talk Pierce into taking me to your theater to see it again."

"That would be great. It's playing for another week, so maybe you can fit it in before Pierce leaves."

Dr. McGovern nodded. "Yes, well, hopefully. He's just so busy, you know. I was sort of hoping that he'd have time to help me decide what I need to bring with me to the retirement home, but we haven't really gotten around to it yet. Maybe you can help me instead. It'll give us a chance to catch up."

Brenna eyed the old doctor suspiciously, wondering if her sisters had already worked him over. "Sure. I'd be happy to. Just call me at the theater—that's where I am most of the time." She dug into the outside pocket of her purse and handed him a business card.

"Wonderful—and thank you. Now, have you seen your sister Kathleen? I'd like to thank her before we leave."

"I believe she's in here," Mary Margaret said as she entered the kitchen, followed by Brenna, Pierce, and his father. Kathleen sat at the table, her feet propped up on another chair while John stood at the sink washing dishes. They both turned and smiled.

As Pierce and Dr. McGovern said their good-byes, Brenna felt Kathleen watching her closely, so she avoided making eye contact. Kathleen seemed to have a natural maternal ability to read her mind. Because Kathleen had five children, Brenna supposed that it was a learned coping mechanism her sister had naturally adapted, but it was disconcerting to be so transparent all the same.

John wiped his wet hands on the dish towel he had tucked into his belt. "So, Pierce. How long do you think you'll be staying in town?"

Pierce glanced over at his father before shrugging. "I'm not sure—"

He was cut off by Dr. McGovern. "He's going to stay around long enough to make sure me and all my pesky affairs are settled." He sent his son a sidelong glance. "Pierce seems to think I'm making up things to get him to stick around a little bit longer than necessary, but it's a fact that it takes a while to tie up a lifetime of loose ends."

"I'll be here at least a month, and longer if you feel you need me." He faced Kathleen and John with a grin that had always made Brenna's heart flip-flop, and it didn't disappoint. "My dog won't recognize me if I stay any longer than that."

Oh, Lord. A whole month. A whole month of avoiding him, of trying to forget about him. Of constant craving for something she could never have. Her heart lurched. A little too brightly, she said, "I'll walk you to the door."

Pierce held the walker while she took the doctor's arm and steered them into the hallway toward the front door. Claire came to stand beside her, and they both waved good-bye as Pierce helped his father navigate the walkway toward their car. She watched the way he handled his father with so much care and patience. His tenderness had always been something he'd kept carefully concealed in the jock world of high school—at least, from everybody but her. To her he had written love letters with words so elegant and poignant they had made her weep. She'd wrapped them with a red ribbon. It had made it easier for her when she dumped them into the Indianola Dam. Maybe it was her longing for them now that made her collect the discarded words and lost sentiments of dead people.

"Man, oh, man—that boy is fine." Claire made the last word sound as if it had three syllables.

Kathleen joined them, resting her chin on Brenna's shoulder, followed shortly by Mary Margaret and Colleen. They stood, unusually quiet, watching Pierce assist his father into the car.

Mary Margaret finally broke the silence. "I was hoping he'd stay longer and play some football. Bet he looks great without a shirt."

Brenna elbowed her sister in the ribs. "Don't you think Dr. McGovern is a bit old for you? And besides, what would Richard say?"

Mary Margaret laughed as she elbowed Brenna back.

Colleen squeezed her way in to be next to Brenna. "Sorry about Elvis, Brenn. I didn't know that he always dressed like that and that his hair wasn't a wig." She patted her youngest sister on the back. "Besides, with that hunk of burning love out there on the sidewalk, I'd say our matchmaking duties are just about over, don't y'all think?" She glanced at her siblings with her hazel eyes, where they all stood huddled around their youngest sister.

Brenna forced her voice to sound light. "I'd say that after Elvis, you owe me one, Colleen. I've just elected you to go have a talk with Aunt Dottie about giving up her car keys. Call an intervention if you need to, but she needs to stop driving today, before she kills someone."

Colleen fisted her hands on her hips. "I guess I deserve that." She yanked on Claire's arm. "Come on. I can't do this alone. You take the keys out of her purse while I corner her."

The two turned away inside, conspiring in whispers their plans to ground Aunt Dottie. Colleen called over her shoulder, "Don't leave without my giving you your surprise, Brenna. You'll just love it!"

Brenna raised her hand in acknowledgment, noticing that everybody had on matching Diamonelle necklaces but her.

John walked up and slid his arms around Kathleen's waist, kissing her on the cheek. She smiled and put her hands on his, their wedding bands winking in the bright afternoon sunshine. His gaze shifted from his wife to the Lincoln poised on the front lawn. "For crying out loud, what the hell—" At a sharp look from Kathleen, he said, "Well, I guess we needed a new mailbox anyway." Shaking his head, he stepped back. "If it's okay with you, I thought I'd bring the horde outside for a little bit of touch football."

Kathleen nodded, turning her head to face her husband. "Just keep them out of my herb garden. I don't think it's quite recovered from the last assault."

"Will do." He gave her another peck on the cheek before disappearing inside.

Mary Margaret linked her arm in Kathleen's. "Come on; I'll help you put the food away. We can talk about this new face cream I just brought back from India that I know you'll love."

Mary Margaret sent Brenna a warning look, and Brenna remained quiet, happy to know that she wasn't singled out to be the only victim. It made her feel a camaraderie with her older sisters, not a familiar feeling.

She stayed in the doorway, glad to have found a few moments of peace. She loved her family, but their boisterousness always made her feel outnumbered in her need for solitude. Staring after Pierce's car as it disappeared around the corner, she allowed herself to sigh. Maybe it would be enough to see him, to speak with him for the short time he would stay in Indianola. Maybe that would be enough to get her through her white-bread existence. Maybe she'd find the elusive forgiveness she'd sought in the last sixteen years to put the ghosts of her past to rest. Maybe.

A warm summer breeze hit her skin, and she turned her face to catch more of it. A dark blue SUV parked on the corner up the street caught her attention. A man sat in the driver's seat, smoking a cigarette, and it must have been the movement of his arm as he tipped the ash out the open window that had caught her attention. The man seemed to see her the moment she spotted him, and quickly raised his window, his face hidden behind reflections of sky and trees.

Her attention was diverted by the familiar chug of Dooley's truck engine approaching from the other direction. He pulled into the bottom of the driveway and jumped out, pausing for a moment with a bewildered expression to inspect Aunt Dottie's Lincoln and its familiarity with the Evanses' mailbox.

He laughed as he sauntered toward her, his hands shoved into the back pockets of his jeans. "Man, wish I could have seen that."

Grinning, Brenna said, "Stick around. Aunt Dottie hasn't left yet, and she'll be fit to be tied when she does." She indicated his truck with her chin. "As a matter of fact, you might want to move your truck to the backyard to get it out of the way."

"If your aunt Dottie's driving, I think Alabama would be safer."

With a laugh, Brenna stepped back out of the doorway to let Dooley pass, belatedly remembering the man in the blue SUV. Craning her head, she turned around and looked, but saw only empty curb where the truck had been. The man was gone.

Shrugging to knock the uneasy feeling from her shoulders, she followed Dooley into the house, shutting the door on the warm summer breeze.

CHAPTER 5

Brenna glanced in her rearview mirror, eyeing the bright red hair of her four-year-old niece, Molly, and the white stick that was connected to the large purple lollipop firmly embedded on the side of the child's head.

Timmy sat next to his cousin in the backseat and was trying to extricate the errant candy, but each effort was met with a loud squall from Molly.

Brenna chewed on her bottom lip as she looked down once more at the birthday party invitation on her lap and the address on the mailbox. The large bouquet of balloons tied to the mailbox would have been enough to convince her that she was at the right place, but she knew Timmy would want her to make sure that he wasn't dropped off at the wrong house.

"We're here, Timmy." She met his worried eyes in the rearview mirror. She had been about to suggest that she drop him off at the bottom of the driveway, but instead said, "You get the present and I'll get Molly out of her car seat so we can walk up together."

Timmy nodded, but his relief was almost palpable in the small car.

Brenna leaned in and unbuckled the car seat, pausing for a moment to revel in the little arms that went around her neck. Mary Margaret had to take her two older boys to baseball practice, and Brenna had agreed to watch the youngest. It was her day off, but she'd already volunteered to take Timmy to a birthday party for Colleen, so she might as well just play aunt for the day. Besides, she enjoyed Molly's company. Most of the time.

She juggled Molly on her hip as they made their way up the sidewalk, Timmy lagging behind and shuffling his feet.

Molly smiled happily despite the purple lollipop dangling from her hair, and played with her aunt's earring, which was now at eye level. "I learnded a new word, Aunt Brenn."

Timmy groaned behind her, matching Brenna's own thoughts. Mary Margaret believed firmly in teaching children everything they needed to know about the human body at a very early age—and to be proud of it. Brenna supposed there was nothing intrinsically wrong with the practice, except for the fact that four-year-olds rarely knew when airing their newfound knowledge was appropriate or not. And it usually wasn't.

Quickly changing the subject, Brenna turned to Timmy. "What's the present?"

He squinted up at her into the sunlight. "It's a clip-on light for his Nintendo and some Braves baseball cards." Looking down at his feet, he mumbled, "He probably won't like it."

With her available arm she pulled Timmy close, her hips and his bony arm jostling each other as they approached the house. "Now, Eeyore, I think those are really cool. If I were an eight-year-old boy, that's exactly what I'd want."

Timmy stopped, his eyes wide and his voice filled with rising panic. "But Scott isn't eight anymore. He's turning nine!"

"It begins with a T, Aunt Brenna." Molly scrunched her face as she tried to remember her new word.

"And I can't wait to hear what it is as soon as you recall it." She turned back to Timmy, who now looked close to tears. Squatting down to his eye level, she put her hand on his shoulder and said, "I think your present is extremely cool. And remember that I'm the aunt closest to your age, so I pretty much know what all the young kids like. I happen to know that Nintendo clip-on lights are all the rage, and the Braves are going to go to the World Series this year—so you are right on the ball. What color is the light?"

"Green." He stubbed the well-worn toe of his sneakers into the brick walkway. "Neon green."

"Excellent choice. I was just about to tell you that that's the most popular of all the colors. I guarantee your present will be Scott's favorite, and, if for some crazy reason it's not, then Scott just doesn't know what cool is."

A lopsided grin puckered Timmy's cheek. "Yeah. Probably."

Straightening, Brenna said, "All right then. Go ahead and ring the doorbell." She eyed the twenty or so Mylar balloons that were jostling one another above their heads like giddy children. "Maybe they'll let you take a balloon home."

Timmy shook his head. "I don't want one."

Something inside made her heart twitch. An old remembrance—of herself. "Why not?"

"It might pop. And then I wouldn't have it anymore."

Brenna stared at him, numb. *Did he learn that from me? Or is there something in our blood?*

Just then the front door opened and Scott's mother appeared. "There you are, Timmy. We were waiting for you before we started the fun."

Brenna gave him a last hug as he disappeared inside, his head hung low. She smiled at Scott's mother. "His mom will pick him up at four."

Waving good-bye, she turned and headed back to her car with Molly bouncing on her hip, her mind deep in thought, and Timmy's words rallying the recesses of her memory. She recalled a family trip to Dauphin Island when she was just seven. She remembered how old she was because it was the last time they had all been together before Kathleen got married. All of her sisters had planned on sleeping in hammocks on the dunes, on that grassy part that was neither beach nor water. Brenna had watched them drag their hammock and stands from the porch, but Brenna had refused to join them. Her sisters thought it was because she was scared. And she was scared—but not of sleeping in the dark next to the ocean's waves and the unseen depths. Instead it had been a fear of disappointed expectations and of inevitable endings. Much better to wonder what might have been instead of knowing what it wasn't.

So she had stayed behind with her father, her nose pressed against the screen porch on the front of the beach house, and listened to the soft calls of her sisters to one another until Kathleen had returned to take her inside to bed. She had been staring up at the full moon as it rose above the swells of the ocean, and her sister had lifted her and taken her into the sand to see it better.

"Kathleen? Why is the moon so big and fat sometimes and other times it's not?"

Her sister had swept her hands over Brenna's forehead to pull back the hair on her face that had escaped her long braid. "It's because the moon stuffs itself with all the world's hopes and wishes, every single night for a whole month, hiding them in those craters until he's full and round. When he's about to burst from being so full, he spills them all back into the ocean to start over again, making him skinnier than God's fingernail."

Brenna had chewed on this for a long while, staring up at the unblinking moon. Finally, she asked, "Is that why my wishes don't come true? Because they fall in the ocean?"

Her sister had knelt beside her, knees cracking. "No, peanut. They only come true if a starfish finds one and hauls it ashore. All the others fall to the ocean floor and become grains of sand covering the endless bottom. And all those whose dreams and hopes become sand find that what they wished for is not what they wanted after all."

Kathleen had picked her up again and brought her inside to put her to bed, and Brenna had lain awake all night, watching the greedy moon get fuller with possibilities and listening to the soft voices of her sisters echo in the cool night air.

"Do something that scares you every day," Brenna muttered as she pulled her car into Dr. McGovern's driveway behind Pierce's rental car. Willingly going into a house where she knew Pierce to be certainly ranked up there with scary things.

She lifted Molly from the backseat and carried her to the door, picturing herself using the child as a shield. With a deep breath, she rang the doorbell.

Pierce opened it after a few moments, his eyes widening when he spotted the little girl whose head nearly obscured Brenna's face.

In explanation, she said, "This is Molly, Mary Margaret's youngest. I'm watching her this morning. Your dad asked me to come by to help him go through his stuff, and he said he didn't mind if I brought her."

Pierce greeted the little girl with a tousle of her hair, then stepped back to allow them in.

"I learnded a new word today." Molly smiled cheerfully up at Pierce.

Brenna quickly whipped out a plastic storage bag of raisins and handed them to her niece. "Here, Molly. Have a snack." She turned to Pierce, trying to keep the desperation out of her voice. "If you could show me where there's a TV, I'll put on *Arthur* and she'll be fine."

Eyeing the lollipop in the little girl's hair, Pierce led them into the TV room. Brenna tried hard not to stare at how nicely he filled his jeans or how his walk hadn't changed. He still bounced on his feet, as if he were crossing a baseball field, and he still used Dial soap. She remembered, briefly, the intoxicating smell of him when she would press her nose into the warm space of his neck, and felt a wave of grief so strong it made her steps falter. Grief for all that she had once had, and all that could never be.

Pierce helped settle Molly on the couch in front of her favorite program. Releasing the child, Brenna felt nearly naked without the protective barrier of the little girl in her arms. Crossing her arms over her chest, she asked, "Where's your dad?"

Pierce looked almost as uncomfortable as she felt. "He was exhausted and wanted to lie down for a bit. He said between the two of us we could probably figure it all out." He picked up a clipboard with lined paper and a pen clipped on top before handing it to her. "Where should we start?"

Feeling like she'd been set up, and wondering which sister was responsible, she smiled brightly. "Well, let's go to the living room. That's usually where the most extraneous furniture can be found, I would think."

Brenna followed his lead across the entrance hall and into a large room with a bay window looking out on the front lawn. Pale yellow ruffled curtains framed the oversize window, like the petals on a sunflower opening up to a picture of the world.

Pierce followed her gaze. "My dad didn't change a thing after he moved in. My mom had decorated our last house, and I guess he felt he didn't know where to start."

She nodded, taking in the old-fashioned furniture and noting the avocado greens and harvest golds of three decades earlier. "I bet your father hasn't stepped foot in this room once."

"Actually, he does. Every night. He pours himself a scotch, then comes and sits at the piano bench."

She noticed the baby grand piano on the far side of the room, behind the sofa. "He plays?"

Pierce shook his head. "No. My mother did." He walked closer to the piano and lifted a framed picture from the top and handed it to Brenna.

She took it and stared at the picture of a woman she had never met, though she knew she would have known her anywhere. The resemblance to her son was strong, and it was especially apparent in the photo. In the black-and-white picture, Pierce's mother held the hand of a boy who was barely past toddlerhood. They both wore frozen smiles, flat and one-dimensional like the models on cereal ads.

"She's beautiful." Looking more closely, she eyed the little boy, the face barely recognizable as the man he'd grown into. "Did your dad ever find out where she went?"

"No." Pierce took the picture and replaced it on the piano. "My dad wants me to take the piano."

Startled, she looked at him. "You play?"

He shrugged. "Yeah. Not as much as I'd like to, but I've been playing since college."

Quietly, she said, "I didn't know that about you."

It took a long time before he spoke. "No, you wouldn't. There's a lot you don't know about me."

She turned around to hide her face and to move on to safer topics.

Pierce continued. "I think just about everything else in here could be sold. There's a few valuable antiques I'll let an antique dealer in New Orleans take a look at, but for the rest I'm thinking garage sale or Goodwill. I doubt there's room for any of it in his apartment at Liberty Village, and he'll probably prefer the furniture in the TV room."

She began making a list of what the room contained, and Pierce came to stand behind her. She felt him, smelled the warm scent of him, knew of his presence before he spoke. "Add the piano. I don't have room for it."

"But I thought he wanted you to have it."

He stared at the yellow curtains without really looking at them. "My apartment in San Francisco is very small."

The words came out of her mouth before she could stop them. "You're staying there? So far from your dad?"

His eyes were dark when he looked up at her. "My life isn't here anymore."

When Brenna looked in his face, she didn't see a bitter man. Instead she saw the hurt and defiant little boy she had first met. The little boy whose first words to her had been that his mother had died. She had known him for about a year before she'd learned that his mother had simply dropped him off for school one day and kept driving, as if she'd forgotten the way home and was trying to find it by never letting her foot off the gas pedal.

"The piano was your mother's. You really should take it. I bet you'd find the perfect spot for it, too."

He looked up sharply at her. "You're starting to sound like my dad." He rubbed his hands over his face, making the hair on his forehead stick up like a young boy's. "Look, I don't want to get into this with you. Not now, not later. I just want you to put the piano on that list, because I don't want it."

She had nothing to say and simply followed him out of the room.

They walked slowly through the house, keeping their conversation to the safe topic at hand, itemizing the bits and pieces of the doctor's life that had once been carefully collected and displayed and now seemed completely expendable. The diplomas and awards went into the right-side column, under KEEP. The menagerie of glass animals in a lit curio went on the opposite side, along with wedding china and crystal that had not been used in over thirty years.

Climbing the stairs slowly behind Pierce, Brenna tried to concentrate on the notepad and not on the way his hair touched the collar of his shirt or how much he had changed since she had last seen him.

Pierce entered a room, and Brenna followed. She stopped in the threshold, blinking. It was a different room, in a different house, but the desk, the chest of drawers, the bed with the handmade quilt were the same. Without touching the bedcovering, she knew what it felt like against her skin as much as she knew what it felt like to be held in Pierce's arms.

She glanced up at him and saw that he was as stricken as she was. She moved her gaze around the room, to the baseball trophies, the Lava lamp, the Atlanta Braves neon sign, the autographed baseball bat. She closed her eyes for a brief moment, transported back in time, and she felt the fumbling fingers of a boy and girl, alone in his bedroom, each wondering how far they'd dare go.

Perhaps every girl's first time was remembered with such clarity of touch, color, and emotion, or maybe hers was only because it had been with Pierce, in that bed, under that poster. It had been the beginning of the end of them, but if she could have called back time, she wouldn't have stopped them.

"All of this can go." Pierce's voice shook her out of her reverie. "All except the baseball memorabilia. I'll pack it up in a box and ship it home."

Brenna struggled to find her voice. "What about the bedspread? Didn't your mother make it?"

"I don't need it." Brushing by her, he left the room, and she could do nothing else but follow.

She wasn't sure when it was that Molly had chosen to join them, but while Brenna stood in the guest bedroom writing down everything that was to be included in the garage sale, Molly appeared at Pierce's side with her arms lifted to be picked up.

Without seeming to think about it, Pierce bent down and scooped the little girl into his arms. Like old friends, she hung one of her arms around his neck while he easily rested her in the crook of his elbow. Brenna stared at the two of them, unblinking, as the thought struck her of what a natural father Pierce would be.

He caught her watching them, and it was as if their thoughts were entwined, each reading the other's. His look became accusing, and she broke the gaze. Moving toward a bedside lamp made out of a crudely constructed birdhouse, she said, "I suppose you want to keep this."

"No," he said softly. "Let's put it in the garage sale."

It didn't occur to her until he had already left the room, the child still clinging to him, that the lamp had once been on the table next to his bed in his bedroom. Ignoring the urge to argue with him, she followed Pierce and Molly down the stairs.

Lifting her purse from the hall table and replacing it with the clipboard, Brenna said, "I think this will give your dad a good place to start. He'll have to do his bedroom himself, since he's sleeping in there right now, but he'll most likely want to bring everything so his new bedroom will be familiar to him."

Pierce shifted Molly in his arms. "He'll be sorry he missed you."

"Right. Like this wasn't planned from the get-go. Was it his idea or Kathleen's?"

Pierce smiled softly. "Does it matter? Besides, you've really been a big help. I think Dad knew he needed somebody objective to go through everything, so he was able to kill two birds with one stone by getting you over here."

"Glad I could help." She reached for Molly, eager to leave.

Molly ignored the outstretched arms and tugged on Pierce's ear. "Testicle." The little girl smiled broadly. "That's the new word I learnded today."

In two steps Brenna had reached her niece and lifted her from Pierce's arms. "That's right, sweetie. Those are the little leg things on a jellyfish."

The little girl scrunched her bright red eyebrows. "That's not what my mommy said. She told me—"

With one swift yank, Brenna disengaged the purple lollipop from the child's hair, making her yelp just once. When Molly saw her candy, she grabbed it from her aunt's hand and stuck it in her mouth, hair and all.

Pierce raised an eyebrow, but it was obvious he was struggling hard to keep the grin from his face. "Smart child. I can see she gets it from her aunt."

"Probably." Adjusting her purse strap on her shoulder, she reached for the door handle. "I've got to go now. Tell your dad I said hi, and to call me if he needs anything else."

Pierce nodded as she opened the door to leave, but his voice held her back. The words seemed reluctant on his tongue, as if they were holding on with both hands. "I was on eBay last night, just browsing, and I came upon an item you might be interested in bidding on. It's an entire collection of letters from a Civil War soldier to his wife. They're still bundled together with a hair ribbon." He shoved his hands into the front pockets of his jeans. "Thought you might like to check it out."

She gripped the door handle, unwillingly breathless, and met his eyes. "Have they been opened?"

"Yeah, I think so. They showed some of the contents—really beautiful handwriting."

"Oh." She kept her disappointment in check. "I'll go look at them. I prefer ones that haven't been opened, but I bet I'd like to take a look at those. And thanks for letting me know."

He shrugged, as if hunting eBay for antique letters were something he did every day. "Just thought you'd be interested."

"I am—and thanks again." She stepped off the porch. Maybe it was the familiar smell of the boxwoods that lined the walkway that made her stop short, searching for words she couldn't quite grasp.

She could feel him watching her from the doorway before she turned her head. "I . . . missed you. I know it doesn't change anything now, but I wanted you to know." She stumbled over her tongue, fighting the urge to cry or laugh; she wasn't sure. "I wanted you to know that I missed you for a long, long time."

Holding Molly tightly, she quickly made her way to her car, feeling him watching her all the way. She didn't look back until she had placed Molly in her car seat and heard the front door slam shut.

Pierce leaned his forehead against the closed door, feeling almost feverish. *I missed you for a long, long time.* He had stood watching her leave, unable to move, while in his head he'd shouted, *But not as long as I missed you.*

He went to the kitchen and took his father's pill tray off the counter and glanced at the large clock over the sink. Time for the next dosage. Knocking gently on the door of the master bedroom, knowing he'd better give his father time to feign sleep, he waited a moment before entering. The old man lay on his back, the TV remote placed conspicuously in his hands.

Pulling a chair close to his father's bed, Pierce poured a glass of water from the pitcher on the bedside table. "I know you're awake, Dad. So just open your eyes and take your medicine while I try to make it clear to you that I am not here to date desperate theater owners in need of a mate." *Especially not one with strawberry blond hair and green eyes and an uncanny ability for breaking hearts.*

The old doctor opened his eyes and looked at his son, and Pierce felt as if he should be wearing shortalls for how old his father made him feel.

"I'm not going to live forever, Pierce. I don't have time to wait until you figure things out for yourself. I don't know what happened that year you went away to college, and I probably don't need to know. But I do know what a life of regret is like. Avoiding choices doesn't make them go away, you know. It only makes you a coward. And I didn't raise you to be a coward."

Pierce handed his father a pill, not meeting his eyes and his father's words echoing in his mind. *But I know what a life of regret is like.* Pierce held the glass up for his father to take in slightly trembling hands. What could his father know about a life of regret? Did he regret marrying a woman who left him and his young son only ten years into the marriage? Pierce had always thought that it was a good thing they hadn't been forced to live with a woman who hated them so much. Regret wasn't a word he ever associated with his mother.

Pierce looked down at the drawn face, watching his father's eyes flutter closed. They'd talk about regrets later. Maybe his father could explain it differently to him, help him make sense of the huge ball of regret he'd carried around for years. But not now. He watched his father's soft breathing settle into a deep rhythm as he stood and placed the glass on the nightstand. Sometimes guessing at answers was so much easier to handle than knowing the truth.

CHAPTER 6

Brenna juggled her scrapbook and bag of supplies as she used her elbow to press Claire's doorbell. She was surprised when Timmy answered the ring, his eyes anxiously peering out the door behind her.

"What are you doing here? Isn't it a school night?"

"I'm thinking the clouds look like there might be a thunderstorm, and Aunt Claire's house doesn't have as many windows as our house. My mom said I could come as long as I rode my bicycle home before bedtime."

Brenna looked up at the fading blue sky and the transparent streaks of clouds, but knew better than to argue. As good as Timmy was at worrying, he was even better at arguing. Instead, she stepped through the open doorway and said, "I had no idea that lightning could come through windows."

"Sure it can. On the news once there was a woman washing dishes in her kitchen sink and she got hit right through her window."

"Did she die?"

His eyes, so much like her own, widened. "No, ma'am. But they said she has a white streak of hair going across her head where the lightning grazed her."

Before she could ask him where he got his news, Claire's twins, PC and Mary Sanford, appeared from the kitchen.

"Wanna come see our new guinea pig?" they asked in unison.

Timmy looked up uncertainly. "Is it near a window?"

Brenna nudged him gently on the back. "Go on, Timmy. If it looks like it's going to storm, I'll come up and make sure everybody's safe, okay?"

She felt his shoulders stiffen under her hand before he nodded slightly. "Okay," he said as he walked slowly toward his cousins with the same enthusiasm one would expect of a condemned man headed for the electric chair.

Turning toward the living room, where her sisters chatted, she heard Timmy ask, "How long do guinea pigs live? I don't think I'd want a pet that didn't live as long as me."

Her heart squeezed a little for the little boy whose thoughts almost always seemed to mirror her own, and yet she couldn't help him any more than she could help herself.

Brenna's sisters were in their usual spots when she entered the room. Kathleen was set up at a card table near the doorway nearest the kitchen so she could easily move between the two rooms with her baked treats. Kitchens were always her domain, regardless of whose house they were in. Claire was parked near the coffee table where the snack bowls were located, so nobody could really tell how much she'd eaten during the course of one of their scrapbooking sessions. Everyone knew perfectly well, but figured it was their sisterly duty not to point out the obvious. Colleen sat in the corner with her laptop so she could periodically keep track of several auctions on eBay. Mary Margaret perched herself on the sofa, watching television. Even though she'd started baby albums for each of her children, she'd never made it past six months for any of them. She brought her albums and supplies each week, but rarely actually worked on any of them. There was something wrong, she said, about freezing memories in a book instead of making them when you were still young. But she faithfully came every week to be with her sisters, and sometimes, Brenna thought, to act as a buffer for her between the older sisters and their matchmaking intentions.

Brenna always used whatever patch of floor was still available. Everyone said it was because she was the youngest of five and was used to making do with what was left, but Brenna knew it was because she liked to spread out all of her letters as if they were stars in the sky, shimmering with possibility. She would touch them, and smell the old paper and ink, then carefully, methodically, place each one in an acid-free sleeve and affix it to a page in her scrapbook. Then, using special archival pens, she would document where she'd acquired the letter and what she thought was written inside the unopened letter.

The talking flowed as everyone worked, the words rising and falling in waves of shared lives and illustrated with scattered photographs. It was mostly the older sisters who talked, while Brenna listened, as she had when she was younger. It wasn't that they excluded Brenna; she liked it that way. In the absence of her mother, the soft murmurings of her sisters had been the arms that rocked her to sleep at night, and even now the sound soothed her like a warm hand.

Mary Margaret, bored with flipping channels with the remote, began her usual stroll around the room, checking on everyone's progress. Brenna stood, too. She'd already documented the letter her brother-in-law John had given her last Sunday, but she'd hit a mental wall when it had come time to write about the contents of the un-opened letter. Her thoughts kept wandering back to Pierce's return to her life, and when she began to imagine what she'd write about the an-tique letter, the words that came were all the lost words she had wanted to tell him.

She joined Mary Margaret over by Claire, who had moved the candy dish of M&M's to her table. She dropped a handful as her sisters approached.

"How's the diet going, Claire?" Mary Margaret scooped up a hand-ful of M&M's and put them in her mouth.

"Not too well. The stress of the Little Miss Crawfish Pageant is enough to kill me. All the other mothers are so much younger than I am and have so much more energy." She frowned and eyed the candy dish. "They're all just so damned perky." She reached over to where Mary Margaret had moved the candy dish and took out a single peanut M&M. "That Tammy Watley is hosting a huge reception at her house for all the pageant coordinators after the event. She's invited all the en-trants and their parents and says she's doing it to thank the people who give such joy to our children. Personally, I think she's just a suck-up and is trying to score points for her Tara."

Colleen looked up from her laptop screen that sat next to her un-opened scrapbook. "Well, everyone knows that Tara Watley has the face of a pit bull, bless her heart. Which is why her mama needs to go the extra mile. Luckily for you, Mary Sanford doesn't need any extra points."

Kathleen spoke without looking up from the page she was working on. "And I don't think wearing tight pants and short skirts is making you look any younger, Claire. Remember, fashion isn't about what's popular; it's about wearing what looks best on you."

Claire stuck out her tongue, but Kathleen missed it as she walked into the kitchen and brought back a tray of small pieces of toast with sliced pears and Brie cheese. Like the good hostess she'd been raised to be, she walked around the room, offering the contents to each sister.

As Brenna took one, Kathleen said, "John said we should all go down to the old post office demolition tomorrow, since Daddy worked there for forty years and was the postmaster for twenty. He said we could take pictures and put them in our albums under 'moments for posterity' or something. I thought it was a good idea."

"What time?" asked Colleen. "I told Bill I'd work at the store until lunchtime, and then I've got an eBay auction that ends at two o'clock, so I need to be back."

Kathleen walked over to Colleen with the tray. "It's scheduled for one o'clock, so you should be able to make it." She took a piece of toast herself and chewed on it thoughtfully for a moment. "You know, before John mentioned it, I hadn't even considered going. But he's right. The old post office was a piece of our childhood, whether we liked it or not."

"Well, I'm not going." Everyone stared at Claire as she leaned back in her chair. "We certainly weren't made welcome there by Daddy, and more than once I felt that the damned post office was his favorite child."

Leaving the tray on the coffee table, Kathleen walked back over to Claire's table and peered over at the pages Claire had been working on. "Don't you think you'd feel better seeing it knocked down?" She reached down and flipped a page in the album, and then another. "You know, Claire, people would think you only had a daughter by looking at your scrapbook album. Don't you have any of PC playing baseball?"

Claire colored. "Of course. It's just . . . well . . . Mary Sanford has been in all these pageants, and we have a lot of pictures. That's all. I'm not picking favorites, if that's what you're thinking." She glared up at her oldest sister. "After being raised by our daddy, do you think for one minute I'd do something like that?"

Kathleen put her hand on Claire's shoulder and squeezed. "No, Claire. I don't."

She returned to her seat and they once again fell into their working pattern, until Colleen said, "Has anybody noticed that hottie in the dark blue SUV that's been hanging around town? He's been to the store several times buying lumber for Mrs. Grodin's screen porch addition. Actually, I think he said he was moving into her empty apartment while doing the work. Have you met him, Brenna?"

Brenna felt the expectant eyes of all four sisters. Colleen had obviously reached the conclusion that the man was young, attractive, probably single, and had all four limbs attached. The thought that he might be a serial killer was tempered by the fact that he was handy with wood and would make a good provider.

Brenna began picking up her things and storing them in her bags. "Um, no. I don't really hang out at Mrs. Grodin's if I can help it. I barely see the neighbors I've got."

She sensed Mary Margaret looking at Kathleen over her head as she spoke. "Colleen, before you start planning the wedding, why don't you let Brenna form her own attachments. I would have hoped you'd learned after the Stumpy incident."

Colleen held up her hand in a defensive gesture. "Look, all I'm saying is that there's this cute new guy in town and he might be Brenna's neighbor. There's no reason at all why she can't just show him some good old-fashioned Southern hospitality and bring him over some iced tea and cookies or something."

Brenna stood and slung her bag over her shoulder. "I've got to go. Beau is off tomorrow at the theater, so I've got to get there early. Good night, everybody—it was fun."

Claire stood quickly, spilling a pile of M&M's she'd apparently been keeping in her lap. "Don't go just because Colleen is being insensitive. Stay awhile longer—you've barely been here an hour. We haven't even gotten to the gossip part of the evening yet."

Brenna kissed her sister on the cheek. "I know, and I hate to miss it, but I'm really not into this tonight. I'm just going to go home and go to bed early."

Mary Margaret slipped up behind her and put her arm around her shoulders. "Come on, I'll walk you to the door."

Brenna turned to Kathleen. "I'll be there tomorrow at one o'clock. I think we should all go." Four sets of eyes turned to look at her. "Because . . . because of Daddy. I think it would be good for us."

Brenna didn't wait for a response but said her good-byes, then allowed Mary Margaret to lead her out of the room. When she opened the front door she was relieved to see clear skies. "Would you mind telling Timmy that there aren't any storm clouds? He was afraid there would be a thunderstorm."

"Sure." Mary Margaret brushed Brenna's hair out of her eyes as she'd been doing since Brenna was a toddler. "You didn't write anything in your scrapbook tonight. I always enjoy reading what you come up with."

"Yes, well . . ." Brenna shrugged and attempted a smile. "I think I'm just tired. I'll do better next time."

"So, you and Pierce McGovern go way back, hmm?"

Brenna knew better than to deny anything to her sister, who had an uncanny ability to see through any lies or half-truths. But instead of answering, she moved down the steps and looked up at the sky. "Do you think the saints really listen to us down here?"

"Yeah. I do. Even Richard does—and he's Baptist."

Brenna's cheek tugged her mouth into a half smile. "Sometimes I wonder. Sometimes I wonder if anybody's listening at all."

Mary Margaret stepped up behind her and put hands on her shoulders. "I'm always here for you, you know. All of us are." She sighed, then stood beside Brenna and looked up toward the sky. "I wish I could have been there for you more when you were growing up. I know how hard it was for you, being alone with just Daddy. I asked him once if you could come live with me after I was married—did you know that?"

Brenna faced her sister, liking the way her eyes sparkled with moonlight, as if they held some secret light. She'd always thought this about Mary Margaret, and knew there was some truth to it. "No. He never mentioned it."

Mary Margaret nodded but didn't look at her. "It was your junior year in high school—when you were so sick with meningitis and had to stay in the hospital. You seemed . . . broken. I wanted to fix you." She smiled a little and touched her head to Brenna's. "But you came back to Daddy's house and eventually you became the Brenna I had known. Almost."

Brenna looked back up at the darkened sky. "Is there anything you

wish for? Anything you want so badly that you lie in bed at night crying for it?"

"No." Mary Margaret's voice was soft in the night air. "I've been
abundantly blessed. I really can't think of one thing I need." She
touched Brenna's cheek. "What about you?"

"There's nothing I need or want." She smiled. "Except for more.
people to come watch movies at my theater."

Mary Margaret was silent for a moment. "Then what do you ask the
saints for?"

Brenna swallowed a sob in her throat, wishing her sister didn't always know the right thing to ask. "That I wouldn't care so much. That
it wouldn't matter that I can't find it in my heart to wish."

She walked past her sister and kept going, embarrassed at her own
admission, and wanting nothing more than the comfort of her sheets
pulled over her head and the whirring of the air conditioner creating
white noise as she drifted into sleep, where nothing really mattered
at all.

The Indianola High School marching band had turned out in maroon-
and-gold splendor for the demolition of the old Indianola Post Office.
Pierce smiled to himself; there had once been a time when he would
have seen this event as something worthy of a marching band, but
maybe the time spent away had turned him into a visitor, and all the
pomp and circumstance arrayed in front of him became merely something to endure.

Yellow tape surrounded the area, and the sheriff was making sure the
crowd of bystanders stood back far enough from the bright yellow
wrecker with the enormous wrecking ball poised, aimed, and ready. A
lemonade stand had been set up across the street as a fund-raiser for the
band, and he bought two plastic cups full, adding an extra ten dollars
to the collection tin. He wasn't exactly sure why he did it, only that he'd
been filled with the memory of Brenna O'Brien playing the flute and
marching in the front row as he tried to distract her with a smile and
she tried not to miss a step. She hadn't always succeeded. He'd stopped

doing it when he found out her father would make her kneel on raw grits for missing notes or skipping a beat.

He handed a cup to his dad. "Go ahead and drink this and I'll get you another one. It's going to be hot, and I don't want you getting de-hydrated."

His dad looked up from his wheelchair, his face shaded by the brim of the old-fashioned hat Pierce remembered his father wearing when Pierce was a little boy. He patted the bag slung over the back of the wheelchair. "I'm a doctor, remember? I brought a couple of water bot-tles. But thanks for the lemonade."

Pierce smiled and nodded. His father had been a single parent be-fore it had become commonplace, and sometimes Pierce hadn't even noticed the absence of his mother. Sometimes.

His father was pointing across the parking lot. "Look—there're the O'Brien girls. Let's go say hello."

Pierce looked to where his dad indicated. Except for Claire, the pe-tite bottle-blonde, there was no question that the women were closely related. It wasn't just in the shape of their faces, or the sharp, pointed nose they all shared. It was more in the way they stood together, the older sisters in an unconscious semicircle around their youngest sister, Brenna, like mini Goliaths in the reverse role of protecting David.

He saw an awkward young man approach the group, and Claire moved forward to introduce him to Brenna. Pierce watched as she greeted the man with a closed grin, and Pierce knew, even after all these years, exactly what she was thinking as she shook hands. She'd be pray-ing to whoever her patron saint of the day was and asking for a re-prieve.

Pierce began to push his father's wheelchair. "Sure. Let's go stand over there. I think they've got the best view of the demolition." He ig-nored his father's knowing look as he quickly pushed him across the street.

The young man had left by the time they arrived, and all five women turned to face him as they approached—all of them, except for Brenna, wore an expression similar to what he'd expect a cat might wear as it waited at a mouse hole.

They were greeted warmly as Mary Margaret took over his father's wheelchair and Kathleen tucked her hand into the crook of Pierce's arm and moved him over to stand between herself and Brenna. He said hello to Brenna and watched a pink flush appear on her cheeks. Not willing to leave her alone, he said, "So, no crusty hair this morning?"

She shook her head slightly, and he could tell she was trying not to smile. "No, not today. But maybe tomorrow. I'll have to check my calendar."

He nodded and looked back to where the demolition ball was about to take aim at the squat brick post office. Pierce watched as Kathleen took a camera out of its case and raised it to her eye. "I like the way you plan your week. Very organized of you."

Brenna was saved from responding by the sound of the band playing a loud staccato drumroll as the wrecking ball swung into action. The crowd instinctively stepped back like children avoiding the oncoming rush of a wave, and the large ball smacked the side of the building. The sound of crumbling brick, breaking windows, and clapping erupted together, but Pierce's attention had been captured instead by the women standing next to him. Each wore a look of what he could only describe as relief, and they had all linked hands as if in that fragile show of solidarity they could withstand the blow from a wrecking ball.

The ball came back again, and this time when it found its mark the roof collapsed in final defeat, bringing the remaining two walls with it. The sound of clapping faded as the band and the crowd began to disperse. Pierce watched as the sisters hugged one another, holding on tightly to sturdy and straight O'Brien shoulders, another family trait. Kathleen raised her camera again, taking pictures of the last breaths of the old building.

He was about to say his good-byes when he heard somebody calling his father's name.

"Dr. McGovern!" A man approached wearing a bright yellow construction hat and a face and body smeared with dirt and dust. Pierce recognized him as Colleen's husband, whose name he couldn't remember. He did recall that he owned the local hardware store as well as a construction business, and it must have been his job to oversee the demolition.

The man carried what appeared to be a large old-fashioned metal cash box, and he held it out to Pierce's father as he drew closer.

"I planned to bring this by today, but since you're here I'll just give it to you now."

The old doctor settled the box on his lap and looked up at Colleen's husband. "What's this?"

The man took off his hat and scratched the top of his head with a dusty gloved hand. "Well, yesterday when we were removing fixtures from the post office, we found a loose tile under one of the counters. It didn't look right to me, so I pried it up and found this."

"But why would you think it belonged to me? I'm pretty sure I've never seen this box before."

"It's a box of old letters. I flipped through them as best as I could and saw that they're all addressed to you."

"Bill, what is it?" Colleen moved to stand next to her husband, followed by the rest of her sisters as they formed a circle around the wheelchair.

Pierce noticed his father's shaking hands as he lifted the lid off the broken hinges.

Bill put his hat back on. "Sorry about that. It was locked and we had to break it open." He added hastily, "I got the postmaster's permission first, of course."

The doctor didn't seem to hear. He was staring at the first envelope, his knobbed finger gently brushing the delicate handwriting on the front. Pierce looked over his shoulder and saw the return address was only a P.O. box, and the letter was addressed to Lieutenant Andrew McGovern, Army Air Corps, Eglin Air Force Base in Pensacola, Florida. *A lifetime ago.* For most of his adult life Pierce remembered his father only as Dr. McGovern, family practitioner and single father, not as a soldier. His father rarely spoke of his war years, and that persona, that soldier of the Second World War, had been buried long ago. Until now, it seemed.

Pierce leaned closer to his father. "Who are they from, Dad? Do you recognize them?"

His dad's eyes were empty, the lenses of his glasses like clear windows reflecting only time. "I've never seen these before."

"Are you sure? Do you at least recognize the handwriting?"

The doctor's voice sounded strained, as if the words he wanted to say were being forced back. "It was so long ago. I don't really remember." He wiped his hand over his forehead. "It's pretty hot out here. I think we should get on home. Thanks, Bill—I'll take a look at these later." He smiled at the women hovering over him. "It was a pleasure seeing you all again. And, Kathleen, thank you for your invitation to Sunday supper. Pierce and I will be there."

"Only if you're feeling up to it." Concerned at the pallor of his father's face, Pierce gently pried the box from him. "You are looking tired—maybe bringing you out in the sun wasn't such a good idea. We'll go home and I'll call your doctor." A knot of worry settled in his throat when his dad didn't complain. Pierce nodded good-bye to Bill and Colleen and the others gathered around them, then pushed harder on the wheelchair, juggling the cash box in his other hand.

"You need some help." Brenna stood next to him and took the cash box. Too thankful to protest, he let her take it.

They walked the four blocks to his rental car; then Brenna followed him to his father's house. When they arrived, she helped to get his father inside and into bed, then stayed with him while Pierce called the doctor.

His father was sleeping when Pierce returned to the bedroom, with Brenna sitting on the side of the bed holding his hand. He'd always liked that about her—her ease in comforting and sympathizing. From a girl who'd grown up without a mother, it had surprised him at first. At least, until he'd met her sisters.

She looked up when he stood next to her. "His breathing is steady and he doesn't seem to have a temperature. I think maybe the heat and the excitement just wore him out." She stood and faced him.

Pierce rubbed his palms against his pants, unsure where to put his hands but knowing that on her shoulders would be a mistake. "Thanks for helping me take care of my dad. You've always been good at that." He was babbling, and he realized that it was because he wasn't ready to see her go. "I always thought you'd be a nurse or a doctor or something."

She picked up a picture in a silver frame that had sat on his father's nightstand ever since he could remember. It was a picture of him as a small boy holding a football and handing it to whoever it was taking the picture. He'd never thought to ask who that had been. Brenna stared at it for a moment before putting it down gently. "Yeah, I thought so, too. And then I decided that I really wanted to stay in Indianola, and then Mr. Miesel put the theater up for sale and I figured it was just meant to be."

He could almost hear a younger Brenna speaking as he watched her pick up her purse and adjust it on her shoulder. *I think the world must be flat, Pierce. Because when people leave this town, they never come back—like they've stepped off the edge of the world. That's going to be me one day. Just watch me.* After the passage of all these years, he could still remember his surprise at her words. Because even back then, Brenna O'Brien had found it difficult to summon the courage to discuss her future. He had liked to think that somehow he was responsible. He had no idea then what that bravado would eventually cost them both.

She faced him, fiddling with the straps on her purse. "Those letters in the box. Do you know who they're from?"

"No. And I'm not sure my dad does, either. He said that he'd never seen them before."

"I wonder how they got there—under the floor in the post office. Like they'd been hidden."

His eyes met hers with the same unspoken thoughts he'd been having since Bill had handed the box to his father.

She turned to go. "Tell your dad I hope he feels better."

"You can stay until he wakes up, if you like. I brewed a pitcher of sweet tea this morning, if you'd like some."

She shook her head without looking at him. "I've got to go open my theater. I've started doing a matinee show each week to get those people who like to see movies on their lunch break or in the middle of the day instead of at nighttime."

"Is that profitable?"

"Depends on how you would define 'profitable.' Am I getting more people into the movie theater to see first-run movies they probably wouldn't have? Definitely. Am I filling the theater and covering my costs? No. Right now I'm just trying to expose as many people as I can to my wonderful theater so they'll know what a treasure it is to the town of Indianola."

He wanted to clap and give her a high five, but he did neither as he continued to lean against the bureau with arms folded over his chest. Her passion for things big and small had always added to her attractiveness, and even after the passage of years it hadn't diminished—neither her passion nor her attractiveness. Warily, he stared her down again until she turned away and headed toward the stairs.

He followed her and opened the front door. When she moved to pass by him, he touched her arm. "Thank you. For helping me with my dad."

Her green eyes smiled at him as she gave a short nod, then walked out onto the front porch and down the steps.

"Good-bye, Brenna."

She didn't stop as she called over her shoulder, "Bye, Pierce."

He watched her walk down the sidewalk as the humid summer air became a time-travel mechanism, bringing him back to the summer of his nineteenth year, when he'd been young and naive and thought that Brenna O'Brien was the one person who could erase the memory of his mother's abandonment and make him whole again.

Slowly he climbed back up the stairs and sat down in a chair that he'd pulled up next to his father's bed, the metal box on his lap. His fingers drummed against the closed lid as he watched his father sleep, beating a tattoo that accompanied the old man's breathing, while Pierce tried not to think too much about why a box of letters addressed to his father had been found beneath the floor of the old post office.

CHAPTER 7

Brenna watched as Claire leaned forward in the front seat of her car and began to rustle around in her beach bag–sized purse. Claire grabbed a cigarette and stuck it between maraschino red lips.

"You'd better not light that in my car. And when did you start smoking, anyway?"

Claire let the cigarette droop from her lips as she spoke. "Since that little Charlene Bennett won the Miss Watermelon Seed crown. Mary Sanford wanted it so badly—it's in the shape of a giant seed and it's got little crystals all over it, so it really sparkles. You just have no idea how upset she is."

"Has she started smoking, too?"

Claire stabbed her hand back into her purse. "Of course not. But Mary Sanford should have won. You should have just heard her singing her heart out when she sang 'Fever.' It was awe-inspiring. Charlene only did a twirling number—and she nearly dropped that stupid baton twice." Rustling around again in her purse, the cigarette still dangling, she added, "Her mom must have slept with some of the judges, is all I can think."

"You let your six-year-old sing a song about sex? In front of other people? Just please don't tell me you covered her face with makeup, too."

Claire remained focused on her purse. "I used appropriate colors—all peaches and pinks. And I did not dye Mary Sanford's hair. Her hair is naturally blond. Unlike that little Charlene, whose hair is probably mousy brown like her mother's."

Brenna eyed her sister as Claire continued her apparent search for a lighter. Several MoonPie and Ho Hos wrappers edged up the sides and took flying leaps from the zipper to the soft leather seat of the Volkswagen. Claire spotted them and quickly crumpled them into a ball and shoved them into the dark recesses of the purse. "At least Mary Sanford will have a better chance at being Little Miss Crawfish. Charlene looks just pasty in red, and that's the required color for the evening gown competition."

Stopping at a red light, Brenna turned toward her passenger. "Look, I'm not going to let you smoke in my car, so you might as well stop hunting for a lighter. Your car will be out of the shop tomorrow morning and you can pollute your own vehicle then."

Annoyed, Claire yanked the cigarette from her mouth and tossed it out the window.

"I guess you missed that part in preschool where they taught you about not littering."

"Oh, quit picking on me, Brenn. I'm upset. Can't you just let me wallow in it? To make matters worse, I'm on that low-carb diet, and it's making me cranky."

Raising her eyebrows at the remembrance of the snack wrappers, Brenna kept her mouth shut as she turned the corner onto Main and found a parking spot near Mary Margaret's emporium. As she put the car in park, Claire faced her.

Reaching toward the chains around Brenna's neck, she lifted one to see it closer. "Which one is this?"

With a sigh, knowing how very few secrets she'd ever been able to keep from any of her sisters, she said, "Saint Eustace."

Claire raised delicately groomed eyebrows.

"Patron saint of difficult situations."

The eyebrows lifted even further.

"I can't really explain, Claire. It just feels as if my life's on a collision course with something, but I don't know what yet. I figured Saint Eustace could help."

Claire nodded slowly and let the medal drop. "I think you're lonely. Do you want me to try to set something up between you and Dr. McGovern's son—"

"No." Brenna cut her off with a sharp shake of her head. "Not him, not ever."

Claire stared at her. "And I suppose you're not going to tell me why."

"We're just not compatible. We can hardly stand to be in the same room together."

"Well, how about Mrs. Venable's nephew—the one who just moved here from Birmingham? I saw him at the grocery store yesterday and got the whole scoop on him. He's tall and good-looking and works for the electric company as an engineer. His name's Jim."

Halfheartedly, Brenna said, "And I suppose you know whether he wears boxers or briefs."

Claire scowled. "What's that supposed to mean?"

"Never mind." She stared out her front windshield, making a note to wash her car. "Does he have a nickname I should know about?"

"Actually, he does. It's Schmott."

"Schmott?"

"Yeah—I guess it's from childhood or something, because as far as I could tell, he's got all four limbs intact." She smiled sweetly at her younger sister. "Would you like me to set something up?"

"Could I stop you?"

"Probably not. I already gave him your number. He might call tonight, so I wanted to make sure you'd be ready."

With a heavy sigh of resignation, Brenna said, "Thanks, Claire. I'll be sure to keep you posted."

Claire opened the door. "By the way, have you talked with Dr. Mc-Govern about those letters? I bet you're just itching to get ahold of them."

Brenna recalled the stricken look on the doctor's face when he'd first opened the box. "Not yet. I know the new postmaster has been to see him, and so has a reporter from the *Times-Picayune* in New Orleans. Mrs. Grodin said that the FBI had contacted the sheriff—something to do with it being an offense to stop mail from being delivered or something." She thought for a moment, remembering how his expression resembled the one her own father had worn when she'd told him about her plans to go to college in Virginia or as far away as she could get from where she was. "I don't know if the doctor is going to want to talk about them."

Claire regarded her sister solemnly. "If those letters were sent during the war, Daddy would have been working at the post office then."

"Yeah. I thought about that, too." Their eyes met, but neither one spoke.

Claire leaned over and kissed Brenna on the cheek before letting herself out. "Let me know if you hear anything. Thanks for the ride, Brenn. I'll see you later."

Brenna waved and put the car into gear. As she checked for traffic before pulling out onto the street, she looked across the median and froze. Parked on the opposite side of the street, directly in front of Bob's Barbershop, was the dark blue SUV she had seen the previous Sunday near Kathleen's house. A man sat inside, wearing a cowboy hat and dark sunglasses, and from the direction his face was turned, she had no doubt that he was looking right at her.

Calmly, she rationalized that he was probably just looking at her car—the only yellow Bug in the entire town of Indianola. But then he nodded his head ever so slightly before raising the window, and she knew without a doubt that his interest had not been in her car.

Pulling into traffic, she quickly went down the one-way street until she could turn around to come back on his side. But by the time she had reached the spot where she'd seen him, the dark SUV was gone. She strained her eyes to see if she could see the taillights heading in either direction, but she saw nothing. He had completely disappeared.

Brenna backed into the door of Bill and Colleen's hardware store, her hands full of two pans of butterscotch pound cake. Mrs. Grodin had been more than generous in sharing her baking pans and utensils and had even offered to help—probably in a conciliatory gesture after the air-conditioner incident. Knowing that she'd need to make twice as much batter for Mrs. Grodin to sample, Brenna had politely declined the help, stating that she could manage just fine. She couldn't resist adding that her air conditioner still needed fixing and that she was going to borrow a tall ladder to remove Mrs. Grodin's air conditioner if she didn't have a replacement by the end of the week.

Dooley stood behind the counter mixing paint for a customer. He grinned at Brenna as she placed the pans on the counter. "This is for you and the other is for Colleen and Bill. It's not enough to thank you for the air conditioner, but it's only my first attempt."

As she turned around, she was surprised to see Aunt Dottie squinting at a copy of *Hardware Today* through her glasses.

"Aunt Dottie! I didn't expect to see you today. How'd you get here?"

Aunt Dottie blinked as if trying to figure out who was speaking. "Oh, hello there, Brenna. Why, I drove, of course. You couldn't expect me to walk in these high heels, now, could you?" She showed a row of perfectly straight dentures.

Brenna glanced out the large front window and saw Aunt Dottie's Lincoln neatly parallel parked at the curb. The front bumper showed a deep dent where Kathleen's mailbox had met its fate.

"I thought Colleen had a talk with you about not driving anymore."

Aunt Dottie's grin never faded. "I didn't fall off the turnip truck yesterday, you know. I saw them coming, so I hid under the dining room table until they'd gone. Timmy helped me."

Brenna looked back at the car to check for bodies still trapped underneath, or at least for further bumper damage as evidence of her parking ability. "But . . . ?"

Dooley stopped the mixing machine and moved the paint can to the counter. "I parked it for her."

"What, dear?" Aunt Dottie dropped the magazine on the floor, apparently forgotten, and approached the counter.

"I said your paint is ready."

Brenna examined the paint before Dooley snapped on the lid and looked at her aunt in surprise. "It's purple."

Her aunt blinked at her from behind the thick glasses. "Isn't it beautiful? I'm redoing my bedroom and thought purple would be lovely. I think the pale yellow that's on the walls now is too old for me."

Dooley and Brenna shared raised eyebrows as Dooley came from behind the counter. Just then the front door opened, the bell ringing in announcement. The back of Brenna's neck prickled, and she knew who it was before she turned around.

Pierce paused for a moment, as if trying to gather why three sets of eyes were firmly planted on him. He nodded briefly at Aunt Dottie and Brenna before addressing Dooley.

"I need to fix my dad's deck—it's all rotted out, and I have to replace it if we expect to sell the house. Dad told me this was the place to come for everything I'd need."

Dooley's face seemed to lose its animation as he looked at Pierce, his brown eyes dimming. Without smiling, he said, "Most likely. Do you have the dimensions of the new deck you'll be wanting to build?" His expression made it clear that he didn't expect any city boy to know anything about building a deck.

Pierce reached into his back pocket and pulled out what appeared to be a pencil drawing, complete with dimensions, of a sizable deck. Without a word, he put it on the counter in front of Dooley as if laying down a gauntlet.

Dooley eyed the plan without comment. Finally he said, "We've got the lumber out back. Do you need to have it delivered?"

Pierce looked at Dooley with a cool expression, as if he'd won round one. "I've got my dad's truck with me."

Bill appeared from the back office jingling a set of keys and greeted everyone with brief nods before turning to Aunt Dottie. "You about ready to go? I'll take you home, and I promise we'll get your car back to you later."

Aunt Dottie blinked up at Bill as if she'd never seen him before, then walked over to where Dooley and Pierce stood facing each other over the counter. "Have y'all met my niece, Brenna? She's single and lookin' to get married. If either of you is single, too, I'd really appreciate it if you'd take her out and give her a chance. She's not so young anymore, but years of living single have sure made her a feisty thing."

Bill muttered something unintelligible before grabbing the paint and taking Aunt Dottie's elbow and forcibly leading her from the store.

Dooley focused his attention on Brenna, making her wonder if he was thinking about color-matching the shade of her face for a lovely red wallcovering.

Smiling, and trying to act as if being embarrassed and humiliated were part of her everyday life, she crossed her arms over her chest and leaned back into a tall circular display of sunglasses. A tall, circular, *movable* display that easily gave way to the pressure of Brenna's weight on it and slid backward before hitting a broken tile on the floor and tipping over, scattering sunglasses across the linoleum.

In the stunned silence that followed, she caught Dooley's eye. It was clear he was trying very hard not to laugh. At her expression he straightened his face, then came to her side to help her pick up the display. Straining his head around it to look at Brenna, he said, "I know she's your aunt, but I think she's one Vienna sausage shy of a can."

Pierce let out a bark of laughter as he bent and grabbed the round knob from the top of the display and shoved it back where it belonged. Dooley gave him a sidelong glance. "Don't worry about this. I'll clean it up."

She held out her hand without looking at either of them "Please don't. I'd rather keep busy and stew in my humiliation by myself. But thanks."

"Are you sure, Brenn? It'll go faster if I help, because I can prevent you from trying on each pair and acting goofy." Dooley tugged on her braid, trying to make her smile, but she shook her head.

"Really—let me do it." She picked up a handful of sunglasses and started to place them back in their holders. Dooley turned and headed toward the back of the store, motioning for Pierce to follow. Pierce paused, wearing a contemplative look. She glared at him, daring him to say something. Instead he coughed slightly, as if swallowing a laugh, before following Dooley.

Turning her back, Brenna listened as their footsteps beat a retreat through the store and disappeared out the back door.

Bending down again, she concentrated on her task, unwilling to shift her focus. The bell over the door chimed, but she didn't look up. She continued stooping to pick up sunglasses and put them away until she felt a presence beside her, and a large, tanned hand held out a wire-framed pair of glasses. "These were over by the door. Figured they belonged over here."

Glancing up, she froze. It was the man in the SUV, cowboy hat and all. As if reading her mind, he lifted the hat from his head.

"I'm Nathan Conley. I'm new in town."

His manners were impeccable and his speech slow and Southern, a lot like the men she'd grown up with and who were now her brothers-in-law. But there was something about him that seemed vaguely familiar. He seemed normal enough, though, that she didn't feel uncomfortable being alone with him in the store.

She took the glasses from him. "It's nice to meet you. I'm Brenna O'Brien."

He nodded, then turned to look around the store, giving her a chance to study him. His hair was a dark brown with no gray in it at all, but wearing the squashed-down look that Brenna always referred to as "hat head." He looked to be in his mid-twenties and had deep-bronzed skin that stretched across a sharp face, with fine wrinkles around the eyes and mouth, as if he'd spent a lot of time outdoors. He was tall and lean, with tightly corded muscles in his arms, and looked exactly like what Brenna supposed a cowboy might look like.

Realizing she was staring, she averted her gaze to stash the last of the sunglasses back where they belonged. "If you need assistance, I don't work here, but Dooley Gambrel is out in the lumberyard right now with a customer. He'll be right back."

The man regarded her for a moment as if he didn't understand what she was talking about or why he was there in the first place.

"Yes, thank you." He put the hat back on his head, and she noticed his left hand was devoid of not only a wedding ring but also a telltale suntan line.

Torn between sticking around to find out who this man really was and the desire to escape before Pierce reappeared, Brenna stalled by digging through her purse and pretending to look for her keys.

Casually, she asked, "Where you from?"

The man looked at her with a level gaze. "Texas. Houston, actually. My mama died recently, and I thought it was time to see the world." He squinted out the large front window. "Nice town, though. Might stay awhile."

She grasped her keys but continued to search through the depths of her pocketbook. "Do I know you from somewhere?" She finally looked up at him, trying to think of a more direct way without coming right out and asking him if he'd been watching her.

As if reading her mind, he said, "You probably think I've been stalking you—but I haven't. Honest." He smiled a sincere grin, and she warmed slightly. "It's just that yellow car of yours—it sort of stands out. Especially with you behind the wheel. Couldn't help but stare."

She heard the back door of the store open and the men's voices approaching. She flushed a little. "Oh, that's okay. I didn't think you were stalking me," she lied. "I've got to get to work. By the way—I own the local theater. You should come check out a show while you're in town." She said a quick good-bye and left before Pierce and Dooley returned.

It wasn't until she was driving away that she realized that he hadn't really answered her question. Nor could she quite understand why it was that he had seemed so familiar to her.

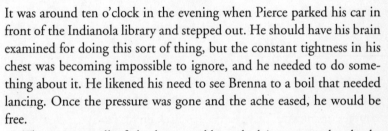

It was around ten o'clock in the evening when Pierce parked his car in front of the Indianola library and stepped out. He should have his brain examined for doing this sort of thing, but the constant tightness in his chest was becoming impossible to ignore, and he needed to do something about it. He likened his need to see Brenna to a boil that needed lancing. Once the pressure was gone and the ache eased, he would be free.

The sweet smell of the honeysuckle tucked in among the shrubs bordering the sidewalk eased the summer evening through his senses, making him pay attention to the night in a way he hadn't done in years. When was the last time he had even taken a walk? He had become so emotionally isolated since his divorce that he had taken to ordering his groceries online and driving the block to the pickup window at the local convenience store to get any last-minute items.

Without his directing them, his feet took him down familiar sidewalks, past houses of old friends and shops that were so interwoven with childhood memories he could almost see the reflection of a young boy staring into the plate-glass windows. He paused in front of Bill's Hardware, remembering seeing Brenna there earlier, and the pain in his chest tightened. But this time it seemed less like pain and more like hunger. Turning away, he kept walking, trying to remember if hunger and pain were two different things.

He heard her before he saw her, trying not to wince at the horrible off-key rendition of the theme from *Gilligan's Island*. Her tone deafness had always been one of her annoying—and most endearing—qualities. That, coupled with her ability to reproduce theme songs from any seventies or eighties sitcom, had always made him want to either throttle her or kiss her. He felt like doing a little of both at the moment as he stared at her from the sidewalk, watching her in the short instant before she knew he was there.

The porch light was on, attracting a swarm of admiring moths, and Pierce could tell Brenna was aware of their activity by the way she was shoved into the corner of the porch swing as far away from the light as she could get.

Abruptly she stopped singing and turned her head slightly to face him. In the quiet night he could hear the bodies of the moths as they threw themselves against the light in complete stupidity, seemingly not knowing what it was they wanted, but killing themselves in an attempt to get it.

"I was taking a walk." He shook his head slightly at how absurd he sounded. He was staying with his father in the neighboring town, it was late at night, yet he was taking a walk and happened to pass by her house.

She stilled the porch swing with one bare foot. He noticed her purse and shoes discarded nearby, as if she had just come home but hadn't yet found the energy to go inside. She stared at him for a long moment before saying, "Would you like to come up and sit for a while? I could get us some iced tea, if you like."

She waited for his answer, her thick strawberry blond hair fluttering around her face as a slight breeze blew through the porch, smelling like rain. Without thinking, he said, "Sure." And then he watched as his own feet walked up the steps of the porch toward her.

Springing up, she was through the front door before he'd even made it to the top step, as if trying to get their tea before he changed his mind. Choosing a seat on the swing on the opposite side from where she'd been, he sat down, clutching the chain to steady himself. He closed his eyes, smelling the summer scents of cut grass and Confederate jasmine, and recalled sitting on another porch with Brenna as her oldest sister handed them iced tea glasses with lemons adorning the rims. As long as he was gone before her father returned home from work, he could relax. And he'd never been caught. Until the time came when his world had shattered and he'd stopped going to her house. Facing her father's anger hadn't mattered anymore. His own anger had been hard enough to deal with.

Within minutes Brenna reappeared with two tall glasses, wedges of lemons impaled on the edges. He avoided touching her fingers as he took the glass from her. Gingerly she backed up onto the other end of the swing, careful not to spill her drink.

He smelled her perfume first, then noticed the silk shirt and skirt and gold earrings. "Have you been out?"

She didn't look at him but kept her gaze focused on the swaying mimosa tree, its leaves brushed by the breeze just enough to show their white undersides. Free to stare at her, he watched as her cheek curved into a smile. "Yep. Just got back from another date from hell."

"Anybody I know?" He took a sip of his tea, hoping it wasn't Dooley.

"Jim Venable. But everybody calls him Schmott."

He raised an eyebrow, the name completely and happily unfamiliar to him. "Schmott? What kind of nickname is that?"

She tucked her feet under her, showing her toenails and chipped pink polish, and faced him, her green eyes catching the light. "That's what I asked. Then wished I hadn't." She took a drink from her glass before continuing. "It seems that while he was on a trip to New Orleans with his buddies, they took a streetcar ride down St. Charles Avenue just for fun. Well, that's what he said, but it was probably because they were three sheets to the wind and couldn't find their cars." She pressed the side of her glass against her cheeks, then turned her face into the wind.

"Jim apparently thought it would be a good idea to stick his head way out of the window of the streetcar. When it collided with a lamppost, that's the sound it made."

"Schmott?" He couldn't hold back a grin.

"Yep—Schmott. And that pretty much sums up my date tonight."

He choked back a laugh. "Sorry. I really am. I'm actually surprised that you take the chance and go on these blind dates. You used to be the kind of person who'd choose to stay home if you weren't sure of the outcome."

Her smile was sad. "There aren't any expectations. That makes it easy."

He smelled her perfume again, and it appeared to coil around his neck and pull him closer. The temperature seemed to rise a few steady degrees, making him imitate her by pressing his chilled glass to the side of his neck. *Thump, thump, thump* went the moths as they hurled themselves at the light.

"Well, at least you'll have good stories to tell your children."

The light seemed to dim in her eyes as she looked at him. "There aren't going to be any. I'm not getting married, remember?" And then she said the words that he had been avoiding for years. They crept out of her mouth with deceptive sweetness, gut-punching him before he could jump up and leave.

"Do you ever wish things would have turned out differently?"

He jerked himself off the swing, thumping his glass down heavily on a small table. He kept his back to her and took several deep breaths. "I try not to live in a world of what-might-have-beens and instead learn to be grateful for the tough lessons."

Her voice was thick. "Is that what our time together was, then—a tough lesson?"

He made the mistake of turning around and looking at her. God, she was beautiful. Even with eyes full of tears, her face alone made him want to touch her. He took a step forward, then stopped. *Thump, thump.* A fat moth, its wings still fluttering in useless animation, fell to the floor, its obsession with the light a fatal folly. He watched the dying moth as it lay on its back, the wings still beating and propelling itself in circles. Even in its last moments, it struggled to reach the light, as if that which brought it death could also bring it salvation. Softly, Pierce said, "It doesn't matter anymore." He stepped down off the porch. "Good night, Brenna. Thanks for the tea."

As he walked away from her the breeze picked up, bringing with it the beginning of rain. Fat drops came down like tears staining the cement, the wind pushing at his back. He was almost sure he could hear her whispered voice directed to his departing back. "It does. I don't want it to, but it still does."

The rain came down harder now and he hurried his steps, anxious to put as much space between them as he could.

CHAPTER 8

Brenna sped her yellow Beetle around the corner onto Main Street, then slid into her usual parking space in front of her theater. Pulling the box of pansies and planting soil out of the trunk, she glanced at her watch. Fifteen minutes late. Earlier she had driven all the way to New Orleans to go to confession, and if it hadn't been for highway construction on I-10, she would have made it to work in plenty of time. She could have gone to St. Andrew's, her local church, but she imagined that after confessing to Father Joe about lust and unforgiveness, she would never be able to face him across the dining room table at Kathleen's again.

She set down the pansies while she unlocked the gate, then picked them up again slowly, frowning. She'd been hoping that the vibrant colors of the flowers in the sidewalk bed would distract the eye away from the peeling paint on the sentinel lions and the crooked marquee. But now, staring down at the delicate petals, she knew her idea was as ludicrous as putting a Band-Aid on an amputated leg.

Putting the flowers down again, she shoved the flat up against the wall and made her way inside to her office. As always, Beau had stacked all the previous night's receipts into a pile on the left side of her desk, along with an itemized to-do list. She picked up the list and read the bold, stringy writing. *Men's bathroom flooded last night during the midnight show. Turned off water and left message on plumber's voice mail to call you this morning. Candy rep called regarding last bill—I told him you'd already mailed the payment. You did, right? Oh—had to cordon off the last row of seats. The supports under the middle seats seem to have snapped or something, and I didn't want anybody getting hurt. Have a great day and I'll see you tonight!*

She dropped the notepad back on her desk without even glancing at the receipts and left her office. Moving through the darkened hallway, she found her way into the grand auditorium, with the thick red velvet curtains and plush seats. Ignoring the duct tape strung across the last row, she walked past them, then sank down in one of the seats on the front row. She stared up at the huge mural on the ceiling depicting the Battle of Mansfield, a Confederate victory fought in Louisiana during the Union's Red River campaign. It had always secretly amused her to see that all the Southern officers were a good deal taller and better looking than their Yankee counterparts, but she'd been charmed nevertheless. The ceiling with its twenty-two crystal chandeliers was unique and beautiful and hers, and staring up at it had never failed to make her feel as if the day ahead held more than just light and darkness.

Except for today. Business had never been great, but it had been sufficient. At least, until major repairs became necessary. She looked up at a fallen Yankee soldier, his eyes rolled up toward heaven and his hand stretched out in silent supplication. She felt an odd kinship with the dying man, except for the fact that, unlike him, she'd have to go on living after the final blow.

She squinted at the top of the large curtain that surrounded the screen, noticing a tear near the top of the rod. With the weight of the velvet, she estimated they had about another three months to go before the entire right-hand side pulled itself away and ended up on the stage. Preferably not during a performance. *God.* She clenched her eyes as if by doing so, she could make everything go away. She'd done that as a girl after watching endless reruns of *I Dream of Jeannie,* until her father told her it was all a fantasy and that things like magic and happy endings could be found only in the movies. It was the only thing he'd taught her that had turned out to be true.

A door closed at the front of the theater, capturing her attention. Standing, she quickly made her way through the theater to the front lobby where she'd come in. Beau was in school, and she wasn't expecting any of her sisters.

"Hello?" she called out.

"Hello?" a male voice answered back, and she jumped at its proximity.

A hatless Nathan Conley turned from where he'd been examining the old floor clock with the large bronze crow perched on top. It was an anomaly as far as theaters went, an item purchased by some long-dead owner and placed in the foyer for no apparent reason except to show the passage of time. But, like the mural, the chandeliers, and even the leaking toilets, it was hers and she loved it.

She stepped back, startled. "What are you doing here?"

He stepped back, too, his hands clutching his cowboy hat over his heart. "I'm sorry," he drawled. "I didn't mean to startle you." He grinned. "Look, I'll go outside the gate and talk there, if you're more comfortable with that."

She shook her head, still surprised to see him. "No, that's all right. But the matinee doesn't start until eleven thirty, if that's what you're looking for."

"Not today. I actually just wanted to see the theater. I'm stomping the sidewalks today looking for a job and figured I'd take a peek inside when I passed by. Old theaters are sort of a hobby of mine—something my mama passed on to me, I guess." His gaze swept across the arched ceiling with its flaking paint across to the mahogany paneling and chipped marble floors. "I have to say that this is probably one of the most beautiful ones I've ever seen."

She warmed to him. His easy manner and his words about her theater put her more at ease. Her cell phone rang, and she unclipped it from her belt to look at the screen. Suppressing a groan, she saw it was the plumber. "I've got to take this. Do you mind hanging around for a few minutes?"

"Sure thing. Mind if I look around?"

She nodded, feeling somewhat less concerned than she might, knowing the vigorous background check Mrs. Grodin did on her boarders. Before Brenna had moved in, she'd been afraid that Mrs. Grodin might turn down her application simply because she'd received a C on her report card in the eleventh grade.

He smiled again, distracting her for a moment before she flipped open her phone to answer it. When she was through getting an estimate that was in the same ballpark as the price of a small car, she hung up and looked around for Nathan Conley. She found him in the auditorium sitting in the middle row, staring up at her mural.

"Wow," he said, then whistled. "This is amazing. You just don't see anything like this anymore, do you? And what a shame that is. What a wonderful, fragile treasure."

She followed his gaze to a fallen Yankee who, even in his death throes, had managed to grab a flag and hoist it aloft in defiance of defeat. "Yeah," she said. "It is." Staring into the eyes of the fallen soldier, she knew that she and Nathan Conley, whoever he was, were kindred spirits.

Brenna began to lead him through the theater, talking about its history. "*Gone With the Wind* was the first movie shown in the Royal Majestic, and it was shown the very first week after the premiere at the Fox Theater in Atlanta in 1939." She heard the pride in her voice but didn't try to hide it as she usually did when talking to her sisters or others who would listen politely with glazed eyes. Pierce had understood. And now she knew that she'd found another person who shared her passion.

"And that clock in the lobby—it's pretty old, and the only thing I know about it is that a previous owner put it in the lobby because of the crow on top. I'm sure it means something, but I've never been able to determine what."

Nathan pursed his lips and nodded. "Well, my mama used to tell me a story about crows. That if you made a wish on one when you saw it take off, and if it didn't flap its wings before it landed again, your wish would come true." He smiled a big Texas grin. "Maybe that owner saw the connection between wishes and fantasy—something we all seem to find at the movies."

Brenna smiled back. "You might be right."

She turned to lead him back toward the lobby. As they passed the small corridor that ran to the bathrooms, she felt her feet squelching on wet carpet.

Nathan stopped and looked down at his feet. "That's not good."

"No, it isn't. I'm thinking I'm going to have to close down the men's bathroom and use the women's as a unisex, because I just can't afford to fix it right now."

He scratched his head. "Well, I worked as a plumber's assistant for a year after high school." After hesitating for just a moment, he reached into the back pocket of his jeans and handed her a white envelope. "Here, why don't you take a look at this?"

"What is it?" she asked as she took the envelope.

"It's a letter of reference from my last employer. Maybe you might want to give me a job."

"A job?" she echoed as she opened the envelope. She briefly glanced at the letter from Donald Black, president of a construction company in Houston that was so big that even she'd heard of it. The letter stated that Nathan Conley was an exemplary employee and that the company hated to see him go. She folded the letter and looked back at the man in front of her, who stood with his hands and hat behind his back like a student getting ready to be scolded by his teacher.

"What did you do in your last position?"

"Construction foreman. I pretty much oversaw an entire job from the permitting to the finish work."

She regarded the surprisingly articulate cowboy standing in front of her, trying to figure out exactly who he was. "So why would you want a job from me?"

He smiled, and again Brenna was struck by something familiar about him. "Our specialty was refurbishing old buildings."

She quelled the little fire of hope and handed the letter back to him. "Look, I can't afford you. Besides, I'm not hiring. I have enough help."

"Really?" His gaze took in the men's bathroom door blocked off with duct tape and the soggy carpet beneath their feet. "I don't think you can afford *not* to have me around." He cleared his throat. "Look, I've been in town long enough to hear about the new multiplex being planned. I've refurbished plenty of old theaters, changing them into restaurants and department stores, to know what happens when a multiplex comes to town. But it doesn't need to be that way. And I think I know enough to be able to make sure you and your little theater here survive."

Brenna crossed her arms over her chest. "Okay. Which sister sent you?"

He regarded her with what looked like genuine confusion. "Excuse me?"

"Never mind. Regardless of how much you need a job, or I need you, I can't afford you. Unless you'd like to be paid in candy bars and popcorn."

"All right."

"What?"

"I said all right. I've got some money saved up; plus I've been doing odd jobs for Mrs. Grodin in exchange for rent, so my living expenses are covered. I don't know how long I'll stay in town, but I figured I'd make myself useful." He stuck his hands in his back pockets and looked up at the chipped gold paint on the tops of the Corinthian columns that flanked the archway leading to the lobby. "Besides, I'm a card-carrying member of the National Trust. It would be a personal affront to see this theater close."

"I don't know. . . ."

He held up his hand. "Think about it. We can work out some kind of plan where I get paid only if one of my ideas makes you some money. I'm living over at Mrs. Grodin's boardinghouse if you need to reach me. But I truly hope you'll consider hiring me on. I really would like to get involved."

She felt her own rallying bugle cry thrum in her head and wondered if this was how besieged soldiers felt when reinforcements arrived. With more confidence than she felt, she said, "Maybe we might be able to work something out."

His eyebrows lifted. "Yeah?"

"Let me have that letter back and I'll do a background check. Then I'll call so we can talk about logistics."

He smiled broadly, unsettling her again. "Sounds like a plan. I'll look forward to hearing from you." He gave her the letter back, then stuck out his hand and she shook it, feeling the rough calluses on his palm. "Oh, and by the way, tell my dad I said hey."

"Your dad?"

"Yeah. Don Black—the president of the company I used to work for."

"Oh. I didn't . . . I mean, you have different last names. . . ."

"Yep. My dad never married my mama, so I've always used her last name."

She squinted at him. "So what on earth are you doing here in Indianola?"

He shrugged. "I guess I just wanted to see the world—at least, the world outside of Houston, Texas. I'd never been anywhere else, and I figured it was time to do it while I was still young and didn't have anything tying me down."

"Okay. Fair enough. I'll let you know." Brenna couldn't help but grin. "Most definitely."

His foot squelched as he took a step toward the bathroom and began shrugging out of his jacket. "Can't say I don't love a challenge."

She thought again of the soldier in her mural, hoisting his flag in the face of defeat, and she smiled at Nathan. "Consider this your employment application."

"Yes, ma'am," he said, and handed her his jacket.

Bone-tired and finding it difficult to put one foot in front of the other, Brenna pushed open the door to Mrs. Grodin's boardinghouse and slowly climbed the stairs to her room. It had been a busy night at the theater, with an almost sellout crowd to see the new Keanu Reeves movie. She leaned against the banister for a moment, then continued her climb. It had been a bittersweet success, however, after Beau had pointed out that once a multiplex opened, it would be nearly impossible to get first-run movies.

Rubbing her lower back with one hand, she made her way down the hallway, squinting in the dim light at her door and what looked like a piece of paper that had been taped to it. Thinking it was a cowardly note from Mrs. Grodin, she yanked it off the door, not really caring if it took a little square of paint with it. Jabbing her key into the lock, she pushed the door open and flipped on the light, kicking her bags inside as she opened the note.

She hadn't seen the handwriting in many years, but she still remembered it. The harsh vertical lines diminished by looping Ys and Gs that had always reminded her of the boy who created them—brash and energetic, but who carefully hid his poet's soul. The same boy who'd cried in film class when they'd watched *Wuthering Heights* and would have broken the nose of any guy who'd ever mention it in his hearing.

Moving to her bed and flicking on the bedside lamp, she read:

Brenna—

I didn't want to bother you at work and I had to stop by anyway to see Mrs. Grodin, whose older brother is at Liberty Village. But I need to talk with you as soon as possible. It's about my dad's letters. Please call as soon as you get a chance. Thanks, Pierce.

As if as an afterthought, he'd included his father's phone number where he was staying, and his own cell number, too. She glanced at her watch. Twelve thirty. The phone call would have to wait until morning, although the waiting would probably keep her awake all night. She wanted to believe that her excitement was only about the letters in the old box, but she was getting too old to lie to herself.

Ignoring her blinking answering machine, she placed the note on her nightstand and got ready for bed. Flinging her new Victoria's Secret bra into her laundry basket and then slipping her cotton nightshirt over her head, she finally crawled between the covers before hitting the play button. One message was from Colleen, asking her to watch Timmy the next day. He was sick and needed to stay home from school. The next was from Dooley, asking her if she had any plans for Friday night. They were having turtle races at Darla's Tavern and he wanted to go. The third call was from Kathleen's husband, John. She'd called him earlier about getting his own human resources department to do a background check on Nathan Conley, and he said that he had the information she needed. He would be working all night at his office on a project, but to call him when she got in, as he was sure he'd need a break.

He answered on the second ring.

"Hi, John—it's Brenna. I can't believe you've already heard back about Nathan."

"It's amazing what the Internet can provide these days. Makes this sort of thing pretty easy—almost makes the HR department obsolete, you know. I mentioned that to Patsy Higgens, our director of HR, and she wasn't amused."

Brenna smiled into the phone. "No, I wouldn't think she would be. So, tell me. Who is he?"

"Well, he's legit. His father really is Don Black from Eagle Construction. My accounting firm's actually done business with them in the past, although I've never met Don face-to-face. And Nathan is really his son."

With a frown, Brenna asked, "So why's he here in Indianola looking for a minimum-wage job?"

She could envision John shrugging his narrow shoulders and pushing his glasses up the bridge of his nose. "Not really sure, except that his dad said that ever since Nathan's mother died last year he's been antsy. Said he needed to 'go find himself' and just left one day with only a full tank of gas, the clothes on his back, and a letter of recommendation in case he wanted to find work. Don was actually relieved when I called, because he hadn't heard from him in a week and was getting ready to file a missing persons report."

"So there wasn't a fight or something that would make him leave?"

"Nope—just the death of his mother, from what I can tell. Don said they were real close."

"Wow. That's interesting." She reached out and picked up the photo by her bed, the only existing picture of her with the mother she'd never gotten a chance to know. Her mother who'd died before Brenna lost her first tooth and whose face she couldn't even remember. The mother that her father had told her she'd killed. She put the picture back. "Do you think it's okay to hire him?"

"Definitely. Seems like a pretty decent guy. Oh, and one interesting fact. He had a full music scholarship to Baylor but dropped out the month after his mother died."

"A music scholarship? Does he sing?"

"No, actually. He plays the piano."

She shook her head, trying to reconcile the cowboy image she had of Nathan with somebody who was good enough on the piano to get a full scholarship to Baylor. "All right then. I'll let him know tomorrow. And thanks—you've been a huge help."

"Anytime, Brenna. Now go get some sleep."

She said good-bye, then thoughtfully hung up the phone. Knowing sleep would completely evade her now, she crawled out of bed and moved to the card table set up in the far corner of her room. She kept her scrapbook open there so that she could add to it during any spare moment.

Sliding the World War I letter that John had given her out of its sleeve, she let her fingers brush over the fading ink. The letter was from Private First Class Cyril Guidry, and was addressed to Mary Alice Guidry of Atlanta, Georgia. *Wife? Mother? Sister?* Closing her eyes, she let her fingers drift to the sealed flap of the envelope, imagining the possibilities of what was written inside. Here, in the dark of her room, she could create her own happy endings like the old black-and-white movies she used to watch in film club. She could walk away afterward believing that the characters really did live happily ever after. That was what she liked the most about movies: never having to deal with the reality of what happened next. Just like her old letters.

Gently placing the letter in front of her for inspiration, she picked up her pen and held it over the scrapbook page, then slowly began to write.

Pierce opened the door to his father's house before Brenna had a chance to ring the doorbell. She wore a pink floral sundress, and her hair had been tamed into a low ponytail. She looked exactly like the young girl she had once been.

She smiled. "I hope I didn't wake you up when I called earlier. It's just that you asked me to call you as soon as possible."

She was babbling, something he knew she did when she was nervous, and it amused him. He stood back and held the door open for her. "Come on in—he's expecting you. We're just having breakfast. Can I get you some coffee?"

Turning his back to her, he led her into the kitchen.

Brenna kissed the doctor on his cheek, then sat down next to him. Pierce poured a cup of coffee and handed it to her black, the way he remembered she liked it. She'd been drinking coffee since first grade, when her father had told her it was time for her to learn to make it for him in the morning. She'd figured that it would be easier to join him than to argue about getting up fifteen minutes earlier.

"Pierce, would you mind getting the box of letters, please?" His dad looked at him over the top of his glasses.

Pierce made his way upstairs to his father's bedroom and picked up the box from the bedside table, resisting the urge to peer inside. His father had forbidden him to look at the letters, telling him that he would explain later. Pierce relegated his father's secretiveness to an old man's idiosyncrasy and carried the box downstairs without opening it.

He set the box in the middle of the kitchen table and leaned back, curious as to what it was his father had thought was so urgent he had to see Brenna O'Brien as soon as possible.

Dr. McGovern pressed a napkin to his mouth. "I understand you collect old letters—is that right?"

"Yes, sir. Since I was about eighteen."

"But you don't like to open them."

"No, sir." She stared down at her nails, all of them chewed down to the quick.

"And I guess you're aware that I just received a box full of unopened letters written to me more than sixty years ago."

Her eyes regarded the doctor steadily. "Yes, I know."

His father was silent for a moment. "My eyesight's not so good now, and I'm going to need somebody to open them and read them to me."

She didn't say anything but looked over at Pierce. Pierce put his coffee mug on the table, afraid of where this conversation might be headed. "I can read them to you, Dad."

His dad wouldn't meet Pierce's eyes. "I know that, son. But you're related, and I'm not sure if the contents of the letters are something you should hear. That's why I wanted an impartial observer, so to speak."

Pierce felt the old anger rise in him again, the same anger he felt when his dad had told him that his mother was gone and wasn't coming back. It was anger borne of knowing that his father wasn't telling him the whole story.

Dr. McGovern put a hand on Pierce's arm. "This has nothing to do with you, all right? Just an old man's whim to spend more time with a pretty girl."

Pierce glanced over at Brenna to see her turning a pale shade of pink. Slightly mollified, he sat back in his chair and took a sip of his coffee. "If that's what you want, Dad, I won't argue."

"That's what I want. And Brenna, I want your promise that anything you read will be kept confidential unless I tell you otherwise."

"I promise," she said, patting the doctor's hand. "I'm not working tomorrow night at the theater, so if you wanted to get started then, I could come over right after supper."

Pierce noted with alarm a slight tremor in his dad's hand that lasted only a moment and then stopped. He couldn't be sure if it was something to do with advanced age or was related to the letters that had waited for sixty years to be read and would now have to wait one more day.

Brenna rose. "I've got to run now—babysitting calls."

As she kissed the doctor on the cheek, Pierce rose too. "I'll walk you to the door."

He held the door open for her and then followed her out onto the front porch. "He's an old man, Brenna. I'll expect you to censor any information in the letters that might upset him. I also think I deserve the right to be told about anything important."

She looked up at him with surprise. "I can't do that, Pierce. I promised your dad that I wouldn't unless he tells me that I can."

He thought the earth was trembling before he realized it was his own legs. He stared at her for a long moment, unable to speak around the rage that seemed to have blocked the words. With great control, he finally managed to say, "Since when have promises ever meant anything to you?"

Her skin paled, reminding him of the way it had looked in moonlight, enraging him even further.

"What do you mean?" she whispered. "I never broke a single promise I made to you."

He leaned closer, his voice low. "You promised to love me forever. You promised to write. You promised that you would never let me go."

Her face seemed so innocent, so incredulous, and he knew he had to leave her then. He stumbled backward and opened the door. Before he could slam it closed, he thought he heard her say something.

He leaned against the closed door with his eyes closed, concentrating on taking deep breaths. It wasn't until he opened his eyes again that he realized what it was she'd said. *I did.*

CHAPTER 9

Brenna headed toward Colleen's house, not even aware of how she got into her car or if she stopped at any of the stop signs. *You promised to love me forever. You promised to write. You promised that you would never let me go.* She parked in her sister's driveway and sat in the car, using the heels of her hands to wipe her eyes.

She grabbed a lipstick tube from the well below her emergency brake and brushed it across her lips to give her face some color. The lipstick had been Claire's idea, and had been given to Brenna with instructions never to be seen without something on her lips, because without it she looked faded. Glancing in her rearview mirror, Brenna stifled a sob. She still looked faded, but at least her lips were orange. Looking into mirrors always made her feel as if she were staring at a ghost—the flesh and the heart long gone, and only a transparent shell left behind. Taking a bracing breath, she opened her car door and stepped out.

She waved to the UPS man as she passed him on the way up the brick walk, then nearly tripped over four medium-sized brown boxes stacked on the bottom step.

With a wary eye on the boxes, she rang the doorbell. Colleen opened the door before Brenna had even removed her finger from the bell. Ignoring her sister, Colleen made a gleeful sound before lifting two of the boxes to carry inside. "Would you mind grabbing those last two, Brenn?"

Following her sister's lead, she dumped the boxes on the dining room table while Colleen fetched a pair of scissors from the kitchen before ripping through the packing tape. "It's a complete collection of authentic gourmet cookware—barely used." She held up a small copper frying pan. "Isn't it gorgeous?"

Brenna peeled back the top of the open box to peer inside at more pieces of copper cookware. "It's right up there with Brad Pitt's face. But you don't cook."

Colleen waved her hand in dismissal. "I can read a recipe, and that's all you need. But I got the best deal on this stuff on eBay, and I couldn't resist." She pulled out a gleaming pot and twisted it upside down, a frown on her face.

"It's a steamer," Brenna supplied, tearing open another box and tugging out a small appliance. She held it up. "A pore vacuum, Colleen?"

Colleen looked up with her arms full of copper lids. "Yeah—they had it for a really low starting bid and I figured, Why the heck not? It's supposed to give you a flawless complexion. You can have it if you like."

Brenna dropped it back in the box without ceremony. "No, thanks. I have called a complete halt to my sisters messing with my face, thanks to Mary Margaret."

Leaning her elbows on the table, Colleen said, "She got you with the face mask, didn't she? She'd already tried to get me and Claire to give it a try. And Kathleen wouldn't let Mary Margaret near her face because of that last incident with the exfoliator. I guess you were the hapless victim."

"Yep. That would be me." Loosely closing the lid on the pore vacuum, she felt her throat catch.

Colleen, who like all of Brenna's sisters seemed to have a special radar where Brenna was concerned, immediately dropped the lids and put her hands on Brenna's shoulders. "What's wrong, Brenn? Did you have a bad date last night?"

Brenna pushed away. She was tired of being the hapless victim. Tired of life-scarring dates, well-meaning sisters, and a pain around the center of her heart that never seemed to go away. Mostly, she was angry at herself for not being able to let go of the young girl who used to wish for possibilities, and having become instead the grown woman who didn't need to.

"No. Not last night. I guess I'm just suffering from the cumulative effect of too many bad dates."

Colleen frowned, then nodded. "I see what you mean. We've got to start looking for a different type of man than we've been setting you up with. What about Nathan Conley? I hear he's started working for you, *and* you live in the same building."

"Stop it. Please. I don't want any more setup dates. They're sucking me dry. And Nathan . . . well, he just doesn't strike me that way."

Her sister continued to stare at her with a concentrated look. "Wilma at the beauty parlor has a nephew your age. He's been married a couple of times, but he's single now. He's a wig salesman and drives through here all the time. Maybe the next time he's—"

"No." Brenna shouted it a little louder than she'd intended, and she regretted the hurt look on Colleen's face. "Sorry, I didn't mean to shout." She sank down in a chair, lacking the energy to argue. She gave her sister a brittle smile. "Sure, have him call me. What's to lose, right?"

Colleen sat down opposite Brenna and patted her hand. "You'll find somebody, Brenn. I know you will."

Brenna stared up into eyes like her own. "Have I ever broken a promise to you?"

"No. Not ever. Kathleen and I used to say that you were too afraid of Daddy ever to be caught breaking a promise or telling a lie."

"I was," she said, flicking her fingernail under an edge of packing tape. She picked up the copper skillet and stared at her hammered-metal reflection, feeling like the scattered bits and pieces of her face that stared back. "Do you remember when I was a junior and had meningitis and had to spend a week in the hospital?"

Colleen closed her eyes for a moment. "Of course I do. It was pretty scary—especially since Daddy wouldn't let any of us close enough to talk to you. He insisted on staying with you every waking moment." She stood and began ripping the taped seams of the boxes to flatten them. "No offense to you, Brenna, but we all figured his concern was because he was afraid of losing his maid and personal servant."

"So nobody came to visit me, then?"

Colleen yanked on a box flap and made a loud ripping sound. "Not that I know of—although my knowledge is limited, since I was living in Baton Rouge at the time and Daddy told me to stay there because you were contagious. But I remember Kathleen being pretty steamed. And then she must have accepted it or something, because that was the last I heard about it. Why do you want to know?"

Brenna shrugged and began ripping the packing tape from a box. "No reason, really. Just that . . . well . . . I was just wondering if anybody came to see me while I was in the hospital. I was too sick to remember, and I was curious."

"The only person still living here then, besides Daddy, was Kathleen. You should ask her—I'm sure she'd remember. She has a memory like an elephant."

Brenna nodded and added a flattened box to the stack in the middle of the table. "Where's Timmy?"

Colleen stilled. "Oh, dear. I forgot I called you last night. I thought he'd be staying home from school today, but he's feeling completely fine now, so I'm sending him. Sorry to get you out of bed on your day off."

Brenna fingered the chains around her neck as she recalled the penance the priest had given her following her last confession. She'd deduct two Hail Marys just for not strangling her sister. But maybe add an Our Father for just wanting to do it. She picked up her purse to leave.

"I'm running a little late this morning, so maybe you could make Timmy's lunch and take him to the bus stop? Bill had to stop by the office-supply place first, so I'm supposed to get to the store early to open it." She gave Brenna a wide grin. "Timmy would love it."

Dropping her purse onto a dining room chair, Brenna headed for the kitchen. "Does he still like peanut butter and jelly?"

"Yes—but without the jelly. And just one slice of bread with no crusts."

Brenna paused with her hand on the silverware drawer. "Why don't I just pack the jar of peanut butter and a spoon? It would save me a lot of trouble, and he'd be getting the same thing."

Colleen's answer was muffled by Timmy's slinking appearance in the kitchen. He wore oversize parachute pants that would probably fit his father and made a swishing noise when he walked. His hands were clutched in the waistband as if to make sure they didn't slide off, and he looked miserable.

She knew better than to say anything. Instead, she bent down to kiss his cheek and then began to make his lunch.

"I have a math test today."

She swabbed a thick layer of peanut butter on the bread. "Are you ready for it?"

"I didn't study. I don't have to."

Brenna continued spreading peanut butter and didn't say anything.

"I'm really good at math. I always get the highest grade."

Without turning around, she could tell that he wasn't finished speaking, so she continued to spread the peanut butter on the single piece of bread.

"Some of the guys . . . um . . . they get mad when I do that. They call me a geek and stuff."

Putting the knife on the side of the plate, Brenna squatted next to Timmy's chair. "Do you know who Bill Gates is?"

Timmy nodded. "He was in last month's *Kid Science* magazine."

"Well, he's a geek. Probably always has been. He's like the richest guy in the world, and the people who used to call him names now cut his grass. Do you know what I'm saying?"

A reluctant smile tugged at his lips. "Yeah. I guess."

"All right. Then ace that test."

She reached across the counter for a paper napkin, then pulled a pen out of her purse and began writing on it.

"What are you doing?"

She paused, the pen over the napkin. "I'm writing you a secret note for you to discover when you're at lunch."

"Don't, Aunt Brenn. Please."

She stood and leaned against the counter. "Why is that? Are you afraid those guys are going to tease you again?"

He shook his head and looked down at his scuffed sneakers. "Nuh-uh."

He didn't speak for a long minute, and Brenna felt her gut tighten. She knew what he was going to say before the words tumbled from his mouth.

"Because I won't know what to do with it after I read it. I won't want to throw it away. And if I bring it home, my mom will."

She remembered a younger version of herself at the dime store with Kathleen. They were at the checkout line, and Brenna was looking at a small display tree of cheap birthstone necklaces.

Kathleen had taken the September one off the rack and held it up. "I'll buy it for you, Brenn, if you like it. It's real pretty."

Brenna shook her head. "No, ma'am. I don't want it."

Her sister had nudged her and tried to get her to take the necklace. "Yes, you do, sweetie. I'll be happy to buy it for you."

The young Brenna had turned her head to block the beautiful blue stone necklace from her sight. "I might lose it, or it could get broken. I don't want it."

She put the pen down with a small snap. "All right, Timmy. I won't." She tried to think of something to say, something that would get him to change his mind and see things the right way. But she couldn't. She wasn't sure she understood it herself.

"Did my mom tell you that I'm getting Mary Sanford's guinea pig? She's allergic and it makes her sneeze and stuff, so she had to get rid of it."

Brenna tried to keep the worry out of her face and she turned to look at him. "You must be very excited."

Timmy began scraping under a fingernail with a butter knife he'd picked up from the table. "They're only supposed to live for five to eight years, but I'm going to love it and take such good care of it that it doesn't die. And I'm calling her Rocky even though she's a girl."

"That's great, Timmy." Brenna tightened the lid on the peanut butter jar. *If only love were enough.* She finished making his lunch, then took him to the bus stop, all the way trying not to remember what happened when love wasn't enough, and what a tough lesson it was to learn.

Pierce pushed his father's wheelchair up the ramp and headed for the theater's ticket booth. It was original to the theater, with room for only one person behind the glass, and apparently still not air-conditioned, judging by the way the teenager inside had sweat dotting his face, and the ineffective small fan blowing small puffs of air in his direction.

He slid a twenty under the glass. "Two for *The Lake House,* please."

The boy wiped the sweat from his forehead with his sleeve. "Sorry, sir. It's not showing tonight."

"Excuse me? I thought it was supposed to be here until the end of the month."

"No, sir. I mean, yes, sir." The boy rolled his eyes. "What I meant is that *The Lake House* will be here until the end of the month, except today's the third Thursday of the month." He smiled as if no further explanation were required.

Pierce raised his eyebrows. "Meaning . . . ?"

"Oh. Sorry. The third Thursday is oldies night, so tonight we're showing *Casablanca* with Humphrey Bogart and Ingrid Bergman. Except tonight we're making it sort of an event. You're invited to dress like your favorite character in the movie, and the high school band will be setting up in the lobby shortly to play forties dance music after the movie, if you wanna dance." He stuck his finger under his starched collar. "I don't normally wear this white suit and bow tie to sell tickets."

Pierce was about to tell him to forget it when his father said, "What a great idea. We definitely want to see it. It's been years since I've watched *Casablanca*."

It had once been Pierce's favorite movie, although he couldn't recall how long it had been since he'd not flinched when a flick of the remote in the middle of the night brought Rick and Ilsa into his living room, along with memories of soft red hair tucked under his chin. Reluctantly, Pierce bought two tickets.

He heard the distinct sound of a piano playing from the lobby as he walked in, and he stopped short as he passed under the chandelier with the missing prisms.

"What do you think, son?"

Pierce stared at the piano, where the man he'd seen at the hardware store was seated on the bench playing "As Time Goes By." "Is that my mother's piano?"

His dad looked up at him with a smile. "Sure is. Brenna asked if she could buy it, since you didn't want it, so I just gave it to her. She and Dooley loaded it up in his truck and here it is. I can't say that I'm not disappointed that you didn't want it, but I couldn't really think of a better place for it to be."

Slowly Pierce pushed his father over to the piano, where Brenna and her four sisters were gathered around the man playing. They were all dressed in clothes from the forties, including Brenna in a hat and suit that was identical to the one worn by Ingrid Bergman in the last scene of the movie. She looked so much like the girl he'd once known that he couldn't help himself. He leaned over to her and said, "Here's looking at you, kid."

Brenna turned to face him, the laughter in her eyes fading when she saw it was him. Recovering quickly, she held up her Coke bottle and replied, "I think this is the beginning of a beautiful friendship."

His dad laughed. "I can see you know the movie as well as Pierce. When he was in high school he could quote the dialogue from the entire movie."

Her smile dipped slightly. "Yeah. Me, too." She turned around to the man at the piano, who had just stopped playing. "Dr. McGovern, have you met Nathan Conley?"

Nathan stood and leaned over to shake the doctor's hand, staring hard into the old man's face. "Good to meet you."

"He's working for me on sort of a consulting basis, I'd guess you'd call it. He's going to help me with a marketing strategy for the theater."

Pierce held out his hand. "I'm Pierce McGovern. Just visiting?"

Nathan shook his hand in a firm grip, and Pierce felt the same hard scrutiny that he'd seen Nathan give his father.

"You could say that. I'm from Houston. I'm taking a little vacation, and thought I'd stay a while in Indianola before moving on."

Pierce dropped his hand, not sure what it was about the man that was making him feel so uneasy. "So, are you in the theater business? You mentioned working on a marketing strategy."

"Nope, I'm in construction, actually. Just have a passion for old theaters, that's all. My mama was a huge movie buff, and I guess it rubbed off."

They continued staring at each other, and Pierce briefly wondered if this was how lions in a cage felt. "And that makes you qualified to help Brenna's theater."

Nathan raised an eyebrow. "Maybe. Not that I'm sharing anything with you, though, since you are, technically, the enemy."

It was Pierce's turn to raise an eyebrow. "The enemy?"

"Yep. Aren't you the one trying to close down the Royal Majestic?"

"Not at all. My company is simply considering building something in this market that it hasn't had before. That's a far cry from closing down a small theater."

"You think so?" Nathan took a step closer.

Brenna moved between them, putting an arm on Nathan that bothered Pierce, though he couldn't exactly tell himself why.

"This was all Nathan's idea—to make oldies night more of an event. It was such short notice that we didn't have time to really do much, but it's a start." She wasn't meeting his eyes, and he recalled the last thing she'd said to him: *I did.*

Kathleen moved to stand by Brenna. She was wearing an old-fashioned beaded gown that was still beautiful, even though Pierce could see that some of the beads were missing and the hem dragged on one side. "Our mother kept all of her old clothes up in the attic, so it was easy finding clothes for us girls."

Pierce's dad coughed, and when Pierce looked down at him he could see that his father's face had paled. "Are you all right, Dad?"

The doctor nodded. "Just . . . tired all of a sudden. I'm thinking that maybe I should skip the movie and go home to rest."

Pierce put his hands on the wheelchair. "I'll take you home."

Claire piped up. "Why don't I take him? Mary Sanford has a fitting first thing in the morning, so I didn't intend to stay long. Anyway, his house is on the way, and I'm a nurse, so I'll take his vitals before leaving him, okay?"

Pierce didn't loosen his grip on his father's chair. "No, but thank you. I'd feel better if I took him myself."

His father laid a hand on top of his. "Don't be ridiculous, Pierce. I'm tired, that's all. I'm perfectly happy to go home with Claire, and I have the cell phone you gave me clipped to my pocket just in case I need you. Don't worry, son. I'll be fine."

Claire brushed aside any further objections and was soon joined by the rest of Brenna's sisters. As always when it came to dealing with them, he felt as if he had just held up his hand to stop a tidal wave, with basically the same results.

Kathleen slipped her arm through his. "I think the movie's getting ready to start, so let's go get seats." She led him into the theater, past a row of seats marked off with duct tape, and put him in the center aisle, second seat in. "Sit here and I'll be right back."

Assuming she'd gone to get something to eat, he settled back in the seat and stared up at the old mural that he used to think was so beautiful. When he'd been assigned his first job with Crown Cinemas to build a multiplex in a rural area, he'd worked feverishly on the plans.

Plans that he realized later would have made the new, modern theater he was supposed to be building into one that resembled the Royal Majestic. He'd even received bids from artists for ceiling murals depicting forgotten moments of heroism from the old classic films. His efforts had been met with nothing but incredulity and derision, and he soon realized that to keep his job he would have to forget the way he thought theaters should be.

He studied the mural above him. It was badly in need of repair, and the soldiers whom he remembered looking so gallant and brave now seemed simply faded, like all the rest of his memories. He closed his eyes for a moment, thinking how odd it was that his memories no longer had any color except for the red of Brenna's hair and the green of her eyes.

He opened his eyes and started, as if he had conjured her from his imagination: Kathleen was doing everything except shoving Brenna into the vacant seat next to him.

"Come on, Brenn. This is a great seat, and Pierce has saved it for you. I know it's your favorite movie, so you just sit back and relax and I'll take care of getting the band set up while the movie's playing."

Brenna seemed to fall into her seat, and they both stared at Kathleen's retreating back. Finally Brenna turned to him and said, "I'd get up and leave if I didn't think they'd bodily carry me back in here."

He looked back at her, unsure of what to say. Instead his eyes drifted to the necklace she wore, visible in the vee of her old-fashioned jacket. Two small oval religious medals hung on a silver chain, and he had a flashback for a moment of him lifting the chain off of her bare chest and kissing the place on her skin where it had lain. "Who are you wearing today?"

Her bitten fingernails plucked at the medallions. "Saint Jude. And Saint Eustace."

"Saint Eustace?"

"Patron saint of difficult situations."

He didn't say anything, afraid to ask what she meant. He was struggling with his own difficult situations. He stared up at the mural instead, into the eyes of the dying soldier, and said, "What did you mean yesterday when you said, 'I did'?"

Her eyes glistened under the light of the chandeliers as she met his gaze without flinching. "I never broke a promise to you. That's what I meant."

He felt the old anger again, but he rationalized it away as he'd taught himself to do over the years—almost convinced himself that none of it mattered anymore. Except that it did. "So why didn't I ever hear from you again after I left for college?"

She pulled on the medallions, stretching the chain taut. "That's not true. I wrote letters every day. I called and left messages on your answering machine." Her voice was very soft. "You never wrote back. Or called."

He felt an undeniable chill creep under his collar. "I did. Every day for a month. I didn't even know you'd been in the hospital until you'd been home for a couple of months. I would have flown down if I'd known. But I didn't."

The lights began to dim in the theater, but they continued to look at each other as if the past would suddenly be revealed in the other's eyes. Kathleen and her husband, John, appeared and handed Pierce and Brenna a huge tub of popcorn and two Cokes, then took the seats directly to Pierce's right. Kathleen whispered loudly, "Mary Margaret and Colleen are handling everything in the lobby, so we get to watch the movie."

Pierce thanked them for the snacks, then sat back, feeling oddly numb. The theater went completely black and he took a handful of popcorn, not tasting it. Nineteen forty-one Morocco appeared on the screen in black-and-white, and he stared at it, not hearing a word but acutely aware of Brenna sitting next to him, and all of the unasked questions that raced through his mind but continued to point in a single, unbelievable direction.

CHAPTER 10

Brenna stared up at the final credits rolling up the screen, reading each line as she'd been taught to do in film club. Pierce stayed, too, as the rest of the audience slowly filed out of the theater toward the lobby, where the strident strains of a saxophone cut through the movie's theme song. Kathleen and John excused themselves and followed the rest of the crowd, and Brenna felt her sister squeeze her shoulder as she passed.

She and Pierce continued to sit in their seats long after the last person had left the theater and the final name had rolled across the screen. She almost expected her own theme song to burst forth, something sad and prophetic, but all she heard was the faint hum of voices and the brass of the high school swing band playing old dance music that nobody knew the steps to anymore.

She felt cold—the same cold she'd felt when she was seven and had fallen through the surface of the ice-covered pond in her backyard. She remembered the slow-motion tiredness, as if she were supposed to close her eyes and go to sleep. And she remembered the warmth around her heart—the warmth that always made her think of her mother. Most of all she remembered how angry she was to be yanked out of the freezing water by a frantic Kathleen and Colleen. She had been so close to seeing her mother's face again that all she could feel as she lay gasping for breath on the bank of the pond was regret. Regret that she'd never get a chance to tell her mother that she was sorry.

Pierce's voice did nothing to warm her. "It's true then? You tried to contact me? And you never knew how many times I called or wrote to you?"

She nodded her head, feeling brittle—an icicle waiting to drop and shatter into a thousand fragments.

He sighed and tilted his head back as if to draw inspiration from the painting above. "There's so many questions I should be asking about how such a thing could happen. How we both could be so easily deceived. But I think we've already come to the same conclusion." He turned toward her. "Your father was a self-serving, selfish bastard. I don't know why, or how he did what he did, but whatever his reasons, they could not possibly justify what he did to us."

Finally she looked at Pierce, but none of the coldness went away. She couldn't defend her father, and had no doubt as to what he would have been capable of. He hadn't wanted her to go away to college, and he hadn't wanted her to fall in love with a boy who promised to take her as far from Indianola as she could get. According to her father, devoting herself to him was a just penance for what she had done to her mother. Even so, for the first time in her life—and contrary to everything her father had always tried to teach her—she had allowed herself to dream, to hope, to love, thinking that would be enough. And, in the end, he'd won. She'd stayed where she was and had come to believe that what her father had been telling her all along was true: that there was no happiness without loss. And the memory of her broken heart was enough to make her tuck her real heart away and live with the shell of what was left. That, along with her family and her theater, was all she'd ever allow herself to need.

She was surprised she could speak past the ice in her throat. "I never even thought my father was somehow responsible. I thought you'd just . . . left."

"Left you? Without any good-bye or explanation? I thought you knew me better than that."

She met his eyes, remembering again the pain of loss, and knew she could never go back. "Maybe . . . maybe he deceived us only because he knew how easy it would be." She swallowed and tried not to blink. "Why didn't you try harder to reach me?"

His eyes were wild, lacking comprehension. "Why didn't *I* try harder? Why didn't *you* try harder? Wasn't what we had worth fighting for?"

She felt a tiny spark ignite her old heart and just as quickly flicker and die. "I don't know, Pierce. Maybe if it had been, we would have both tried harder. Maybe if we had loved each other enough, we would have found a way to reach each other. What if my father knew that it wasn't strong enough, and in the end was actually doing us a favor?"

Pierce stood suddenly, his seat flipping closed as he stalked down the row away from her. He rounded the row of seats and approached the stage. As he leaned against it, she watched his hands clench and unclench, as if they, too, were unsure.

She stood, too, but didn't approach him. The sound of Glenn Miller's big-band hit "A String of Pearls" danced into the theater, along with the sound of laughing voices, and Brenna wished she were with them instead of here amidst the wreckage of old dreams.

"You know that's not true."

"Then why haven't we spoken to each other in almost sixteen years?"

His head jerked as if he'd been struck, and he stared at her for a long moment. "I don't know," he said, defeated.

"Don't you think that things always happen the way they're supposed to? That we're merely pawns in God's plan and that we always end up where we're supposed to be? Maybe we didn't love each other enough and that's why we aren't together now. Maybe what happened then was easier for us to handle than if we'd gotten married and discovered too late that what we felt for each other wasn't enough."

He speared his fingers through his hair, making her want to smooth it down with her own hands, but she stayed where she was.

"God's plan? I haven't been to church in a long time, but I can guarantee that your father's machinations had nothing to do with anybody's plan but his own. And now you're telling me that all the pain, grief, humiliation, and recrimination I've felt over the years have been for the best. That what we had wasn't ever real and doesn't even matter anymore." He let out a mirthless laugh. "It's like when Scarlett pours out her heart to Rhett, telling him she's just realized that she's always loved him and wants to start over, and he basically tells her to go to hell." He walked over to her, his eyes narrowed. "What you're really saying, though, is that you allowed your father to spoon-feed you a lot of crap until you believed him. And you know what, Brenna O'Brien? You will always love your fears too much ever to take a chance on happiness and risk disappointment."

She raised her hand to slap him, surprised at her own violent reaction. Drawing in a quick breath, she stilled her hand and let it fall to her side.

He didn't flinch. "The truth hurts, doesn't it?" he said softly, then began to walk away. Pausing for a moment, he said, "Don't worry. I'll leave you alone. I'll get my father settled and then I'll leave, and you can crawl back into your lonely little shell again."

Brenna watched him walk away, the hurt and pain pulsing inside of her like the living, breathing child they had once talked about having. "Why did you divorce your wife?" She wasn't sure why she'd said that, only that she felt a childish urge to hurt him as much as he'd just hurt her.

He faced her again, his eyes hard. "Because she wasn't you," he said before quickly walking out of the theater.

Brenna watched him leave and pass Kathleen with a curt good-bye. Kathleen looked from Pierce's face to Brenna's and ran toward her sister. It was clear from her expression that she had heard most of their conversation.

Kathleen touched Brenna's cheek, and Brenna was surprised to see her fingers come away wet. "Oh, Brenn," Kathleen said as she held out her arms, and Brenna fell into them as she had so many times as a child. "I'm so sorry, Brenn. I'm so sorry."

Brenna cried on her sister's shoulder, feeling the sequins of her mother's evening gown against her cheek and smelling the laundry detergent and Youth Dew perfume that reminded her of her childhood, and didn't think to ask what Kathleen was so sorry for when all she could feel was simply emptiness.

Pierce found his father sitting in the dark amid packing boxes and rolls of bubble wrap, holding the box of letters in his lap. Moonlight streamed into the room from the window, the curtains having been removed and donated to Goodwill. His father's face appeared younger in the pale blue light, as if the beams had somehow erased all the lines and sorrows caused by a wife's abandonment and a lifetime of healing the sick and comforting the dying.

Dr. McGovern didn't look up as Pierce found a place to sit on a large box without turning on the light. "How are you feeling?"

"Tired, that's all. I think I've just been waiting here for my energy to find me so I can take myself up to bed."

Pierce nodded as he looked around at what remained of his father's life, the mismatched pieces of furniture and the hulking shapes of the boxes like a city of memories. "I'm sorry you had to leave before the movie, but I'm glad you're feeling better."

He felt his father's eyes on him and he was glad of the darkness. His father always seemed to have an ability to know his son's thoughts, but it had been a long time since Pierce had had any thoughts worthy of sharing.

"Did you have a good time with Brenna?"

"Please, Dad. It's not like that with us, so don't get your hopes up."

His father was silent for a moment. "Is it because she's a woman or because she's Brenna O'Brien?"

"There's a difference?"

His dad snorted. "Yeah, I'd say so. The more suitable they are, the farther you try to run. Your mother might have left us, Pierce, but that was about me and her. They won't all abandon you, you know."

Pierce searched for a change of topic, and his gaze fell on the box of letters. "Have you heard any more about where those came from?"

A light from the window reflected in his father's eyes for a moment before Dr. McGovern turned his head. "They're from an old friend who used to work at the post office. They were sent and returned when I was missing in action, so I guess the post office was the best place for them. Then I suppose they were just forgotten. Until now." His dad looked up again, the odd light glittering in his eyes. "The guys investigating are okay with it, since my friend's been dead for years. And the press has lost interest, luckily. I can't say I'm disappointed. I'm too old for that kind of excitement." A flash of white illuminated his teeth as he smiled.

"Good." Pierce stood and moved to the window. "Do you still not want me to read them? I don't really think Brenna O'Brien is the best person for the job."

Dr. McGovern was silent for a long moment, and the sounds of the tree frogs in the pine woods behind the house invaded the shadowed room. The hall clock, not yet disassembled for moving, ticked off the minutes in the hallway. "Yes, Pierce. She is. I know it doesn't make sense to you right now, but all I'm asking is that you'll give in to the whim of an old man."

His father's voice sounded faded in the darkened room, as if part of him had already gone. Panic welled up in the back of Pierce's throat as he remembered all the years he'd lived apart from his father, all the years he made excuses not to come home only because he didn't want to be reminded of the mother who wouldn't be there. It suddenly seemed so important to talk to his father, to know him not just as a father, but as a man, too. As the young man he'd once been and the soldier he'd become. And the doctor he'd been for most of his life. Swallowing, Pierce moved to the ottoman next to his father's chair and took the old man's hand.

"You said something the other night. Something about living with regret. Was it me, Dad? Did I ever cause you regret?"

His father squeezed his hand. "No, Pierce. Not once. I never had any doubt that you were the one thing in my life that I did right."

Pierce reached over and clasped his father's hand between his own. "Then what did you mean?"

Dr. McGovern took a long time to answer. "When I was a young man—long before you were born—I made certain . . . choices. At the time, I thought I was doing the right thing." He gently pulled his hand away and let it rest on the box of letters. "I don't know if it was youth or ignorance or a little bit of both. Doesn't matter really. I had to make a leap of faith. But what I didn't realize at the time was that I wasn't leaping with both feet."

Pierce leaned forward, noticing how his father's voice kept getting fainter and fainter. "What do you mean?"

The old man continued. "Well, to make a leap of faith you must wholly commit to your choice. I didn't. It's like that Robert Frost poem about two paths and how you must choose between them because you can't do both. And reversing direction is not an option." He leaned his head against the back of the chair, and the ticking clock continued to mark the passing of the minutes. "I tried to keep a leg on each path— an illogical thing from all perspectives. I ended up hurting innocent people." He turned to face Pierce. "That's what I regret. Not leaping with both feet."

Sitting back, Pierce contemplated his father's words. "What choice, Dad? What choice didn't you commit to?"

His father patted the letter box. "In due time, son. You'll know when you're ready to know."

Pierce stood, too tired to argue. It seemed to him that he'd spent the entire evening walking through the minefield of his past, the effort leaving him with nothing but weariness and the old desire to escape. "Come on, Dad. Let's get you into bed."

He helped the doctor stand, then firmly gripped his father's arm, feeling the fragility of the old bones, the sound of the ticking clock loud in his ears. He faced his father in the darkness. "In case I never told you, you've always been the best of fathers. I know it wasn't easy without Mom around, but you never let me down. There was never a time when I was growing up, or even now, that I didn't think you'd always be there for me." Pierce swallowed. "I guess I'm sort of giving you a very late thank-you. But I wanted you to know that despite my mother's leaving us, you gave me a great childhood."

Frail, knobbed fingers patted his arm. "I love you, son."

The words took Pierce by surprise. Not because he'd never heard them before—his father had always ended their telephone conversations with them—but because for the first time Pierce felt the need to answer back.

"I love you, too, Dad."

Pierce reached over and flipped on a lamp, the light creeping into the shadowed corners of the house and dispelling the darkness as he gently led his father up the stairs.

When Brenna's alarm went off she was still fully dressed from the night before, and she'd filled several pages of her scrapbook with neat, spidery writing. The need to escape into a stranger's life and away from the mess of her own had preempted sleep, where no escape was possible.

She stood and stretched, feeling stiff and sore, and looked ruefully at the crumpled jacket and skirt that she'd worn all night. She had thought about taking it off and putting on her nightshirt so she'd be more comfortable, but wearing these clothes had felt almost like having her mother's arms around her. All her memories of her mother were based on old pictures and her sisters' stories, but she had clung to the sense of her mother's presence all during the long night. They'd helped her focus on writing instead of dwelling on what her father had done to Pierce and to her, and how the passage of years had done nothing to ease the ache and everything to firm her resolve never to have a vulnerable heart again.

After quickly showering and dressing, she stood in front of the drawer with her saint medallions and paused for a moment. Then she unfastened the chain around her neck and slid off the Saint Eustace medallion, replacing it with Saint Genevieve. She grabbed her purse and let herself out of the building as quietly as possible, not wanting a confrontation with Mrs. Grodin. In the mood she was in, she was afraid she'd inflict bodily harm.

Brenna sped down Main Street, glancing at the clock on her dashboard. This was Aunt Dottie's morning for grocery shopping, and Brenna had drawn the shortest straw among her sisters, earning the privilege of playing chauffeur. She slowed in front of her aunt's house, trying to figure out why Dooley had his head under the lifted lid of the old Lincoln, and why Aunt Dottie was sitting in a lawn chair on the sidewalk in front of her house, watching him. Dottie wore a dress splashed with huge sunflowers, in direct contradiction to the overgrown garden in front of her small, pink house that sported nothing but weeds and an impressive assortment of garden gnomes and various animal statuary.

Brenna parked her car at the curb and approached Dooley. She waved to her aunt, then bent close to Dooley, pretending to look at the confusing road map of wires. "What's going on, Doo?"

He looked at her, his brown eyes lit with laughter and completely negating the stern expression he was trying to give. "I should be asking you who gave her my home phone number." He turned back to the engine. "But I guess I should really be asking who removed the spark plugs."

Brenna stifled a laugh. "Whoever it was should win some sort of peace prize."

Aunt Dottie called from her chair. "How much longer, Dooley? They're having a special on dog food at the Piggly Wiggly and I don't want to miss out." She squinted at him through her thick glasses.

Dooley raised his eyebrows. "She has a dog?"

"Um, no. But she's really into specials."

Dooley nodded and turned to Aunt Dottie, whose hat was adorned with fringe balls the color of her sunflowers, which danced around her head like swarming bees when she moved. "We're going to need to replace some parts, ma'am, and since this is an older model, it could take a while for them to come in—about two or three weeks."

Brenna elbowed him and said under her breath, "Longer."

"Um, maybe closer to eight or nine."

Dottie sank into her floral dress, looking like a wilted sunflower. Even her fringe balls stilled. Brenna walked over to her and kissed her on the cheek. "Don't worry, Aunt Dot. I'm here and I've got my car and I'll take you wherever you want to go. I don't have to be anywhere for another three hours, so I'm all yours until then."

"I don't want to be a burden."

"Not at all. I needed to go to the Piggly Wiggly, too, and we can keep each other company while we shop. Besides, I need to pick your brain for some good movies for oldies night. I've got to plan for the next two months, and I don't know where to begin."

Her aunt brightened. "*Wuthering Heights*. We definitely need to have *Wuthering Heights* first. Laurence Olivier is what your niece Marie would call a hottie." Aunt Dottie squinted at Brenna. "Maybe we can find you a nice young man while we're there."

Unfortunately, Dooley made the mistake of joining Brenna at the lawn chair, and her aunt shifted her attention to him. "How about him?"

Dooley stood next to her, wiping grease off his fingers. "Pardon me?"

"Are you married yet?"

"No, ma'am. I've been saving myself."

Brenna elbowed him, but when he looked at her she didn't think it was laughter she was seeing in his eyes.

He turned back to Aunt Dottie. "I'm afraid that the woman I want won't have me."

The old woman held up her hand, and Dooley gently lifted her from the chair. "Have you asked her?"

"No, I haven't. See, as long as I don't ask her, I still have the possibility that she might say yes. If I ask and she says no, then it's all over."

Aunt Dottie blinked at him from behind her glasses. "That didn't make a lick of sense." Dooley began to lead her to Brenna's car. "Do you know my niece Brenna? As far as I can tell, she hasn't had any sort of relations with a man in years, and if she's not careful she's going to turn into a bitter old person, just like her daddy."

"Aunt Dottie . . ." Brenna tried to interrupt before any more personal observations of her sex life were aired in front of the one person to whom she used to think she could tell anything.

Her aunt continued. "He was my brother, God rest his soul, but he was one bitter man. Like a human lemon, he was. Being married to a person who can't love you as much as you love them will do that to you, I guess."

Brenna stopped in the grass. "What?"

Aunt Dottie stopped, too, her expression thoughtful. "What were we talking about?"

"My parents."

"Oh, yes, your parents. Lovely couple. Five lovely daughters, all of them married except for the youngest." She paused for a moment. "Your daddy sure was ornery, though. Most people thought it was because of him not being allowed into the Army on account of his bad knees. But I know that's not true because he was ornery long before then."

Brenna shook her head, refusing to delve further into the muddy conversation, if that was what it had been. She made a mental note to tell Kathleen that they might need to look into an assisted-living facility for Aunt Dottie.

They had reached Brenna's car, and Dooley helped Aunt Dottie into the passenger seat, Dooley carefully ducking her head so she wouldn't mess up her hat. Brenna slid into the driver's side, unable to meet Dooley's eyes. She waved a quick thanks without looking at him and pulled away from the curb, feeling as if her heart, which she'd spent so much time wrapping in flour, had suddenly been thrown into the frying pan.

Brenna marched through the landscape of her day with single-minded determination. The busier she was, the less time she had to think. The ground beneath her feet no longer seemed as solid as it had even a week before, and she had the strangest feeling that her earth had tilted, sending her careening downhill. She struggled to stay upright and not think too much about Pierce's words or how much she knew them to be true.

She'd helped Dottie shop, successfully steering her aunt away from the dog food and any conversation that involved Brenna's love life. As an added bonus, she also had the next four months planned for oldies night at the theater. She didn't really believe that oldies night would pull her theater out of the sinkhole it was in, or even help it survive increased competition. But it was something to keep her busy and stave off the inevitable.

After settling her aunt at home, she'd driven to the theater, where she'd found not only the bathroom plumbing fixed, but also a notepad full of great ideas from Nathan as to how to increase attendance, as well as a tentative time line on various repairs. She'd sat at the chair in her office for a long time, weak with relief and close to tears. When the phone rang, she'd been in such a good mood that when the beauty shop owner's out-of-town nephew asked her on a date, she said yes without hesitation. Even his suggestion that they go bullfrogging didn't faze her until much later. Now she was heading to Dr. McGovern's, but the restlessness that had dogged her all day caused her to make a quick stop first.

The church parking lot was empty except for a navy blue Buick. Brenna parked next to it, realizing it was Kathleen's from the ACCOUNTANTS NEVER LOSE THEIR BALANCE bumper sticker that Brenna had dared one of her nephews to put on his mother's car. She'd wanted to put it on John's, but he had to drive to work each day.

The dark coolness of the vestibule embraced her with wax-scented air, and colored light filtered through the stained-glass window. She crossed herself with holy water before entering the sanctuary. This was the church she'd been baptized in, and had received the sacraments of First Communion and reconciliation. It was also the church where her mother's funeral service had been held, but all Brenna could remember of that was the smell of flowers, and even now the scent of roses made her cry. Now it was the place she frequently came for peace of mind and quiet prayer, a place where she could look into her heart and not be afraid of what she saw.

The sweet smell of burning incense and candle wax hung heavily in the air, a mixture that filled Brenna with both comfort and apprehension. The church was where she confessed and atoned for her sins, so it could never be a complete sanctuary for her.

She didn't see Kathleen at first, but instead followed the sound of whispered prayers to the bank of small candles to the right of the altar. Her sister knelt before them, wearing the old-fashioned veil that hardly anybody wore anymore except the staunchest Catholics raised on tradition and guilt.

Brenna knelt in a pew behind Kathleen and drew out her rosary beads and began the Apostles' Creed while half listening to her sister. The intermittent words were familiar to her, probably because there weren't many prayers she hadn't been taught during her thirteen years in Catholic school.

". . . my sisters and other near relatives, my Jesus, mercy and relief through thy sacred wounds . . . all for whom love or duty bids me pray, my Jesus . . ."

Brenna looked up, startled, realizing it was the prayer for souls in purgatory that Kathleen was reciting.

". . . those who have suffered disadvantage of harm through me . . ."

Brenna's rosary slipped in her fingers, and she lost track of where she was on the first decade of Hail Marys. She strained to hear as Kathleen mumbled the prayer and Brenna tried to fill in the missing words from memory.

". . . parents who failed to watch over their children, my Jesus, mercy and relief through thy . . . Those who are in purgatory because of me, my Jesus, mercy and relief through thy sacred wounds. My own poor soul when I shall have to appear before thy judgment seat. Eternal rest grant unto all of these, O Lord; and let the perpetual light of thine countenance shine upon them. Amen."

Brenna's rosary fell through her fingers to the marble floor, and Kathleen's head jerked around. Their eyes met, and Brenna could see that Kathleen was crying. Kathleen never cried; she was the soother of tears, the one responsible for making all things better.

Her sister made the sign of the cross, then moved to sit next to Brenna. "I didn't expect to see anybody at this time of day." She looked away to wipe her eyes, then turned back with a smile. "I'm very hormonal these days—it must be the change of life." She laughed, but it wasn't a laugh Brenna had ever heard before from her sister.

"Are you sure that's all it is?" Brenna felt unsure in her role reversal, as if she'd been asked suddenly to play a part in a play she'd never rehearsed.

Kathleen nodded. "Yes, that's all. How about you? Are you feeling better?"

"Yeah. I'm fine. What you saw last night between Pierce and me . . . well, it's all in the past. He won't be in town too long, anyway, so we'll just have to muddle through for a while."

Kathleen picked up the silver chain from around Brenna's neck. "Saint Genevieve?"

"Patron saint of disasters."

"I know. But yesterday you were only at difficult situations. Was last night really such a disaster?"

The prick of tears stung her eyes, and she couldn't respond.

"I heard, you know. About the letters. About what Daddy did." Kathleen lifted Brenna's chin and met her eyes. "Do you still love Pierce?"

Brenna squeezed the ebony beads she'd retrieved from the floor but felt no comfort from them. "I don't . . . know. I can't anymore."

Kathleen held both of her hands, squeezing them tightly. "Don't let Daddy win this one, Brenna. He's been dead too many years to still rule your life. And he was wrong about so many things. I only wish—" She stopped, her lips closed firmly as if physically holding in the words.

"You only wish what?"

Kathleen looked at her for a long moment. "That you find your own happiness. And that you stop looking at letters of people who died long ago to tell you what it is."

Brenna stood suddenly, her restlessness overpowering her and spilling over into anger. "I thought you understood."

Kathleen stood, too. "I do. More than you know. That's why I'm trying to help you not throw your life away."

Brenna shoved her rosary into her purse and walked out of the pew. "Just because I choose to live my life differently from you does not mean that I'm throwing it away."

Brenna kept walking, her arms jerking with anger, until she got to her car, avoiding her reflection in the rearview mirror. It was only when she was almost at Dr. McGovern's house that she realized she'd forgotten to ask Kathleen why she'd been saying prayers for the dead.

Dr. McGovern greeted her warmly when she knocked on his door and surprised her by kissing her cheek. "Come on in, Brenna. Please excuse the mess, but the movers don't come until Friday, and the packers finished sooner than they expected. I guess I got rid of more than I thought I would." She followed his slow progression with his walker into the living room, where a Frank Sinatra record played on an old-fashioned record player in the corner. There was something familiar about the song. She didn't recall the lyrics or even the melody; it was just a presence in her memory.

"Do you like Old Blue Eyes?" Dr. McGovern asked as he indicated the sofa for her to sit.

"Yes," she said. "I mean, I think so." She smiled, confused. "At least, I think I do. I don't have any of his albums, if that's what you mean."

"Your mother did," he said as he slowly lowered himself into the recliner. "She was a wonderful dancer, too. She always said she'd have to marry a man who could sing or dance."

She thought about her father for a moment. "But she didn't, did she?"

"No, I don't guess she did." He smiled. "Can I get you some sweet tea or a Coke before we get started?"

"No, but thanks. Maybe later." She looked at the table by his chair, where the box of letters sat. "May I?"

He nodded, and she stood to get the box and the letter opener that lay next to it. She paused for a moment, the box heavy and solid in her hands. "It's strange," she began, then stopped.

"What's that?"

"It's just . . ." She went back to the couch and sat down. "It's just that I've never opened the letters I collect."

The doctor leaned back in his chair. "Sort of like watching a tennis game and finally realizing that you'd enjoy it a lot more if you were actually playing."

Brenna recalled what Kathleen had said, her words echoing the doctor's. *Find your own happiness . . . stop looking at letters of people who died long ago to tell you what it is.* She shifted uncomfortably in her seat. "I wouldn't know. I've never played tennis." Her face formed a lopsided grin. "Couldn't stand the thought of losing, I guess." She looked down and studied her hands resting on the box of letters, realizing how stupid she sounded, and how grateful she was that the doctor didn't say anything.

Gently, Brenna lifted the lid and stared inside, smelling the old paper and fading ink and briefly feeling like Pandora. The letters lay in a stack, not bound by twine or a rubber band. She looked up at Dr. McGovern for guidance.

"I organized them in the order they need to be read," he said. "I used a magnifying glass to read the postmarks, and it gave me a terrible headache. I'm glad you're here so I don't have to go through that with the contents of the letters." He smiled warmly at her, but her restlessness remained.

"Did you figure out who they're from?"

He nodded slowly, his eyes averted. "An old friend who used to work for the post office. They must have been sent when I was MIA, which I suppose is why they were found where they were."

Setting the open box on the table near her, she picked up the first letter and the letter opener, and with a deep breath, sliced open the envelope and began to read.

February 3, 1942

Darling, she began, then looked up, startled. "Your friend was a woman?"

The doctor nodded. "Yes, she was. When all the men enlisted, most of the women took the jobs the men had to leave, just so Indianola could function."

Brenna returned to the letter and began to read again.

Darling,

    It has been fifty-four hours and twenty-two minutes since I last saw you. I guess I didn't realize how much I'd miss you. But every time I look at the clock, I can't help but think what you would be doing here at that particular time. It's silly, I know, to be looking backward like that when you made me promise to think only of our future. But I can't help it. I miss you.

Brenna glanced at the bottom of the letter to see the name of the person who'd written it, but the letter was signed only, *Me.* "Is this from Pierce's mother?"

He didn't respond immediately. "No. I hadn't met my wife yet."

Brenna leaned forward, curious. "So, who is this?"

His eyes seemed shadowed. "She died a long time ago." He looked away, avoiding her curiosity, and she knew she'd pressed on an old bruise that maybe even he'd thought had long since been healed. She cleared her throat.

    Mama has really become involved in the war effort. She has me take my little brother's Radio Flyer wagon and go door to door collecting newspapers and the aluminum wrappers from chewing gum. It's dreadfully boring, but then I stop to think that I'm somehow indirectly helping you, and that makes me knock on the next door. The hardest thing, besides saying good-bye to you, is that Mama has confiscated all my nylon and silk stockings. It's humiliating to go barelegged like a little girl, but all the women are doing it and are proud of it. I guess I just need to buck up and be proud of it, too.

You-know-who has asked me out dancing next Friday night. I wish you'd allow me to wear my ring so everybody would know that I'm taken. I know you want to have a huge announcement party when you return, but it would make my life so much easier now.

Oh, darling, I'm sorry to be burdening you with my troubles when you need to focus on receiving your commission and your wings. Please just tuck this letter next to your heart and know that I miss you and I love you. And when you stare at the moon tonight, know that I'm staring at it, too, and thinking of you.

Bye,
Me.
P.S. I told him no.

Brenna folded the letter and tucked it back inside the envelope, then looked at Dr. McGovern, a question on her lips.

He was leaning back in his chair, his eyes closed, and she thought that he was asleep until she saw his hand clench into a fist and then relax.

"Would you like me to read the next one?"

Dr. McGovern nodded.

She pulled out the next letter and began to read.

February 5, 1942

I know it's been only two days since my last letter, and I didn't really expect a response from you by now, but I couldn't help but feel devastated when no news from you waited in my mailbox this after-noon.

A soft groan came from Dr. McGovern, almost sounding like a sob. "Doctor? Are you all right?"

With his eyes still closed, he nodded. "I'm fine. Just . . . nostalgic. Can we stop for now? I promise we'll do more next time, but not tonight."

Disappointed, she pushed back the question that had been lingering in her mind: Who was she? "Are you sure? We only read the one, and I don't have to be anywhere."

The old doctor shook his head. "No. I'm sure."

Brenna slid the envelope on top of the stack, then closed the lid of the box. "All right, then. When would you like me to come back? I'm working at the theater in the morning, but I can come by here afterward."

Dr. McGovern slowly raised himself from the chair. "That sounds fine. I'll be here."

"Can I get you anything before I leave?"

"No, I'm fine. Pierce will be back soon."

"I'll let myself out." She kissed him on his cheek and said good-bye, eager to leave before Pierce put in an appearance.

She shut the front door behind her but stood there for a moment, chewing on her fingernail. There was a niggling thought in the back of her brain that she couldn't quite retrieve—something to do with the letter she had just read, something that didn't quite jell with what Dr. McGovern had told her earlier.

Her hand slipped to the Saint Genevieve medallion around her neck, finding scant comfort there as she walked slowly to her car, her restlessness following her like an afternoon shadow.

Pierce sat back behind his steering wheel, the engine long since cooled, and watched as Brenna paused for a long moment outside his father's closed door, then thoughtfully walked toward her yellow Beetle, fingering one of those medallions she always wore. He wondered which one it was tonight, and if there was one for broken hearts and illogical thinking.

When he'd first seen her car at the curb, his instinct had been to drive around until she'd left. He'd even thought about calling his father and giving him the news to tell Brenna, but he had given up on that idea. He could talk to her once more. Once more, and that would be enough to last him forever.

As she neared her car he pushed open his car door and stepped out. "Brenna."

She froze, as if her mind had been miles away and she only just now realized that she was standing on the cracked sidewalk in a small Louisiana town. Her hand wrapped around the medallion as she stared at him, waiting for him to speak.

"I need to talk to you."

He almost laughed as he saw her give a quick glance at her car as if measuring her ability to reach it before he got too close.

"I thought we'd already said everything that needed to be said."

"This isn't about us. It's about your theater."

Her eyes widened. "My theater?"

He looked down at his feet, noticing how the grass spilled over onto the white cement sidewalk and reminding him of similar summer nights growing up, when he'd run barefoot on sidewalks like this one while playing hide-and-seek with neighborhood children. And it reminded him of a younger Brenna. She'd never known where to hide, so he'd find a good place for her first, then find one for himself—which usually meant that he was found first. He glanced back up at her, realizing that she was still looking for places to hide, but that she no longer needed him to do it. She'd built the dark corners inside her own head, and stood in them, where she hoped nobody would find her.

"I wanted you to hear this from me first. I had a conference call today with my boss. I'd already sent in my feasibility study and had discussed it with the planning board. It looks like the multiplex is a go."

"Oh," she said, more like a defeated puff of air. "Congratulations." She turned away from him and began walking toward her car again.

He followed her, feeling like a fool. He'd already told her what he needed to, so why was he still talking? "This doesn't have to be bad news for you, you know. You're smart. You'll figure out a way. Like your oldies night—that's something that we could never do."

She turned to face him again. "I only filled half the theater. That won't even pay my electricity bills. I make most of my money from showing first-run movies. You and I both know that I won't get first-run anymore if there's a multiplex in the next town."

He took a step toward her. "There are other ways, Brenn. It doesn't have to be the end of the Royal Majestic." A warm breeze blew at them, tumbling dead leaves across the asphalt and whipping up Brenna's hair.

"Why would you care, Pierce? You've got what you wanted. So why don't you go away somewhere else, where you can gloat?" She opened her car door and slid in behind the wheel.

Why *did* he care? He wasn't sure of the answer at all. Maybe it had to do with the memory of a young girl who was once strong enough to take a leap of faith with him but had somehow disappeared in the long years between then and now. Still, he grabbed hold of her door so she couldn't close it. "Do you remember what you told me before? About how you missed me?" He took a deep breath, unsure of what would come out next. "I missed you, too. For a long, long time."

She stared at him with her lovely green eyes, the shadows behind them making them even darker. He stepped back and she looked away before closing her door. He stood on the deserted street as she pulled away from the curb, then continued to stare down the empty street long after her car had disappeared around the corner.

CHAPTER 12

When Brenna arrived at the theater the next morning, she was surprised to find the front gate already open and a tall ladder propped against the front of the building. Piano music filtered out to the sidewalk where she stood, and she smiled in recognition. Humming to herself, she made her way into the lobby, where Nathan sat at the piano and had his head bent over the keys, his eyes closed.

Leaning against the piano, Brenna began to sing along with the lyrics to "Moon River."

Nathan looked up at her with a broad smile and joined in for the end of the refrain with a surprisingly strong baritone.

When the last note had faded, Brenna said, "From *Breakfast at Tiffany's*, right?"

"Bull's-eye," Nathan said, closing the piano lid. "It was my mama's favorite movie, and that theme song was the first piece of sheet music she ever bought me. I must have played it a thousand times before she figured out that I could probably play other things, too." He gave her half a grin that didn't light his eyes.

"I love the movie, too. I had to do a final exam project in film class my senior year in high school, and *Breakfast at Tiffany's* was the movie Pierce and I were assigned." She stopped for a moment, a fleeting memory returning. "Pierce hated that movie as much as I loved it, and whenever he heard 'Moon River' he'd leave the room." She met Nathan's eyes. "I always wondered about that. We usually shared the same taste in films and music."

"Maybe it reminds him of somebody he doesn't want to be reminded of."

"I thought so, too. Probably his mother. She played the piano—this one was actually hers."

Something flickered in his eyes and then, just as quickly, was gone. "So, you and Pierce are old friends, huh?"

Brenna felt her cheeks pinken. "Yeah, you could say that."

"I would guess more than friends. Whenever the two of you are in the same room together, you're both pretty prickly."

Brenna shifted uncomfortably. "That's one way to put it, I suppose. We sort of dated in high school. We weren't real public about it because my dad didn't approve. But it's been over for years."

He raised his eyebrows at her as if he expected her to continue. She pointed to the piano. "You're really good, you know." She looked down at his long fingers that rested on the closed lid, remembering his callused hands. "Your father said you had a full music scholarship to Baylor."

He grabbed his cowboy hat off the bench next to him and stood. "Yep. Sure did. Thought at the time that's what I wanted."

"Did something happen to change your mind?"

"You could say that."

It was her turn to raise an eyebrow, and when he didn't say anything else, she said, "I guess there're some things we're just not going to talk about."

He regarded her for a long moment without speaking, then turned to where the bright yellow of her car could be seen outside the theater's entrance. "That's your car, right? I see it at Mrs. Grodin's boarding-house all the time. I'm thinking you knew all along that we're neighbors."

"I figured we'd run into each other eventually. I would have mentioned it up front, but I didn't know you very well at first and I didn't want to tell you where I lived in case you were a stalker or something."

He smiled a devastating smile, something that on another man might make her look twice. But on Nathan it just made her roll her eyes. He continued. "Hey, if I were a stalker, I would have figured out where you lived first."

"Yeah, I suppose so." She crossed her arms. "Have you ever been bullfrogging?"

"Sure. Did it a lot as a boy. Why?"

"Well, I'm going on a blind date tonight, and the guy's asked me to go bullfrogging."

Nathan covered his mouth with his hand for a moment and

coughed, although it sounded suspiciously like a smothered laugh. "I see. Well, I'll be honest and say I've never really considered the activity as something I'd want to do on a date." His mouth twitched. "All I can say is that you should wear tall boots and nothing that would bother you if you got mud on it."

He moved across the lobby and bent down to retrieve a broken corner of a tile and held it up. "Don't want anybody tripping on this. I'll see if I can find a good enough match for now. Oh, by the way, you might have noticed the ladder outside. I thought I'd straighten the marquee—it's been bothering me."

Brenna rested her elbows on the piano, her restlessness creeping up on her again, remembering that she'd come in early to take an inventory of the theater's assets. She needed it now so she could figure out if there was anything she could sell right away to help with the monthly payments to the bank that she was barely making now. If worse came to worst, she figured she'd need the list later, when she was forced into foreclosure.

She kept her eyes down, unwilling to look around the lobby in all its faded glory, and afraid she might cry. She felt somehow that she had been entrusted with the survival of the Majestic and had failed, and she already felt enough shame and recrimination without looking around to confirm the proof of her failure. "You might want to save your energy, Nathan. It's official; the multiplex is a go."

He continued as if he hadn't heard her. "I'm going to go check out the roof later and see if I can stop the leak that's messing up the corner of the mural."

She walked to the center of the lobby and put her hands on her hips. "Did you hear what I said? The multiplex is a go. We won't be able to hang on." To hear the words spoken out loud startled her as much as if they'd been shouted at her. "I'm going to lose my theater." The words fell heavily from her mouth, as if by finally saying them, she recognized them to be true. The solidarity of her family and her love for the theater that had sustained her for all those years suddenly seemed to be planted on shifting ground, and she had as much footing in her life as if she were standing on quicksand.

She didn't realize she was crying until Nathan handed her a tissue.

"You gotta stop that, Brenna. Crying's a lot like trying to scoop up the ocean with your hands. It's not going to get you anywhere."

His voice was angry, but when she looked up at him she could tell that his anger wasn't directed at her. "We're going to beat this Pierce McGovern at his own game. Do you hear me? We're not going to let him win again."

Brenna wiped her eyes, hardly recognizing the man in front of her as the placid Nathan she'd come to know. "What do you mean, 'again'?"

He lowered his voice so that it sounded like the slow Southern drawl she recognized. "He's already broken your heart once. I don't want to see him do it again."

She managed a small smile. "I appreciate your fighting spirit, Nathan, but I don't think it's going to do any good. Maybe it would be best just to cut our losses and move on."

"No," he said, his voice firm. "I'm going to pretend that I didn't hear that. I haven't known you that long, Brenna, but you're Irish through and through. You're just not built to be a quitter."

"I'm not a quitter." She sighed, her heart silent in her chest. "I just don't have any fight left."

He grabbed hold of both her shoulders and looked her in the eye. "Then let me do all the fighting right now. When you find your spirit, you can come join me. But you've got to give me everything you've got left. My mama always told me that you can't fight a fight with only half a heart." He shook her gently. "Do you love this theater?"

"Yes!" she said, her voice echoing in the marble-floored lobby.

"Then remember that every time you hit a setback. Shout it if you need to. But one thing's for sure—we're not going to let that bastard win."

A quiet throat clearing turned their attention to the entrance. Pierce stood there, holding her pink fleece sweater. He walked across the lobby toward her, his face unreadable, and handed her the sweater. "The father of 'that bastard' asked me to bring this to you in case you needed it this morning. You left it on the back of your chair last night." He sent an appraising glance toward Nathan, then looked back at Brenna. "He's expecting you at eleven. I'll make sure to be gone until one o'clock."

He turned to leave, his heels clacking against the marble tiles, then stopped. Facing them again, he said, "I'm not the enemy here, you know."

Brenna and Nathan remained silent, making a mockery of his words.

Brenna watched him leave, wishing that seeing him in her theater didn't bring back all the happy memories of times they had spent there together, and another part of her glad that it did.

As good as his word, Pierce was gone when she knocked on Dr. Mc-Govern's door. An iced tea pitcher and glasses sat sweating on a tray on the coffee table, and as Brenna poured a glass for each of them, she noticed that the stacks of boxes she'd seen the last time hadn't changed. "Weren't the movers supposed to come yesterday?"

Dr. McGovern took the offered glass and sat back in his recliner. "Yes, they were, but there's been a little problem." He took a long sip. "I decided that the one-bedroom apartment I had booked is really too small for me. I don't want Pierce sleeping on the couch every time he comes to visit, so I've asked for a two-bedroom."

Brenna sat down, her hands clutching her iced tea glass, anticipating his next words.

"Unfortunately, one won't be available until next month, so I'm going to have to wait."

"But what about all your things? Everything's packed up."

The doctor shrugged. "I don't need them. I guess as a person gets older it's easier to see what's really necessary in life, and that whatever's left is just debris." His eyes met hers, and she had the brief impression that he wasn't talking about moving boxes.

Her hands chilled against her glass, but she didn't move them. "Will you need extra help moving, since Pierce has to go back home?"

A look that could have passed for amusement crossed over the doctor's face. "No, Brenna. I've asked Pierce to stay awhile longer, and he's arranged it with work. He says it works out anyway, since he wanted to be on hand for the final permits and groundbreaking for the new movie theater. They'll be able to get started immediately, because the land was already zoned commercial."

The chill in her hands crept up her arms, and she shivered. Finally putting the glass down, she rubbed her hands on her pants and picked up the letter box that was still where she'd left it the time before. "Shall we get started?"

Dr. McGovern nodded as he leaned back again in his chair and closed his eyes, his still-full glass resting on the table beside him.

Brenna picked up the second letter she'd begun before and began to read.

February 5, 1942

Darling,

I know it's been only two days since my last letter, and I didn't really expect a response from you by now, but I couldn't help but feel devastated when no news from you waited in my mailbox this afternoon. Oh, I know I'm being unreasonable, but how I long for just a single word from you. It would make your absence a little bit easier to bear.

I passed your mother's house today and saw her blue star flag in the window. How proud she must be to hang it and let everybody know that she has a son fighting for his country. There are more and more windows with blue stars each day, and I pray each night that this war will be over before any of them become gold stars.

I know the flags are to honor the mothers, but I wish there were something I could have to let people know that my heart is no longer with me but was given to a soldier who is far from home.

Write to me, darling. I miss you.
Me

Brenna slowly folded the letter and slipped it back in its envelope. "Are you ready for the next one?"

Without opening his eyes the doctor nodded, and Brenna reached inside for the third letter.

February 6, 1942

Darling,

After posting my letter from yesterday, I realized how maudlin it must have sounded to you, so I've decided to write another one today just full of happy news.

Jacquie Barnett—do you remember her? We were in the marching band together, and she now works at the post office with me—is in the family way. We were all surprised, since she and Frank were married only a week before he was shipped off for training, but we're all so happy for her. She's moving in with Frank's mother, and I hope that works out all right, and I can only imagine the comfort that they will give each other.

Mayor Lafayette has instituted blackouts starting at six o'clock in the evenings. It's hard doing things by candlelight, but my mama makes it fun. She's making socks for the soldiers and teaching me how to knit, and each sock I make I think of you. We listen to Edward R. Murrow every night on the radio during dinner. Mama makes Joey and me leave the room when bad news from the front comes on, but I've been creeping back in to listen. I want to know when this war will be over and when you are coming back home to me.

My love, before you go to sleep tonight, press your hand against your chest to feel your heart beat and know that it is my heart you feel. There is not a moment that ticks by that I am not thinking of you and wishing you were here.

Me

P.S. You-know-who has been stopping by each evening after work and sits on the porch with me. He's asked about you several times and wanted to know if I'd heard from you. I don't know why, but I lied and told him I'd received a letter from you each day you'd been away. I don't know why I did that, and I hope you will forgive me, but I know in my heart that you are thinking about me, and I needed to make him know this. I am living on hope now, darling, and it's a very thin meal, indeed.

Brenna stopped reading and glanced up at Dr. McGovern. He looked asleep, but then he opened his eyes and looked at her. His gaze seemed far away, as if Brenna and the living room had ceased to exist.

"Who was she?" Brenna asked.

The doctor didn't answer right away. Finally he said, "A woman I loved a long time ago." He sat up, placing his elbows on the arms of his chair. "We were supposed to be married, but then I enlisted and was sent away for training." He paused, swallowing. "I think at the time a lot of us boys thought that we'd whip the Germans and be back home in a month." He steepled his old hands in front of him, as if in prayer. "I left in the middle of my senior year at LSU, thinking I'd be back in time for graduation. I don't think any of us thought we'd be gone so long."

Brenna set the box aside and knelt in front of Dr. McGovern's chair. "How long were you gone?"

He leaned back again, his movements quick, as if he'd forgotten he was no longer a young soldier. "Three years. After I received my commission and wings as an Army Air Corps pilot, I was transferred overseas to fly B-25s. I was shot down over the English Channel and held in a German prison camp for the last year of the war."

Brenna put her hand on his sleeve and felt a slight tremor under her fingers. "Did you ever see her again?"

His eyes were bleak when he looked at her. "Yes. When I got back."

"But you didn't marry?"

He shook his head. "No."

Brenna waited for him to say more, almost knowing that he wouldn't. She was curious, but it wasn't her place to intrude. Standing, she patted his sleeve. "Do you want me to read another one now?"

He gave her a soft smile. "No, Brenna. I think that's enough for today—two seems to be my limit." He looked up hopefully. "Maybe tomorrow?"

She smiled back. "I can be back at the same time, if that's all right with you."

"I'm not going anywhere." He surprised her by grabbing her hand. "And thank you, Brenna, for doing this. I can't tell you how thankful I am."

"I should actually be thanking you, Dr. McGovern. I've enjoyed reading them. It brings me back to another era. But . . ." She was about to tell him that the opening of each envelope made her restless, the same way that winding a jack-in-the-box had made her feel as a child; the cold anticipation of knowing that something was about to pop out at you.

"But what?"

"Oh, I was just going to say how unfamiliar it was to me to actually slice open the letters."

He smiled again. "Maybe you'll get used to it and want to open all the ones you've been collecting."

She squeezed his hand. "Maybe. I'll see you tomorrow then."

They said their good-byes and Brenna left, pausing on the front step to make sure she didn't see Pierce's car, then headed to her own. Her thoughts kept going back to the sad eyes of an old soldier and to the woman he'd left behind.

It was almost ten o'clock by the time Brenna lugged herself up the porch steps of Mrs. Grodin's boardinghouse. She was covered in so much mud she was afraid to smile in case some of it flaked off into her mouth. Walter had dropped her off at the corner, worried that the delay of actually bringing her to her doorstep would cause the ice in the chest to melt and spoil his frog legs.

The site of Dooley Gambrel sitting on the porch swing made her pause on the top step. "Hey, Doo. What are you doing here?"

He was grinning his beloved half grin—the same grin he'd used when he'd dumped the bucket of crickets in Troy Beaudreaux's truck after Troy had pinched Brenna's rear end in algebra class. "I was close by, since I had to close the store." His grin widened. "Thought you might need some moral support."

She collapsed on the step and began tugging at her boot. Dooley joined her and easily slid one boot off, then the other. Then he reached over and flicked a clump of mud that hung from the tip of her nose. "Thanks," she said, easing one muddy sock off her foot and then the other. She stretched out her jeans-clad legs, afraid they'd dry in a bent position and she wouldn't be able to stand again. "How'd you find out about tonight's fiasco so soon?"

Dooley handed her a longneck bottle stuffed into a leopard-print coozie with fringe—presumably one of Colleen's eBay finds—and she took it gratefully. "Your date came into the store earlier to get some supplies and mentioned where he was going tonight and that he was bringing you. Colleen thought you might be needing this when you got back, so I volunteered to bring it to you. She also said that for you, all beer is on her for the rest of the year."

Brenna tilted her head back and gulped the cold beer, not caring how it tasted. She needed a buzz and she needed it quickly.

He handed her a brown packing envelope. "And this was on the doorstep, too."

She took the package and saw it was from Victoria's Secret. Her newest guilty pleasure had finally arrived. In the past she would have taken it out and shown Dooley, but something had changed between them, and she wasn't sure when.

"I've been thinking, Brenn."

"About what?" She stuck the package behind her, then placed the top of the bottle against her cheek in a vain attempt to cool off.

"About you. About us."

She looked at him, glad to be feeling the first effects of the beer that would hopefully dull what was promising to be an uncomfortable moment.

"Yes?" she asked, her tongue sticking to the roof of her mouth. She tilted the bottle back again, surprised to find it already empty.

"I think I've come up with a solution to all the dates from hell you seem intent on pursuing."

Even the little stab of anger she felt was dulled by the beer, and she grinned. "I don't pursue them."

"Yeah, well, you don't exactly discourage them, either. Or if you do, not strongly enough so your sisters know to leave off."

"Hey, you got another beer?"

"Do you really need another?"

In response, she indicated her mud-streaked hair and face, and her stiffening jeans.

Reluctantly, he reached around to his side and opened a cooler, then handed her another bottle. "That's your last one, Brenn. You know what beer does to you, and I won't be responsible."

She took the bottle, then stuck her tongue out at him, feeling remarkably better after doing so. "Thanks," she said as she tried to replace the bottle in the coozie and repeatedly missed the opening. With a sigh, Dooley took it from her and did it instead.

After a long swig, she looked at him again. "So, what's your solution?"

He took his baseball hat off and ran his hands through his light brown hair, and she found herself really looking at Dooley Gambrel for the first time in years. He had somehow grown up into a good-looking man without her noticing.

"Why aren't you married, Doo?"

She could tell he was trying to look irritated, but the light in his eyes made her smile brightly at him.

"Could I ask the questions, please?"

"Sure," she answered before draining the second bottle. She leaned her head against his shoulder and felt his arm pull her closer.

"Doo?"

He sighed heavily. "Yes?"

"What's your real name? I've known you forever, but I don't think I've ever known your real name."

He sighed again. "Dudley Harrison Gambrel the Fourth."

She snickered against his shoulder. "Yep. I see now why everybody calls you Dooley."

He nudged her gently with his elbow and laughed lightly. "Are you done now? Can I talk?"

She closed her eyes, feeling incredibly sleepy—the combination of the beer and Dooley's presence as comfortable as an old and familiar blanket.

"I think we should get engaged."

Wide awake now, Brenna sat up. "What?"

"Well, nobody would make you go on any more blind dates if they thought you were engaged, right?"

"Uh, no, but—"

"And you wouldn't have to hide at Kathleen's Sunday gatherings anymore. You could actually stay inside the house and eat."

"Yeah, but—"

"And your aunt Dottie and the rest of your family would stop asking you embarrassing questions about your love life."

Brenna felt completely sober as she stared at her best friend, remembering what he'd told Aunt Dottie. *The woman I love won't have me.*

"It could be just for a little while—just to give you some breathing room."

"You mean like a fake engagement?"

He shrugged. "Sure. I mean, why not? You'll get everybody off your back, and me . . . well, I'll get to tell everybody that somebody as fine as Brenna O'Brien has agreed to be my bride."

"This is *not* a good idea, Dooley. I love you—you know I do. Your friendship means too much to me to do something like you're suggesting—regardless of how tempting it might be. And I love you even more for suggesting it." She looked down at her lap. "I would never want to hurt you."

He gently took hold of her hands. "Come on, Brenna. It could be fun. Think about it—no more hunting bullfrogs. Or kissing them either." He winked. "Remember when we were teenagers, how much fun we used to have playing pranks? When was the last time you had fun, huh? And I won't get hurt—promise. I'll even be the one who officially breaks it off when we're done, if you want me to."

She looked into his eyes. "Why are you asking me this, Dooley? Really."

His eyes were open and honest, but he didn't answer her right away. Finally he said, "Because for the longest time you've been like a person sleepwalking through life. I figure you could use some waking up. I also figure you could use fewer dates from hell. Sort of a two-for-one deal, I guess." He looked away for a moment, and when he looked back he was grinning. "Plus, I'm hoping that you'll get used to the idea and agree to marry me after all."

"Dooley!"

"I'm kidding, Brenn. I know it's not like that between us. Really, I'm just trying to be a good friend."

She sighed, more tempted than she'd care to admit. *The woman I love won't have me.* "No, Doo. Absolutely not."

"Just say yes, Brenna. No strings attached. Promise. And you won't have to have another night like tonight."

As if to punctuate his words, a clump of mud fell from her hair and landed on their joined hands.

"This sounds like such a bad idea I can't believe I'm even considering it."

Dooley leaned close to her. "Call it a leap of faith if you like—I'll do the leaping, and I'll drag you with me until you can find your own footing."

She looked into his earnest brown eyes, unwilling or unable to see past her hurts of the last weeks and instead seeing a way out, regardless of how temporary, and she felt her resolve weakening in the face of his simple earnestness. "Okay, Dooley. But we end it the minute either one of us has had enough, right?"

"Right."

"Like I could end it tomorrow if I wanted to, right?"

"Right," he said, smiling his wonderful smile that had always made Brenna feel as if she were the most beautiful girl on the planet.

"Okay, then. It's a deal." She leaned forward and planted a kiss on his cheek, smearing mud on his face.

He reached into his back pocket and pulled out a black velvet ring box. "I thought you could wear this to make it more official." He opened the hinged top, revealing an old platinum setting with three small emerald-cut diamonds. "It was my grandmother's."

Brenna felt like crying in the face of Dooley's intensity and her own eagerness to deceive, but she held out her hand anyway. After brushing away some of the dirt, Dooley slid the ring on her finger.

"Congratulations," he said softly.

"You, too."

He stood, punching her gently on the shoulder as he always had as a way of saying good-bye. "I should be going."

"Bye, Doo. Thanks for the beer. And the ring," she added hastily.

He shrugged, then bent to retrieve his hat and the cooler. "Glad I could help. Guess I'll see you Sunday at Kathleen's."

"Are you sure you can handle that? They might swarm."

He smiled widely. "Yeah, they might. I can handle it."

"I'm sure you can. Good night, Dudley Harrison Gambrel the Fourth."

His eyes were sad behind his smile. "Good night, Brenna McKenzie O'Brien."

She watched him walk away, his gait so achingly familiar, then stared down at her new ring, recalling something he'd said about a leap of faith, and wondering if she'd ever have the strength to make one again.

CHAPTER 13

Pierce pulled his car up to the curb in front of Aunt Dottie's house, marveling at the assortment of plastic flowers in the front bed and the large red Lincoln with missing wheels parked in front. Since the rest of the O'Briens were heading to Kathleen's right after church, Kathleen had asked Pierce to pick Dottie up, since he passed her house on the way.

His knock was answered by Aunt Dottie, who peered up at him through thick glasses as she stuck her head around the door.

"Do we have a date? I don't recall my calendar saying I had a date."

"Uh, no, ma'am. I'm here to drive you to Kathleen's for Sunday supper."

Pulling the door open fully, she reached up and touched her large straw hat, which strongly resembled a brimming fruit bowl. "That's right, I'm wearing my Sunday hat. I'm a bit confused, is all, seeing as how I went to Mass yesterday at the senior center." She leaned forward, whispering in a conspiratorial manner, "Didn't like that at all. Filled with lots of old people, don't you know." Grabbing Pierce's arm and squeezing his biceps, she said, "It's a shame we don't have a date, though. Do you dance?"

"Yes, ma'am. I can jitterbug and shag with the best of them." He looked down at the old lady whose green eyes and spirit reminded him so much of how Brenna used to be. It was none of his business, really, how Brenna chose to live her life. Still, he couldn't help remembering a girl who used to celebrate the anniversary of the release date of the movie *Gone With the Wind* as if it were a national holiday, who laughed at the Three Stooges, and who had once told him that she would love him forever. Now she collected letters from dead people and owned a theater that seemed to be falling down around her ears, almost as if she believed that was all she was entitled to from life.

He patted Aunt Dottie's arm as he helped her down the steps. "I would be honored to go on a date with you."

She giggled, and he couldn't help but smile. "Oh, no, we couldn't do that. You're Brenna's beau. I wouldn't want to interfere with true love." They had reached the car. She dropped her hand and turned toward him. "My brother did that, you know. I had my own special beau, but my brother didn't approve." She looked Pierce squarely in the eye. "I never married because of him. And a day doesn't go by that I don't regret not fighting harder for what I wanted. Regret is a horrible thing to live with." She poked her finger into his chest. "Always remember—the road to hell is paved with regret."

Pierce thought for a moment. "I think that's supposed to be, 'The road to hell is paved with good intentions.' "

"What? Why are we talking about hell?"

"No, ma'am, we aren't. I believe we were talking about regret."

"Regret? Oh, yes." She paused for a moment, her eyes distant until they focused on her wheelless car in front of them. Her large chest rose and fell with a heavy sigh. "I regret not having a car to drive."

He opened the car door and paused, looking at the ancient Lincoln. "What happened to your car, Miss Dottie?"

She squinted up at him. "I don't rightly know. I just woke up yesterday morning and that's what I saw. Kathleen's husband said it could take months to get the wheels replaced, on account of it being so old. I'm thinking about getting one of those cute yellow cars like Brenna's. Do you know my niece, Brenna? She's single, you know."

He helped her into the backseat behind his father, making sure her hat didn't get squashed against the doorjamb. "Yes, Miss Dottie. I know Brenna," he said as he closed the door.

As he turned the ignition, his father faced the backseat and greeted Aunt Dottie. "That's a beautiful hat you're wearing, Dorothy."

"Thank you, Andrew. I must say that it makes me feel like a young girl again." She leaned forward as if to get a better look at him and, to Pierce's surprise as he watched in the rearview mirror, she touched his father's face. Her fingertips ran across the deep wrinkles on his cheek as if trying to make them disappear. "When did we get so old, Andrew? It seems like yesterday when we didn't have so much gray hair, doesn't it?"

The doctor took Dottie's fingers and squeezed them tightly. "It does, Dottie. It really does."

"I still have that letter for you, you know. You're never going to know what's in it until you open it."

His father cleared his throat before kissing her hand and letting go. "Thank you, Dottie. Maybe soon."

"Better make it sooner than later. You know the road to hell is paved with procrastination."

Both Pierce and his father turned their heads toward the backseat, then looked at each other without saying a word. Pierce waited to ask his father later about the letter, almost afraid of whatever tangent Dottie might head off into if he were to ask in front of her.

When they reached Kathleen's house, a rowdy game of touch football had already started in the large front lawn. John and Kathleen came out to the car to help him with his father and Aunt Dottie. As Pierce unloaded his father's walker from the trunk, John joined him.

"Thanks for driving Dottie."

"My pleasure. I think my dad enjoys her company. They've known each other practically their whole lives but don't get to see each other very much." Pierce closed the trunk. "I'm assuming you know what happened to her tires?"

"Damned straight I do, and I'm not proud of it. Some idiot at the dealership called her to let her know her spark plugs were in instead of calling me first. That would have given us a long reprieve. Instead, we had to stoop even lower and steal her tires."

Pierce lifted his father's walker. "Better talk with the Volkswagen dealership, then. She's planning on buying one of those new Beetles."

A look of horror crossed John's face. "God help us all," John said under his breath before leaving to help Kathleen walk Dottie inside.

Pierce set the walker in front of his father and walked beside him as they slowly made their way to the front door. "What was Dottie talking about—about the letter?"

Dr. McGovern slowly shook his head. "Who knows? Poor Dottie. They really should think about putting her in an assisted-living facility. She seems fine most of the time, but then others . . . well, she just gets confused." They took a few labored steps. "I think she'd heard about the letters they found at the post office and just got her stories mixed up."

Pierce nodded his head, knowing that what his father had told him was completely possible, but having had enough conversations with Aunt Dottie to not completely discount her, either.

When they entered the living room, it appeared that everybody who wasn't playing football out front was gathered in a circle in the front room. Brenna stood in the center of the small crowd and was holding out her left hand, where something glittered on her fourth finger.

He felt like he had when he was eight and had fallen out of a tree. He hadn't been able to breathe for a long moment, and in that time he knew he was going to die and, with the pain in his chest slicing through him, he wished that he would.

His breath had come back to him in a single, painful rush, and he found himself doing that now as he watched Brenna O'Brien show off what appeared to be an engagement ring. Kathleen moved up beside him and slipped her hand through his elbow. He nodded perfunctorily.

"Surely not Schmott?" he asked.

"Of course not. It's Dooley Gambrel. Do you know him?"

He managed to keep the surprise out of his voice. "Yes. She looks happy."

"Not really."

He looked down at the small red-haired woman with surprise. Of all of Brenna's sisters, Kathleen was the one most like a mother to her. When he and Brenna had been secretly dating, Kathleen had been the only one in whom Brenna had confided. He'd been surprised the first time Kathleen had shown up at his house with a message from Brenna. When he'd asked her why she would defy her own father for her sister, she had said simply that the best thing for Brenna would be to get as far away from their father as possible.

"Why don't you think she's happy?"

Kathleen looked up at him with hauntingly familiar eyes. "You know that better than I do, Pierce."

He fought to keep his breathing even. "Then why's she marrying him?"

"Because she'll never have to worry about him breaking her heart."

She patted him on the arm, then excused herself to the kitchen. Not able to stand and watch anymore, he escaped to the front yard, where he hoped a lot of sweat and bruises might help him forget the sight of Brenna showing off her ring and erase, at least for a time, the old ache around his heart.

Brenna finally looked up when she knew Pierce had gone. She had sensed him when he entered the room but hadn't been able to meet his eyes, afraid she'd see her own doubts and recriminations there.

Colleen moved close to her and slung an arm around her shoulders. "I'll start checking eBay for wedding dresses for you, all right? You can get a brand-new Vera Wang for a steal if you know where to look and how to bid."

Brenna pulled back, horrified that she hadn't anticipated this. "You don't have to do that, Colleen. I thought I'd wear Mama's dress." She hadn't really thought about it at all, but that was the first thing that came to mind.

"You can't do that, Brenn. Daddy gave it away in one of his fits after Mama died. None of us wore it."

"I'd forgotten that."

"Yeah, well, you were just a baby. But I remember it—and of all the mean-spirited things he ever did, that was probably the one thing I could never forgive him for."

Brenna studied Colleen's face, recalling one of the only conversations she'd ever had with her father about her mother. *I want a picture of her, Daddy. Just one picture. I don't even know what she looked like.*

She's dead, Brenna. She didn't try very hard to stick around for you or for me, so I don't see a reason to keep pictures of her to remind us. Besides, she got the diabetes when she was pregnant with you and that's what killed her. Can't see why you'd want to be reminded of that.

Kathleen had been the one who'd given her the photo of Brenna and her mother. Brenna had kept it under her mattress her entire childhood until her father died. On the day of his funeral she'd pulled it out, and it had rested on her bedside table ever since.

Timmy ran into the room, frantically searching the baseboards and peering under the furniture. "Have y'all seen Rocky?"

Colleen planted her hands on her hips. "Why isn't she in her cage?"

"PC and Mary Sanford wanted to see her run. So I took her out. Have you seen her?"

"You took her out? I told you that I would only allow you to bring her to Aunt Kathleen's if you kept her in the cage."

"Mama, not now!" Timmy wailed.

Slightly chagrined, Colleen said, "No, I haven't seen her."

Timmy took off at a run, with Colleen calling out behind him, "We're not done with this conversation, young man."

Brenna looked down at her feet, afraid of what she might see. "Does he mean Rocky the guinea pig?"

"Yep, the very one—it was Mary Sanford's, but she had to give it up because of allergies. In a million years I wouldn't have given Timmy a pet, but I think this is the best thing I've ever done."

"What do you mean?"

Colleen pursed her lips for a moment. "You know how Timmy avoids anything that might end in disappointment? Well, that's why we never got him a pet, because pets can live only so long."

Uneasy, Brenna looked to the doorway where Timmy had disappeared. "So how is this good for him, then? Guinea pigs don't live that long. And if he can't find Rocky, Rocky's life expectancy will be drastically reduced, I would think."

Colleen looked pointedly at her sister. "Sometimes it takes kind of a baptism by fire to help us make the leap over whatever bump has been blocking our way. I don't know if it was in the way Daddy raised us with the 'glass is always half-empty' attitude, or maybe it's in the blood, but we O'Briens are a stubborn lot. We seem to need a good hard kick in the pants to get us moving in the right direction." She put her arm around Brenna again and began steering her toward the front porch, where the other three sisters were gathered to watch their men and off-spring play football. "Remember how Mary Margaret broke up with Richard because Daddy threatened to disinherit her? She gave in so easily, I think in part because she figured she'd never have to face the ins and outs of marriage with Richard if she never married him. Which is pretty stupid once you get down to it, but that's Mary Margaret." Colleen rolled her eyes. "But then she was so miserable that she realized she'd rather be with Richard and risk one day losing him than lose him right off the bat."

Brenna forced a smile and held out her left hand. "Hey, I've made the decision to get married. I've moved forward by my own volition— discounting the discarded bodies of all those men you and the others have thrown at me over the years."

Colleen stopped in front of the screen door. "Brenna, I don't know about the others, but you're not fooling me. There's more going on here than what meets the eye. I can only hope that you know what you're doing and that when all's said and done, you really have done something to change your life."

Stung, Brenna pulled away. "My life is just fine, thank you. I wish you and the rest of my sisters would stop trying to live my life for me."

"Well, somebody has to, since you won't."

"I have my theater and my family. And now I have Dooley," she added hastily. "I have everything I need." She tried to bite back her next words, but her anger was acting like wind on a fire and there was no going back. "I don't think you're qualified to give me advice on life's lessons, Colleen, because *I'm* not the one jeopardizing my life savings by spending it all on eBay. Don't think I haven't overheard any of your arguments with Bill."

Colleen stared at her and then, unbelievably, began to smile. "Welcome back, Brenna. I haven't seen you this worked up over something in a long, long time. Maybe marrying Dooley is the right thing after all."

Her anger doused by surprise, Brenna turned abruptly and pushed open the screen door, Colleen following behind. Mary Margaret, Kathleen, and Claire were standing by the porch railing sipping sweet tea and giggling like schoolgirls. Brenna moved over beside them and peered into the front yard, where half of the men and a few of the boys had removed their shirts.

Claire elbowed Kathleen. "Tell John there's such a thing as a tanning booth. I swear I'm going to go blind looking at the sun reflecting off his chest."

Mary Margaret leaned down, resting her elbows on the railing. "You're one to talk, Claire. Buzz strongly resembles Casper. And although I don't think I would have noticed if we didn't have some new chests to stare at, I would say all of our men could benefit by hitting the gym once in a while." She squinted, holding her hand over her forehead to block the sun. "Gosh, Claire, is Buzz *pregnant?*"

Claire snorted. "With beer, maybe. When I told him I really admired a six-pack, he went to the store and bought one. Doesn't slow him down, though, if you know what I mean. Sometimes a little cushioning can be nice."

They all laughed, except for Kathleen, who'd stepped back from the railing and moved to stand beside Brenna. "I guess that now you're an engaged woman, we don't have to censor our conversations anymore." She tucked Brenna's hair behind her ear, but Brenna didn't respond, remembering their argument at the church.

Kathleen handed her a glass of tea. "I just poured this—would you like it? There's more in the kitchen, and I'm heading that way in a minute anyway."

Brenna took it for the peace offering it was. "Thank you," she said, and turned her attention to the game in the yard that seemed to be getting louder and louder with the shouting of men and the yelling of children.

Colleen let out a low whistle. "That man is fi-ine. I think we should go hide his shirt so he can't put it back on."

Brenna didn't have to ask whom they were talking about. She watched as Pierce gained possession of the ball and began running toward the makeshift goal line. From her conversations with his father, she'd learned that Pierce had become an avid sailor while living in California. It was evident in the fading bronze of his skin and the taut muscles. She could imagine it, too; he probably liked to sail in stormy weather just to prove to himself that he could. He'd always been that way. She wondered, too, if he'd given up football and his love of poetry when he'd married and moved to the West Coast. He would have assimilated well there, with his sailing skills and easy charm. And his new wife who hadn't been her. He'd said that to her when she'd asked him why his marriage hadn't lasted. *Because she wasn't you.*

There was a collective groan as Brenna and her sisters watched Nathan and Dooley tackle Pierce at the same time. Claire nudged Brenna. "They've been doing that all through the game. It's like they're singling him out for some reason."

Pierce was on the ground now, still in possession of the ball. John, the most fair-minded and even-tempered of all of Brenna's brothers-in-law, was playing a double role as referee and ran into the melee.

Claire continued: "Dooley doesn't look so bad without his shirt on, either. Way to go, little sister."

For the first time, Brenna actually looked at Dooley, first embarrassed that she hadn't already done so and then embarrassed that she did. He was tall and lanky, with smooth muscles, and certainly worthy of being shirtless, but she had to look away. Although she'd never had a brother, she was pretty sure that was the way she would have felt if she'd seen him without his shirt.

Pierce was on his feet now, and Brenna couldn't stop herself from looking at him again and remembering the way her head fit in the space between his neck and shoulder and how his skin tasted under the warm sun. And how it had felt to be touched by him and held in his arms. All the things she'd lost and taught herself not to remember were suddenly right in front of her, so near she felt she could stretch out her hand and grab them, but somehow she seemed to be seeing it all through a plate-glass window, where everything on the other side was simply out of reach.

Kathleen was standing next to her again, this time holding a cloth dampened with cold water. That was so like Kathleen—always anticipating everybody's needs. "Are you okay, Brenna? Too much sun?"

Grateful for the distraction, Brenna took the cloth and held it to her face. "Thanks, Kathleen. I think I've been working too hard at the theater and not getting enough sun. I'm just not used to it, I guess."

"That must be it," said Mary Margaret behind her. "That Dooley Gambrel sure looks fine without his shirt. Who would have thought?"

"Yeah," said Brenna, keeping her eyes focused on Dooley. "Who would have thought?"

Pierce was waiting in a rocking chair on his father's porch when Brenna arrived to read more letters. Her first impulse was to turn and run, but instead she slowly climbed the stairs and stopped at the top. "Hello, Pierce."

"Hello, Brenna."

"Is your dad all right?"

"He's fine—waiting inside for you, as a matter of fact."

Confused, she said, "Oh, I only thought . . . Oh, never mind." She moved forward to knock on the screen door.

"Never mind what?"

Brenna held back a retort. Pierce had never been able to drop a subject or to ignore the obvious. She'd grown up with a father who preferred silence and four sisters who preferred pretending everything was fine, and Pierce's forthrightness had always been one of the things she'd loved most about him. Without it, she never would have realized that she wanted a lot more out of life than what her father wanted for her.

She looked at him now, wondering where that naive girl had gone and why she had never known to miss her until Pierce McGovern walked back into her life. "It's just that you said you'd leave me alone until you had to go back, that's all. I figured if you were here when I stopped by, there was something wrong."

Pierce hooked his leg around another rocking chair and pulled it closer to him. "Have a seat."

"Your dad—"

"You're early, so you've got a few minutes. Have a seat. Please."

Slowly she sat down in the rocker, keeping to the edge so she could leave quickly.

"I didn't get a chance to chat with you at Kathleen's today, and I wanted to offer my congratulations on your engagement. When's the big day?"

She could smell the beer now. "You've been drinking."

"Damn right I have. Why the hell do you think I'm here instead of in my car and a thousand miles away?"

"I wouldn't know. I don't keep track of you."

"You sure were this afternoon." He leaned toward her and she sat back. "I was remembering things. Something about you seeing me shirtless made me remember." He grinned, but it wasn't a pleasant grin. "Made me remember going to the beach with you and being in the backseat of my dad's car."

She started to stand but he held her back. "It made me remember a girl who used to take chances and wasn't afraid to love somebody with all of her heart."

I remember, too, she wanted to say, but her throat was thick with disappointments and heartbreak, and the words couldn't find their way out. "Please stop," she said instead. "I've grown up, Pierce. I'm not that girl anymore. I've got different priorities now."

He leaned forward, the beer smell on his breath strong. "That's the problem, Brenna. You didn't grow up. You grew sideways—or worse, you grew down. You're more repressed and naive than you ever were. You told me that your theater means everything to you—but what have you done? You've hired a drifter from Texas like he's a magic pill. What's that all about? Why aren't you calling in the forces? Working your ass off instead of doing what you've always done? Because you're right about one thing—you're going to lose the first-run movies. Have you thought about alternatives? Or are you sticking your head in the sand so that when my multiplex opens up you're caught by surprise? And your family—you say that besides your theater they're the only other thing you need. Well, I've got news for you, Brenna O'Brien: If they're going to sit back and let you marry Dooley Gambrel, they don't give a damn about you."

Brenna felt the strange urge to get into crash position, as if she were on an airplane getting ready for a bumpy landing. She felt light-headed and nauseous, just as she'd felt when she was in third grade and had seen Willie Norton hit by a bicycle when crossing the street. He'd lain there, unmoving, the wind knocked out of him while the world continued to swirl about him and the other children who had witnessed the accident.

She forced herself to stand. "Why did you have to come back? Why can't you just go?"

He stood, too. "Because who else is going to make you look in a mirror? Your dad's been dead for a long time, Brenna. Isn't it time to start really living your own life?"

She grabbed the back of the rocking chair and squeezed it to stop her hand from shaking. "I am. I'm getting married. I'm starting a new life."

Pierce only snorted, then pulled something out of his back pocket and handed it to her. "Here. I got this for you. I was in New Orleans yesterday selling some of my dad's things to an antiques dealer and saw a bunch of old letters shoved in a shoe box in the back of the store. Against my better judgment, I went through them, letter by letter, until I found one that had never been opened."

She looked down at the faded brown ink on the sepia paper, noting the marks on the envelope. "It's Civil War—occupied New Orleans. It's from a Confederate prisoner."

He pressed it into her hand. "Take it—it's yours."

She started to protest, but he put it into her hands and closed her fingers over it. Then he leaned closer to her, and she wanted to close her eyes and simply exist in the scent of him. "Open it," he whispered in her ear. "Open it, Brenna. I'll stay here with you while you do it."

A cool breeze moved across the porch like a soft hand pushing her in a direction she didn't want to go. She shivered, although it had nothing to do with the wind. "No," she whispered. "I don't want to."

He stepped closer and she did close her eyes, feeling him without touching. "Open it," he said again.

She shook her head, her eyes still closed.

"I gave up too easily once, Brenna. I won't make the same mistake again."

He tilted her head and kissed her softly on the lips, and all the pain and wonder of her first real love swelled through her, but she remained still with her eyes closed as she listened to him move off the porch. When she finally looked, he had vanished into the early evening, leaving her shivering in her thin sweater and trying hard not to remember what it had once been like to see life as full of possibilities.

CHAPTER 14

Dr. McGovern was not in his usual spot in the chair beside the large picture window when Brenna entered the house. Instead, she found him at the kitchen table with a worn paper grocery bag spilled on its side, its contents strewn over the surface.

Dr. McGovern looked up at her over his bifocals. "Hello, Brenna. I'm sorry—I didn't hear you at the door."

"That's all right. I was trying to be quiet in case you'd fallen asleep."

He indicated the kitchen chair next to him. "Have a seat. I was just going through some of my old war memorabilia. I guess the letters have made me a bit nostalgic." He rifled through a pile of old black-and-white photographs, then pulled one out and handed it to her. She studied the picture of five airmen wearing leather bomber jackets and goggles strung around their necks. Their arms were loosely thrown over one another's shoulders, and they stared at the camera with smiling youth and casual enthusiasm.

"That was the day we all received our commissions. The next day we were sent overseas."

She brought the picture closer, trying to determine which of the young pilots had been Dr. McGovern. She sought a man who looked like Pierce, tall and broad-shouldered, with a cocky grin and determined eyes. She pointed to a man squatting on the end of the row. "Is this you?"

She held the photograph in front of him and watched him try to focus. "Yep, that's me. Younger and greener than I ever remember being."

Brenna looked at the newspaper clippings and photographs, at the belt buckle and embroidered ribbons and medals, and what looked like a menu written in Italian. It was like a time machine to another era, and she felt a little thrill at having the privilege of experiencing it. It was similar to the way she felt about her theater: a small portal to escape this life, if only for a short while.

"Where did all of this come from?"

The doctor looked up from a stack of letters that had been bound together by rubber bands. "Mostly from my mother. I found the bag when I was cleaning out her closet after she died. A lot of it I sent to her during the war. The rest were things I brought back and at some point put them all together."

"You flew planes in the war, right?"

"B-25s. I was stationed in England for the first part of the war and led bombing raids across the Channel."

She studied the old man in front of her with the wrinkled skin and shaking hands, trying to picture him flying a B-25 bomber headed inside enemy territory. "How old were you?"

"Nineteen. Still wet behind the ears."

Brenna leaned closer. "Who are those letters from?"

He held her gaze. "Me. I wrote them to my mother during the war."

"Oh." She sat back down. "I just assumed that because . . ." She stopped, not sure how to continue.

"You thought that because I hadn't written to my fiancée, that I hadn't written to my mother, either."

Puzzled, she nodded. "Yes. I'm . . . surprised." She looked back at the stack of photographs. "Are there any pictures in there . . . of your fiancée?"

At first she didn't think he would answer. He sat in his chair for a long time, staring at the letters. Finally he looked up and said, "I don't think so. My mother wasn't aware of my engagement. There wouldn't have been any reason for her to keep pictures of us."

Brenna nodded, her fingers sifting through the discarded remnants of an old life, finally realizing what it was she was searching for. "Is there a picture of Pierce's mother in here? I've only ever seen the one that was on the piano. Pierce was just a baby."

Dr. McGovern shook his head. "I didn't meet her until I came back from the war, so there wouldn't be any pictures of her in there. Besides, the ones I had I gave to Pierce. I'm not sure what he did with them."

She remembered an eight-year-old Pierce who stubbornly claimed that his mother was dead long after it had become known that she had left her family willingly and, as it turned out, permanently. She wondered if he had even kept any of her pictures.

Brenna saw a flash of something shiny tucked underneath the bag and pulled it out. It was a soldier's dog tag listing all vital information for Lieutenant Andrew McGovern. But what held her attention was the religious medal that hung from the same chain, larger than the ones she wore. Placing the medallion in her palm she studied the face of the saint on the front.

"Saint George?"

He nodded. "Patron saint of soldiers."

"I didn't realize you were Catholic."

"I'm not. It was a gift from somebody who was."

With a bitten fingernail, Brenna flipped it over. Moving it closer, she read,

> Hope is the thing with feathers
> That perches in the soul,
> And sings the tune without the words,
> And never stops at all.

She knew those words. They'd been in a dog-eared book of poetry that Pierce had given her long ago. "Emily Dickinson. Did your fiancée give you this?"

Slowly, he nodded. "Yes. And to this day I remember exactly what it was that she said when she gave it to me." He lowered his head and didn't speak for a long time, as if he were conjuring the strength he needed to get the words from the recesses of his memory and bring them out into the light of day. "She said, 'Take this and keep it close to your heart, that you might live in the protection of Saint George.'" He took a deep breath. "'And when you feel it against your heart, know that it is my heart that is touching yours and that it will never be whole without you.'" He shuddered and she saw him swallow. "And her last words to me were, 'Come back to me. I'll wait for you forever.'"

Brenna looked away. They were both silent for a long moment, listening to the distant ticking of the hall clock. At last, Dr. McGovern spoke. "Why don't we leave all of this for now and go read some letters? Are you up to it?"

She forced a smile. "Of course." She stood and helped him out of his chair, then led him into the living room. The box sat where it always was, on the table by her chair, and she plucked the letter that sat on top and began to read.

March 5, 1942

Darling,

It's been a whole month now since you left. I haven't written recently because I've been hoping and hoping for a letter from you so that I could respond to anything you had to say. But still nothing! What is wrong? When we said good-bye, I knew in my heart that what I was feeling was completely reciprocated by you. I don't think I could have been wrong.

Oh, darling, please forgive me for all of my doubts. I'm so lonely and I miss you dreadfully. And I do have some Very Important News to share with you. I'm hesitating to tell you in a letter, especially when I'm not sure if my letters are even reaching you. Please, please, please let me know if you're all right and if you've been getting my letters. I'm so eager to share my news with you! Please write soon.

With all my love,
Me

As Brenna gently folded the letter back into the envelope, she glanced up at the doctor. As was his habit while she was reading, his head rested on the back of the chair and his eyes were closed. She knew he wasn't sleeping, and also knew that he would expect her to continue with the next letter. After sticking the first letter into the bottom of the pile, she pulled the next one off the top.

March 10, 1942

My darling,

Still no word from you. I'm going to pretend that my letters are still in transit—which can take forever now with the war on—or that you've been too busy with earning your wings to respond. I understand, darling, I do. It's just that I so need to hear from you now more than ever.

I stood behind your mother today at the store, waiting to get our sugar rations. She was very warm toward me, which made me feel better, although still a bit guilty. I had your ring on a chain around my neck the whole time, but I'm quite sure she didn't notice it. I did ask if she'd heard from you, and she said that she'd received several letters the first few weeks you were gone and then nothing since. She did mention that you had asked her to say hello to me for you and to ask me to write. I'm hoping this means that you hadn't received my earlier letters yet, but have now. I double-checked with your mother that I had the correct address just to make sure. I'm hoping when I go out to my mailbox today I'll find a stack of your letters that have been winging their way to me all the while I've been pining for you.

Things are getting tight here already. We have to wait in line to buy just about anything—like sugar and coffee, even shoes! They've even started requiring us to turn in our old toothpaste tubes before we're allowed to purchase new ones because they're made with metal. The cherry trees along Main Street are in full bloom, and the high school band has begun to practice again in the square for the upcoming commencement exercises. I hope I'm not boring you with all these things, but they all remind me of you, and I'm hoping that by telling you about them, they'll make you remember me, too, and to always keep in your mind a picture of what you have to come home to.

I have a new haircut. I went ahead and cut it so that it looks a little bit like Lauren Bacall's. I wasn't sure at first, but my friends say it's very flattering. I do hope you like it. I met a new friend who works at the beauty shop. She visits the post office often to see her *brother and we always chat. She said she'd give me a good deal if I let her cut my hair. I was feeling so low that I agreed. I do hope you like it.*

Mother is calling me for dinner so I must close. It is becoming urgent that I hear from you. Please, please, please do whatever you can to get a letter to me.

I love you.
Me.

Brenna folded the letter back into the envelope, then leaned forward with her elbows pressed against her knees. "Dr. McGovern?"

He opened his eyes and looked at her. He'd taken his glasses off, and for a moment she thought she could see the young airman he'd once been.

"What was her name? I feel as if I know her, but I don't even know her first name."

A corner of his mouth lifted in a half smile. " 'Me' was sort of a nickname I gave her, and it stuck. I don't think I ever called her anything else."

"But what was her real name? Does she have family still living in Indianola?"

He closed his eyes again. "I'm very tired now, Brenna. Do you mind letting yourself out?"

Disappointed, Brenna put the box on the table and stood. "Of course not." She pulled an afghan off the back of a sofa and placed it gently over his legs. "Is there anything I can get for you before I leave?"

"No, thank you. Pierce will be back soon. He's been real careful about leaving before you get here and arriving right after you leave."

"Yeah, I noticed."

His eyes were open again, and he was staring at Brenna with a sharp intensity. "I remember the first Christmas after he went off to college, he came home and asked me for his mother's engagement ring. She'd left it when she . . . she went away. It was a lovely ring, a family heirloom. Had stones in it from both of my grandmothers. I assumed it was for somebody up at college, since to my knowledge he'd never dated anybody here." He paused for a moment, and Brenna tried not to squirm. "I'll admit I was surprised when no engagement was forthcoming. And when he did get engaged four years later, he didn't give Diana that ring."

Brenna swallowed. "Oh, well. He must have had his reasons. Maybe he sold the ring."

"No, he didn't. He gave it back to me. For safekeeping, he said."

"Oh." Brenna tucked her hands into her front pockets, unsure of what to say. "Well, if that's all . . ."

"I'm an old man, Brenna. And I know when you count the years, I've been alive on this earth for a very long time. But the truth of the matter is that life is short. Too short."

The incessant ticking of the clock in the hallway vibrated through Brenna, bringing back the restlessness that had seemed to plague her since Pierce's return. She grabbed her purse. "Good night, Dr. McGovern. I can't come tomorrow, but what about Tuesday at the same time?"

He nodded, his eyes steady on her, preventing her from turning away. "Of all your mother's daughters, you're the most like her. Did you know that?"

She shook her head, trying to remember the face of the woman in the picture by her bed.

"You all looked like her, although you more than the others, but you inherited her spirit. Even as a baby, she would say that about you. You were relentless in getting what you wanted, trying again even if you failed. She loved that about you. She thought she'd finally managed to produce a daughter who wouldn't be cowed by your father."

Brenna swallowed and clutched at her purse straps. "No one ever told me that. Thank you."

"No, Brenna. Thank you. I can't tell you how much I've enjoyed your company. You've made the past easier to face."

She regarded him for a moment, trying to find the courage to ask her next question. Finally, she asked, "Did you ever find out what it was that she wanted to tell you?"

He gave her a faint smile. "Good night, Brenna. I'll see you Tuesday."

She knew enough not to press him, but she wouldn't drop the subject, either. If it wasn't revealed in the next few letters, she'd ask again. Besides, according to her mother, she was supposed to be persistent.

"Good night," she said again, turning away with a smile, trying once more to remember the face of the mother who had once thought that she was the daughter most like her.

Pierce stood in the street in front of the Royal Majestic, admiring the newly straight marquee sign, and the almost-matching tiles that had been fitted into spaces where broken tiles had been before. Even the lions out front gleamed with new black paint. It was patchwork, though, like holding your finger in the hole of a dam. He knew he wasn't responsible for Brenna's current financial woes, but he did know that he would, in fact, be responsible for pulling the final rug out from under her feet.

He stepped back to admire the Gothic stonework at the top of the building, remembering briefly standing there with his mother when he was a small boy and feeling the euphoria of childhood enthusiasm—the same enthusiasm that quickly turned to cynicism as the boy grew older.

"Come to gloat?"

Pierce turned to see Nathan Conley emerging from the theater, a wide grin on his face that did nothing to put Pierce at ease. He stifled his disappointment. He'd wanted to talk to Brenna and avoid this Nathan person entirely. For all his cowboy swagger, there was something about Nathan Conley that set Pierce on edge.

"I've actually come to see Brenna. Is she here?"

"Yes, actually, she is. But she's busy. Can I take her a message?"

"This will only take a minute." Pierce stepped aside to move past Nathan but found his way blocked. Not willing to get into an altercation in front of the theater, Pierce stopped.

"I have something to give to her that I think she'd like to have."

"Sounds great. Why don't you give it to me and I'll be sure she gets it."

Pierce took a deep breath, determined to remain civil. "Look, I'm not sure what your problem is or why you think you need to protect

Brenna from me, and I don't really care." He raised the cardboard port-folio he'd brought with him. "I was going through some of my father's things and found these old pictures of the Royal Majestic. My mother was a bit of an amateur photographer and she loved the theater, so she took a lot of pictures of it."

A flicker of interest shone in Nathan's eyes as Pierce opened the folder, holding it so Nathan could see the photos.

"This one here is Greta Garbo. There's actually quite a few pictures with movie stars in them. I think somebody had a connection to one of the studios or something. Anyway, there's a lot of photos of this theater from the last six decades."

"Can I?" Nathan asked, indicating the folder.

"Sure."

Nathan took the folder from Pierce and continued to look at the pictures, slowly flipping through them and studying them as if they held some sort of clue he was supposed to be looking for.

Pierce continued. "I thought these would be nice to hang in the lobby."

Nathan closed the folder. Almost grudgingly, he said, "These aren't too bad. And you say your mom took them?"

"She was a big movie buff. Loved everything about them—especially the theme music. I have a whole box of movie-theme sheet music, actually, and I was about to take it to Goodwill."

An unusual light lit Nathan's eyes, and a tic started in his jaw. "No, man. Don't do that. We could use it here."

"Really?"

"Really. Not that I'm going to tell you why, of course." He winked, and Pierce figured Nathan was trying for a lighter tone. "But if you're going to get rid of them, you might as well give them to us. Unless you're afraid of a little competition."

Pierce eyed the man in front of him, realizing they were the exact same height, and wondering how they had become somewhat adver-saries without really knowing each other. "Look, Nathan, I don't know if you or Brenna have thought about this, but there're other options than being in direct competition with my theater. If you did something different, something that a big corporate multiplex can't do . . . some-thing that would appeal to a small-town mentality . . ."

Nathan studied him. "You think so? And what makes you think that Brenna will listen to you? You're the guy trying to run her out of business."

"Nathan? Who are you talking to?"

They both turned to see Brenna walking toward them, pausing in front of the box office to dump a pile of movie posters. She seemed defeated, somehow. Maybe it was in the slump of her shoulders or the light he couldn't see in her eyes. Did he do this to her? No sooner had the thought hit him than he dismissed it. He knew that it had begun the day her mother died and her father had become her only parent.

Pierce moved toward her. "I brought some old photos of the theater that I thought you might want."

Her startled look surprised him until he recalled what he'd said to her the last time he'd seen her. *I gave up too easily once, Brenna. I won't make the same mistake again.* And then he'd kissed her. God. What had possessed him to do that? He'd like to think it was the beer and not his inability to let her father win, and maybe, just maybe, because he had loved her once and probably always would.

She took a step closer to Nathan. "You could have left them with your father. I'm going there tomorrow night."

"Yeah, I know. I just . . . I wanted to give them to you myself."

Nathan handed her the folder, and Pierce watched as she opened it, her face and eyes brightening as she studied each picture. Her expression reminded him of the old Brenna who had been a member of the film club all through high school while her father believed her to be in a youth Bible study. She broke into a smile, and he couldn't help but smile back.

"Look at the marquee sign in these pictures—it's like a list of the biggest movies since the forties. And real movie stars, here in Indianola! And look—who is this?"

Pierce moved closer to look over her shoulder. The picture showed the marquee advertising *Guess Who's Coming to Dinner,* and the reason he probably hadn't noticed the woman standing on the sidewalk underneath the large sign was because on the other side of the picture were picketers denouncing the movie as indecent. He leaned closer, catching Brenna's scent. He recognized the woman immediately and jerked back.

"That would be my mother. Apparently she didn't take all the photographs."

Brenna looked more closely, a small smile teasing her lips. "You look just like her, you know. She's wearing a hat, so I don't know about her hair, but that's definitely your face."

He quickly reached over and flipped the picture to the next one and she looked up, startled. "I'm sorry. I forget sometimes. I like to look at the picture of my mother and try to see what parts of her I have."

Pierce looked into her eyes, seeing again the motherless child he had known and realizing maybe for the first time how very much alike they were in that regard. "I never did," he said softly, knowing it for the lie it was.

Nathan stepped forward and gently took the folder from Brenna. "If you like, I'll get them framed for you. I'll look for a self-framing shop that will save us some money. Maybe we can have a big unveiling event or something."

She raised her eyebrows. "An event?"

"Yeah. We can talk about it later."

Brenna placed a hand on Nathan's arm. "I need to speak to Pierce. Would you mind calling the roofing contractor back and telling him that we're going to have to wait on those repairs but that we'll call him when we're ready?"

Nathan looked from Brenna to Pierce, then back again. "Sure thing." He raised the folder. "And then I'll go see about getting these framed."

"Thanks," Brenna said, and they both watched Nathan walk away, the swagger in his step making him look all the more like a cowboy.

Pierce spoke first. "I wanted to apologize for last night. I had too much to drink and didn't know what I was saying." He stopped, then forced himself to continue and get it over with. "And I apologize for kissing you. I shouldn't have done that—especially with you being an engaged woman."

A pink flush spread over her cheeks. "Oh. Okay. Well, that's what I figured. You know, since you'd been drinking."

He rubbed his jaw, feeling the short stubble. "I don't drink much anymore. Guess I wasn't used to it." He searched around for something to say, wanting to stay while at the same time wanting to run as far away as he could. His gaze rested on the old grandfather clock with the brass crow. "Did you ever find out anything about this clock? When you were in high school, you used to tell me that this clock was your favorite thing about the theater, and that one day you would buy the Royal Majestic just so you could own the clock."

Brenna had crossed her arms over her chest as if to build a barrier between them, but a small smile cracked her lips. "It wouldn't be the Royal Majestic without it. Sort of like the ravens at the Tower of London—they say that if the ravens disappear, there wouldn't be a monarch on the British throne."

He smiled back, feeling seventeen again. "Did you ever make it to London to see the ravens?" They had spent his entire senior year talking about the trips they would make, and watching movies that were set in foreign countries. Brenna had wanted to see the world, or at least what else there was outside of Indianola, Louisiana.

Her smile faded. "No. I never did."

He couldn't think of anything to say to that, so he said good-bye and turned to go.

"Pierce, wait."

He faced her again, embarrassed at how hopeful he felt.

"When were your parents married?"

He thought for a moment. "Nineteen fifty-six. Why?"

She shook her head. "Oh, nothing really. Just a question I had after reading your father's letters. He's always so tired when I'm done that I haven't had a chance to ask many questions."

"Have you learned anything important? I mean, anything you're allowed to share with me, that is." He was ashamed at the sarcastic tone in his voice, but his father's rejection still stung.

"Only that you once asked him for your mother's engagement ring and that you never gave it to anyone."

His jaw clenched. "Anything else?"

Her eyes met his. "And that love is fleeting."

He frowned but didn't drop his gaze. "Funny. I thought you'd already learned that from experience."

Not wanting to hear her answer, he turned abruptly to leave, almost running head-on into Dooley Gambrel.

"Congratulations, Dooley," he said. "And good luck. You're going to need it."

Pierce walked away, wondering if what he felt about Dooley was really pity or something else entirely.

CHAPTER 15

Brenna sat in her car with the air-conditioning blasting, trying to find the energy to gather her scrapbooking supplies and walk up to Kathleen's front door. She stared at the street in front of her, trying to imagine where it might lead if she simply put her car in drive and didn't stop. Even as she leaned forward to turn off the ignition, she knew she no longer had whatever it took to make her care enough to do it.

Not bothering to ring the doorbell, she let herself in and made her way to the large kitchen in the back of the house. She followed her sisters' voices and paused inside the doorway, taking in the scene of the women spread around the large kitchen with scrapbooks open. Even Colleen's laptop was closed, although Brenna suspected it was only temporary. Colleen might suffer from eBay withdrawal if she didn't check an auction or two at least every hour. Brenna looked around, surprised by the presence of Aunt Dottie, who stood by the stove wearing an apron and stirring something pungent.

Brenna greeted everyone and began laying out her things, the effort exhausting her. Mary Margaret leaned her elbows on the island counter, where she was perched on a stool. "You look tired. I've got some great new vitamins in the store. Come by tomorrow and I'll give you a starter pack."

Brenna smiled wanly. "If you think that would help. I don't know what's wrong with me these days."

Claire paused with a handful of chocolate-covered peanuts close to her mouth. "Well, you're newly engaged. We can probably guess why you're so tired." She winked and the others smiled.

Kathleen left her spot at the kitchen table and stood by Brenna. "Here," she said, sliding a small box toward her. "I thought you might like this."

Brenna took the box and opened it, finding a silver medallion nes-

tled in cotton. "Saint Agnes," she said, smiling. "Patron saint of engaged couples." She didn't have the heart to tell Kathleen that she'd already bought one, but hadn't decided if she should wear it or not. "Isn't
she the one who had her breasts cut off by her jilted suitor?"

Kathleen was already removing the chain around Brenna's neck, her
lips pursed. "Yes. And she survived her ordeal with tranquillity, which
is why I think she'll be a good patron to help you through your engagement and wedding planning. I'll go ahead and put this on so you can
wear it home."

"Thanks," Brenna said. She wrinkled her nose. "What's that smell?"

Dottie turned from the stove. "I'm making cabbage stew. My brother
always made sure I had plenty on hand during any family crisis."

"There's a family crisis?"

Dottie looked at her, her eyebrows furrowed. "Isn't there?"

Brenna looked toward Kathleen for help, but her sister just
shrugged. Colleen glanced up from her scrapbook. Quietly, she said,
"Maybe she's referring to the fact that Dooley and Brenna haven't had
sex yet."

All heads turned toward Colleen. "What?"

"Well, according to Brenna's neighbors, Dooley hasn't once spent
the night. Our little sister is being a good Catholic girl—or Dooley is
showing a great deal of restraint."

Brenna looked down at her scrapbook, seeing the unopened letter
Pierce had given her. "Stop it. Please. I will not talk about Dooley in
that way, so leave it alone."

Mary Margaret patted her arm. "You're right." She sent a warning
glare to the other women. "And I do want you to stop by tomorrow, all
right?"

Brenna nodded.

Dottie spoke slowly and deliberately, as if recalling old words not
spoken in a very long time. "He's missing in action. My brother asked
me to make my soup to take over to her house. I always make this during a family crisis. The strong smell gives you something to hold on to
so your mind stays with you." She continued stirring as everyone else
looked at her. "I've had to make this damned soup too many times, I
think."

"Who's missing in action, Aunt Dottie?" Brenna's fingers found the Saint Agnes medallion.

Dottie glanced over her shoulder at Brenna, an odd glint in her eye. "Well, according to your sisters, that would be Dooley."

Her sisters laughed, but Brenna continued to stare at her aunt's back, trying to unravel her words. She had long since realized that listening to Dottie was a bit like playing Scrabble: If you sorted through the scrambled letters long enough, you'd eventually come up with a word that made sense.

Everyone bent over their scrapbooks again, except for Colleen, who had snapped open her laptop for a seven-thirty auction. Kathleen stood to pass around stuffed mushrooms and paused by Colleen. "How much money are you spending on eBay these days?"

To Brenna's surprise, Colleen colored. "I'm not really keeping track of it. Why do you ask?"

Kathleen placed a stuffed mushroom on a plate for Colleen, then walked on. "Oh, no reason, really. Just wondering if you were aware, that's all."

Colleen kept her eyes focused on the screen. "Well, it's none of your damned business."

Everyone paused for a moment, trying to remember the last time Colleen had snapped at anyone besides her children.

Brenna looked down again at the old envelope in her hand, recalling when Pierce gave it to her. *Open it.* She had been tempted to do it. With him standing next to her, she thought she could. But she'd known, even in that brief moment, that she could no more open that letter than she could tell Pierce that she wasn't sure she believed everything she'd told him that night in the theater. That everything had happened the way it should have. She'd been praying to her saints every night to make her not care, to believe what she wanted to, but the only answer she'd received was silence.

She flicked at the corner of the envelope, then spoke out loud to nobody in particular. "Does anybody remember the time when I was in the hospital with spinal meningitis?"

Mary Margaret and Kathleen glanced at each other before Mary Margaret spoke. "Kathleen was the only one living here at the time. For those of us living close enough that we could come, Daddy discouraged us because you were in ICU and couldn't have visitors. Kathleen called us every night, though, and kept us informed of your progress. We would have been here in a flash if she thought we needed to be here."

Brenna flicked the envelope again with her fingernail, trying to pull up the piece of information that had been bothering her. "I'm just trying to figure out how Daddy could have kept everybody away. How even my phone calls to Pierce were never received. I gave him my letters for Pierce to mail, so it's easy to figure out how those never made it, but I don't understand the rest."

Claire looked up from where she'd been trying to re-create one of Mary Sanford's tiaras in paper cutouts. "What are you talking about, Brenna?"

Brenna gave her a withering glance. "Let's just all get it out in the open, okay? You four never keep anything from one another. You're all like a PA system every time you hear some news. So, I know that Kathleen has told you that Pierce and I . . . dated during high school. And what Pierce and I figured out only recently—that somehow Daddy managed to keep us apart while I was sick. And that . . . and that was why Pierce and I never saw each other until he came back home last month."

All pairs of eyes looked at her, but no one spoke.

Brenna continued. "I just can't figure out how he did it. And why."

Mary Margaret stood. "Well, I can tell you why. With the rest of us grown and having our own lives, you were the only one around whom he could control. He was a lonely, bitter old man, and he couldn't stand the thought of you going, too."

Dottie, who had taken her place next to Kathleen at the kitchen table, bent over the new scrapbook Kathleen had set before her, using Kathleen's box of stickers to begin making a collage on the open page. She pulled out a sticker of the Eiffel Tower and stuck it in the middle of the page. "You were the one most like your mother, you know, before she married your father. She was funny and silly and did things without thinking sometimes, but always with joy in her heart. And then she died. I think it was her only defiance of him: to die first." She picked up a sticker of a tennis racket and covered the top of the Eiffel

Tower with it. "I don't suppose she realized what she was doing to poor Brenna by doing that. Maybe she knew that Brenna was enough like her to survive anyway."

Brenna took a gulp of water from her glass, her mouth suddenly dry. "She had diabetes that she got when she was pregnant with me. It got worse and she died of complications. That's what Daddy always told me." She glanced around at the faces of her sisters. "So how could you say that she just decided to . . . die?"

Slowly and deliberately, Dottie began decorating the top of the page with multicolored sparkly balloons. "There're some people who decide to die but keep on breathing anyway. Don't know what's worse, really."

Kathleen placed her hands atop her blank scrapbook page and eyed Aunt Dottie with a stern expression. "Mama had a heart attack, brought on by her Type II diabetes going on too long unnoticed. She didn't just decide to die." She leaned back in her chair, her eyes closed. "And of all the mean things Daddy ever did to any of us, laying the blame for Mama's death on an innocent six-year-old child is unforgivable. It took all of us years to make you understand you had nothing to do with it." She glanced over at Brenna. "Although sometimes I think you still carry around that guilt."

Brenna looked down at her chewed fingernails with a soft smile. "I kind of like the idea of Mama deciding to die first just to defy him. I don't remember much about her, but that's the sort of person I do remember when I think of her."

Brenna stood, her scrapbook forgotten, and began pacing the room where her sisters were bent over their own work but conspicuously not really doing anything. She paused next to Kathleen, whose pages were beautifully bordered but no pictures had been attached. In the years Brenna had been scrapbooking, she'd never seen Kathleen actually put photos in her album. She'd spent months organizing her photos and decorating her pages, but the final act of displaying the photos seemed to be beyond her. It was almost as if Brenna's oldest sister were undecided about displaying her past for everyone to see. Which was ridiculous, really; Kathleen had the perfect life, and her completed albums would simply be objects of envy.

Brenna picked up a loose photo of Kathleen and John on their wedding day, the bride radiant. "Why don't you go ahead and start with this one? It's really the beginning, right?"

Kathleen shrugged, not looking at Brenna. "I haven't decided yet. Soon, though." Kathleen smiled down at her page, and Brenna walked away, still restless.

She moved to the stove and picked up the wooden spoon to stir the pot, turning her face away from the smell. "I just can't figure out how my phone calls weren't received. I remember getting an answering machine when I called Pierce, but how could Daddy have intercepted those calls?"

Colleen slid off her stool and moved toward the coffeepot and began pouring coffee. "Did you dial the number yourself?"

Brenna thought for a moment. "No. I was still too sick. Kathleen did. I remember Daddy got her the number from me to dial and then she gave the phone to me."

"And what was the message on the answering machine?"

"It wasn't Pierce's voice. It was one of those automated computer voices."

All of her sisters looked up at her, and Brenna felt a little sick. "How incredibly stupid of me." She put her face over the steaming soup pot, not bothering to fight the smell because she desperately needed something to hold on to.

Mary Margaret left her album of mostly blank pages and put her arm around Brenna. "You were really young. Why would you suspect your own father of such a thing?"

Brenna nodded, breathing deeply the smell of the stewing cabbage. "Have you tried to explain all this to Pierce?"

Brenna stirred briskly, splashing hot water on her wrist but not feeling it. "He figured it out, so he knows. But I told him that it didn't really matter anymore, because it was so long ago. I told him that things had worked out the way they were supposed to."

Dottie stood and moved next to Brenna, taking the wooden spoon and stirring. "You would sure make your father proud, dear. But I don't think your mother would recognize you anymore."

Brenna stared at her aunt for a long moment before turning away. As she passed Kathleen's table, she saw that her sister had begun penning a poem in calligraphy. It was a loose page, not attached to the book, as if Kathleen wasn't sure where it should go. Leaning over, Brenna read:

> Hope is the thing with feathers
> That perches in the soul,
> And sings the tune without the words,
> And never stops at all.

Startled to see that same verse again, Brenna asked, "Where did you find that?"

Kathleen gave her a delicate shrug, then continued with short, deliberate strokes of the calligraphy pen. "It's from a small book of poems I've had since I was a child. I'm not even sure where it came from. I just remember it being on my bookshelf tucked in with all my children's stories and fairy tales that Mama used to read to me. It's Emily Dickinson, I believe."

"Yes, it is," Brenna said absently as she moved back toward her chair, where she settled in to begin staring at the sealed envelope in front of her again.

Claire leaned forward on her elbows. "I'm in the mood to talk about Brenna's wedding. It's been so long since there's been a family wedding I can hardly remember what all's involved. Have you picked a date yet?"

Brenna sat back in her chair, resigned to discuss her wedding that would never take place. Without thinking about it too much, she realized she'd rather do that than stare at a sealed envelope and try to determine what might be inside. For the first time since she'd begun collecting old letters, she felt like a child picking at a Band-Aid, yet afraid to see what lay beneath.

She smiled brightly at Claire. "No, not yet," she said as she tucked the envelope into her scrapbook. "But we're thinking early fall," she said as she snapped the book shut.

Pierce sat at his father's kitchen table, the surface still littered with old photographs, newspaper clippings, and letters. They had taken to eating at the kitchen island so they wouldn't have to interrupt their sorting by clearing the table. He picked up a newspaper picture of his father with three of his friends in their pilot uniforms. The caption read, *Four Indianola Men Earn Their Wings*. The faces of the men were young and smiling and incredibly optimistic. Pierce put the photo down and leaned back in his chair, wondering if he'd ever been like that.

Scrubbing his face with his hands and feeling the bristles on his chin, he looked at the clock over the sink. Three o'clock in the morning. He groaned and rubbed his eyes, wishing he could feel tired. No, that wasn't the word. He was exhausted, just not sleepy. He hadn't been a good sleeper for years. Not since his mother left him and he'd learned to stay awake through the night, listening for her return. But ever since he'd run into Brenna on his first day back in Indianola, he'd had even less sleep than normal. He'd finally realized it was because he'd been afraid that his dreams of her would return—the same dreams he'd had for years and that only recently had stopped. They were always about her and him, and he would dream they were at the Royal Majestic staring at the ceiling mural and even sometimes at the magnificent old clock that stood in the foyer of the old theater. And he was happy in the dreams, and never tired, and he'd loved having the dreams. He just couldn't stand to wake up from them.

The sound of his father's walker scuffing the kitchen floor startled him, and he quickly stood to help his father to the table.

His dad patted his hand after Pierce had seated him. "What are you doing up so late?"

"I guess I should be asking you the same question. Did I keep you awake with the kitchen light on?"

"No. Just couldn't sleep. I think that happens a lot with old people. It's like we're aware that time is short and don't want to miss out on anything."

"Don't talk like that, Dad. You've got years to live. I'll think you'll sleep a lot easier once we get you moved over to Liberty Village. That way you'll never have to worry about house upkeep or anything, really."

His father grinned. "You think so, huh? I guess since you don't have children you wouldn't understand this, but let me tell you that as long as I have a child, I will always have something to worry about."

Pierce sat back down and put his feet up on the opposite chair. "Have I really given you so much to worry about?"

"Oh, not a lot. Just when you married Diana. And when you divorced her. And when you didn't give her your mother's ring."

"I gave it back to you, Dad. I didn't lose it."

"I know. That's not what worried me. What worried me was the fact that you hadn't chosen Diana to wear the ring."

"Dad, let's not go into this now. Please?"

"Why not? It doesn't look like either one of us is doing much of anything else right now."

Pierce simply looked back at his father, not willing to start the conversation, but quite sure that his father would have no such reservations. He was right.

"So, why didn't you give the ring to Diana?"

Pierce sighed, reluctantly reliving painful decisions over a decade old. "Because . . . because when I'd asked you for the ring originally, it was going to be for another woman."

Dr. McGovern nodded slowly. "Brenna O'Brien?"

Pierce's eyes widened. "Yes. How did you know?"

"I'm old, Pierce. Not blind or stupid. You never brought her home to meet me, but I knew there was somebody special. You were gone a lot, and I recall lots of whispered phone conversations. I knew there was no reason you would ever keep something like a girlfriend from me, so I figured it had to be Brenna. She would be the one who would need to keep it under wraps because of her father." He waved his hand through a stack of clippings, spreading them out like a fan. "He and I . . . well, we were never friends. He would never, ever allow one of his daughters to date a son of mine." He met Pierce's gaze. "And then you went off to college and asked for the ring, and I waited and waited and nothing happened. Then you married Diana and returned the ring."

Pierce passed his hands over his face again, and his eyes felt gritty with exhaustion. "Yeah, that's pretty much it."

"Really? You think that's the end of the story?"

"Of course it is. Brenna's engaged to Dooley Gambrel and I have a life out in California. As soon as the groundbreaking permits are approved for the new cinema and you're settled into your new place, I'll be going back there. I'll be back frequently to visit with you and to monitor the progress on the cinema, but that's it."

"So that's it."

Annoyed at his father's smugness, Pierce snapped, "Yeah, that's it."

His dad actually smiled. "So who was that you were talking to on the phone earlier today while I was napping?"

Pierce sat up. "I thought you were sleeping."

"I was. But then I heard you on the phone, so I got up and opened the door so I could hear you better."

With a reluctant smile, Pierce said, "Sorry. I didn't mean to wake you."

"Not a problem. But your conversation did make me curious as to why you'd be speaking with somebody from the National Park Service about a theater you don't even own."

Pierce stood and pulled out two glasses, then began to fill them slowly at the sink. "Just guilt, I think. Her theater is going to have a tough road once my cinema opens. And she's not doing anything serious to save it. Patching it up here and there isn't going to do anything. She needs the big guns. So I figured that I could at least help her out."

"Does she know you're doing this?"

Pierce shook his head. "She'd never accept my help, and that Nathan guy would hardly give me the time to explain. I figured I could just set the balls in motion and then walk away. Everything else should take care of itself."

He placed the glasses of water on the table and sat down again. "All I did was contact a friend of mine who works for the National Park Service. I've had dealings with him before when I had to move historical buildings to build some of our multiplexes. Anyway, if Brenna's theater can be put on the National Register, she'll be eligible for tax credits and a few other benefits that could really help her. My friend said he'd contact Brenna directly and schedule a visit—and not mention my name."

"And you think that will solve everything."

"I'm not trying to solve anything. I'm just trying to help out somebody I used to care a great deal for."

His father studied him for a long moment before finally speaking. "Why didn't you give her the ring?"

Pierce spun his glass in the puddle of condensed water that had formed on the table. "It was a huge misunderstanding. Her father found out about us and put a stop to our relationship without either one of us knowing. We each believed the worst of the other. And that was the end of that."

"And that was the end of that."

"Why are you repeating everything I say?"

"Because it seems to me that you need to hear it yourself to understand how utterly ridiculous you sound."

Pierce stood abruptly and put his glass in the sink. "I'm going to bed now. Do you want me to help you upstairs or are you going to stay down here?"

His dad raised his glass in salute. "I'm not tired. I think I'll just stay down here and sort through some more of these newspaper clippings."

"Okay. Then I'll see you in the morning."

"Good night, son."

"Good night, Dad."

He made his way upstairs, still not in the least bit sleepy, and his feet dragging to the beat of the incessant ticking of the old clock.

CHAPTER 16

It was stupid to continue circling the block waiting for Pierce to leave, Brenna thought, especially in her rather conspicuous yellow VW Beetle. On the fourth pass, she gave up and slid her car up to its usual spot, on the curb.

She felt a mixture of relief and disappointment when she didn't see him waiting for her on the porch. Gently she rapped on the front door and entered, finding Dr. McGovern in his usual spot, but this time he was holding the box of letters.

"Good morning," she said.

He held his fingers to his lips. "Pierce is still sleeping. He had a late night."

She raised an eyebrow, trying not to let her imagination wander too far. She sat down. "Oh. All right. Does this mean we need to postpone our reading for another time?"

"No. I think he's down for the count. And I'm eager to continue. I've been sitting here with these letters for over an hour now." He smoothed his hand over the lid, like a magician conjuring flowers from a handkerchief. "It's odd really. I know who sent these letters, and I know they were intended for me. And I even know how everything turned out. But somehow there's something about all of these unread letters that makes me feel as if there's a whole world in here filled with possibilities. As if the history isn't already written. As if there're no rights or wrongs until each letter is opened and read. I even toyed with the idea of not reading any further, as if by stopping now I could somehow control what would happen."

Brenna's knees hurt, and when she looked down she saw her fingers digging into her bare skin. She lifted her fingers, seeing the nail marks.

"It's a bit like time traveling, isn't it?"

Brenna could only nod, but stood to take the box that Dr. McGovern now held out to her.

"But it's all an illusion. A self-indulgent illusion to believe that we are anything more than impartial bystanders. This morning, as I was flipping through the letters, I finally understood that by reading them or by not reading them, I still wasn't going to change the outcome of what's contained inside." He sighed and leaned his head back against the crocheted headrest on his chair. "I suppose being forced to face my past will make me feel less of a coward. One would think an old man would be immune to these kinds of things." He closed his eyes as he always did as a signal for Brenna to begin reading.

Brenna regarded the old doctor quietly, and wondered again why he had never written to the woman whom he'd promised to love forever. Carefully she pulled out the next letter and began to read.

May 1, 1942

Today is May Day, and the maypole has been erected in the town square and people are all dressed in bright colors and celebrating spring as if there isn't a war on at all. But if you look closely, you'll see patched clothes and ill-fitting shoes and no nylons whatsoever. It's like me—from the outside I look fine, but if you look closer, you can see that I am simply shattered.

My new friend from the beauty parlor is doing her best to help me cope, but I'm afraid it's useless. I'm simply at a loss as to how to continue. I get up each morning and stare at myself in the mirror, and it's like I have no idea how to comb my hair or brush my teeth. There seems to be no meaning in any of it at all.

I've been out walking and to the movies several times since you've been gone. I'm not trying to make you jealous, just wanted to let you know that I'm trying really hard not to turn inward so that you recognize me as the fun-loving girl I was when you left. I know the two of you have never been friends, but he's very nice and courteous to me, and he knows that my heart is engaged elsewhere, but I do appreciate a man's touch at my elbow. I sometimes pretend that he is you so that I don't feel so all alone.

It is now nearly three months since you left, and I'm afraid that I can't keep my secret much longer. I need to hear from you soon, as there are decisions we must make. Even if you now think that our love was a mistake and you want no part of me, I need to hear it from you. It will break my heart, but at least I will know and will be able to proceed with my life in the best way I know how.

Write to me, my love. Please. I die a little each day waiting to hear from you.

Me

Brenna looked up from the letter, feeling the desperation in the woman's voice and wanting to cry. Dr. McGovern sat watching her, his eyes steady and alert. "It's hard to hear, isn't it? It would be so easy to put the rest of the letters away so that we can imagine that her soldier comes home to her and that everything ends well, wouldn't it?" He grasped the arms of his chair and leaned forward. "But that wouldn't be reality, and how can we ever expect to learn courage if we are never forced to face reality?" He leaned back again. "Read the next one, please."

She noticed that his hands were shaking before she saw that her own were, too. Slowly she opened the next letter, the crackling of the paper loud in the silent room.

May 10, 1942

Darling,

Spring is quickly disappearing, the flowers fading and falling as the heat of summer approaches. I'm glad. Spring is the season of hope, and I'm beyond hope now. I want to see the bright colors fade from sight and wilt in the heat. It is how my heart feels, and I need to feel kinship with something, as I have never been so lonely in all my life. I'm surrounded by a loving family and friends, yet I am all alone.

I have told my secret to my new friend, but she's the only one. I'm sorry, but I needed someone to confide in. She told me that a decision needs to be made about my future, and that I need to give you an ultimatum. She's right, of course, although I once told you that I would wait for you forever. Well, that was when only two people were involved. I don't want you to think I'm the kind of person who breaks promises; yet the circumstances have changed, and I need to.

If I haven't heard from you by May 30, then I will know that you've had a change of heart and that you are setting me free. I will grieve for a long, long time, but at least I will know.

Me

Brenna was crying this time as she looked up. She was surprised, too, at the anger she felt. "Why didn't you write to her, Dr. McGovern? Did you just stop loving her and couldn't tell her?"

He shook his head, his face slack. "I never stopped loving her. To this day I still love her and will until I die."

"Who, Dad? Who are you talking about?"

They both looked to where Pierce appeared on the stairs dressed in jeans and a T-shirt and barefoot, his hair evidence that he'd just awakened. Brenna quickly brushed the tears from her face and waited for Dr. McGovern to answer.

"A woman I used to know."

"My mother?"

Dr. McGovern shook his head. "No. This was several years before I met your mother."

Pierce continued his descent, then paused at the newel post. "So this woman you were saying you would love until you died was not my mother."

The old doctor didn't flinch. "No."

Pierce moved to stand closer to his father. "I guess this would mean that you still loved this other woman even while married to my mother."

"Yes. But if you're asking if I ever had an affair, the answer would be no. We respected each other too much for that."

Pierce blew out a puff of air. "I see. Was this other woman married, too?"

"Yes."

"And were you ever planning on telling me the whole story?"

"When I know what that is, I'll tell you."

"Dad, I'm an adult. I can take whatever is in those letters with an adult maturity."

"Trust me, Pierce. Please. You'll understand in time."

Pierce seemed to notice Brenna for the first time. He looked at her but didn't smile. "I'm about to go brew a fresh pot of coffee. Would either one of you like a cup?"

Brenna hastily stood and placed the box on the side table. "No, thank you. I've got to run. I'm meeting Dooley to take Aunt Dottie shopping."

She said good-bye to Dr. McGovern and allowed Pierce to lead her to the door.

"How's he doing?" Pierce asked, his hand on the door, blocking her way.

"Your father?"

"No, Dooley."

"He's fine. Thank you."

"You still planning on getting married?"

"Of course. Why do you ask?"

"Because you're not wearing your engagement ring. Most brides-to-be are never seen without it."

"It's too big and needs to be sized properly. I don't want to lose it."

"No, I'm sure you don't."

She stood awkwardly in front of the door. He'd dropped his hand, but she still felt as if she couldn't leave.

He was standing close enough that she could smell the sleep on him, and she was suddenly sixteen again in the back of the doctor's Buick. Pierce's voice brought her back to the present. "It's oldies night again, isn't it? What's playing?"

"*Since You Went Away.*"

"Ah." He nodded. "Nineteen forty-four, right? Best picture nominee with Claudette Colbert and Shirley Temple."

"Nine nominations but only one win—for best score."

"I just might have to come see that."

She slipped her purse strap over her shoulder. "You know where to find it," she said, not meeting his eyes and reaching for the door handle.

"How could I ever forget?" he asked softly, and she turned her head to find his face very close to hers.

She quickly let herself out of the door. "Good-bye, Pierce," she said without turning around as she walked briskly down the steps toward her car.

Brenna honked her horn outside the hardware store and waved to Dooley. He left the store and approached her with the slow swagger that had always made her smile. "Hey, Doo—you ready for shopping and lunch with Aunt Dottie?"

He warily eyed her car. "As ready as I'll ever be. But do you think we could take my truck? I don't have a lot of pride, but I think being seen in that macaroni-mobile would pretty much empty all my reserves."

Brenna rolled her eyes but laughed. "Whatever. Just know that Aunt Dottie will be sitting up front with you and will most likely be asking you all sorts of questions as to when her car will be ready to drive again. Make sure you have some answers ready."

As he walked to his truck in front of them at the curb, he patted his shirt pocket. "I've been working on that all morning and took some notes. Do you have any idea what an oxygen sensor is?"

"No clue."

"Neither do I. I saw it on a Ferrari parts list, so I'm guessing Miss Dottie doesn't either. Anyway, that's what her car's missing, and it's going to take a while to get it from Italy."

"Dooley—she drives a Lincoln. They're not made in Italy."

He held the passenger door open for her. "I know that, and you know that, but I'm not completely sure Miss Dottie knows that."

Brenna smirked. "I wouldn't bet on that. Just be sure to be prepared with an answer in case she asks why you're ordering parts for her Lincoln from Italy."

He shifted the gear into drive and the truck lurched forward. "It's bound to be easier than explaining why she found her four car tires in Kathleen's garage."

Brenna laughed, then relaxed back into her seat as Dooley drove

them to Aunt Dottie's house. She stared out at the familiar scenery of
the town she'd spent her entire life in. Dooley turned down a street
Brenna usually didn't travel, and she sat up with surprise at the large vacant lot on the corner.

"What happened to the Flahertys' house?"

"They sold it to some hotshot lawyer from New Orleans. His wife
grew up here and always wanted to retire in Indianola. So, they bought
the Flahertys' house, knocked it down, and I hear they're going to build
a small replica of the governor's mansion on this lot and the next. They
just bought that one and they're going to knock down the house so
they'll have enough room to build."

"But that's terrible! It won't fit in with the other houses around it.
When did this happen?"

"Six months ago, Brenn. Where've you been?"

She didn't answer, but sat back in her seat again. Six months ago?
Why hadn't she noticed or heard about it? She began to stare out the
window in earnest, really noticing things she hadn't bothered to look at
in years. When had she become so complacent that she didn't see that
there were fewer of the beautiful live oaks that bordered the residential
streets, or notice the new cream paint and green shutters on the city
hall? Or that Mr. Williams's barbershop had closed and was now a sushi
restaurant and the corner dime store was now a day care?

Closing her eyes, she tried to think back to when the familiar had
become invisible and when she'd begun to see nothing outside her family and her theater. She opened her eyes abruptly, trying to quell the
feeling of drowning, of pulling her feet through water. Of sitting at the
top of a hill without the thought of rolling forward.

"Are you okay?" Dooley slid the gear into neutral and pulled up the
parking brake in front of Aunt Dottie's house.

"I'm fine. Just . . . thinking."

"About our wedding?"

"No, but I should be. How much longer should we carry this out? I
know it's only been a week, but still . . ."

Dooley leaned his forearms over the steering wheel. "Well, have
your sisters quit trying to set you up on dates?"

"Yes, but—"

"Have you had any dates from hell recently?"

"No, but—"

"Can you enjoy family gatherings again without fear of being hit on by some weirdo who looks like Elvis?"

Brenna smiled. "Yes, but—"

"Well, then. Seems to me we should just keep at it."

"It just feels so . . . wrong. I still feel as if I'm taking advantage of you."

He looked at her with a wicked grin. "I *wish* you'd take advantage of me."

She blushed. "You're sounding like my sisters. Apparently it hasn't gone unnoticed that we haven't spent the night together."

"We could fix that right quick."

"Doo, quit." She slapped him lightly on the arm. "We could, you know. I mean, with you in a sleeping bag on the floor. Like we used to do when we were kids."

Dooley switched off the ignition and opened his door. "Exactly what I was thinking," he said as he shut the door and headed up the walkway to get Aunt Dottie while Brenna crawled into the backseat.

As they headed toward Mary Margaret's Motivations and Grocery Emporium, Dottie turned to Dooley. "When's that part going to come in for my car? I feel so bad making everybody drive me around."

"I'm glad you asked, Miss Dottie. I checked that out on the computer this morning. Apparently an oxygen sensor is a delicate instrument and has to come all the way from Italy. I'm afraid it could take three to four weeks."

Brenna poked him in the shoulder from the backseat.

"Maybe closer to eight or nine. We'll have to see. Italians can be pretty fickle about timing."

Aunt Dottie just stared at him for a few moments but said nothing. Dooley pulled the truck into a space in front of the store, and as Brenna was helping her out, Dottie said, "Your beau isn't the same beau you were with last time."

"This is Dooley, Aunt Dottie. We're engaged, remember?"

"Engaged in what?"

"To be married."

Aunt Dottie blinked several times, as if trying to make the words register. "What happened to the other beau?"

"I didn't have another beau. Unless you mean Dr. McGovern's son, Pierce. But he and I weren't . . . aren't . . . well, he's not my beau."

"You can't marry both of them, you know. Well, nowadays maybe you can. But back in my day, you married once and that was it." She reached her hands to her head, feeling for her hat. "It's a good notion—if you married the right person in the first place. That didn't always happen, of course. Like people marrying because they had to, if you know what I mean."

Dottie leaned heavily on Brenna's arm as she was led to the entrance to the store. "Did you ever have a beau, Aunt Dottie?"

Brenna watched in surprise as her aunt actually blushed. "Oh, yes, I did. We were to be married. But then he went off to war and that was that. Your father didn't approve, you see, so there was no wedding before my sweetheart left."

A tingling began behind Brenna's ears and she stopped walking, Dooley almost running into her from behind. "Was it Dr. McGovern?"

Dottie's eyes widened behind her glasses. "Who is?" She glanced back at Dooley. "No, Brenna, that's your beau. And I'm thinking I'm too old for him, anyway."

"Aunt Dottie, who were you supposed to marry?"

"Oh, I'm too old to get married, dear. Too late for me, I'm afraid." She turned away from Brenna and began to make her way up the front steps. "All these years have taught me how to fill the empty spaces, or at least not notice them so much." Brenna grabbed her elbow to stop her aunt from falling back to the first step. "Which is why I'm thankful for all my nieces and nephews." She sent Brenna a glance from the corner of her eye. "Except when they try to take my car away from me. I'm a perfectly good driver, you know."

Brenna was saved from answering by Mary Margaret, who opened the door and helped Aunt Dottie across the threshold. Aunt Dottie was immediately drawn to the trays of pearlescent and metallic marbles at the back of the store. She began to hold them up to the light from the window with gloved hands, examining them like an explorer would examine a globe.

Dooley stood with his hands shoved in his pockets while Mary Margaret examined him with a similar intensity. He looked uncomfortably from one sister to another while no one spoke. Finally he said, "Um, I'm going to go check out the latest paperbacks while you two chat. Let me know if you need help with Miss Dottie's shopping list."

Brenna nodded as Mary Margaret linked her arm with Brenna's and led her to the front of the store, past the display of curry mixes tucked among boxes of sweet corn bread mix and the shelf of saris made of traditional Indian fabrics as well as Lycra and washed denim.

Mary Margaret indicated a bar stool in front of the counter and began pouring a cup of coffee. She put a teaspoonful of a yellow powder into it and stirred before sliding it across the counter toward Brenna.

"It's a vitamin powder—part of that vitamin pack I was telling you about. You put a scoop of this into your morning coffee and then take a few pills throughout the day. You'll feel energized in no time. I've been taking them for over a month, and even Richard can tell the difference." She opened her mouth as if to say more, but then stopped, a pink flush covering her cheeks. "Anyway, I thought it might help you."

Brenna took a sip of her coffee, grimacing at the chalky taste. "That's really awful. I don't think I could stand to do that to myself every day."

"Oh, it's an acquired taste. You'll get used to it."

Putting the cup down abruptly, Brenna said, "That's kind of like saying that if you get punched in the face every day, you'll eventually get used to it. I'm sure that's true, but it's still going to hurt like hell, just as I'm sure this will always taste like chalky mud." She pushed the mug away, her persistent restlessness now mixing with anger—anger at her own inertia, and anger over her sisters' manipulations and eagerness to help in a situation they could never understand.

Mary Margaret raised her eyebrows at Brenna. "Well, I think you need it. You really are looking tired and exhausted all the time, Brenn. We have to do something to fix you."

"I don't need you to fix me. And I don't want more of your vitamin crap. It won't help me, and I'd appreciate it if you would just stop trying." Brenna stood and shoved the bar stool under the counter, the legs squeaking loudly against the unpolished wooden floor.

Mary Margaret leaned across the counter, her eyes steady on Brenna. "What did you just say?"

"I said that I don't want any more of your crap and to stop pushing it on me like I'm some helpless guinea pig. Let me solve my own problems for once."

Brenna wasn't sure if her sister was angry or amused, because Mary Margaret kept her expression placid for a long moment, much as Brenna had always imagined a priest's face would look on the other side of the confessional. Then, very slowly, a smile crept over her sister's face.

"Brava, little sister. Brava. It's about time I started hearing your voice again. It's been a long time. Too long."

"What?"

Mary Margaret took the full cup off the counter and dumped it into the sink. "Well, it's just that I was beginning to think that you didn't have any opinions about anything anymore. It's good to know that you do." She paused, thinking for a moment. "No, let me take that back. I know you have your own opinions, but you usually don't express them for the sake of not ruffling feathers. Daddy taught you that, I think. And when you have to have your way, you do it furtively, so that whoever's wishes you're going against won't find out. Like when you joined the theater club and Daddy never knew. I only found out when I ran into your theater teacher—who happened to be the same one I'd had when I was in school—and she told me about it."

Mary Margaret placed the mug in the sink and turned to Brenna. "So, I guess what I'm saying is that I'm glad you've found your voice. You should use it more often."

Brenna took a deep lungful of air, all her restlessness, annoyance, and anger rising to the surface like fatback in a pot of beans. "You're doing it again," she shouted, not really caring who heard her, but definitely liking the way it felt to raise her voice. "Stop telling me what I should or shouldn't do!"

She felt rather than heard a button pop off the front of her blouse at the same time she spotted Dooley and Aunt Dottie emerge from their respective aisles.

"Nice bra," said Mary Margaret, winking and sliding a safety pin across the counter.

Brenna looked down and saw her new red velvet Desire bra that had just arrived in the mail the day before. She clutched at her blouse to close it but not before Dooley and Aunt Dottie had received an eyeful.

Dooley turned away, but Aunt Dottie just plopped a big bag of marbles onto the counter and said, "Your mama loved to wear beautiful lingerie under her clothes, too. It was her way of defying your daddy, you see. He didn't like her to wear showy clothes, but there wasn't much he could say about her unmentionables." She slapped her wallet on the counter. "Now tell me how much these marbles are and I think I'm done with my shopping."

"But . . ." Brenna held up her list and Dooley took it, indicating he'd take care of it.

"Two cups of decaf, please," a deep yet familiar voice said from behind her.

Brenna quickly stuck the pin in her shirt, then turned to see Pierce trying very hard not to look at her blouse.

"Hello again, Brenna. My dad wanted to purchase tickets to tonight's movie now, so that he won't have to wait in line. Is the theater open yet?"

She nodded, trying to pretend she didn't have a safety pin holding her shirt together. "Beau Ward should be there to help you out."

He nodded. "Thanks," he said to Mary Margaret as he slid a few bills toward her. He picked up the two Styrofoam cups and turned to leave but stopped, facing Brenna again. "About this morning . . ."

She held up her hand. "I'm not passing judgment on your father, and I don't think you should either. I don't know the whole story, and neither do you. I don't . . . understand any of it, really. But as I read the letters, I feel as if a tragedy is unfolding in front of me and I can't do anything to stop it."

His blue eyes regarded her steadily, reminding her what it was that first made her fall in love with Pierce McGovern. "I know the feeling."

Brenna turned away. "Good-bye, Pierce."

Instead of leaving, he took a step closer to her. "You might want to repin your shirt before you leave. As nice as the view is, I don't think you want to go outside like that."

Brenna looked down at her shirt and saw that she had pinned one side of her blouse to the bra, leaving the other side gaping open, her breasts neatly framing her Saint Agnes medallion. She simply blinked at Pierce as he said good-bye and left. She held her hand up to Mary Margaret. "Not one word from you, please."

"I wouldn't dream of it. You're doing a good enough job on your own right now."

Brenna quickly fixed her shirt again, then helped Dottie count out her money for her marbles and other purchases. As she and Dooley assisted Aunt Dottie to the car, the old woman turned toward Brenna. "You like old letters, don't you?"

"You've seen my scrapbook, right? I like to collect old letters, remember?"

"Oh, yes. It's a bit odd, don't you think?"

Brenna bit her tongue before she said something about the plastic flowers in Dottie's front yard or her outrageous hats. Or her inability to follow a line of conversation.

"I have an old letter."

"You do? Have you opened it?"

Aunt Dottie tucked her chin into her neck in indignation. "Of course not. It's not addressed to me. It would be rude to read a letter not addressed to me unless I had permission."

Dooley opened the passenger side of the front cab of his truck for Aunt Dottie as Brenna swallowed her irritation. "I'm sorry—I thought you meant that the letter is yours."

"What letter?"

Brenna bit her lip, drawing blood. "Never mind," she said as she tucked Aunt Dottie into the truck and closed the door. As Brenna crawled into the backseat, Aunt Dottie turned to Dooley. "Young man, could you please explain to me why parts for an American car need to come all the way from Italy?"

Brenna met Dooley's amused expression in the rearview mirror and turned away before she laughed out loud. She continued to stare out the window and see the landscape that had seemed to change in front of her without her noticing, until she closed her eyes so she wouldn't have to see it anymore.

CHAPTER 17

Pierce stood at the kitchen window, watching as fingers of light reached across the sky, burning holes in the early evening. The leaves on the trees outside seemed to tremble with portent, unable to contain their excitement at the change in the atmosphere. He imagined he could smell the burned ions of spent electricity in the air as thunder rumbled the foundations of the old house, making the windows shake.

In all the years he'd lived away from the South, he had missed the thunderstorms the most. As a child he'd loved them because it meant being comforted by the soft arms of his mother. After she had gone, he'd loved them in a defiant sort of way. He'd go to the large picture window in their living room and face his fear of the light and noise, as if telling the world that he hadn't really needed his mother's comfort after all.

Of course, there were storms in California. But not the sort of earth-shaking, sky-trembling renewal of a Louisiana thunderstorm fed with thick humidity and the sweat of old warriors, where one could almost believe that when the rain stopped, a wrecked soul would be found whole again. Now, as he stood at his father's window, he could still almost believe that his mother would walk back through the door and that the abandoned little boy who lived inside of him could finally find peace.

He heard his father's slow tread behind him. "I thought you were napping."

"I was. Hard to sleep through a storm like that, though."

"Yeah, I guess it is." They had not had a chance to speak yet. His father had disappeared into his bedroom as soon as Brenna had left. Without turning to look at his father, Pierce said, "Who was she, Dad? Who was this great love of yours?"

His father sat down at the kitchen table, but Pierce remained at the window listening to the clatter of rain against the glass.

"I was very young. Only nineteen when I met her. Heck, I was only twenty when I went to war. I thought I knew everything then, that twenty was old enough to call myself an adult. Believe me, when you're eighty-three and looking back at your life, you'll realize how much of a child you still are in your twenties."

Pierce crossed his arms and leaned back on the window, listening to the rain and trying to see his father as the young man in the pictures he'd seen. His father had been past fifty when Pierce was born, already an old man in Pierce's eyes. It was almost like talking about another person when his dad spoke about his youth.

"Anyway, she was only sixteen when we met. Her parents were very protective and considered her too young to date—especially not a boy who was three years older than she. But there was something about her . . . something so special. We shared the same interests; we loved to do the same things. We could sit and talk for hours, reading poetry out loud or just holding hands. She was bright, and funny, and smart—she simply sparkled from within. She put light in my life, and I knew I could never live without her. So we kept our love a secret. We would go out with a group of friends and then separate ourselves so we could be alone together."

His dad picked up an old photograph from the table and stared at it with blank eyes, almost as if it were a portal back to the past. "When the war started and I enlisted, we became secretly engaged. We pledged our undying love to each other and parted, thinking we'd only be separated for a few months until the war was over. Oh, how naive we all were."

A crack of thunder rent the late-afternoon sky, and Pierce could almost feel the change in the air, the soft, healing balm of cleansing and renewal. He moved from the window to sit at the table with his father.

"And then what happened?"

Dr. McGovern sat back in his chair, his eyes still focused on the photograph in his hand. "I didn't hear from her for a long time. I was at Eglin for almost six months before I was shipped overseas but never received a single letter from her. I was in England for six months before I was shot down over France and was MIA for the rest of the war. I was actually in a German POW camp, but information was dicey then. It wasn't until the end of the war before my own mother knew what had happened to me."

"But her letters—she did write you. But you never got them."

"No. I didn't. I had no idea she was writing to me. My mother wrote to me and mentioned in passing that she'd seen her with another man. I thought the worst."

Pierce flattened his hands against the table. "So her letters somehow were delayed, and somehow they were never delivered and were buried at the post office all this time."

"Something like that."

Pierce glanced at his father, an elusive thought bouncing around in the back of his head that made him think that there was more to the story, but he knew his father had said all he was going to say about it. Leaning forward, he asked, "What happened when you came back?" Lightning swathed the sky and the light over the table flickered for a moment before going out completely. They sat in the now-silent house, absent of the whir of the air conditioner and the hum of the refrigerator, and listened to the rain pelt the house.

He felt his father's eyes on him in the dark shadows of the kitchen. "She was married."

Pierce stood, scratching his head. "It doesn't seem to me that she was such a great love, Dad, if she could so easily marry somebody else."

"I never said she did it easily."

"Did you speak to her? Did she give any explanation?"

"Son, sometimes we make decisions because it seems to be the only path visible at the moment. It's only later that we see there was more than one path, but the others were blocked from our vision at the time. That's the thing with hindsight, you see. Even if you can see it clearly, there's no going back. It's at that point we need to turn around and stare ahead and make a new life."

Slowly, Dr. McGovern stood and gripped his walker. "I tried to do that, you see, when I married your mother. I thought I loved her enough. What I didn't realize was that when I married her, I was keeping one eye straight ahead, but the other was firmly fixed in the past."

"A leap of faith, but with only one foot."

His father looked at him, his lip quirked. "Exactly. Glad to know that something I've said to you over the years actually stuck. I know you're an adult, Pierce, but sometimes I think how very much you still need to learn."

Pierce turned away, his gaze catching on the box of letters in the other room, and he knew he had to try again. "What happened to her letters, Dad? How could they never have reached you?"

"How, indeed?"

The light flickered back on, shining down on them in a weak yellow glow. "I want to read them. I think I should."

His father regarded him for a long moment. "All right. But only the ones that Brenna has read to me so far. I'll give them to you later. For the rest, you can sit with us and listen as she reads."

"How about I just read them to you, instead?"

"Because I like the sound of her voice. Besides, it would be too much like making her put down a book in the middle of a scene. I think she wants to know what happens next."

"Don't we already know what happens? You married my mother and had me. End of story."

"Is it?"

"I don't know, Dad. You tell me. What else is there to know?"

"Brenna will be here tomorrow night at eight o'clock. Come and listen. Right now, I need to go get dressed for the movie. Give me ten minutes, all right?"

"Sure, Dad. Can I help you up the stairs?"

"I got it. I like to pretend I'm not so old now and again. Although I might need help getting down. I'll give you a shout."

Pierce nodded and watched his father's slow progress up the stairs, trying to picture him again as the young man with a broken heart, and thinking of the woman he married but could never love enough.

"I'll be here," he said softly, remembering his mother and wondering for the first time if maybe her departure hadn't been about his own inefficiencies but because of something else entirely.

Brenna turned her face up to the rain, letting the coolness of it wash over her, soaking her skin and making her blouse stick to her body. She watched the lighting flit its way through the sky and didn't flinch as she usually did. Her father had taught her that lightning contained demons trying to come down to earth to possess unclean souls, and throughout her childhood she'd cowered during storms. Until she'd met Pierce and he'd taught her how to stare down her fear of wild light and thundering clouds with only his arm to protect her.

She felt cleansed, somehow—rejuvenated. It had started in Mary Margaret's store, where she'd turned her inner turmoil into anger and unleashed it on her sister. What had Mary Margaret called it? *You've found your voice.* Yes, that was exactly what it was. She'd found her voice, something she hadn't even realized she'd lost. She wasn't sure if she could sustain it, or even what to do with it. She only knew that it was something different in her life, and something different to her at that moment was a lot like the miracle of electric light streaking from the sky to touch the earth.

She made her way through the front door, giving Mrs. Grodin's door her customary knock to complain about her air conditioner. As usual, there was no response. Reaching into her purse, she pulled out the pad of sticky notes and began writing.

I'm giving a formal complaint to the Better Business Bureau as well as seeking legal counsel for breach of contract unless I have a new air conditioner by the end of this week.

Brenna didn't sign it. If Mrs. Grodin couldn't figure out who'd sent her the note, then too bad. She turned away and marched up the stairs. Damned right she'd found her voice.

After showering she dressed carefully, deciding against the Ingrid Bergman–inspired suit she'd worn to the showing of *Casablanca* in favor of the long silver sequined gown with the plunging neckline. She wore her Victoria's Secret lace plunge bra to add to her nonexistent cleavage and had to lean forward in her mirror to appreciate the effect.

Feeling more hopeful than she had in a long time, she threw on her raincoat and drove to the Royal Majestic, parking across the street to be able to take in the whole picture. The tailoring shop and the small department store that flanked the theater were still hanging on, not thriving but not starving, either. It had long been the owners' hope that a re-furbishment of her theater would bring revitalization to Indianola's an-cient Main Street and make it possible to do more than just exist.

Trying hard to hold on to the ebullience of wearing her plunge bra and sequined dress, she stared at the flickering marquee, where only half of the lights were lit. Nathan had explained to her that it wasn't the bulbs but some sort of electrical short that would need the attention of a licensed electrician. A bit of the shine slid off of her evening, even seeming to dim the sequins on her dress. Pulling her coat close around her, she crossed the street and entered the theater.

She was early, and only Nathan and Beau were there ahead of her. Nathan sat at the piano playing "Lara's Theme" from *Doctor Zhivago*. He wore a fedora low on his forehead, giving him the appearance of a gangster from the thirties. She took a quick second glance, wondering who else he reminded her of. When he looked up, she saw he'd drawn on a fake pencil-thin mustache, and when he winked the resemblance was gone.

Beau threw a worried glance toward the sky. "I hope it stops raining soon. You know how bad this weather can be for ticket sales."

"I know." Brenna shivered and ran her hands up and down her arms. "At least my whole family is coming, last time I checked. That'll be worth something."

"Yeah—but they're all half-price tickets. I think you should make them pay full price. They'd still come, you know, because they have to."

Brenna sent him a sidelong glance. "Thanks, Beau."

"Yes, ma'am."

She started to argue with him again about calling her "ma'am," but let it rest. There was enough turbulence in the atmosphere already.

"Miss O'Brien?"

"Yes, Beau?"

"I almost forgot. The band director called. The band can't come tonight on account of the lightning. Mr. Bassett said he didn't want to take any chances with all those brass instruments." He smiled broadly. "I think that's okay, though, because Mr. Conley is doing such a great job on the piano nobody will notice. Not that there will be anybody here, anyway."

Brenna was relieved from delivering a blistering speech about Beau's pessimism by the appearance of her sister Claire. She shook the rain off of her umbrella as Brenna scanned the space behind her. "Where're Buzz and the kids?"

"Mary Sanford has a pageant this weekend, and we didn't want to keep her up late. And you know how hard it is to get a babysitter on a weekday." She smiled brightly, her flaming red lipstick shining in the dim light of the foyer. "But I'm here."

Brenna kissed her sister on the cheek. "Great. Thanks for coming. Um, go ahead and get something to eat and grab a seat. I've got some work to do in my office before the movie starts."

Brenna waddled to her office as fast as the close-fitting skirt of her dress would allow, then quickly shed her wet coat. She sat down in front of her computer and flicked it on, willing the feeling she'd had earlier, while staring up at the stormy sky, to return. She pulled up the figures for the day's receipts from the matinee showing and closed her eyes. She couldn't afford a night like tonight. With those kinds of numbers, she'd have to pay Beau from her own pocket.

She tried to find her voice again, but could hear only the roar of the wind pushing against the sides of the building. She rifled through the papers on top of her desk until she found the folder Nathan had given her. Inside were various ideas he'd come up with to generate revenue, and the projected cost associated with each one. She'd barely glanced at them, unable—or unwilling—to recognize that she had a problem.

A brief rapping sounded on the door before it was opened by a frantic Kathleen.

"Mary Margaret just called my cell. She's at the hospital. Aunt Dottie had to be taken to the emergency room. She swallowed something, but Mary Margaret didn't say what it was. Anyway, they're taking her in right now to have her stomach pumped, and I think we should all be there."

Brenna stood immediately and grabbed her coat. "I'll drive. Beau and Nathan can handle things here."

On the way out, they grabbed Claire while Kathleen called Colleen and asked her to meet the rest of them at the hospital.

In any other situation Brenna would have laughed at the picture they must have made entering the hospital: she in her sequined dress and her other sisters wearing something from their mother's attic straight from the 1940s. She almost expected the lights to dim and the colors to fade so that everything appeared to be in black and white.

They were ushered into a deserted waiting room, where a worried Mary Margaret sat on a beige vinyl chair staring at an unopened copy of *Car and Driver*. She stood when they entered and enveloped them all in a hug before everybody found a seat to collapse into.

Kathleen spoke first. "What happened?"

Mary Margaret frowned and looked at Brenna. "Remember earlier when you were in my store with Aunt Dottie and she bought all those marbles?"

Brenna nodded.

"Well, for some reason yet to be determined, Aunt Dottie took it upon herself to swallow them. All of them. She's having her stomach pumped right now to remove them. The doctor says her throat will be sore for a while and she will need to have a restricted diet, but she should be fine."

Brenna struggled to understand. "She swallowed marbles? But why? Why would she do such a thing?"

Mary Margaret shrugged. "I'm not sure. She was in so much pain when I drove her that I didn't ask, and then they gave her something for the pain, so she was less coherent than usual after that. She was going on and on about filling up empty spaces, and an envelope that's not addressed to her. Oh, and Italian car parts. I think she might have been delirious."

Claire leaned forward. "Do you think that she was trying to . . . to hurt herself?"

"You mean commit suicide?" Kathleen asked.

Mary Margaret shook her head. "I don't think so. I'm not sure, since I didn't really get a chance to speak with her, but I got the feeling that she was just . . . experimenting. Seeing what would happen, I think."

Colleen crossed her arms over her chest. "I've been telling y'all for years that we need to put Aunt Dottie into an old-folks home. She has never really been in her right mind, you know, and getting older hasn't really helped."

Softly, Brenna said, "I don't think so, Colleen. She's always been in her right mind—which is different from yours or mine, but it's all hers. I don't really see that she's acting any different now than she did twenty years ago. She just has a different . . . perspective on life, I think."

"I'd say so." Claire stood and began slowly walking around the room, straightening piles of old, dog-eared magazines. "Remember when we were little—before you were born, Brenna—and Mama and Aunt Dottie would take us to the beach? Daddy hated the beach, but Mama loved the sun and the sand, and the time she spent away from Daddy, I think. The few times Daddy went with us just weren't as much fun. But when Aunt Dottie was there it was a little like going to Disney World."

Claire smiled to herself as she leaned against the single window in the gloomy room and raised the metal blinds so they could see the grimy, rain-streaked glass. "Aunt Dottie would make up skits where we would all be mermaids, and each one of us would have a part. One year she even made us sequined bathing suit tops to wear as our costumes, remember that?"

Kathleen smiled, too. "Yeah, I remember even back then thinking how racy it was to have a two-piece bathing suit, even if the top came all the way down to our belly buttons. Except yours, Claire. You were always so small. I remember your top was practically a one-piece on you."

Claire faced her. "Yeah, and Aunt Dottie had somehow missed your growth spurt. I remember your top barely covered your nipples. I thought the guys on the beach would have heart attacks from all their ogling."

Brenna stared at her oldest sister, trying to imagine the straitlaced, prim and proper Kathleen wearing anything that didn't button up to the neck. Kathleen looked away and didn't comment. Instead, she said, "There's a cafeteria downstairs. I'll go see what's edible and bring it up with some coffee." Without waiting for an answer, she left the room.

Claire returned to stare out the window. "Daddy threw away our bathing suits when he saw the pictures Mama had taken with her new camera . . ." Her voice trailed away. "Aunt Dottie never came to the beach with us again, ever."

Colleen tucked her legs underneath her on the beige vinyl seat. "Remember how after Mama died, Aunt Dottie had sleepovers at her house for us? She'd let us stay up past our bedtimes and watch late-night movies. They were always the old movies, and she said they were our mother's favorites. We didn't really care—we were just so thrilled to be up past eight o'clock. And her romance novels—remember those, Mary Margaret? They were banned in our house, but Aunt Dottie let us read them as long as they never left her house."

"Oh, yeah. I remember those," said Mary Margaret. "I think I learned from them everything I know about sex. You know, I've always wondered why she never married. We've all seen the pictures of her as a young woman, and she was beautiful. She would have made a great mother, too, although I think having her as a surrogate mother helped us all."

"She had a boyfriend—before the war," Brenna blurted out. "She told me. And that Daddy didn't approve and then her boyfriend went away to fight."

Mary Margaret leaned forward in her chair, her elbows on her knees. Her high-heeled 1940s pumps had long since been discarded. "Did he not come back?"

"I wasn't able to get an answer from her. You know how she can be about answering a direct question." She tried to smile, but felt it wobbling on her face. "I guess I've always taken for granted that she would be here."

"I think we all have," said Kathleen, entering with two large bags of food and a tray of coffee cups.

In a silence unusual to all of them, the sisters distributed the food and coffee and ate without speaking. Brenna kept her eyes down, her thoughts focused inward. She wondered if they were all thinking of other times they'd been at the hospital. First with their mother, when Brenna was small and only remembered being allowed to eat the candy from the machines on the first floor without anybody scolding her, and how she'd gotten a stomachache and had been at home with Aunt Dottie when her mother died.

And then they'd gathered there when their father had had his final heart attack. The atmosphere then had been more of relief and guilt than grief, and the same beige vinyl that assaulted her now had been almost welcome in its austereness then. It was as if her father had chosen to die as he had lived: without ornamentation or wasted emotions.

Mostly she wondered if they were all thinking of the time Brenna herself had been there, when nobody had been allowed to come see her except for Kathleen, and how that still seemed to burn a hole in her heart, the gaping hole that had been left there by her mother's death and only temporarily filled by her sisters and then Pierce before being dug up and emptied again.

Kathleen stood and began moving chairs. The other sisters joined in until all the chairs had been pulled into a circle, where they sat and joined hands and prepared to wait for news of Aunt Dottie. It wasn't something they all agreed to do, just something that came naturally to them. As Brenna looked around at the familiar faces, she felt grounded, somehow; as if here in this circle of sisters she'd found her place in the world. She felt that within this circle, despite their differences and her own restlessness, she would always find her home. She looked down at her hand entwined with Kathleen's. Yes, this was nothing new—probably something she'd always taken for granted. But it seemed that now, with so much to lose hanging in the balance, she found herself believing that no matter how hard she fell, these hands would catch her to soften the fall.

A nurse tapped briefly on the door. "Excuse me, is there a Brenna O'Brien here?"

Brenna looked up groggily, wondering if she'd really dozed or if she was just exhausted from being awake for almost twenty-four hours. "I'm Brenna O'Brien."

"Dorothy O'Brien is awake and in recovery and is asking to see you."

"Is she all right?"

"The doctor will be in shortly to speak with all of you, but, yes, everything appears to be fine, and all of the foreign objects have been removed from her stomach."

"And she wants to see me? Just me?"

"Yes. Just you." The nurse frowned. "She was quite clear on that point."

With a hasty glance back at her sisters, Brenna stood and followed the nurse, the woman's squeaking rubber-soled shoes making a duet with the tapping of Brenna's heels across the blue linoleum floors.

The nurse turned to her. "I'm not sure how coherent she is. She keeps talking about her Sunday hat, and being missing in action, and something about Laurence Olivier." She paused outside a closed door. "But she did say your name very clearly and was adamant that she speak with you before she went to sleep."

Opening the door, the nurse added, "Obviously she's still under the effects of the anesthesia. Just hold her hand, let her know you're there. Don't bother talking to her about anything important, as she won't remember any of it. I'll be back in five minutes." As she turned to go, she said, "Oh, and she said something about engine parts from Italy. Go figure."

A smile creased Brenna's face as she entered the recovery room, wishing she'd brought her Saint Raphael medallion for Aunt Dottie, and just as quickly wondering if her indomitable aunt Dottie would ever need the intercession of saints.

CHAPTER 18

When Brenna entered the room, Aunt Dottie's eyes were open. Without the thick glasses she appeared to be a different person. But as Brenna approached and saw the large green eyes and the soft white hair, she recognized her beloved aunt. She stopped by the side of the bed and held Dottie's hand, amazed how soft it still was, and suddenly remembering this same hand holding her behind Dottie's back, protecting Brenna from her father's anger and his thin-tipped belt.

Brenna leaned over and kissed the pale cheek. "How are you?"

Her voice was very soft and slow. "I'm fine, thank you. They won't let me wear a hat in here, though, so if you wouldn't mind speaking to one of those horrible nurses about it, I'd appreciate it."

"Yes, Aunt Dottie." Brenna leaned closer, trying not to notice the needle in her aunt's other arm, or the breathing tubes in her nose. "Why did you do it? Why did you swallow all those marbles?"

Dottie closed her eyes, and for a moment Brenna thought she had gone to sleep. But then she sighed heavily and said, "All those empty places inside of me. I thought the marbles would . . . fill the empty spaces and I could finally feel full."

Brenna sat heavily on the side of the bed, unable to stand. She found herself gasping for breath, as if she'd run a long, long way. She swallowed heavily before she could speak. "Oh, Aunt Dottie—what empty spaces? What haven't we given you?"

She looked at Brenna now, her green eyes soft and lovely, reminding Brenna of the beautiful woman Dottie had once been. "I loved him, you know. I should have married him. But my brother said it would never work, that we would grow out of love too quickly and have nothing left. And I believed him. I believed him when he said that it was better to wonder than to know." Dottie closed her eyes again as if the effort of speaking had exhausted all her energies.

Still, Brenna pressed on. "Was it Dr. McGovern, Aunt Dottie? Was the man my daddy wouldn't let you marry?"

"I have a letter for him. Did he tell you that? I'll never open it because it isn't addressed to me. That would be very ill-mannered, and my mama raised me to have good manners. Don't wipe your nose with your sleeve, child. Find a handkerchief."

Brenna grabbed a tissue from a box by the bed and dabbed at her nose. "What empty spaces did you want to fill, Aunt Dottie?"

Large green eyes peered up at Brenna. "Nothing's ever going to fill the hole left by your great passion. You've got to fill it somehow."

"I don't understand," Brenna said softly.

"No, I didn't think you would. You've always done it backward, dear. You figure out the outcome first and live your life as if that's the only way. Your daddy taught you that, same as he taught me. But you've got to relearn that part of life. It's like learning to breathe all over again."

The nurse tapped on the door and poked her head in, holding up a finger to indicate one more minute.

Brenna held her aunt's hand again, like a lifeline to understand things that had never been clear to her. Softly, she asked, "Why did you want to see me instead of the others?"

The old woman lifted her head off the pillow, her eyes intent on Brenna's. "Because you're the one I wanted to warn about swallowing marbles. They don't work. And it hurts like hell." She collapsed against the pillow and closed her eyes.

Brenna glanced back at the nurse, who nodded, reassuring Brenna that everything was all right. Gently, she disengaged her hand from her aunt's and began to walk away from the bed.

"My purse. Please have the nurses give you my purse so you can take it home with you. I don't want anything happening to it."

Brenna returned and placed a gentle kiss on Aunt Dottie's forehead. "I'll take care of it. Anything else?"

"Fix my car," she said, her eyes drooping and her voice groggy. "There's bound to be a parts place closer than Italy." Her voice died, followed by gentle snoring. Brenna kissed her again and left, a small smile on her lips.

She wasn't able to tell her sisters anything new, only that Aunt Dottie seemed fine but was groggy and mostly incoherent. This seemed to satisfy them, so they began making decisions as to what to do next. It was determined that Kathleen would take the first shift and stay in the hospital while everybody else went home to change and sleep until it was their turn to come back and keep watch. Colleen offered to drive Brenna, and as they drove home in the breaking dawn, Brenna sat in the front seat, holding Aunt Dottie's purse close to her chest.

Colleen yawned, then smiled as she flicked on her blinker and turned out of the hospital parking lot. "I think you can put the purse down now, Brenn. Nobody's going to take it."

Brenna relaxed her grasp a bit. "I guess not. It's just that . . . well . . . it reminds me so much of her. She's had this same purse since I was a girl." She smoothed her hand over the worn black leather, remembering how she'd always thought of Aunt Dottie's purse as her magic bag. For whatever ailed Brenna, Aunt Dottie had always had the remedy somewhere in the recesses of her purse: a dollar bill, an aspirin, a tissue, a lipstick, candy, notepad and pencil, and once even a screwdriver. It suited the role her aunt had played in her life: the surrogate mother in whose hands Brenna had found every refuge. And never once had she thought that Aunt Dottie would have empty spaces aching to be filled.

Brenna hugged the purse to her chest again, missing her aunt. "I'll call Father Joe tomorrow and have him add Aunt Dottie to the prayer list."

"I'm sure Kathleen's already seen to it."

"I'll call him just in case."

Brenna turned her head away, ashamed at the sharpness in her voice and not really sure why. She sensed Colleen looking at her, but continued to stare out the side window until they came to Colleen's house. Colleen was about to drive past it to take Brenna home, but pulled into the driveway when Brenna spotted Timmy on the front steps waving at them.

He was still in his pajamas as he ran out to the car, and Brenna could see that he was crying.

Alarmed, Colleen grabbed his shoulders. "What's wrong, Timmy? Is somebody hurt?"

He nodded, great gulping sobs shaking his thin body.

Colleen knelt in front of him. "Who, Timmy? Who?"

"Rocky," he choked out.

Visible relief washed over Colleen's face. "Your guinea pig? Your guinea pig is hurt?"

"She's not moving. I think she might be . . ." Another sob racked his body, and he was unable to finish.

Brenna touched Timmy's head. "Is the cage in your room? I'll go up and check, okay?"

He nodded, and Brenna let herself into the house and up the stairs, taking each step one at a time to somehow postpone the inevitable.

The large white wire cage sat on a table in the corner of the room. From where she stood in the doorway, she could make out a still, dark, furry form in the corner of the cage. She approached it slowly, waiting for it to move. The guinea pig was on her side with her small, dark eyes open. Tentatively, Brenna stuck her hand inside and ran the backs of her fingers down Rocky's side, feeling the soft fur and the stiffness underneath.

She moved her finger toward the tiny pink mouth, waiting for Rocky to lick it, but the animal remained motionless, as if in a deep sleep. She heard Timmy's bare feet running up the stairs, then stopping at the door to his room.

"Aunt Brenna—is Rocky okay?"

Brenna took two slow breaths before turning around. "I'm sorry, Timmy. I'm so sorry."

Instead of his face crumpling, as Brenna had expected, a dry-eyed Timmy moved to stand beside her at the cage. As Brenna had done, he put his hand inside and patted the soft brown fur. "I thought she was sleeping."

"She looks really peaceful, doesn't she?"

Timmy nodded as his fingers gently stroked the furry body. "I feel bad. I didn't want her at first. I didn't want a pet at all, because they always die. My best friend, Mark, had a dog that got hit by a car, and I couldn't understand why he wanted another one if they're just going to die on you like that."

He continued to stroke the fur, swallowing to hide a lump in his throat. "But I really liked Rocky. She used to squeak really loudly when I'd come home from school and she'd hear my voice. Like she was happy to see me or something." A tear dripped down his cheek and landed on his arm, but he continued petting Rocky as if he hadn't noticed. "And she used to just sit in my lap while I did my homework, kind of like she was keeping me company."

"Sounds like she was a good friend to you."

"She was." He sniffed loudly as his body shook. "And I'm not mad that Mary Sanford gave her to me, even though I only had Rocky for such a short time."

Brenna put her arms around her nephew and held him close, feeling his tears soak into her mother's sequined dress. "But why would you be mad at Mary Sanford?"

"Because at first I told her that I didn't want Rocky since one day she would die, but Mary Sanford made me take Rocky anyway."

Brenna wrinkled her brow, trying to understand his eight-year-old's logic. "So you're not sad that Rocky died?"

Timmy shook his head. "I'm sad that she's dead—but I'm not sad that I got to play with her and have her with me as a friend. Even if it was for just a little while. If I'd never been forced to take her, I never would have learned how much I loved her."

Brenna continued to hold him as he cried, and wondered why she also felt like crying. Timmy drew a long, shuddering breath. "It's like Rocky was telling me that it's okay to have fun for just a little while, even if you don't know what's going to happen next. Like jumping off the high dive at the pool—when you don't know if the water is going to be warm or cold and it doesn't really matter, because it's so much fun just jumping."

Brenna got down on her knees and stared into the pale green eyes of her favorite nephew, finally admitting and understanding why he was her favorite. She held back her own tears and offered instead a wobbly grin. "It's like learning to breathe all over again, isn't it?"

Timmy pulled back to look into her face and smiled. "Yeah. Sort of."

She pushed his red hair out of his eyes. "We'll have a really nice funeral for Rocky, okay? Then we can all pay our respects and say good-bye."

Timmy nodded and put his head against her again, and they stayed that way for a long time while Brenna took deep breaths, marveling at how easy it was to fill her lungs with air and breathe it out again.

Pierce put his feet up on the desk in his bedroom, the same desk he'd used since first grade, and rubbed his hand over his face. His father's old letters were scattered across the surface of the desk, and a few had drifted to the carpet, where they remained near his feet.

He tapped his finger against the signature on the letter in front of him. *Me.* His dad had told him only that it was a nickname, and really no help at all in determining the identity of the letter writer. Despite constant proddings, the old doctor had continued to be evasive. It had become very obvious to Pierce that he and Brenna would have to put their heads together to figure it out. And it didn't escape Pierce's notice that this had probably been his father's intention all along.

He stood, stacking the envelopes into a pile and trying to push back the restlessness that had crept up on him while he read. He wanted to know more, and he wanted to know the truth; but mostly he found that he wanted to hear it from Brenna's mouth. Gathering the envelopes in his hands, he went downstairs.

Brenna was seated in her usual place in the chair across from his father. Pierce paused for a moment, watching her. Her whole body almost vibrated with anticipation, the air around her seeming to shimmer, as if she had suddenly discovered that the world outside brimmed with possibilities. He watched, amused, as her fingers tapped on the armrest, beating along with her impatient foot as it bounced up and down on her crossed knee.

"Good morning," he said as he crossed the room and handed her the letters. She looked up at him and actually smiled, the strain of all their previous encounters somehow missing. He couldn't resist and let his gaze drop down to her chest, as if checking to see if she'd remembered how to button correctly. She blushed when she realized what he was doing, but it didn't make her stop smiling.

"Good morning," she said in return.

He continued to look down at her. "You seem to be in a very good mood this morning. Did you have a great night at the theater last night? Dad and I were there, but we didn't see you."

"Actually, it was a horrible night. I was just telling your dad that I was at the hospital for most of the night with Aunt Dottie. She'll be okay, but it was a lot of worry there for a while. And then Timmy's guinea pig died, and now I have a funeral to plan. But I think Timmy's going to be okay."

"So why are you smiling?"

She looked down at her hands that rested on the letters he'd given her, at the chewed fingernails that had never changed since he'd known her. "Because I have plans. For my theater. Nathan has given me a folder full of them, and I finally feel as if I can actually start implementing them. It's been a long time since I've had plans for anything, really." She didn't meet his eyes when she said this.

"Well, if you don't count wedding plans, right?"

She looked startled, as if just now recalling that she did, in fact, have wedding plans. "Right. Of course."

Pierce moved to sit on the couch. "What happened to Dottie?"

Brenna laughed nervously. "She . . . she swallowed a bunch of marbles."

"Accidentally?"

"Apparently, yes. She said that she was . . ." Brenna glanced over at his father, as if for encouragement. "She said that she was trying to fill in all the empty spaces inside of her."

It was silent for a moment before the doctor spoke. "Only Dottie O'Brien. She's always been one of those people who has extraordinary solutions to ordinary problems. I think you young people today would say that she 'thinks outside of the box.' I suppose that's why she's always been one of my favorite people."

Pierce caught Brenna's eye before they both turned to stare at his father. He met their gaze without comment. Finally he turned to Pierce and asked, "Did you finish reading the letters?"

"Yes, I did. And I have a few questions—"

His father interrupted. "Wonderful. Then we're ready to start. Brenna has to get back to the hospital, so I don't want to keep her."

Again Pierce's eyes met Brenna's, and he was once more transported back through the years to when a look like that from Brenna O'Brien would make his knees weak. With some surprise, he realized that things hadn't changed much, regardless of the passage of years.

Brenna lifted a letter from the box, opened it carefully, and began to read.

May 29, 1942

Darling,

I have been awake all night thinking of you. It feels so wrong to be demanding attention from you right now—now, when you will be sent in harm's way to fight for our country and for the freedoms that all of us have taken for granted for so long. I am so very proud of you, darling, that I could almost burst with it. Mrs. Greeley has four gold stars in her window now. Four! All of her handsome sons have been killed in action, and my heart aches for her. Do you remember Robert, her youngest? He was in my grade at school and was the spitball king—known far and wide for his accuracy. He always had a joke, and I never saw him without a smile on his face. I can't believe that he's gone forever and that he and his brothers will never walk through their mother's door again. Yet, when I see her she walks tall and proud, and says that she knows her sacrifice will not be in vain.

I wish I could be like her. But my heart is so heavy with dread. I pray each night for your safety and for God to give me hope, but I'm quickly running out of time. And here I am writing the most important letter of my life, and I spend most of it procrastinating by writing about other things. But the time has come, I think, to write what has been pressing on my heart.

I had hoped to tell you this in person, but I'm afraid that that time will never come, so I am forced to tell you in this letter. Darling, I'm going to have a baby. You and I are going to have a child. I can't say that I am ashamed or unhappy about this news, only saddened that you aren't here to share it with me. I believed you when you asked me to marry you, and I can feel no shame that we conse-

crated our love with our bodies before we stood together in a church. Whatever you decide to make of this news is up to you. I don't know why I haven't heard from you, and I can only hope and pray that it's not because you've forgotten me, because, as you now know, this is no longer just about you and me.

In the darkest hours when I cannot sleep, I plan our wedding, because it's the only thing that keeps me sane and away from my worries. I've also come up with the Old Testament reading for our wedding Mass. It's always been a favorite of mine, and I hope you will allow me to choose it. It's from the book of Ruth. "Entreat in me not to leave thee, and to return from following after thee, for whither thou goest, I will go."

Brenna's voice cracked and she stopped reading. Neither he nor his father said anything as she cleared her throat and continued.

"And where thou lodgest; I will lodge: thy people shall be my people, and thy God my God."

Darling, I am clinging to the barest thread of hope. Please write. Please, please, please, please, please. I am swallowing my pride and begging you. For the sake of our child, please write to me.

I love you,
Me

Brenna stood abruptly, the box of letters spilling to the floor. She wiped her eyes with the heel of her hand. "I can't read any more right now. I've got to go."

Without another word she fled from the room, and before Pierce or his father could react, the banging of the front door echoed through the house.

CHAPTER 19

Brenna had managed to calm down by the time she reached the hospital, only to become agitated again when she found that Dottie had already been discharged and sent home with Kathleen. Driving faster than she knew she should within the town's limits, she and her VW Bug flew to Kathleen's house.

Kathleen answered the door before Brenna had a chance to knock. She had her finger raised to her lips to tell Brenna to be quiet as she opened the door further for Brenna to enter.

Disappointed at having to wait to speak with her aunt, she reluctantly followed her older sister into the kitchen. "How is she?" Brenna whispered after she'd sat down at the counter.

Kathleen began pouring two cups of coffee. "Well, she's sleeping right now. She should be in the hospital, but the damned insurance wouldn't pay for another day as long as she was stable. So they released her. I mean, she's an old woman—a stomach pumping is much more serious for the elderly." She slapped her hands down on the counter and took a deep breath. "She's doing fine, and Claire said she'd stop by after her shift to check on her." Kathleen took a sip of coffee and shook her head. "I still can't believe it—that she swallowed all those marbles! Daddy used to always say she was crazy, and now I'm beginning to think he may have been right."

"No—don't say that."

Kathleen started at the harsh tone of Brenna's voice, and quickly put down her cup of coffee, sloshing the hot liquid over the side.

Brenna picked up her napkin and began sopping up the spilled coffee. "I'm sorry. I didn't mean to shout. It's just that after seeing her in the hospital, I realized how much she means to us. To me. And how her special way with things is what made my growing up bearable."

She stared down into her cup, seeing the warped reflection of her own face. "In the hospital, she said she's been trying to . . . fill in the empty spaces in her life. And it made me think that it was our turn to make her life better. To fill in any of the missing parts."

Kathleen rested her chin on her hands, smiling softly at Brenna. "You sound like Mama, you know. She and Aunt Dottie were more like sisters than just sisters-in-law. Mama always stuck up for her when Daddy was on one of his rants, and always made sure Aunt Dottie was part of our lives even though Daddy didn't want us spending any time with her. It was the only thing I ever remember Mama putting her foot down about. I've always wondered what it cost her."

They stared at each other for a long moment in the silent kitchen before Brenna spoke. "Was Aunt Dottie ever married? Even for just a little while?"

"No, never. I mean, obviously she was around long before I was, but she still has her maiden name, and I know there was never anybody around when I was a child. Why do you ask?"

"Just something I read in Dr. McGovern's letters. I can't really say more—except that I think they had a secret engagement before he went to fight in the war, and she got pregnant. Supposedly she was already married when he got back from the war."

"But that doesn't make any sense, Brenna. She doesn't have a child, for one thing. And surely we would have known if she'd ever been married. Have you asked her?"

Brenna rolled her eyes. "Of course I've asked her. But that's a lot like asking the clouds to stop raining or the grass to stop being green. You never get the answer you're expecting."

Kathleen laughed. "No, you surely don't. Have you asked Dr. McGovern?"

"His answers are almost as evasive as hers. That's why I rushed right over here. I need to talk to her—I need to find out the truth so that I can help her. Maybe it's not too late for her to find her passion." She smiled ruefully at Kathleen. "That's what she said to me. That nothing will ever fill the hole left by your great passion."

Kathleen stood abruptly, taking both coffee cups. With her back to Brenna, she began pouring fresh cups. "And you and Pierce—was he your real passion?" She placed Brenna's cup in front of her but remained standing, looking out into the front yard from the window over the sink.

Brenna held her fingers around her cup, feeling the heat seep into her skin until she could feel the burn, as if she needed to be reminded that she still could feel. "I try not to think about it. Mostly, when I do, I feel only pain. And there is nothing—*nothing*—that will make me want to relive that kind of pain again."

Kathleen faced Brenna, her eyes serious. "Do you forgive Daddy?"

Brenna stared long and hard into her cup, as if expecting the answer to appear. "I don't know. Maybe he saved me from worse heartache later on. Maybe I never would have found my theater and decided to make it my life. Who can say? Maybe Daddy was right when he said it was better to wonder than to know for sure."

"But do you forgive him?" Kathleen leaned forward, her voice urgent.

Brenna looked up sharply. "No. I can't. I know it's a sin, but I can't forgive him."

Kathleen sat back, clearly agitated. "Did you ever think that some-times people do things because they feel they have to? That they don't have any choice?"

"There was nobody making Daddy do what he did. He had his own selfish reasons for keeping Pierce and me apart, and there's no excuse. And I'm surprised that you, of all people, would look for excuses for him."

Kathleen looked back at her with eyes wide. "What do you mean?"

"Just that you're the oldest. You'd been around him a lot longer than any of us were and had probably seen more."

"Yes, I guess you're right." Kathleen seemed to slump a little in her chair. "I suppose I was just wondering if you thought that some sins were forgivable if they had been committed, perhaps, to hide an even greater sin."

"What? What greater sin did I commit? Sleeping with Pierce outside of marriage? Was that why Daddy punished me?"

"No, Brenna. That's not what I was talking about. I just wanted you to think that no person is unblemished by sin. And that penance and retribution can be far worse for the sinner than the person they have sinned against."

"I don't know, Kathleen. I never saw Daddy suffer for anything he did."

Kathleen studied her for a long moment. Then quietly she said, "Some people never show their suffering on the outside. They keep it to themselves so nobody else can see."

Brenna started to ask her what she meant when Aunt Dottie called out from an upstairs bedroom, "Kathleen!" Her voice was strong yet strained.

Brenna put a hand on Kathleen's arm. "I'll go see what she wants. I need to talk with her anyway."

Kathleen surprised her by putting her own hand over Brenna's and squeezing. "All right. Just let me know what she needs. In the meantime, I'm going to pour her some sweet tea—diluted, of course. I swear the woman drinks a gallon of it a day."

Brenna was relieved to see Dottie's complexion less pale and the familiar glasses on her nose. She walked over to her aunt and kissed her lightly on the cheek. "You're looking better. How do you feel?"

With a raspy voice she said, "The same way you'd feel, I expect, if you'd had your stomach pumped to remove thirty-eight marbles." She blinked her wide green eyes behind the thick glasses. "I'm thirsty."

"Kathleen's bringing you some sweet tea. Is there anything else?"

"My purse. Have you seen my purse?"

"I have it, Aunt Dottie. I left it in the car but I can go get it before I leave, okay?"

Aunt Dottie nodded solemnly. "I have something in there for you."

Curious, Brenna sat on the edge of the bed. "What is it?"

"I don't remember. But I'll know it when I see it. I think."

"Okay. Well, thank you." She took her aunt's hand and waited for the large eyes to focus on her again. "Aunt Dottie, I need to ask you a personal question. I hope you realize that whatever you say to me will be kept in confidence, all right?"

"All right. Shoot."

Brenna drew a deep breath. "Have you ever been pregnant?"

Aunt Dottie's eyes were serious as she looked into Brenna's. "Cross your heart and hope to die, stick a needle in your eye?"

Brenna would have laughed if the subject hadn't been so completely serious. "Sure."

"I'm waiting."

"For what?"

"You have to cross your heart."

Dottie waited patiently while Brenna made the motions.

Brenna leaned in closer. "Well?"

"Well, what?"

After a deep breath, Brenna asked again, "Have you ever been pregnant?"

Dottie's brows knit, and she frowned as if she were deep in thought. Finally, she said, "No. At least, I don't think so. I might have put on a few pounds over the years, so some people might think I'm pregnant, but I'm quite sure that I'm not."

"No, Aunt Dottie. I don't mean now. I mean before—when you were younger. Before the war."

"Oh, yes. I was young then. Was that your question?"

Brenna bit her tongue to keep from shouting. She decided to try again. "Did you and Dr. McGovern ever date—before the war, that is?"

Dottie shook her head. "He wasn't a doctor then. He didn't go to medical school until after the war."

"Yes. But did you and he . . . did you ever have a relationship together?"

"He was in love, you know. So in love back then. It was almost too painful to watch."

"What was too painful, Aunt Dottie?"

"How badly a heart can break. And what a person has to do so they don't die from it."

"Like what?"

Dottie turned her head toward the window, where the afternoon sun angled the light through the window, turning her white hair to yellow again. "Like telling your heart to love where it doesn't. Your heart is not a brain, you see. It can't be forced to do what it won't. Your brain can lie to itself, but your heart never can."

Kathleen entered the room with a glass of tea and a bowl of soup and set them on the dresser. Brenna helped her prop the old woman up against fluffed pillows before putting a bed tray over her lap. Kathleen gently placed the bowl and glass on the tray, then opened up a linen napkin and placed it across Aunt Dottie's chest.

"I'm afraid it's just clear broth. Your doctor said it would be a few days before you can handle solids again. Would you like me to feed you?"

Aunt Dottie regarded her with a blank expression. "I'm old, Kathleen, not dead. I'm sure I can manage."

Brenna hid her smile at Kathleen's shocked look. Kathleen smoothed her hands over her pleated pants. "Well, then, while you eat I have a surprise for Brenna. Wait here, and I'll be right back."

Brenna began following Kathleen to the door. "And while you're doing that, I'm going to run out to my car and get Aunt Dottie's purse—she was asking for it."

Aunt Dottie looked up from her bowl of soup. "I was?"

"Yes, remember? You said you had something for me in your purse."

"I do. Do you know where my purse is?"

Brenna bit her lip again. "I'll go get it." Before her aunt could say another word, Brenna ran out to her car and back, barely pausing to yank the purse off her backseat. She had just placed the purse on her aunt's bed when Kathleen returned, a white satin-and-lace confection of a dress draped over her arm.

"What's that?" Brenna stayed where she was, afraid to touch the dress, knowing what it must be.

"I'm thinking it's a wedding dress. When we were going through the attic to find Mama's old clothes to wear for oldies night, I found it wrapped in tissue at the bottom of one of Mama's trunks. And I know it was hers, because look here at the label." She held the neck of the dress up to Brenna. *Made expressly for Mary Everly.*

"But I thought you said that Daddy gave away her wedding dress after she died."

"He did—which is why I'm not sure why this dress was up there. At first I thought it might not have fit, so she had to have the other one made, but then I figured this might have been a cotillion dress. Those dresses had to be white, too, and a lot of them looked like wedding gowns."

Brenna stepped forward, gingerly touching the delicate lace on the bodice. "It's beautiful."

"I thought so, too, and it looks like it would fit—which makes sense, since you and Mama were built the same. I thought maybe you could try it on, and if you like it, this could be your wedding dress."

Brenna's hand snapped back. "Oh, I don't know. . . ."

Kathleen handed the dress out to her. "Just go try it on. You can use my room—Aunt Dottie and I will wait here—but call me if you need any help."

Brenna heard her voice in the back of her head, the one that was telling her to shout out the word *no*. But then she looked at Kathleen's face, and thought of Dooley, and pushed the voice aside.

"All right," she said, taking the dress. "I'll go try it on."

She walked down the hall to Kathleen and John's room and closed the door. She leaned against it for a long time, looking at the antique four-poster bed with the antique quilt spread over the top, the large wedding photo hanging over it, and all of the pictures of their children that were scattered around the room in various frames. When Brenna was a child, this room had been her father's room, and one she avoided. But now it was the heart of the home, and one in which Brenna had learned to seek sanctuary. Until now.

Gently she laid the beautiful dress on the quilted bedspread, noticing the fine embroidery work on the skirt of the gown and across the delicate cap sleeves and princess neckline. It was exactly the kind of dress Brenna would have wished for her own wedding. With a wry smile, she realized that her dream had come true: This was to be her wedding dress, regardless of whether or not she actually had a wedding.

She took off her clothes, carelessly discarding her jeans and blouse on the floor, and slipped on the dress. There was a small zipper in the back, hidden by false buttons, making her realize that even if the dress had been custom made, it had been made on a relatively limited budget.

With eyes closed, she faced the mirror over the dresser, afraid to look and see the girl she had once been, the girl with dreams and possibilities. Afraid, even, to find that maybe that girl was too far out of reach to find again even now, when Brenna thought she might be worth finding.

Keeping her eyes closed, she turned and left the room, taking a deep breath before joining Kathleen and Aunt Dottie. Both women stared at her as she paused in the doorway, and didn't say a word.

Brenna laughed nervously. "Is it see-through or something?"

Aunt Dottie's hand fluttered in front of her face. "You're the spitting image of your mama. The very spitting image."

Kathleen walked toward Brenna, her eyes bright. "You're beautiful, Brenna, in your own right. But it's almost like this dress was made for you." She hugged her sister. "I think we need look no further—we've found your dress."

"Great," Brenna said, trying to mean it. She wanted to blurt out the truth then, but something stopped her. Maybe it was because she was embarrassed that her subterfuge had carried on for so long. Or maybe it was because a part of the girl she had once been still lived inside of her—the girl who'd dreamed of marrying the man she would love forever, and traveling with him around the world until they reached the edge of it together.

Brenna looked over Kathleen's shoulder to the bed, where Aunt Dottie was struggling to dig through her purse. Kathleen quickly moved over to her. "Aunt Dottie, you shouldn't be doing that. Let me."

She reached for the purse, but Aunt Dottie held it back and pulled something from it. "I found it, Brenna. My little surprise for you." She pulled out a long silver chain upon which a small oval medallion hung.

Brenna moved toward the bed, aware of the dress swishing around her ankles like the soft hands of her mother. She took the chain from her aunt and held up the medallion to see it better. "Saint Monica?"

Aunt Dottie collapsed against her pillow, exhaustion from her efforts evident on her face. "Patron saint of unanswered prayers."

Kathleen crossed her arms. "Is that appropriate for a bride-to-be?"

"Sometimes," Dottie said as she turned her head toward the window and closed her eyes.

After removing the bed tray, Kathleen stood quietly watching the old woman sleep. "I hardly know what to think about Aunt Dottie anymore. Sometimes I believe she's on top of things and understands more than even I do. And then others"—she turned and began walking toward the door before pausing in the doorway with the tray in her hands—"I feel like she's in her own little world, a place where her reality doesn't intersect with ours."

Brenna fingered the Saint Monica medallion, a small smile on her face as she watched her sleeping aunt. "I don't know. Sometimes I wish I understood things as well as she does."

She ignored Kathleen's glance as she hurried out of the room to take off the beautiful wedding dress before she, too, realized how it seemed as if it had been made just for her.

When Brenna rushed into the theater foyer, she startled Nathan from his perch atop a ladder near the old grandfather clock with its brass crow, and for a moment it appeared he would topple off. To their mutual relief, he regained his balance and climbed down to greet her. It was only after he'd reached the bottom rung that she saw Dooley, who had been crouched in the corner near the snack bar with some sort of tool he'd apparently been sticking into the woodwork.

He stood and approached her with the same smile she'd been warming to for most of her life. It had never failed to be the brightest part of her day, and as he reached her she hugged him, catching him off guard. Apparently thinking her public display of affection was for Nathan's benefit, he gave her a quick peck on the mouth before pulling her close with one arm.

"Get a room, y'all," Nathan said sternly, his tone softened by a smile. "I'm a single man and I don't want to be corrupted."

Embarrassed, Brenna pulled away, then indicated the tool in Dooley's hand. "I'm glad to see you, but what are you doing here?"

"I worked the last two days, so Bill gave me the day off. Thought I might pop over and see you. When you weren't here, I asked Nathan if he could use some help."

Brenna turned to Nathan. "I thought you were supposed to be checking the ceilings for water damage from the storm."

Nathan shoved his hands into his pockets and gave Dooley a quick glance. "Well, we did. I went up to the attic to see if any rain had come in."

"And?"

"And I'd say that quite a lot of rain got in. The floor of the attic is saturated, but the worst of it appeared to be right over this spot here. Dooley and I searched for someplace where the water might have come out on this floor, but we've been unable to find it. We've been checking the baseboards and plaster for dampness, and it doesn't look good."

"What does that mean?"

Again, Dooley and Nathan exchanged glances before Dooley spoke. "It looks like the water might be running between the walls. What it means is that you could have wood rot, or mold—or both. It's hard to tell without knocking out some walls. When was the last time you had an inspection?"

She shrugged. "I think about a year ago. The man who came was a good friend of Kathleen and John's. I don't remember him being too picky." The familiar feeling of lethargy crept up on her again, but she pushed it away, focusing instead on Aunt Dottie's words about finding her passion. "So how long will it be before we know for sure? And how much would something like that cost to repair?"

This time Nathan stared down at his cowboy boots. After taking a deep breath, he met her eyes and said, "More than you've got."

She braced herself, unwilling to let go. "What about insurance? Couldn't we submit a claim?"

"Well, Brenna, I just paid the premium. You and I both know that the only way you've been able to afford your premium by keeping it so low is by having your deductible really high. Now, I'm only saying this because you've given me access to your accounting books, but, to be honest, you can't afford the deductible."

Brenna focused on pushing back the panic. "But there's no immediate problem, right? I mean, there's no danger to anyone in the building, right?"

Nathan shook his head. "Not as far as I can tell, but I'm not an expert. I've done remodelings, but I'm not the one who determines what needs to be remodeled. You're going to need an expert. I just don't know how you're going to pay for one."

She walked around the lobby while thinking, absently running her hands against the beautiful marble columns, the burled mahogany of the ticket window, finally coming to a stop in front of the grandfather clock. "I could get a bank loan. And I could sell shares in the theater's profits to investors."

Nathan moved to stand in front of her. "Well, as my daddy always told me—you can't borrow money unless it looks like you don't need it." He gestured toward the shabbiness of the lobby around him. "And you look like you really, really need it."

She looked around, taking it all in, and knew he was right. Despite their temporary patches, the lack of funds was still painfully obvious. She stuck her hand out and snapped off a chip of peeling paint from the wall and stared at it for a long time, her mind lost in thought. She was amazed to find her thoughts drifting to her aunt Dottie, wondering what her aunt would tell her to do. Slowly, Brenna stopped spinning the paint chip as a small smile played on her lips. "I've got a little money saved from my grandmother. What if I emptied out all of my savings and used it to pay for cosmetic work—like plaster and tiles and new plumbing in the bathrooms? I've been going over your ideas, Nathan, and there're lots of great things in there I think we could do if we had some money. I'm thinking that if I drew up a business plan with a revenue projection incorporating a lot of your ideas, and then showed it to the bank and potential investors, it might make us more attractive to them—especially if the theater is cleaned up a bit first. Then we'd have money not only for new events at the theater to bring in more revenue, but also for all the long-term capital costs, like a new roof, and new wiring, and repairing the mural."

Dooley nodded. "Definitely. Not only that, but I think you should temporarily close, then have a grand reopening where you invite bank officers and potential investors to get them all riled up and excited about giving you money. Something about people dressing up always seems to make them want to open their wallets."

Brenna smiled broadly. "Why, Doo, I always knew you were smart, but I never guessed you were a marketing genius, too."

Dooley shoved his hands into his back pockets and grinned. "Well, I am just four credits short of my business degree. I keep thinking I should go back and finish up."

"And I'm thinking that's a very good idea."

Dooley pinched her gently on the arm. "Okay, who are you and what have you done to Brenna?"

Nathan crossed his arms as a slow grin grew on his face. "Well, now,

I'd say you've seen the light. Do you care to share with us what's got you so fired up all of a sudden?"

She leaned against Dooley's shoulder, seeking and finding comfort there. "Just something Aunt Dottie told me. Made me realize that this was something I've got to do."

Nathan stared at her closely. "Well, it's about time. I've been wondering why my folder sat unread on your desk. I wish I'd known that it would have only taken swallowing a few marbles to get you to take a look."

"I wouldn't say it was that easy, Nathan, but it certainly was illuminating."

Nathan rubbed his hands together. "All right then, let's get busy. First, let's put some fans up in the attic and do some patchwork to prevent more rain from coming in. Then you and I should sit down and crunch some numbers so we can figure out how soon we can get the Royal Majestic fixed up enough to have a grand reopening. Then comes the fun stuff—picking which of my ideas you want to present to investors, along with cost estimates and revenue projections."

"Sounds like a plan," Brenna said, feeling hopeful and optimistic for the first time in years.

Dooley handed his wood tool back to Nathan. "Doesn't sound like you'll need me here. I guess I'll go on home and finish up some projects I've been working on."

"I'll see you later, then," Brenna said as she leaned over to kiss him on the lips again just to see him blush. Then she turned and walked toward the auditorium to stare up at her mural for inspiration, concentrating on taking deep breaths and letting them out slowly, as if she were learning how to do it for the first time.

CHAPTER 20

Pierce stood beneath the old magnolia tree in Colleen's backyard, waving away the gnats that circled his head, having been given the dubious honor of being a pallbearer at a guinea pig's funeral. Dooley Gambrel stood on his other side, holding up his own end of the shoe box. If Pierce hadn't felt such an overwhelming antagonistic yet unprovoked yearning to slug the other man in the jaw, they might have shared a really long, hard laugh over a beer.

Brenna's entire family formed a circle around them as Brenna moved into position at the base of the tree, with the large family Bible under her arm. Kathleen pulled up a lawn chair next to Brenna while her husband, John, escorted Aunt Dottie into it. Timmy stood at Brenna's side, surprisingly dry-eyed. A small hole had already been dug in the ground beneath the giant tree, the earth placed in a neat pile beside it.

Brenna pulled Timmy close to her and began to speak. "Thanks, everybody, for coming. As you all know, Timmy's little friend Rocky has gone on to live in the great parsley field in the sky. She was a good and loving friend, and it is only fitting that we lay her to rest with the proper ceremony."

She opened the Bible and began to read from the Twenty-third Psalm. " 'The Lord is my shepherd. . . .' "

"Who died?"

Everybody turned toward Aunt Dottie, who was looking around with a confused expression.

Claire moved to stand next to her aunt, her high heels stabbing into the soft ground.

"Timmy's pet guinea pig died, Aunt Dottie. We're having a funeral for her."

Aunt Dottie sat back in her chair. "Well, then. That's nice. I know all about funerals. Weddings, too. Don't matter which—someone's always getting buried."

" 'I shall not want . . .' " Brenna continued, her cheeks reddening.

As she spoke, Pierce watched her, unable to look away. Something about her had changed. He wasn't sure what it was, although he thought it had something to do with the return of the old light in her eyes and the way she pushed back her shoulders. Whatever it was, she reminded him of the way she used to be: the girl with the bright eyes and indomitable faith in all of life's possibilities. The girl who made up new endings to sad movies and poured her father's coffee every morning and learned to drink it even though the smell of it made her nauseous; the girl who would have a funeral for a small rodent only because it would mean the world to her young nephew. But mostly, the girl who loved an old theater enough to make it her own regardless of the odds, and who still might, if she were willing to try, make it succeed. If anybody was able to pull off a leap of faith, it would be Brenna O'Brien. If only she could believe it herself. If only he could be here to see it.

His neck prickled, and he broke his gaze away from Brenna and turned toward Dooley. Dooley was looking at him hard, his brows knit and his teeth clenched.

Pierce leaned over and spoke quietly. "Is the box too heavy for you, Dooley? If it is, I don't mind holding it myself."

Dooley narrowed his eyes even more. "Stop staring at her. You look like a hunter with a five-point buck in your sights. You had your chance, but now she's spoken for."

Brenna's clear voice continued to read the psalm. " 'He maketh me to lie down in green pastures. . . .' "

Pierce looked down at the small box resting in his hand, the weight so small and so inconsequential compared to the weight of love in a young boy's heart. "You must not know Brenna very well if you think that either one of us could ever make her do anything. Changing her mind would be like counting raindrops—only harder."

Dooley grunted in a kind of acknowledgment. "You hurt her real bad once, and I've been here with her ever since, trying to pick up all the pieces. She's finally starting to snap out of it, so leave her alone. Let her go."

"I wish I could," Pierce said, watching Brenna as she was now, yet remembering her with longer hair spread over his chest as they quoted the dialogue from *Cat on a Hot Tin Roof.* "Believe me, I wish I could."

" ' . . . and I will dwell in the house of the Lord forever,' " Brenna finished, closing the Bible. "It's time now to lay Rocky to rest." She indicated Dooley and Pierce to move forward and place the shoe box in the grave.

When the box had been set inside the hole, Timmy approached with two bunches of parsley and gently laid them on top of the box. "Goodbye, Rocky," he said, his voice cracking.

They all remained silent while Timmy stood looking in the open grave for a long moment. Finally he turned to his mother and said, "I think I want a dog next."

There was a smattering of laughter, but Aunt Dottie's voice rose above it. "Whose wedding is this, anyway?"

"It's a funeral, remember, Aunt Dottie? We're burying Timmy's pet," Kathleen said as she helped Aunt Dottie up from her chair.

"I've been to lots of weddings. Never my own, sadly. I was at yours, Kathleen. I wore my pink silk dress with the large white polka dots. Never could find a hat to match, but I liked it anyway."

Kathleen began to lead Dottie toward the house, and Pierce fell in behind them, allowing Dooley to walk with Brenna. "Yes, you were at my wedding. And you did look lovely."

"Can't understand why people take vows at weddings when they never intend to keep them, though."

Kathleen stopped short, her face very still. "What are you talking about?"

Dottie continued walking. "Don't you know what polka dots are? They're big round spots and I like to wear them on dresses and hats. And I don't think I'd be allowed to wear either if you ever decide to put me in one of those old-people homes."

Pierce noticed that Brenna had stopped walking, too, and they all stood where they were, watching Aunt Dottie walk slowly through the grass toward the house.

A phone rang from inside and Colleen reappeared on the back steps, her hand held over the mouthpiece of a cordless phone. "Hey,

Brenna—Beau's on the phone, and he wants to talk to you. He says the painter called and he can be at the theater this afternoon. Wants to know when he can expect you."

Pierce watched as Brenna nearly skipped to the phone. He caught up to Aunt Dottie and took her arm. By the time they entered the kitchen, everybody was gathered around a smiling Brenna.

"Okay, everyone, this might be a little premature, but I wanted to let you all know my plans so you won't be surprised." She clasped her hands together and waited for everyone to be silent. "I'm closing the theater—just temporarily—to get some much-needed maintenance done. Then I'm going to have a grand reopening—with a huge celebration and lots of publicity. I'm thinking a *Gone With the Wind* theme would be perfect, and I've got lots of ideas, but I'm going to need everybody to pitch in. I'll give you free tickets to the reopening and half-price tickets in perpetuity to pay you back, because I'm not going to have a penny to spare to actually pay you." She smiled at the smattering of laughter.

She turned to Colleen. "If you could start scouring eBay for antebellum costumes for men and women, that would be a big help. And Claire, I'll talk about this in detail later, but I was hoping to have a date night every Friday, where parents can come and leave their kids in a fun, supervised play area while they watch a movie. I was hoping you could start talking to people—maybe even some of your sisters"—Brenna smiled and looked around—"who might be interested in earning some extra cash." She turned to Mary Margaret. "Since you're so handy with needle and thread, I was hoping you could help me with redecorating the lobby and creating some of the props for the reopening. And Kathleen . . . well, since you're good at everything, I thought maybe I could run some of my ideas by you and you could offer some suggestions."

Mary Margaret hugged Brenna tightly and leaned in closely. "You go, girl. I think you've found your voice for real."

Pierce stood back with Dottie while Brenna accepted hugs and cheek kisses from her sisters and their husbands and children, listening to the confusion of voices while everyone shouted out ideas and suggestions until Kathleen finally told everybody to be quiet so she could get out a notepad and pencil to write everything down.

Pierce felt Dottie sag on his arm, and he quickly found her a chair by the window and got her a glass of sweet tea. "Do you need to lie down?"

"No, I'm fine. My knees get tired now and again, that's all." She raised her glass in Brenna's direction. "About time, don't you think?"

"About time for what?"

"For that girl to use the good sense she was born with." She blinked at him behind her thick glasses. "Speaking of using good sense, when are you going to stop this business about her marrying that Gambrel boy? Don't get me wrong—he's a good catch. But he's not the one for her."

"Why would you say that, Miss Dottie?" He felt itchy under his collar, and twisted his head so he wouldn't have to meet her eyes.

"How's the old doctor?"

Pierce looked back, not really sure if she had forgotten his question or if she knew exactly what she was doing by changing the subject.

"He's well, thank you. They've had a two-bedroom unit open up, so he'll finally be moving in two weeks. I think he'll feel better about the whole move once he's settled in."

"Did you tell him I have the letter?"

"No, Miss Dottie. I haven't had the chance yet. But I will. Can I tell him who it's from?"

She smiled softly, transforming her face so that for a moment Pierce felt that he'd caught a glimpse of the young beauty she had once been. "He'll know."

He sat up straighter. "Miss Dottie. Did you and my father . . . well, did you and he ever have a love affair?"

"Have you seen the movie?"

At Pierce's confused expression, she added, "You know, *Love Affair*?"

Pierce contemplated the old woman in front of him, again wondering if she really were confused or simply avoiding what she didn't want to discuss. "The old one with Irene Dunne and Charles Boyer or the remake?"

"The old one, of course. The remakes are never as good."

"I'd have to agree with you there. And, yes, I've seen them both. Very sad story."

Aunt Dottie nodded sagely. "According to Hollywood, the best love stories are those that end badly. Don't see why people seem to think that's the way it should be in real life."

Pierce sat up and ran his fingers under his collar again. "What do you mean?"

Dottie leaned forward, her eyes narrowed. "Do you really believe that Scarlett got Rhett back? Or that Ilsa ever returned to Casablanca for Rick?" When Pierce didn't respond, she said, "I don't think so either." She leaned even closer. "But I do believe that a love can be saved by a single letter if only the person it's meant for is strong enough to open it."

"It's a love letter?"

"Terrible movie, that. *Love Letter*. Wasn't sure if it was supposed to be a drama or a comedy. Didn't like the ending at all."

Pierce leaned back in his chair and allowed his lungs to slowly fill before letting the air out again. "You watch a lot of movies."

"Yes, I do. Always have. Your mother liked movies a lot. She used to give me a discount on my tickets when I came to the theater because I came so often."

"My mother worked at the Majestic?"

"Her grandparents owned it for years. They were the ones who put that old German clock in the lobby. They'd inherited it from some relative, but it wouldn't fit in the house, so they put it in the theater instead. Guess it was easier to sell the theater with the clock than move it." She laughed with a girlish giggle that made him look at her again, trying to see what he'd seen before.

Pierce looked down at his hands, so different from his father's short, blunt fingers. "I didn't know that. My father . . . well, we've never really talked a lot about my mother or her family."

"And why is that, dear?"

Pierce glanced around, hoping somebody would come to his rescue, but everybody was still milling around Brenna while Kathleen jotted ideas down on her notepad. He rubbed his hands on his thighs. "Uh, mostly because she left us when I was a little boy and we never heard from her again."

Dottie took a delicate sip of iced tea. "And you think that meant she didn't love you."

Pierce scratched his neck and stood. "Miss Dottie, I need to leave. Will you be okay right here?"

"No, I won't. Please take me over to all the commotion and find me a seat. I hate not knowing what's going on."

Repressing a sigh, Pierce helped Aunt Dottie stand, then led her to the table where everybody had gathered. As he gently grabbed her elbow to lower her into a chair, she faced him, blinking her magnified green eyes. "Sometimes walking away is the only way a person can show how much they really love someone."

Dottie sat and turned away while Pierce stood still for a long moment, her words like fragments of glass scraping at his memories. Finally he stepped back and said his good-byes and left, all the while wondering why he hadn't dismissed the ramblings of an old woman, but instead had found himself wishing with a glimmer of hope that somehow she had spoken the truth.

Still in her funeral clothes, Brenna sat at the card table in her room with her opened scrapbook in front of her. Gently she slid a yellowed envelope out of the acid-free plastic sleeve and held it in the palm of her hand. She plucked at the old wax seal, testing it and teasing it as if it were a snake in a hole, waiting with dreaded anticipation for it to pop out at her.

She slid her fingernail around the seal and along the envelope flap. Her fingernail found a small opening at the top and she flicked it up, tearing a small hole at the corner. Enough of a hole to slide a letter opener in and slice it open.

She allowed the envelope to slip from her hand onto the table. She stared at it for a long time, trying to find the will to open it. Brenna felt sure she had changed; that she was again in control of where her life was headed for the first time since she'd been in the hospital and had nearly died. She was moving beyond her past: her bitter father and the loss of her mother, her love for Pierce, and her need to hold the possibilities of unopened letters in the palm of her hand.

Her fingers brushed across the front of the envelope, and Brenna willed them to pick it up, to tear at the envelope, and to pluck out the letter inside to read it. But her hands lay immobile beside the unopened letter on the table, as if unable to decide if knowing were truly better than wondering, and whether the imagination were always brighter than the truth.

Frustrated, Brenna slid her chair back and stood. After grabbing her purse and keys she left her room, banging on Mrs. Grodin's door just for spite as she passed by it. She thought of knocking on Nathan's door, but changed her mind when she heard the chain saw in the backyard. She rarely saw him in the boardinghouse they shared, since he worked for Mrs. Grodin whenever he wasn't working at the theater. She had teased him once about being a workaholic, but Nathan hadn't found it funny. She'd begun to see that his need to stay busy was for the same reason she did: to stay ahead of invisible demons that always seemed a mere step behind.

She parked her car in the driveway next to Pierce's car, knowing he'd be waiting inside with his father. Resisting the urge to check her lipstick in the rearview mirror, she headed toward the door and knocked.

Pierce opened it, seeming surprised to see her. "We weren't sure you'd come today."

She stepped inside the foyer to stand beside him. "I gave your dad my schedule, and this afternoon is definitely on it."

"No, we know that. It's just that after last time, we weren't sure you'd be back."

"Oh," she said, remembering storming out of the door before they could see her cry. "I just . . . well, I've decided I can't pass judgment until I know the whole story, and your dad won't tell us the whole story until we've finished reading the letters, so I'd better continue. There's only one left, you know."

"Actually, there're two. Aunt Dottie says she has one for him, too."

"How did you know about that?"

"She told me. She tells me lots of things, and I realized that if you're not listening carefully, you're going to miss something."

Brenna nodded, smiling reluctantly. "Yeah, I've noticed that." Tilting her head, she regarded him closely. "Do you think Aunt Dottie wrote all those letters? That she and your dad were lovers?"

He closed the door softly. "I asked her that very question yesterday, and she was very evasive. I have no idea what to think."

"I've asked your dad, too, and he's equally evasive. Maybe he wants us to draw our own conclusions by having us both read the letters. But if he and Dottie really were lovers, why can't he just tell us? It's not like it would have any effect on us now."

"Except there was a pregnancy."

"True—which means I could have an older cousin somewhere. But does it really matter? It's all in the past, and none of it means anything anymore."

He put a hand on her arm. "That's not true, Brenna. Our pasts make us who we are. As much as we try to run from them, they're always a part of us."

She pulled away. "I have to believe that's not true. Because if it is, then trying to change is pointless."

"No, Brenna, trying to change is just about learning from your past. There were good things, too, you know." He smiled softly. "Like the backseat of my dad's Buick." He touched her cheek briefly, then let his hand drop. "And watching old movies from the back row of the Royal Majestic. I'll never forget that. And I don't think you should, either."

She turned away without saying anything and walked into the living room, where Dr. McGovern waited in his recliner. She greeted him with a kiss on his cheek, settled down in her usual chair, and picked up the letter box. "This is the last one."

The doctor nodded. "I know. I counted them and I've been keeping track. And I'll admit that I even considered not reading it." His eyes reddened, and he dropped his gaze to his lap. "Except I realized that not knowing wouldn't change anything." He took two slow breaths, then looked back up at Brenna. "So go ahead. Let's read the last letter."

Slowly Brenna pulled the letter off the top of the opened stack. After hesitating briefly, she began to read.

May 30, 1942

Darling,

Do you remember in our eighth-grade history class when Mrs. Anderson taught us about Julius Caesar invading Gaul and crossing the Rubicon? Of all the things I've learned in school, I've always wondered why that particular lesson has stayed with me. And now I know, because I'm faced with my own Rubicon, and I must find all my courage to be able to move forward.

I've been told to conserve paper by writing in between the lines of old letters, but since I don't have any from you, I'm being extravagant and using a clean sheet I took from my father's desk. This will be my last letter to you. Your silence has told me everything that I need to know. Just know that I have loved you with all of my heart, and that I will until the day I die.

Remember the book of poetry you gave me? I've been reading it a lot lately, trying to hear your voice reading them to me, and trying to find comfort in them. But the only thing that would bring me comfort now would be your arms around me.

I've received a marriage offer, and I've said yes because I have to. I will start showing soon, and I don't want my family to be disgraced. When he asked me, I told him about the baby, and he was understanding and said that it didn't matter. He told me he loved me, and that was enough.

If you should return—and I will continue to pray that you do— I will acknowledge you on the street, but I will be a faithfully married woman and I will not seek you out, and I trust that you will do the same. The baby I carry will be my husband's, and I hope that you will never say or do anything to the contrary.

I will entrust your ring to my friend for safekeeping and ask her to return it to you when you come home. But I will keep your book of poetry and will cherish it in secret always, because it will remind me of the happiest days of my life.

I'm going to borrow from Shakespeare, because I could not express any better the way I feel right now as I sit trying to close this final letter and attempting to keep my tears from smudging the ink. You see? I'm still the foolish girl you said you loved. There are some things I suppose will never change.

"I love thee, I love but thee with a love that shall not die. Till the sun grows cold and the stars are old."

Good-bye forever, my darling.
Me

Brenna looked up at Dr. McGovern, but his hands were held over his face. She dropped the letter and the box and moved toward him, knowing that no words of comfort existed to ease the heartache of an old heart.

A horrible gasp of air emitted from between his fingers, and Brenna looked away, unwilling to see a grown man cry as if the sun had suddenly disappeared from the sky. Her hands wandered aimlessly, like moths looking for light, but found nowhere to land. Folding them in her lap she dipped her head, horrified at what she was witnessing, yet completely impotent to fix it.

She felt a hand on her shoulder, and she turned to see Pierce standing by her side. "I think it best that you leave now. I'll take care of him."

She nodded, almost relieved. Standing, she said a brief good-bye to both of them, then left, nearly stumbling to the door. She'd walked almost six blocks before she realized she had headed in the wrong direction and left her car behind.

Brenna looked around, seeing her surroundings for the first time. She was in the town square, where they still had the maypole dance every May and where the World War monuments rose up from the earth like old warriors. Brenna walked toward the World War II obelisk and touched the brass plate with the list of names, wishing she knew the name of the woman who'd written the letters so that she could imagine the name added to the brass plaque. She hadn't been a soldier, yet the war had killed a part of her just the same. Slowly she slid down to the marble step and sat until she heard the courthouse bell ring the five-o'clock hour.

CHAPTER 21

It was almost dusk before Brenna returned for her car. His father had gone to bed to nap, and Pierce had sat out on the front porch to wait for her.

She was barefoot, carrying her sandals in one hand as she strolled slowly down the sidewalk. If he hadn't been expecting her, he would have thought it was a young girl walking toward him. There was still so much the same about her, and he wondered how she had managed to stay so young. Maybe the secret lay in the unopened letters she collected, a sort of Dorian Gray portrait in which all the troubles of the passing years laid waste to the paper and lives contained within the envelopes, leaving her own face unscathed. Dorian Gray had sold his soul for the privilege, and Pierce knew that Brenna's price for an uncluttered life had been almost as high.

She saw him, and he stood as she approached the front steps. On impulse he held out his hand to her. "Come with me. I'll show you the greatest seat in the house for watching the sunset."

Brenna surprised him by slipping her hand into his, the same slight hand with the bitten fingernails he'd remembered, and he led her to the backyard. The house had been built on a slight rise, and previous owners must have cultivated something from the earth that now lay stale and untended under the late-summer sun. But what had once been a man's hard labor was now Pierce's clearing to watch the clouds battle it out with the stars to turn the day into night.

Two ancient Adirondack chairs with a matching side table had been placed in a small dirt circle where grass refused to grow, and which Pierce had found convenient for wedging his beer cans into for impromptu coasters.

They sat down and Brenna pulled her bare feet up, wrapping her arms around her knees. Pierce noticed the chipped pink nail polish on her toes, and the red velvet-and-lace strap of her bra where her tank top had slipped off her shoulder. Brenna O'Brien had always been about surprises and contradictions—an irresistible combination, if one could overlook her stubbornness to see things she didn't want to see.

"How's your dad?" She held a cupped hand over her forehead to block the fading sun from her eyes.

"He was pretty upset, but he didn't want to talk about it. He said he was tired, and I brought him upstairs to nap. I just checked on him before you arrived and he was still sleeping."

She nodded. "At first I felt so angry with him for not writing her back. And then I realized that he'd never received those letters—but why? There's so much to this story that we don't know, and I'm not sure who to ask, or even if I have any business asking. I've tried with both your dad and Aunt Dottie, and neither one of them will tell me anything. But this horrible thing happened to your father and another woman, and I can't believe that somehow, even after all this time, we can't fix it."

Pierce leaned over the arm of his chair and snagged a handful of grass outside the circle of dirt. "You can't fix everything, Brenna. Some things just need to stay broken while the rest of the world marches on."

"Do you really believe that?"

He let a blade of grass drift back down to the ground. "Do you really believe that everything is fixable?"

She turned away and looked up, where shades of purple had moved in to mix with the reds and oranges of the summer sky. "I don't know what I believe anymore. I just know that you terrify me, while Dooley makes me feel safe. And that I love going to work in my theater every day, and the thought of not having it anymore is unbearable to me. And that I realize that when I imagine my future twenty years from now, I don't see anything different from the way it is right now, right this very minute."

"And that's a good thing?"

She faced him, and he was surprised to see tears in her eyes. "Yes, Pierce. That's a very good thing. A life without pain and grief and heartache is a very good thing. I've seen it, done it, been there and bought the T-shirt. I can't go back to that. Ever."

A burst of whirring erupted from cicadas hidden in the boxwoods and trees around them, singing their last chorus before nightfall. The sound had always reminded Pierce of the nighttime prayer his mother taught him. *Now I lay me down to sleep. I pray the Lord my soul to keep. If I should die before I wake, I pray the Lord my soul to take.* It was as if the cicadas were shouting out their glory one last time in case they didn't make it through the night. It saddened him, but it encouraged him, too, reminding him that it was never too late to find the one thing in your life that made you shout with being alive.

He grabbed another fist of grass. "My wife was once sent on an assignment to South Africa to do a story on the diamond trade. She found it incredibly enlightening—in more ways than one. It was on that trip that she met the cameraman who is now her husband. But besides a new boyfriend, she also brought back a lot of interesting information. Do you know how diamonds are made?"

She gazed steadily at him, the light turning her green eyes transparent.

He didn't wait for her to answer. "They're made of a single element—carbon. But, over millions of years, the carbon had to undergo incredible pressure—something like a minimum of four hundred pounds per square inch—and cook to at least seven hundred degrees. The amazing thing is that if there's not enough pressure or heat, instead of a diamond, plain old graphite is made. Imagine that—instead of the world's most indestructible and beautiful thing, you get just graphite. Something to make pencils with. Sure, pencils are nice and useful. But they aren't diamonds."

"Why are you telling me this?"

He opened his fingers, letting the grass fall slowly to the ground. A few stubborn blades clung to his skin, much as he would imagine old dreams finally leaving the places they had grown up in. "I don't know, Brenn. I really don't know." He met her eyes. "It's not important. I'll be gone in another month or so and you can forget me again."

Her hand reached for the silver medallions hanging on a long chain around her neck. "I never forgot you."

"But none of that matters anymore, right?"

Brenna didn't say anything for a moment and stared at the medallions in her hand. "I'm glad you came back—I am. I'm glad we had a chance to talk about what happened and to understand that we can't blame each other. And your being here has also helped me realize that I need to make some changes. You've helped me see that the Majestic is my passion, and that I need to fight for it."

The sky shifted colors, the sinking sun slowly stealing the golds and yellows and leaving only purples and grays to entertain the moon. She stood as if to move closer to the sky. "I had good news today. Somebody called from the National Park Service to ask me about my theater. They're going to send some people to come take a look and evaluate it from a historical perspective. He said that if it's listed on the National Register, I'd be eligible for tax credits and other incentives that will help me with finances to restore it, and to even protect it in the future." She pulled her shirt strap up over her shoulder, then folded her arms across her chest. "I tried contacting them once, to see what I needed to do to get it listed, but I didn't follow through. I'm not really sure why. It was like I was asleep and now I'm not."

"And you think it's all about your passion for your theater."

"Yeah. I do. And it's enough for me."

"What's going to happen if you lose the Majestic?"

She closed her eyes. "I'm not going to let that happen." Her fingers shifted again to the medallion around her neck. "The phone call from the Park Service from out of the blue means that finally one of my saints is listening."

Pierce stood, too, and moved to stand next to her. "Yeah. You must be right." His eyes followed her to the show of light and shadow in the sky. Softly, he quoted, " 'Play the sunset. Close your eyes. One, two, three, four.' "

Bridget looked at him, her eyes widening in surprise. "From *Mr. Holland's Opus*. Nineteen ninety-four, right?"

" 'Ninety-five. Close."

She faced the sky again. "So you're still watching movies and memorizing dialogue to impress me."

"Something like that." He watched her cheek crease with a smile. "Watching movies reminds me of you. Of being with you. It's like grilled cheese and tomato soup. Or fried chicken with biscuits and gravy. It's nice to be reminded once in a while of how young and naive we once were."

She didn't say anything, but she stopped smiling. Leaning toward her again, he said, " 'One man's sunset is another man's dawn. I don't know what's out there beyond those hills. But if you ride yonder . . . head up, eyes steady, heart open . . . I think one day you'll find that you're the hero you've been looking for.' "

She looked back at him with knitted brows.

"From *An American Tail*. Don't tell me you never saw it. It's a classic."

"Of course I've seen it—it's animated. I have a bunch of nieces and nephews, and I've seen just about every animated movie made in the last fifteen years. I . . . I was just surprised that you'd seen it."

He shrugged. "I lived down the street from an old theater in San Francisco. I'd go every Sunday afternoon and watch whatever was showing. The owner had really eclectic tastes."

She laughed. "That's pretty funny. You spend all your time building newer and bigger cinemas, but you still prefer watching movies in old theaters. I hope your boss doesn't find out."

"Me, too," he said softly.

"Did your wife enjoy going?"

"No. I always went alone. Got my Junior Mints, Coke, and popcorn with extra butter and watched movies all afternoon."

She smiled again but looked away. "I always get the same thing. Still. It's odd how some things stay the same while everything else changes."

A last strip of light streaked across the sky as the crickets began with their night noise. He moved closer to her. "Some things will never change, no matter how much we want them to."

She looked at him, startled to see him so close. "Don't, Pierce. Please."

He touched the side of her face, just to see if it still felt the same. "Why? It doesn't matter anymore, remember?" He brushed her lips with his, and her skin tightened under his fingers.

She pressed forward, her arms winding around his neck as she kissed him back, and he was seventeen again, under a younger sky—a sky filled with the same stars.

He felt her break away and watched as she stepped back. "My father was right about you." Her chest rose and fell, as if she'd run around the house and back. "He told me you'd only break my heart. And you did. And now all I've got left is a little piece I managed to keep whole, and I'm saving it for my theater and my family. Don't take what's left."

Pierce took a deep breath, trying to order all the thoughts slamming through his head. "And you, Brenna, will always love your fears more than anything else. Let them go."

They stood staring at each other in the gathering gloom of nightfall until she turned and walked quickly away, leaving her abandoned sandals in the dirt clearing that encircled the chairs.

Brenna gathered with her sisters at Kathleen's house, her scrapbook dutifully opened in front of her. She'd even brought photographs to attach to new pages that didn't contain old letters: old pictures of her theater that she'd copied from the ones Dr. McGovern had given to her and that Nathan was having framed to be showcased in the lobby on the night of her grand reopening.

It had been nearly three weeks since she'd last seen Pierce or his father. She'd called several times to check on the doctor, but hadn't spoken with Pierce at all. Claire, who knew all the town's gossip apparently by osmosis, had learned that Pierce had finally moved his father into the assisted-living facility and then returned to the West Coast for a short business trip. Brenna was simultaneously relieved and disappointed, and refused to dwell on either possibility. The Royal Majestic was taking up all her time, and she was glad of the distraction.

But she dreamed of Pierce. Disturbing dreams filled with a sky at sunset, his voice angry and challenging, his hands strong and persuasive, pulling her down to an earth that had suddenly become cool, dark water filled with stars. It was only after having dreamed the same dream for the third time that Brenna realized that the stars were from the mural in the theater—stars she no longer noticed because their yellow brightness had been extinguished by years of rain running from the roof and onto the ceiling.

Dottie shared a table with her and was, as usual, decorating blank pages with stickers and die cuts with no apparent rhyme or reason. She was also working on another batch of cabbage soup, and even all the potpourri and candles Kathleen had burning couldn't eradicate the odor. Apparently there was a family crisis brewing that nobody was aware of except for Dottie.

Brenna looked up from where she was spacing out her photographs for one of the pages. "Isn't Colleen coming?"

Kathleen and Mary Margaret shared a quick exchange before Mary Margaret answered. "She went over to Greenwood to use one of their Internet cafés. Apparently Bill took away her laptop because she was spending too much on eBay."

Kathleen added, "If Bill calls, we're to tell him Colleen's in the bathroom and she'll call him back."

Brenna looked at her two sisters. "And you two are okay with this?"

Mary Margaret finished sticking down a picture of her and Richard with their two youngest children atop an elephant in India. As far as Brenna could tell, it was the only photo so far in the album. "Of course not. She knows it's wrong, so telling her won't work. We'll probably have to wait for the crash-and-burn phase for her to come to us, and then we can help bandage her up and make things better."

Brenna grinned at the matter-of-fact attitude, realizing that they were absolutely on track. Years of sisterhood had honed their skills of family bonding and subterfuge. "I guess I should feel guilty. She was able to find the most unbelievable dresses for us on eBay for the grand reopening—which, by the way, I'll be calling y'all for fittings as soon as they come in. Oh, and she also found the most authentic Yankee and Confederate uniforms for Nathan and Dooley. I'll let them fight over who gets what."

Mary Margaret came to stand behind her, looking over her shoulder. "I'm almost finished with the drapery panels for the water-stained wallpaper in the lobby. I'm wondering if I should have bought more fabric and just covered the whole lobby."

Brenna shook her head. "No—we really just wanted something temporary to hide the stain. We were going to pull down the wallpaper and repaint, but the painter said the plaster under the paper had been damaged and we'd have to replace the entire wall. Since I can't afford that yet, we decided to do something cosmetic for now. The rest of the wallpaper is good enough. Gives kind of a vintage feel, you know?"

Mary Margaret reached down and picked up one of the old theater photos. "It's nice to see you putting something else in here besides your old letters. Who took these?"

"Pierce's mother took most of them. Her grandparents used to own the theater—did you know that?"

"I might have once. Makes sense, I guess, seeing what Pierce does for a living now. She must have inspired him in some way."

Kathleen's husband, John, joined them in the kitchen. He approached his wife's chair and bent to kiss her cheek. He laid his hands on her shoulders and gently rubbed them as she placed her hands over his. Brenna looked away, feeling peculiarly as if she'd been spying on an intimate moment between new lovers. As long as Brenna could remember, it had been that way between Kathleen and John, even now, after so many years of marriage and five children.

Mary Margaret picked up another photo. "You've got eleven pictures—are you going to have enough pages for them all?"

"Actually, I've got twelve." Brenna laid them out on the table, surprised to realize she had only eleven. "I know there's twelve—I counted them when I gave them to Nathan to make copies. That's odd." She reached for her bag on the floor and began searching inside. "It must be in here—and if it's not, then I must have somehow dropped it when I picked the pile off of my desk at the theater before putting them in my bag."

She stacked the photos and began looking at each one, trying to determine which picture might be missing. She'd gone through it twice before she realized which one. "That's funny—I would think I'd find it first. It's the photo I've enlarged the biggest because I want it to go on a wall by itself. It's a picture of a protest here in the sixties of a controversial movie and, incidentally, Pierce's mother happens to be in a corner of the photo."

Mary Margaret lifted the back cover of the scrapbook to look underneath it. "It couldn't have gone far—I'm sure you'll find it."

"I'll ask Nathan about it when I get back to the theater. He's the one in charge of getting them framed."

Claire pushed back from her chair and headed for the triple-layer chocolate torte Kathleen had made. She picked up a large knife and began cutting. "To hell with my diet. I can't take the stress anymore." She placed a large slab of cake on a plate and picked up a fork. "I'm sitting here all these hours poring over my scrapbooks so Mary Sanford will have all these memories stored forever; I'm spending tons of money on her outfits and lessons for all the pageants; I'm spending all my time when I'm not working at the hospital chauffeuring her around to all her events. And what do I get? Nothing, I tell you. Absolutely nothing. Not even a single thank-you. All I get from Mary Sanford are the words 'I'd rather stay home and play with my friends.' Can you imagine?" She shoved a huge bite of cake into her mouth.

Nobody said anything, and Claire remained by the cake eating, helping herself to a second piece when she finished the first. "Do you have any Diet Coke, Kathleen? I've had enough sweet tea to make my eyeballs float."

Kathleen went to the refrigerator while Brenna focused on her scrapbook, making sure to save room for the missing picture. She organized two facing pages with four of the photos, and saw she had enough room to write something next to a photo of the Royal Majestic on its opening night. The gowns and hairstyles shimmered with old glamour, while the couple in the foreground seemed to be posing in the middle of a dance step. Brenna pulled back, an idea forming in her head.

"Does anyone remember that quote about 'the light fantastic'? I know it's about dancing, and the excitement of going out on the town at night, but I can't remember exactly how it goes. I thought it would be a beautiful quote to caption this picture."

Kathleen stuck a wedge of lemon into Claire's glass of Diet Coke and handed it to her. "It's from 'L'Allegro' by John Milton. It's in the book I was telling you about last time—the poetry book with that Emily Dickinson poem you were looking for."

"Do you know where it is? I'd love to find that quote."

"It's still in Marie's bedroom, on the bookshelf by her bed. I'll go get it."

While Kathleen was gone, John cut himself a piece of cake and stood with Claire as he ate it. "Peyton Charles was great at Friday's game. Two touchdowns in the first quarter—really amazing."

"I know—and I missed it. I had to take Mary Sanford to Birmingham for the Little Miss Sweet Potato Pageant. Buzz told me all about it, though."

Kathleen reappeared with a leather-bound book, its binding wearing off at the edges. "Here it is," she said as she handed it to Brenna.

John moved closer to Brenna's table. "How ancient is that book, Kath? I remember you reading from it to our oldest children, and I thought the book looked old then."

"I really have no idea. I've had it for as long as I remember. Maybe Mama gave it to me."

John reached for the book and opened the front cover. "Maybe it was your mother's. The copyright date is nineteen forty-one."

As he handed it back to Brenna, a small folded note fell out from between the pages, landing in the middle of Brenna's scrapbook. Without thinking, she picked it up and unfolded it. She'd only read the words *Kathleen—when can I see you again?* before Kathleen snatched the note from her.

"That's from an old boyfriend. Don't think you should be reading it." Her voice was tight, belying the smile she wore.

John put his arm around her shoulders. "Sweetie, I don't remember you ever having a boyfriend besides me. Who's it from?"

Kathleen shrugged dismissively and shoved the note into the pocket of her skirt. "Nobody you know."

Claire grinned wickedly. "Is it the guy you always met up with at the beach?"

Kathleen flushed hotly but didn't answer. "Can I get anybody something to drink? John brought us a bottle of wine, if anybody would like some."

John glanced at his watch and kissed Kathleen on the cheek. "Gotta go—boys' poker night." He turned to Mary Margaret. "I promise not to tell Richard's congregation that he's gambling—unless he fleeces me again, like he did last time."

Everyone pretended to work on their scrapbooks until he left. With the sound of the front door closing, Claire asked, "Is that note from

Paul, Kathleen? Isn't that the name of the guy from the beach house next door to the one we always rented in Dauphin Island?"

A pale white line formed itself around Kathleen's mouth. "Yes, actually. It was."

Claire leaned back in her chair and whistled. "Whoo-eee. He was fine. Real fine. I think that he was one of the reasons Daddy said we couldn't go to the beach anymore."

Mary Margaret leaned forward on her elbows. "Didn't he come to Indianola once—right after you and John got married? I remember you telling me that he had somehow found out you were getting married and had come to see you to see if he could change your mind. But by then it was too late."

Kathleen stood by the stove, her back to her aunt and sisters, and stirred the pot of cabbage. "Something like that. It was so long ago that I barely remember."

Brenna watched her older sister stir the pot, seeming not to notice the noxious odor drifting up to her face. "Have you ever wondered what you would have done if he had arrived earlier?"

Kathleen's arm stopped. "I supposed Paul will always be my one regret. But I try not to dwell on regrets or thinking of what might have been. John and I have had a good marriage. How can I say I wish things had been different?"

Claire sat up. "Read the letter, Kathleen. It's been so long since I've heard a love note—unless Brenna wants to share any from Dooley—I'd love to remember what young love is all about."

Brenna noticed the stiffening of Kathleen's shoulders as Mary Margaret stood. "That's private, Claire—leave her alone. Actually, I want to hear the 'light fantastic' quote. Did you find it, Brenna?"

Brenna flipped through the pages, noticing the worn edges and stains on the paper as if this were a much-loved and treasured book. Almost toward the end, she found the poem and read it aloud.

> And love to live in dimple sleek;
> Sport that wrinkled Care derides,
> And Laughter holding both his sides.
> Come, and trip it as you go

On the light fantastic toe;
And in thy right hand lead with thee
The mountain-nymph, sweet Liberty;

She smiled. "It's perfect. And I think that 'Tripping the Light Fantastic' will be the theme for the reopening. We can use it on our tickets and brochures—even the invitations I'm going to be sending out."

Mary Margaret nodded. "If you like, I can stencil it in gold on the wall next to the picture. I think it will make a beautiful statement. Then, after the reopening, we can frame a new picture of you and Dooley in your antebellum duds in a grand waltz stance to hang next to it."

Kathleen turned, a tight smile on her face. "That's an excellent idea. I'm surprised Brenna hadn't already thought about it."

Brenna looked down at the book again, wondering absently if the brown spot in the corner was from an old teardrop. Kathleen was right: Brenna *had* thought of the idea, only it hadn't been Dooley with her when she'd pictured it in her mind.

She looked up. "It's settled then. Two weeks from tomorrow we will be genteel Southern ladies and we will all be tripping the light fantastic."

"Look out, Indianola," said Mary Margaret as she put her arm around Brenna.

Brenna smiled but kept her eyes focused on Kathleen by the stove, the word *regret* reverberating in her head, and remembered Kathleen in church praying for forgiveness for the dead. For the first time, Brenna saw her oldest sister as not only a surrogate mother, but as a woman who'd had a life before Brenna: a woman who knew something of regret.

CHAPTER 22

Pierce paused outside the Royal Majestic, Brenna's yellow sandals latched onto his fingers. He read the sign posted out front: THE ROYAL MAJESTIC IS TEMPORARILY CLOSED! JOIN US FOR OUR GRAND RE-OPENING SATURDAY, SEPTEMBER 5. TICKETS ON SALE NOW! Pierce looked up to where a banner had been hung over the archway entrance. COME TRIP THE LIGHT FANTASTIC; CELEBRATING SIXTY-SEVEN YEARS AS INDI-ANOLA'S PREMIER ENTERTAINMENT VENUE.

"Did I hang it straight?"

Pierce started as Nathan appeared from the dim foyer, a hammer and nails in his hands.

"Looks great. Did you come up with the wording, too?"

"Nope—that would be Brenna and Dooley. She's quite the creative one, and Dooley . . . well, who would have thought that he'd be such a marketing genius?"

Pierce nodded. "Who would have thought?" He held up Brenna's sandals. "She left these at my dad's, and I've been meaning to return them. But with my dad's move and then my trip out to the West Coast for a few weeks, I never got around to it. Is she here?"

"Sorry—you just missed her. She's having her final fitting for her Scarlett O'Hara dress. She made me and Dooley draw straws as to which uniform we were supposed to wear, and I lost."

Pierce raised an eyebrow. "So, you're going to be the guy in gray?"

"Nope. I lost, remember? I'll be in Federal blue."

"Hey, just be glad she's not making you wear a corset and pan-talettes. In third grade she had me dress up as a sheep so she could be Little Bo Peep at the school talent show."

Nathan shook his head. "Man, that's harsh."

"Tell me about it. Mark Whittier still has the scar on his face where I hit him for baaing at me." Pierce's attention was drawn to the framed photographs behind Nathan. He moved into the foyer, recognizing the prints hanging on the wall. "These are the photos I gave Brenna, aren't they? The ones my mother took."

Nathan paused for a moment before following Pierce. "Yep. They sure are. It was Brenna's idea to blow them up and frame them for the reopening. Her sister did this fancy lettering, and I thought it turned out real nice."

Pierce stood in front of the picture with the two people dancing and read the stenciling: TRIPPING THE LIGHT FANTASTIC. He smiled to himself. "I remember my father reading me the entire poem when I was a kid. 'Come, and trip it as you go, on the light fantastic toe.' That's as much as I ever remembered."

"That's the theme for the whole evening; it's on all the invitations and stuff."

"Yeah, I saw that on my dad's. I hope Brenna understands that I'm going to have to come with him. He can't get around by himself."

"She knows. She was going to send out a separate invitation to you, but I told her to save herself a stamp." Nathan held up his hand and shook his head. "What I meant was that I knew you'd be coming with your dad. We're watching our pennies, and I figured that was a small expense she could do without."

"Thanks. I think." Pierce glanced around for the one print that had stayed in his mind from the first time he saw it. "Where's the one of my mother? There was a protest and she was in a corner of the photo."

Nathan hooked his thumbs into his belt loops. "I don't know. I remember it being in the stack you gave us, but I don't know what happened to it. I put in a complaint at the photo shop, since they must have misplaced it or something. I'm sure it'll turn up."

Pierce eyed Nathan, wondering again why the man seemed so familiar. "Okay, I give up. What's going on?"

"What do you mean?"

"Well, you haven't been belligerent or inadvertently hostile since I've been here. Did you have a lobotomy, or have you somehow decided I'm not as much of a jerk as you first thought?"

Nathan crossed his arms over his chest. "It's only that I know that the National Park Service doesn't just happen to call somebody who's in financial straits and who might be able to benefit from some incentives the government could offer."

Pierce raised both eyebrows but didn't say anything.

"Seems to me somebody must have planted a bug in somebody's ear to get the ball rolling."

"And you're mentioning this to me because . . . ?"

"Oh, don't worry about it. I won't tell Brenna. I just figure that somebody who'd do something like that couldn't be all bad."

Pierce simply looked up at the freshly painted ceiling. "The thought of this place being boarded up or worse—turned into loft apartments—makes me ill. My mother's grandparents used to own it. I guess that's why I've always felt a strong connection. I would hope that it would be around for more generations to enjoy."

"So, it's all about the theater and nothing to do with Brenna?"

Pierce walked out of the foyer and turned around to look at the smooth stucco facade of the old building. "It's always been about her. I don't have a single memory of this theater that doesn't include her." He eyed Nathan again. "But I have no idea who might have put a bug in somebody's ear. I've been out of town."

"Right. Well. I hope it works out. By the way, the people from the Park Service are going to be here the day of the reopening. Hopefully we'll have some good news to announce that night."

Pierce didn't respond. Instead he asked, "Have we met? Ever since you've come to town, I've had a feeling that I've seen you someplace before."

"Nope. I never forget a face, and I know for sure that I've never seen you."

"You've never been to Indianola?"

Nathan's face remained blank. "Nope. Never. But I will say that there's something familiar about you—but not in the way you're thinking. You remind me of Brenna. You both sort of have that desperate look about you—like you're looking for something but can't find it. Maybe it's because you were both raised without your mothers."

"How did you know about my mother?"

Nathan shrugged. "Small town. People talk."

Pierce studied him for a moment longer before letting his gaze drift to the large grandfather clock that had been pulled into the middle of the foyer. Its top had been draped with a flower-covered sheet, making it look like a tall blooming tree in spring. He remembered what Dottie had said to him, about the clock belonging to his mother's family. He approached it, admiring the burled mahogany and elaborate brass fittings. "This is a beautiful clock. How on earth did you move it?"

"Wasn't easy, that's for sure. We had about eight men—and Brenna."

Pierce rubbed his hand against the wood before turning to go, almost forgetting the sandals in his hand. "Oh, I don't want to forget these. You can just stick them in her office. She'll know where they came from."

Nathan took them with the crook of his finger. "Sure thing."

"And tell Brenna I'll be here for the reopening. That way you'll save me a phone call to RSVP."

Nathan tipped his ubiquitous cowboy hat. "I'll do that."

Pierce nodded again, then left, still not able to shake the feeling that he had met Nathan before, and wondering how an almost-stranger could name the look Pierce had seen facing him in the mirror ever since he was eight years old.

Brenna looked up from her bedroom mirror at the tapping on her door. Narrowly missing a small side table with her wide hoop skirt, she practiced sashaying as she went to answer it. Throwing it as wide as she could with her skirts in the way, she smiled brightly at Dooley, looking uncomfortable and itchy in his Confederate gray uniform. "You look great! I'm starting to see what makes all those women swoon over a man in uniform."

Dooley stuck his finger into his collar and gave a scratch. "Yeah, well, they don't have to wear the thing. And these boots are killing me. I just hope I don't accidentally slice off somebody's leg with this saber. Are you sure I have to wear it?"

"You look wonderful—and don't you dare take off the sword. It gives you a distinguished flair—just the foil for my simpering Southern belle." She tried to execute a twirl, but got stuck between the open door and her dresser.

She ushered him inside. "I'm just about ready—I need you to put my pearls around my neck. I've been trying for the last fifteen minutes, and I can't get the clasp."

He moved to stand behind her at the mirror and took off his gloves to pick up the string of pearls. Gently he placed them on her neck and clasped them behind her. Their eyes met in the mirror as Dooley let his hands rest on her shoulders. She stared at their image in the glass as if it were a portrait and their identities unknown. She'd like to think they were a couple in love, reunited at the end of the war, much as she imagined the lives of the writers of her letter collection. But in this case she knew the characters in the story; knew they weren't in love and didn't have any real drama between them that would even be worth writing about. And she couldn't quite decide if that was a good thing or a bad thing.

She smiled at him. "You're a good friend, Doo, for dressing up and playing escort. I'll pay you back one day—promise."

He smiled back but his eyes were flat. "Can't wait." He stuck his fingers inside the neck of his jacket again. "Damn, this uniform's hot. And I'd better not be the only guy wearing one."

"Well, Nathan will be wearing his—just a different color. He won't be dressed yet, because it's still early. Speaking of which, he called about an hour ago. The guys from the Park Service are at the theater now. I waited around for them all morning, but they got delayed in New Orleans and only just got there." She glanced around for the little satin purse she'd bought to go with her dress. Spying it on the bed, she picked it up and threw a lipstick inside. "So, to make a long story short, that's why I had you get dressed now instead of later. I knew it would take me forever to get dressed, so I figured I'd go ahead and get it done before I headed back to the theater and see what they have to say. And there's no way I could have gone alone—so thanks for coming." She placed her hand on her corseted abdomen. "I don't know if it's the nerves or this danged corset, but I feel like I could throw up."

Dooley raised his eyebrows. "Well, in that case, maybe we should take your car."

Brenna elbowed him as she squeezed past to get to the door. "Like I would fit. As it is, I'm thinking I might have to ride in the bed of your pickup truck if all these petticoats are coming with me."

He held the door for her and helped push her through the opening. "I'm sure we'll make it work. Can't say I don't love a challenge."

"Then let's go," she said as she walked past him toward the stairs. She banged on Mrs. Grodin's door out of habit as she passed by, then waited for Dooley to open the main door for her before the ordeal of squeezing herself into the front of Dooley's truck.

It was nearly half an hour later by the time they made it to the theater. Brenna kept glancing at her watch in frustration. She'd really wanted to spend the time with the men from the Park Service to point out all the fine elements of the theater. She'd hated leaving before they got there, but she needed to be ready to play hostess on what she hoped would be one of the most important nights of her life. She glanced at her watch again. Her sisters would be arriving any minute, and she'd barely get there in time to double-check on the decorations and schedule for the evening.

Dooley put a warm hand over hers. "Stop fussing. I can almost hear that hamster wheel in your head. Everything will be fine. You've got me, Nathan, Beau, and your sisters to help out, so just have a glass of wine when we get there and relax. Remember, you're supposed to be charming potential investors tonight, not worrying."

She was about to respond when she noticed his face tighten as he stared at something straight ahead. She followed his gaze and blinked twice, as if to make sure that the two fire trucks blocking the street in front of the Royal Majestic were really there. The lights in the marquee were dark, as was the rest of the building. Broad spotlights from the two trucks threw light over the scene like confetti, reflecting off the glass ticket window and the freshly painted gold columns.

Twin fingers of panic and despair wrapped themselves around her, real enough that she found it difficult to breathe. She registered no flames shooting out of the roof at the same time she spotted all four of her sisters outside on the sidewalk in their antebellum gowns, looking like wilted gardenias in the summer heat. Nathan and Beau seemed to be having an animated conversation with Mr. Archer, the fire marshal. He stood stoic and immobile, much as he had appeared to her as her eighth-grade civics teacher, occasionally shaking his head to whatever it was that Nathan and Beau were saying to him.

"Oh, God, this can't be good," Brenna said, clutching the wool sleeve of Dooley's jacket. "Help get me out of this truck."

Dooley leaped from his seat and rushed over to Brenna's side. She was sure the sight of her with her skirts over her head and Dooley trying to wedge her out of her seat would have been a humorous one if only she didn't feel the way she'd felt the first time she'd run to her mother's room for comfort and found it empty.

When Nathan spotted her, he ran across the street as if to stop her before she came any closer. He grabbed hold of her shoulders, his large hands gentle. "I tried to call you on your cell so you wouldn't have to see this, but I didn't get an answer."

Without taking her eyes off the entrance to the theater, where firemen were coming and going, she held up the silly piece of satin and lace she'd been using for her purse. "It wouldn't fit." She tore her gaze away from the theater and met Nathan's eyes, surprised to see him looking as sad and panicked as she felt. "What's going on? Where are the Park Service people?"

"I'm sorry, Brenna, it all happened so quickly. I waited until the last minute to call you, because I thought I could handle the situation. But it got out of control." He took his cowboy hat off and rubbed his fingers through his hair.

Dooley stepped forward. "What got out of control? What's going on?" He began unbuttoning his jacket and then placed it around Brenna's shoulders before she realized she was shivering. Her sisters approached, forming a circle around them, their bright, flowing dresses a contrast to their tight and drawn faces.

Nathan's large Adam's apple bobbed before he spoke, sounding surprisingly like he was close to tears. "They've condemned the building, Brenna. The guys from the Park Service were all excited at first until they went up to the attic. They drilled a hole in the floor to get a better look at the structure underneath." He paused, as if unable to continue.

Dooley's chin stuck out, surprising Brenna with his show of determination. She wasn't sure if she'd ever seen a look on Dooley's face that wasn't a neutral or good-natured one. "Come on, Nathan. Not telling us everything isn't going to change anything, so just spit it out."

Nathan glanced at Brenna as if for confirmation, and she found the strength to nod. "Tell me, Nathan. I can take it." She was lying, of course; the truth was bound to wound her in ways she no longer thought possible. But already the numbness had begun to creep up on her, as frost does on winter windows, spreading silently until all the glass is covered, all sound and light diffused.

"Remember the storm last week and all the water we found in the attic? Well, we patched the roof, but apparently water's been coming inside for years. There's advanced wood rot on the supporting beams, and standing water near live electrical wires. They've already shut off the electricity to the building to avoid the risk of fire." He looked down at his boots. "Mr. Archer said it's a miracle that nothing's happened already." Reaching into his back jeans pocket, he pulled out a business card. "This here's from David Welch, one of the guys who were here this afternoon. He apologized for having to leave, but he'd still like to talk with you. He said he was impressed with what he saw and thinks there's still hope to restore it. Said something about helping you find a buyer who could afford to rehabilitate it."

Cars had started arriving for the grand reopening and were silently crawling toward them, until a fireman directing traffic explained what was going on and they drove away. The sound of splintering wood reverberated off the pavement, and she looked at Nathan.

Nathan softened his voice. "They're breaking down the wall and trying to shore up the load beams, as well as eliminating any risk of fire. It's a mess inside, and I don't want you to see it."

She stared at him mutely, knowing that to see the Majestic in a gutted state would kill part of her, but still needing to see for herself. Breaking away from Dooley's arm, Brenna moved through the circle of her sisters and approached the building.

"Don't go in there, Brenna. It's dangerous." Mr. Archer smiled with compassion, and it made her want to cry, but she couldn't find the tears. They were frozen, she supposed, like the rest of her. She stared at the bright bouquets of balloons tied to the open entrance gate and at the sign she'd been so proud of. COME TRIP THE LIGHT FANTASTIC! GRAND REOPENING TONIGHT!

She heard her name shouted from across the street, and she turned to see Pierce running toward her. It seemed the most natural thing in the world to allow him to embrace her, and she let some of his warmth puncture the numbness encroaching on her heart. The fact that he was wearing a tuxedo somehow reached into her frozen mind, and she even had the presence of mind to ask, "Where's your father?"

"I left him in the car. The fireman told me that the reopening tonight had been canceled and to go home, but he wouldn't tell me why. What happened?"

Her body shuddered. "They've condemned the building. It's not safe for anybody to be inside."

She felt him stiffen. "How did Mr. Archer reach this conclusion?"

"The guys from the National Park Service were here today to inspect the theater. They called him."

"No good deed goes unpunished, does it?" he said quietly, looking toward the blacked-out foyer where the old clock still stood, its brass crow reflecting in the harsh light of the flood lamps.

"What?" she asked.

"Nothing," he answered, shaking his head.

They both turned toward the sound of running feet, and then Brenna felt Pierce being knocked away from her.

Nathan faced Pierce, his hands held in tight fists. "Are you happy now? Did you tell her? Did you explain to her that this is all your fault?"

Brenna glanced at Pierce, confused. "What is he talking about?"

Nathan took a step toward Pierce, and as they faced each other in the dim light, their profiles looked identical, as if they were two halves of the same body. She shook her head to clear the image and faced Pierce. "What is he saying? How is any of this your fault?"

He looked at her but didn't meet her eyes. "I called a friend in the National Park Service to get them to send somebody down here. I thought it could only help you. I had no idea that something like this could happen. It never even entered the realm of possibility."

"Oh," she said, glad for the numbness as she stood looking into the dim foyer, staring at the odd glow from the brass crow. "Oh," she said again, unable to formulate any words into the feelings slowly being taken over by the growing frost inside of her.

Nathan pulled back his fist, taking Pierce unawares and knocking him off his feet with a blow to the abdomen. Nathan stood over him on the ground, his teeth clenched. "I don't want to see you anywhere near Brenna or this theater, do you hear me? You've caused enough damage."

Brenna had enough presence of mind to be shocked at Nathan's re-action, and somewhere in her numb mind it occurred to her that Nathan's lashing out at Pierce had very little to do with the Majestic.

Pierce coughed and clutched at his stomach, but didn't try to get up. Nathan took a step back, and his gaze fell on the clock and its brass crow and his fists slowly eased open before he looked back at Pierce. "Maybe you should start praying real hard that there's been a horrible mistake and the Majestic will reopen tomorrow. Or start making wishes. See that crow in there on that old clock? My mama used to tell me to go find a crow and watch it fly from its perch and make a wish. If it didn't flap its wings before it landed again, your wish would come true. So go find a crow and start wishing."

Pierce stared up at Nathan and coughed again. "My mother used to tell me the same thing."

Nathan stared at him for a long moment, his fists unclenching. "Did she now?"

Dooley rushed over to the two men and helped Pierce stand. "Stop it," he said. "Can't you two see that Brenna's upset enough?"

He turned to Brenna. "I'm going to take you home; there's nothing you can do here. Kathleen said that she'll go talk to Mr. Archer and see if there's anything they can salvage from your office. I'm going to ask that they throw a tarp over the piano and the clock to keep them safe from falling debris and water."

She nodded. Her mind screamed in protest, trying to convince her body to run into the building and get everybody out of her theater and to leave her alone. Instead, she allowed the ice to close over her heart as Dooley led her to his truck. She looked back only once, and her gaze was captured by the winking brass crow of the clock. It almost seemed to her that the crow had become a beacon in the darkness, and even when she closed her eyes she still saw it. She leaned her head on Dooley's shoulder and let him take her home.

CHAPTER 23

When they arrived at Mrs. Grodin's boardinghouse, Brenna finally opened her eyes. "Come sit with me on the porch swing. I don't want to be alone."

Dooley nodded and then helped her out of the truck. He held the swing steady so she and her skirts could find purchase on the seat before he sat beside her. Somehow she managed to kick off her shoes and pull her feet underneath her before moving her head to rest on Dooley's shoulder again, a position she realized she'd assumed fairly often in the course of the last twenty-four hours.

She stared up at the full moon, the same vibrant moon she'd stared at a mere few hours before, thinking then that it held in its bright, shining face all of her hopes and dreams for her Royal Majestic. She closed her eyes now, allowing the moon glow to bathe her skin, but unwilling to face the betrayal of its glittering light.

"What are you going to do now, Brenn?" Dooley's hand gently stroked her hair, in the same way he'd stroked her hair after she'd been hit by a softball in PE in fourth grade, and when she'd come home from the hospital after she'd almost died of spinal meningitis and he'd held her while her heart broke. It startled her to realize that Dooley Gambrel had been the one friend to stick around and help her pick up the pieces.

Brenna reached for the medallions around her neck, but her fingers grasped only her mother's pearls. She had a brief, clear recollection of being held as a child by her mother and grabbing at the same strand of pearls. Maybe her whole life she'd been searching for the mother with the pearls, reaching for her and grabbing only air. That was how she felt now, as if she held only air in her arms and in her heart. The one thing she could feel that was real was Dooley's hand stroking her hair.

"Let's get married, Doo. For real. Let's go ahead and set a date—the sooner the better."

His hand stilled on her head. After a long moment, he quietly asked, "Why, Brenna?"

She looked up into his face, into his warm brown eyes that had always made her feel safe. "Because I love you. Maybe not in the way that you love me—not yet, anyway. But that will change. I know it will. I think what we have between us is what makes a marriage work; we actually like each other, because we've been friends forever. You're my best friend, Dooley." She looked down in her lap, not able to read what was in his eyes and not sure that she really wanted to. Softly, she added, "And because you'd never break my heart."

He lifted her chin to force her to look at him again. "I have loved you my whole life, Brenna. And because of that I don't feel that I can analyze your change of heart right now. All I want to do is say yes and to hell with your reasons why we should and my reasons why we shouldn't. I guess I really am selfish, after all. So, yes, Brenna O'Brien. I want you to be my wife." He disengaged himself from her and stood. Kneeling down on one knee in front of the porch swing, he asked, "Will you marry me?"

Brenna smiled broadly, feeling small cracks form in the numbness around her heart. She took his hand in hers. "Yes, Dudley Harrison Gambrel the Fourth, I will marry you."

He let out a whoop, and if he'd still been wearing his hat, Brenna was sure he would have thrown it in the air. Instead, he pulled her to her feet, took her in his arms, and kissed her. The stars didn't fall from the sky, nor did the moon move to set low over their heads, but in his arms she felt beloved and safe, and that was enough.

"Well, it's about time," came a low voice from the front door. The large bulk of the elusive Mrs. Grodin created a shadow in the entranceway. "I've been hearing y'all were engaged for a while, but this is the first time I've seen proof of it. Congratulations."

They pulled apart and faced Brenna's landlord. Dooley put his arm around Brenna and hugged her to his side. "Thank you very much, Mrs. Grodin."

"When's the happy day?"

Dooley and Brenna glanced at each other and said in unison, "Soon."

Brenna laughed, the sound hollow, as if it were echoing against solid ice. "We'll let you know."

"I hope you do. I'll need to find another tenant, unless y'all are planning on moving in here." She raised her eyebrows. "If you decide to do that, I might throw in a new air conditioner as a wedding gift."

Dooley coughed into his hand to stifle a laugh. "Thank you, Mrs. Grodin. We'll let you know."

Mrs. Grodin shuffled forward, her slippered feet rasping against the wooden floorboards, and reached her hand out toward Brenna. "Now, come on in, Miss Brenna. While you're living under my roof I've got your reputation to think of, and there will be no hanky-panky on my watch. Now, say good night to your beau and come on inside."

Mrs. Grodin looked up as if to give them privacy, and Dooley gave Brenna a quick kiss. "You've made me the happiest guy on the planet."

Mrs. Grodin grabbed her arm and tugged. "Okay, you two, that's enough. Come on inside now."

She allowed Mrs. Grodin to pull her into the house with just a quick good night to Dooley. Slowly she climbed the stairs up to her room, marveling at how different her life had become since she'd last descended the same stairs. She paused outside her door, trying to gauge her feelings. Yes, the numbness had worn off, but it seemed to have been replaced by a new kind of numbness; it was as if she were stuck in neutral with no momentum to push her forward.

After turning her key in the lock, she opened the door to her darkened flat and began flipping on lights. She stood in the middle of her room, then slowly walked to the closet where the wedding dress hung. She'd think about what to do about the Royal Majestic later; she had a wedding to plan. It made her feel a little bit like Scarlett O'Hara, putting things off until tomorrow, but if she were to survive, she had to divert her thoughts.

She pulled the wedding dress from the hanger, examining the tag again. *Made expressly for Mary Everly.* Brenna frowned, an elusive thought niggling the back of her brain. What was it about her mother's name? It wasn't the first time she'd seen it, of course. When she was in grade school, Brenna had practiced writing out her mother's name over and over, as if somehow by writing it, it would make her mother a real presence in her life instead of just a face in a photograph.

Carefully she hung the dress on the back of the closet door so it would be the first thing she saw when she woke up. Bending down, she picked up a poster from the grand reopening that she'd hoped to have framed for her room, and shoved it under her bed. Tomorrow would be another day, she thought with a brittle smile—one without heartbreak and disappointment. She'd already seen enough to know she wouldn't go down that road again.

She left her clothes in the middle of the floor and climbed into bed, staring at the wedding dress hanging on the door until the morning sun turned the white lace yellow.

On his way to Mrs. Grodin's boardinghouse, Pierce stopped in front of the boarded-up theater. He got out of his car to peer through the pad-locked gate, and could see the large framed pictures that Brenna had been so excited about. He wondered why they'd been left behind, but thought he knew. If he'd been the gambling sort, he would have bet that Brenna hadn't once been back to the theater since that night. She was the only person he knew who would deny the existence of something simply by not looking at it.

Across the wood panel that covered the entrance were spray-painted the words *Closed indefinitely*. Up above the entrance, somebody had mercifully removed the grand reopening signs as well as the posters that had lined the front of the building. It was like watching the funeral of an old friend, and Pierce had to turn away before he did something to embarrass himself.

He got back in the rental car and drove to Mrs. Grodin's. He used the buzzer outside to try Nathan's room and was rewarded with an immediate answer.

"Hello?"

"Yeah, um, Nathan. This is Pierce McGovern. Do you have a minute?"

There was a short pause. "Sure. Come on up. First door on the left at the top of the stairs."

As Pierce climbed the stairs, he glanced to the other side of the hallway, to where he knew Brenna's room was located, but turned to the left. Nathan was standing in the open doorway as Pierce approached and held it wide for Pierce to enter.

Pierce glanced inside, but didn't enter at first. "What? No interrogation? No punches to the gut? I hardly feel as if I'm in the right place."

Nathan shook his head. "Man, I'm really sorry about that. I guess we were all a little emotional that night." He held the door open farther. "Actually, I've been expecting you to visit. Just sooner." Nathan led the way inside.

"I've been in California." Pierce glanced around the apartment. It was a small room, furnished sparsely with an iron bed, a desk, and a chest of drawers, and a door that led to what Pierce figured must be a private bath. He turned to face Nathan. "But something's been running through my brain ever since you slugged me, and I can't let it go."

Nathan stood near the closed door, his hand still on the doorknob. "What's that?"

"Something you said to me right after you hit me—about watching a crow fly and making a wish."

Nathan didn't move. "Is that so?"

"It's just that I thought it was an odd coincidence your mother would have told you that. I've never heard it before except from my own mother."

"Yeah, well, the world is full of coincidences."

Pierce stared at him a little longer. "Yeah, it sure is."

Nathan pushed off from the closed door. "Wanna beer?"

"Sure, thanks."

In the corner near the window sat a small table with two chairs. Nathan indicated for Pierce to take one, then took the other after grabbing two beers from the minirefrigerator.

Facing Nathan, Pierce asked, "You said you'd been expecting me."

"Thought you'd want to know about Brenna."

Pierce nodded and took a long swig from his beer. "How's she doing? I've called and left messages, but she hasn't returned any. I've only been in town for a couple of days, and I've buzzed her door several times, but I haven't gotten an answer."

"That's probably because she's been living at Kathleen's while they're planning her wedding. Everything's gone pretty fast."

"Oh. So she and Dooley have set the date?" Pierce forced his voice to remain neutral.

"Yep—October tenth, this coming Saturday, as a matter of fact. It happened kinda quick. Right after the grand opening, actually. I'm surprised you didn't know."

"I haven't been here, remember?" He glanced around the room, noticing the bare walls. "What's happening with the Majestic?"

Nathan tipped his chair back, his long legs stretched out in front of him, and brought the bottle to his mouth. "Nothing much. The guy from the Park Service gave Brenna the name of a man who might be interested in purchasing the theater and restoring it. He's apparently loaded and does this kind of thing for a hobby. He's got about a dozen theaters on the register already. Otherwise, Indianola's going to have to tear it down. Not good for the town or other businesses having a condemned building in the middle of their main street, you know?"

"Look, what happened with the Park Service was an accident. I would never hurt Brenna like that. I'm still racking my brain trying to find a way to help her out of this."

"She won't accept your help."

"I know. But that's too damned bad. I can't just walk away."

"She's marrying another man. Why don't you let the two of them take care of it?"

Pierce leaned forward. "Because Dooley Gambrel doesn't know the first thing about the Royal Majestic. I do—from the first movie premiere to the last, to the pattern on the carpet in the auditorium, to the fabric of the curtains—hell, I could probably recite from memory the eye color of every soldier in that damned mural." He took a deep breath. "What I'm saying is that the theater is a part of me. It has been ever since I was a boy and went every weekend with my mother. They're actually some of the few memories I have of her."

Nathan stood abruptly, then went to the small refrigerator and retrieved two more beers. "So why'd you want to see me?"

Pierce took the bottle, then leaned forward, his elbows on the table.

"The old grandfather clock that was in the lobby—do you by any chance know where it is so I can get a picture of it?"

"It's still there at the theater, but covered with a tarp. Your daddy's piano, too. Too heavy to move far, and besides, we have no place to put it." Nathan slid his chair back. "But I can save you the trouble. Brenna had me take tons of pictures from the interior of the theater to help with her proposal for investors. I happen to know that there's about a dozen of the clock. If you want, you can have them all. Don't think she'll be needing them now."

Nathan stood and moved toward the desk, where he slid open the top drawer and pulled out a stack of photos. Pierce stood, too, and began walking toward Nathan, but his foot kicked something on the floor. Looking down, he spotted a duffel bag half-filled with clothing. Partially covered by a T-shirt was the black-and-white photo of his mother taken outside the Royal Majestic. Leaning over, he retrieved the photo, and when he looked up Nathan was regarding him carefully.

Pierce straightened, the photo clutched in his hand. "I guess this means the picture was never really lost."

"Guess not."

"Do you mind telling me what's going on?"

"I do, but I bet you're going to make me."

"Yeah, you're right. So, what's this doing in your bag?"

Nathan shrugged. "I don't have a job anymore. I was packing so I could go back home."

Pierce rolled his eyes. "Please, no bullshit. Just tell me about the picture."

Nathan lifted his chin and eyed Pierce steadily. "I don't have any pictures of my mother when she was younger. I thought I should have it."

Pierce waited for the shock to roll over him, but it didn't happen. It was almost as if he'd known for a long time, had seen all the clues and understood them without being consciously aware of them. Suddenly so many things made sense. *My mama used to tell me to go find a crow and watch it fly from its perch and make a wish. If it didn't flap its wings before it landed again, your wish would come true.* "Are you saying that this woman in the photo—my mother—is also your mother?"

"You're pretty smart, Pierce. Must run in the family."

Pierce sat down on the edge of the bed. "How long have you known?"

"When Mama died last year, she told me you were still alive. See, I always knew I had a brother—but she told me you had died as a little boy. And I wanted to see for myself the boy I had grown up to hate."

"How could you hate me? You didn't even know me."

Nathan shrugged. "Trust me, it wasn't that hard. Growing up, I always felt my mother was comparing me to a perfect kid who never made mistakes. It's hard to spend your whole life falling short."

"Were you ever going to tell me?" Pierce indicated the partially packed bag at his feet. "Or were you just going to leave?"

"I was debating that. See, it's hard to go from hating somebody to finding out that they're not so bad after all. And finding that they're definitely not perfect."

Pierce gave a half-cocked grin. "Thanks—I think."

"I just wasn't sure you'd want to know about Mama. Brenna told me how her leaving still tears you up inside."

Pierce looked down at the photo, his thumb brushing over the image of the young woman who would become the mother he would love and lose. "Yeah, you could say that." He faced Nathan again. "So, my mother talked about me?"

"Yep. A lot. Her last words were about you, actually."

Pierce waited while Nathan crossed the room to the table and stared out the window. He took a deep drink from his beer. "She told me you were alive and asked me to find you so I could tell you that she was sorry. Sorry for leaving you. But she also wanted you to know that she did it out of love for you."

Pierce couldn't keep the sarcasm out of his voice. "She deserted me because she loved me? How did she explain that?"

"She loved your father very much. It didn't take her long to discover that he was in love with somebody else. No, he never had an affair, if that's what you're thinking, but he didn't need to. It's very hard to love somebody so much and know that they will never love you back. It did things to her—bad things. She said she even thought about killing herself, but she didn't because of you and the way it might affect you." Nathan began picking at the label on his bottle, the small paper flakes floating slowly to the ground. "She even thought about taking you with her, but she loved your father too much to do that to him. Your father loved you, too, and it would have killed him to have you taken from him."

"So she just walked out of our lives. Just like that. Without a glance back."

"No, man. It wasn't like that at all. She looked back every day. She tried to start a new life with my dad, and I think she was hoping to replace you by having me. But that never really happened. You were everywhere—in framed pictures around the house, in stories she'd tell me, in all her memories. And even though I thought you were dead, I resented how much she still loved you. It feels incredibly stupid now, but for a young kid, you were a tough act to follow."

Pierce glanced back down at the duffel bag. "And you were going to skip town without telling me any of this?"

"Actually, I had a plane ticket to California. I was going pay you a visit on my way back to Texas. But now you're here, so I don't have to."

Pierce shook his head. "This is a hell of a lot to swallow right now." He placed the picture on the bed and stood. "I've got to go." He stood and moved to the door.

Nathan followed. "What about Brenna?"

"What about her? She's getting married on Saturday, remember?"

"Yeah, I remember. Just wondering if you did."

Pierce studied Nathan for a moment, seeing again the familiarities, but this time understanding where he'd seen the blue eyes before and the broad cheekbones. He saw them every time he looked in a mirror. Without another word he turned and left. But before he reached the bottom step, he heard Nathan's footsteps racing after him. "Wait—you forgot these."

Nathan held out the stack of pictures. "You wanted the picture of the clock, remember? Maybe these will help."

Pierce took the stack.

Nathan continued. "She was my mother, too, you know. She loved that theater. Talked about it all the time. I'd like to help if I can."

Slowly, Pierce nodded. "All right. Just stick around to make sure Brenna doesn't make any rash decisions about the theater until I get back."

"Where are you going?"

"To New Orleans. I should be back before Saturday." He turned to leave but paused. "Thanks. For telling me."

Nathan nodded. "Have a good trip, and I'll see you when you get back."

Pierce said good-bye, then left, trying to pay attention to the sidewalk in front of him, but seeing only the once-forgotten memory of his mother holding him up to the ticket window at the Royal Majestic, and telling him that she would love him forever.

He sat in his car for several minutes, staring out the windshield without really seeing. *Her last words were about you.* Then he remembered something Aunt Dottie had told him after Rocky's funeral: *Sometimes walking away is the only way a person can show how much they really love someone.*

He passed his hand over his face, searching for the place in his heart that he'd kept the bitterness of his mother's abandonment and felt instead the emptiness of it. Not really emptiness, though; it had been filled with something else. *I have a brother.* The thought brought a glimmer of a smile to his lips. "I have a brother," he said out loud this time, as if saying it somehow lent credibility to such an outlandish thought.

Still smiling, Pierce flipped through the stack of photos until he came across several of the old clock from different angles. Carefully, he placed them on the seat beside him and put the car in drive.

CHAPTER 24

Brenna sat in her mother's wedding dress at Kathleen's dressing table as her sisters bustled around her like butterflies around honeysuckle. Claire had a curling wand wound close to Brenna's scalp, close enough that it made Brenna try to twist away.

"Stop fidgeting, Brenn. You're going to mess up your hairdo. I call this one my 'Paris Hilton at the Oscars.' " Claire slid the wand out of a ringlet of curls and stood back to admire her handiwork. "I did it for Mary Sanford for the Miss Boll Weevil Pageant, and she came in first place."

Mary Margaret stepped closer and held up her brush. "Unless you want Brenna to resemble Little Bo Peep, we need to brush out some of these curls."

"Don't touch a hair on her head!" Claire brandished the hot curling wand like a weapon, and Mary Margaret stepped back. "I'm not done. A masterpiece takes time, you know." She lowered the wand and took a deep breath. "Now, just leave me alone and let me do my work. I promise you won't be disappointed."

Brenna met Mary Margaret's dubious gaze in the mirror as her older sister stepped back. "All right. But I get first dibs with a hairbrush when you're done and she hates it."

Claire stuck her tongue out at her sister, then proceeded to wrap more of Brenna's hair around the wand.

Brenna watched her sisters through the mirror as they stood in their slips and panty hose and put on makeup. She was a young girl again, on the periphery watching as her older sisters prepared for a date or a football game; always their sister, but separate. Was it because they'd had a mother's guidance and she hadn't? Was it because she was always looking to find in them the thing she missed, even though she hadn't had it long enough to really know what a mother's touch was like? But she felt the absence, and still did. It made her feel fragile, afraid to touch the world around her.

She examined her hair in the mirror, the same hair as her mother's, although now it would have been white or gray, and remembered something Aunt Dottie had said. Something about her being the most like her mother. Brenna brushed her hands across the delicate lace on the skirt of the wedding dress and tried to feel like the woman who would take her five daughters to the beach despite her husband's disapproval and was defiant enough to die first.

Instead, she felt the numbness creep up on her again, the spidery veins of crackling frost sealing over her nerves, insulating her emotions. And she was glad for it. After experiencing the loss of the Majestic, she never wanted to really feel anything again.

"Close your eyes, Brenn," Colleen said as she stood in front of Brenna's chair with an eyelash curler.

She did as she was told and kept her eyes closed as she felt the tugging on her hair and skin as her four sisters wreaked their magic on her numb body.

"Who's getting married?"

Brenna opened her eyes to see Aunt Dottie being escorted into the room by Kathleen's daughter Marie. Marie rolled her eyes but smiled. "Brenna is, Aunt Dottie. She's marrying Dooley Gambrel."

"Who?"

"Dooley Gambrel," said Marie, louder.

"Who's Dooley Gambrel? Have I met him?"

"Yes, Aunt Dottie. You've met him."

"Why's he marrying our Brenna?"

Kathleen approached and took Dottie's arm. "Because he loves her, Aunt Dot. That's generally what happens when people love each other."

"Not always," said Aunt Dottie as she settled into her chair. "People get married for all sorts of reasons. Sometimes they have to, if you know what I mean."

Kathleen began ushering her daughter out of the room. "Thanks, Marie. Tell your father that Brenna will be ready in about fifteen minutes and to have the car ready. And please ask him to vacuum the front seat if he hasn't already."

With a reluctant look behind her, Marie left the room as her mother quickly shut the door.

"And sometimes," Dottie continued, "people who love each other don't get married—not to each other, anyway, but that's a whole 'nother story. Speaking of which, I have something for the bride." She opened her ubiquitous purse on her lap and began rummaging through it. Two plastic Baggies filled with ice and containing two slender objects, wrapped in foil, fell out and onto the floor. Mary Margaret knelt and picked them up and handed them to Dottie, who immediately took the foil items out of the Baggies and placed the Baggies, filled with ice, back in her purse.

Mary Margaret blew warm air onto her hands. "Why are they in Baggies with ice, Aunt Dottie?"

"I keep them in my freezer."

After a brief pause in which the sisters eyed one another, Mary Margaret asked, "Is it food?"

"No, silly. Why would I keep food in my purse? I keep important items in my freezer so that I always know where they are. And I keep them in Baggies so they're easier to find." She held up one of the foil-wrapped items. "Is Dr. McGovern coming to the wedding? I have a letter for him."

Brenna turned, her gaze falling on the elusive letter. "He's coming, Aunt Dot. Buzz has been sent to bring him to the church."

"Why can't his handsome son bring him?"

Brenna faced the mirror again. "Because he's in California."

"No, he's not. He stopped by to visit with me yesterday. Such a lovely boy. But all he wanted to do was talk about you."

Brenna met her aunt's unblinking eyes in the mirror before dropping her gaze to her hands in her lap.

"Well, no matter. You're marrying somebody else, so why should you care if Dr. McGovern's son is back in town? I just hope I remember to give this letter to his father when I see him at the wedding." She placed the encased letter back in her purse and held out the second item. "This is what I was looking for—it's a little gift for Brenna for her wedding day."

Mary Margaret took it and brought it over for Brenna to unwrap.

The foil still held the frosty temperatures of Aunt Dottie's ice-filled Baggies, making the edges stiff and brittle and difficult to open, especially with fingers already numb. When the foil lay open in her lap, she looked down to discover a delicate gold filigree necklace, just long enough to rest in the middle of her chest once Mary Margaret had fastened it around her neck.

"It's lovely, Aunt Dottie. Thank you."

"It was your mother's, so there's your 'something old' you need to wear." Her eyebrows knit as she raised her hand to her head. "Where's my hat? Has anybody seen my hat?"

Kathleen left Brenna's side. "I'll ask Marie to go look for it. Is it the polka-dot hat? The one you like to wear for weddings?"

"Oh, no. Not that one. I wanted to wear my black one today. And I could have sworn it was on my head."

Kathleen's smooth forehead furrowed. "A black hat, Aunt Dottie? To a wedding? Are you sure?"

Dottie glanced at her eldest niece with annoyance. "Yes, dear. I'm very sure that I especially want to wear my black hat to this wedding."

Brenna stared back at the mirror, watching as the light from the window made the gold chain shimmer, almost as if her mother were gently making her presence known. She moved her gaze back to Aunt Dottie, who was staring at her unblinking through her thick glasses.

A knock sounded on the door, and Kathleen's husband, John, stuck his head in the room. "Your car and chauffeur are ready, Brenna," he said, winking.

Kathleen helped her stand and moved her to the full-length mirror in the corner so she could see the whole effect for the first time. Her hair and makeup were flawless, the red in her hair shimmering under upswept curls and drifting waves.

"You did a beautiful job with my hair, Claire. Thank you."

Mary Margaret moved to her side, appreciatively eyeing the curls and waves. "Not too bad, Claire. Glad to hear that years of beauty pageants have finally paid off."

Claire sent her sister a sidelong glance but didn't say anything.

Colleen handed Kathleen a circlet of flowers that she placed on Brenna's head and secured with bobby pins while Claire fussed around them, warning them not to mess with her masterpiece.

Kathleen then placed a rosary in Brenna's shaking hand. "These are mine, so you have your 'something borrowed.'"

Mary Margaret slipped an ivory-colored cuff bracelet around Brenna's wrist. "And I bought this for you in India on my last visit as a birthday gift, but I figured you could use it today. So there's your 'something new.'"

"And don't forget this!" Colleen brandished a puff of blue satin and white lace from a UPS bag she'd placed on the floor. "It's your garter— and it's Vera Wang. I won it on an eBay auction yesterday and had them overnight it. Isn't it gorgeous?"

Mary Margaret turned to her sister. "Aren't you supposed to be banned from eBay?"

Annoyed, Colleen said, "But I had to do this for Brenna. She needed something blue. And I won't tell Bill if you don't." Kathleen and Claire held Brenna steady as she lifted her foot for Colleen to slide on the garter.

All the sisters stepped back from the mirror to allow Brenna a chance to see herself. She smiled and nodded and thanked her sisters, and all the while she was afraid the frosty cracks would begin showing through her skin and her eyes, or that they would hear the hollowness of her voice. When she spoke her thanks it was as if the sound bounced off walls of ice that filled her heart, echoing from her aching chest.

Still smiling, she turned toward her brother-in-law and took his arm, allowing him to lead her to the waiting car.

Brenna and John sat in the front seat, while Kathleen, Aunt Dottie, and Aunt Dottie's black hat filled the back as they led the slow procession of cars to the church. As they passed the theater she looked away, studying instead the late-morning shadows on the buildings across the street. She felt a hand on her shoulder and, when she turned to see, was surprised to find Aunt Dottie's gloved hand there. Softly she patted her aunt's hand, then turned back around to stare out the windshield, watching as the church steeple loomed in the distance.

Brenna spotted Dooley's truck in the parking lot, the prerequisite decorations of whipped cream and beer cans tied to the back making her wince. John stopped the car at the curb in front of the church and looked at her. "Are you ready?"

Brenna nodded, unwilling to speak and have her voice give her away.

They poured out of the cars like jelly beans onto the pavement in their brightly colored wedding clothes, Dottie's black hat a beacon in the crowd. They all began to climb the steps ahead of Brenna and John, since John would be giving her away and they'd be the last to enter the church. She'd wanted a small wedding and had chosen Kathleen as the maid of honor. Dooley's younger brother, David—affectionately known as Davey until he'd reached the age of thirteen and could phys-ically enforce the use of his correct name—had been chosen as the groom's best man.

John gently tugged on her arm and Brenna looked up, startled, aware that everyone, with the exception of Dottie and Kathleen, had al-ready made their way inside the church. With a nod she slowly began to climb the steps, gradually aware of the sound of a siren in the dis-tance becoming louder and louder. Before she reached the top the sound had become more insistent, and she and John turned in time to see Nathan in his truck skidding to a stop at the curb with Pierce rid-ing shotgun, a detachable siren on top of the roof. The sound had stopped, but they were now flashed with a strobe light of red and white.

Pierce jumped out, and Brenna could see from the pallor of his skin and the tightness around his eyes that something was wrong. She let go of John's arm and began running down the steps. "What is it?"

"It's my dad. He couldn't get out of bed this morning, like his body had started shutting down or something. They've moved him to Memorial Hospital in Greenwood." He grimaced. "It's not looking good—the doctors don't think he's going to last much longer. But he's asking to see you; he says it's important." His gaze skipped over her dress and behind her to where John, Kathleen, and Dottie were wait-ing. "I'll understand if you want to wait until after your wedding, but I thought you'd want to know."

She looked past Pierce's shoulder toward Nathan, trying to sort through the jumbled words in her head. "Why is Nathan here?"

"He's the one who found him; he'd come for a visit—long story, but I'll tell you later. Anyway, Nathan is a volunteer firefighter in Texas and keeps his siren in his truck. He offered to come with me to get you."

She didn't think twice as she skipped down the remaining two steps. She wasn't thinking of her internal numbness, or even all the guests now sitting in the pews or Dooley at the altar. A small fissure of warmth erupted inside her as she thought of Dr. McGovern and the letters. "I'm coming now," she said as she slid into the middle of the front seat. Before Pierce crawled in beside her, she called out to John, "Can you let Dooley know? He'll understand and will make my excuses to the guests."

"I'm coming, too," Aunt Dottie shouted as she began descending the steps.

Kathleen held her back. "There's no room. After John tells Dooley, we'll drive over with you."

Pierce shut the door and Nathan turned on his siren again and the three of them sped away down the street past the old church where her mother had been married and past the boarded-up Royal Majestic toward the hospital where a dying man lay, more evidence of the passage of time and Brenna's inability to stop it no matter how hard she tried.

Nathan dropped Pierce and Brenna off at the main doors to the hospital with promises that he'd be up as soon as he'd found a parking spot. The nurses recognized Pierce, and their faces registered no surprise at Brenna's wedding dress as they led them to Dr. McGovern's room.

Another nurse was writing something on a clipboard when they walked in, and gave Pierce a terse smile as she left the room.

Brenna barely recognized the shriveled old man in the hospital bed as Pierce's father. Gone were the broad shoulders and cocky smile of a World War II flying ace. Instead, all that remained was a hollow shell full of rumbling breaths and old memories held together by the tubes and needles protruding from both arms and his nose.

Dr. McGovern caught sight of Brenna in all her wedding finery and smiled, transforming his face and making Brenna feel as if maybe this wasn't the end after all. Then her gaze took in the needles and tubes again and she had to try very hard to smile back.

Pierce pulled a chair to the side of the bed for Brenna to sit in, and

he stood behind her as she reached for his father's hand and held it between hers.

She leaned forward. "I'm here, Dr. McGovern. I came as soon as I
heard."

He smiled again, and years seemed to fade away from his face, leaving a glimmer of the man he'd once been. "You are so much like her. So
very much." He pointed a shaky finger at the gold filigree chain around
her neck. "I recognize that. There's a picture. . . ."

His hand slid away, and Brenna looked at Pierce in alarm, but Pierce
shook his head. "He's just catching his breath." Pierce moved to the
other side of the bed, facing Brenna.

"Thank you, Brenna, for reading my letters to me. I wanted you to
read them for yourself more than I wanted to hear them."

Brenna's eyes met Pierce's before returning to his father.

"Your mother was a good mother, Brenna. She just didn't get the
chance to be a mother to you for very long. And I'm afraid you've suffered a great deal because of it. That's why I wanted you to read the letters. So you'd understand."

He closed his eyes, his breathing soft and shallow. Brenna leaned
forward, her brows knit with worry. "Understand what?"

Instead of answering, he reached up and touched her eyes, forcing
them closed as his fingers pressed against the lids as if he were anoint-
ing them. "Sometimes when you make yourself blind, you miss all the
beautiful and good things along with the bad. Stop being blind,
Brenna. Open your eyes." His hand dropped to his side.

Her eyes flickered open, and she could still feel his soft touch upon
her. "But what does this have to do with my mother?"

"She would have told you the same thing. I loved her, you see. I
never broke my promise to her because I still love her. And I wrote to
her every day. I don't know why she never received my letters." He
paused, his hand tightening on Brenna's. "I can only think that your father intercepted and destroyed them. He hated me because he knew
your mother loved me. He would have wanted no reminder—although
I don't think he could bear to destroy her letters. He loved her too, you
see. I imagine he liked to pretend they were written to him, which is
why he kept them. Or maybe he had a guilty conscience and couldn't

bring himself to destroy them." The old doctor took long, deep breaths, trying to restore the energy it had taken to speak.

Brenna sat back, her body seeming to vibrate within her skin, threatening to shatter. Her fingers flew to her mouth. "ME. They were initials, weren't they? For Mary Everly." Her eyes brightened, and she felt her mouth working as she tried to form the words. "She was my mother. ME was my mother." She bit her lip, trying to focus on the hospital room and the dying man but seeing instead a box of old, unread letters. She was ice again, yet now she felt as if she were falling and nearing the ground. "Why did you let her marry my father? Why didn't you try harder to reach her? Oh, God," she said, covering her face with her hands, not feeling her cheeks, only the warm wetness of tears on her fingers.

A trembling hand rested on her head. "Brenna, hope is the easiest thing to give up and the hardest thing to hold on to. Hold on to it always, or you risk losing everything. And then you spend the rest of your life either looking backward or looking forward wearing blinders."

Lifting her head, she took his hand and held it to her cheek. *I wrote to her every day.* Acknowledgment and grief swirled in the space between them as Brenna realized what this man had lost. Softly she asked, "What happened to the baby? Did you ever find out?"

Pierce took his father's other hand, and Brenna watched his attempt to remind his father of his son's presence and to hold his father to this world.

"Dottie told me about the baby as soon as I got back to Indianola. She thought I should know." He closed his eyes briefly. "The baby was stillborn. A little boy. It was the only conversation about us that Mary and I had after I returned. I had to talk to her, you see. But she held to her vows and wouldn't see me again except as the family doctor—and that's only because I was the nearest doctor in almost fifty miles. But that was after more than ten years later when she was pregnant with Kathleen. I've always speculated why it took so long to start her family with your father." He sighed. "She was a strong woman, your mother. Much stronger than me." Dr. McGovern's voice became raspy as if he couldn't put enough air behind the words.

Brenna looked up suddenly. "There's one more letter. Aunt Dottie

has it. She must have been the friend Mama talked about in her letters."
She looked up at Pierce. "She might be here already, and I know she has
it in her purse."

She stood. "You need to stay here with your father. I'll go."

He nodded. "Hurry."

The light green corridors of the hospital passed in a blur as she went
in search of the waiting room, oblivious to the stares of strangers as she
ran past them in her wedding dress. After two wrong turns she accosted
a passing nurse, who led her to the right room. Nathan was there, along
with all of her sisters and brothers-in-law. Aunt Dottie sat with her back
straight and her purse primly in her lap. She'd left her black hat, and
her white hair shone under the harsh fluorescents. She held a foil-
covered envelope in her hand.

Brenna struggled to take the time to give a quick greeting and reassurance to everyone that Dr. McGovern was still alive as she approached
Dottie. She knelt in front of her chair. "The letter, Aunt Dottie, the one
you said you have for Dr. McGovern. Can I have it now?"

"I was wondering what was taking you so long." She handed her the
foil package. "I was Mary's friend, you see. That's why she trusted me
with her last letter to him. Tell him . . ." She blinked rapidly behind her
thick glasses. "Tell him that she'd ask me every week if he'd read it yet,
and I'd have to tell her no. She never stopped asking. Up until the week
that she died, she never stopped asking."

Brenna took the foil and impulsively hugged the older woman. "You
were a good friend, Aunt Dottie. I'll give it back to you if he still doesn't
want to read it, all right?"

"He will. He's going to see her again soon, so it won't matter now,
will it?"

Brenna swallowed past the thickness in her throat. "No, I don't
guess it will. Thank you." She turned without speaking to anybody else
and rushed through the door, somehow remembering the way back to
Dr. McGovern's room.

At first the old man seemed to be sleeping peacefully with Pierce still
holding his hand when Brenna entered the room. She held the foil
package up to Pierce. "I have the letter."

Pierce stared at it for a moment. "Why is it wrapped in foil?"

A small bubble of a laugh escaped through her tears. "She kept it in the freezer so she wouldn't lose it."

She handed him the letter as he sat down on the edge of the bed nearest her. "Oddly, that makes sense." He peeled away the foil folds, gradually unearthing a pale yellow envelope with only the name *Andrew* scrawled across the front.

Brenna leaned over to speak with Dr. McGovern again. "Aunt Dottie wanted you to know that Mama asked every week if you'd read it yet. She never stopped asking."

The old doctor nodded slowly, and Brenna wanted to stop there, to let him die in peace—to allow her to continue only to wonder instead of knowing the truth. She moved her hands to her neck, grasping her mother's necklace, surprised to find her skin warm and pliable beneath her fingertips. She'd expected cold, hard ice, because that was what she imagined she was fighting when she tried to move her lips to speak.

Almost whispering, she asked, "Why did you never read it?"

He opened his eyes and looked at her with clear lucidity. "Because I was afraid. Afraid to know that she didn't love me anymore, that she was happy with somebody else. That perhaps she had never really loved me after all. If I never opened the letter, then I would never have to know the truth. I could keep believing that she would love me forever."

Pierce cleared his throat. "Do you want to read it now, Dad?"

"Let Brenna."

At Brenna's nod, Pierce handed her the letter. Slowly she ripped open the envelope with a chewed fingernail, and when she took out the letter, a small wrapped tissue fell out. Opening it carefully on her lap, she unveiled a small lock of very fine blond hair. She held it in her flattened palm, each strand of hair full of light and memories filling her hand, yet weighing nothing at all. After glancing up at Pierce again, she began to read.

November 5, 1945

Darling,
Yesterday was the first day I've seen you since you went away to war more than three years ago. It seems more like three centuries, yet sometimes I think it could only be three minutes.

Before I saw you yesterday, I thought that I had finally relegated you to my past. I'm very busy, you see, taking care of my house and husband, and all my community and church activities. People say that I have so much energy, and I just nod because I could never tell them that I'm simply keeping my mind occupied so that I don't have to think about you or our little boy. I miss you both, you see, and I can't allow myself to dwell on all that I have lost. I once read, "Beware the barren soul of a busy life." I think they were writing about me.

I was managing so well until you walked back into my life. There I was, leaving the market, and there you were. I didn't quite know what to say because I thought I was dreaming. We all believed you dead for so long, since the last we'd heard you'd been shot down. And then you reappeared from the grave, and it was all I could do to stop myself from throwing myself at you.

You're much thinner than I last saw you, and there are lines on your face that no twenty-three-year-old should have. You looked dearer than ever to me, and I wanted to hold you and kiss you and tell you that everything would be all right. But the crowd outside Murphy's Market and the gold band on my finger prevented me from doing so.

Instead, you shook my hand like an old friend and asked me about our baby. I told you he had died, but what I didn't tell you is that he lived for two hours and died in my arms. And he looked like you, with the big gray eyes and a white, downy fuzz on his head. Before they took him from me, I cut some of it to give you. It's wrapped here in tissue.

Pierce picked up the piece of tissue and brought it to his father. The old doctor touched the wispy strands of hair as if stroking the head of a child, all the while nodding as if he understood.

Brenna noticed something else poking out from the corner of the envelope and reached for it. "There's more." She pulled out an old black-and-white photograph of a young woman. Around her neck, almost hidden from the camera, hung what appeared to be a diamond solitaire ring on a gold filigree chain. Brenna's hands reached for her own necklace, identical to the one in the photo. She let her fingers drift across the picture and felt the air absent her lungs, as if she had died a little. "That's my mother," she managed. "That's Mary Everly." She covered her mouth with her hand and closed her eyes for a long time, remembering all the other letters she had read, and allowed herself to cry. *Mama. Oh, Mama.*

She felt Pierce's warm hands on her shoulders. "Brenna, I'm sorry. I'm so sorry." He knelt in front of her. "I'll finish, if you like."

She shook her head. "No. I want to." With a deep breath she picked up the letter again and resumed reading.

But it was your question as to why I never wrote to you that left me gasping for air. I wrote often, yet you said you'd never received my letters. How can this be? And when I asked you why you never wrote, you claimed that you had. So what has happened to our letters? How can fate have been so cruel?

I'm trying to make sense of all this, trying to find rhyme or reason or even meaning to what happened to us. I know our love is as strong as it once was, and I can't help but wonder how we allowed these barriers into our lives to separate us.

Dorothy O'Brien, my good friend and now my sister-in-law, once told me that it is our life's goal to find our passion and work toward it, not allowing anything to stand in our way. To give up too easily leads to regret, yet trying and then failing can lead us to second chances if we do not accept it as a failure, but a chance to learn.

I should have waited for you, regardless of the consequences. I should never have married. He is good to me and loves me, but I wonder how long he will be patient with me while he waits for me to return his affections. If he asked me today, I would tell him never, for I no longer have a heart to give. It belongs to you and always will.

Perhaps it would be best for both of us if I should set him free. That is my thought when I ask you this: Will you come away with me? It would mean leaving this town and all we hold dear. But we would be together always. I have no children, and nothing to hold me here. Please, please say yes. I can't imagine the bleak years to come, knowing that you won't be in them. I'm giving this letter to

Dottie, and after you've read it you can send your answer through her. Whatever you decide, I will abide by it. If you do not choose me, then don't grieve for me. I will try to find a new passion to pursue. As you once taught me, I will take a leap of faith with both feet and see where I land. But the choice is yours; do not cheat us both by deciding not to choose at all.

I am only twenty-one years old, yet I feel as if I already have a lifetime's worth of knowledge. It's as if the war years have made all of us grow up much too fast, and face life challenges that should be reserved until we are much older.

But I cannot regret what I have learned. Regardless of what you decide and what becomes of us, it will not change this belief, and whatever children I may have, I will try to teach them this: that life is meant to be more than existence. Fight for and hold on to your passion, whatever it is, but surrender gracefully when the passion is well spent. For it is through loss that we learn, and grief that we grow stronger, and living that we learn how to love. Everything is a choice, and by avoiding choices, one not only ensures that a wrong decision won't be made, but also steals a soul's chance to live, to learn, and to love.

I will wait to hear from you. Every day I will wait. But when the waiting time grows too long, I will surrender you and take a leap of faith in another direction, and I will be lost to you forever.

But I will never stop loving you.
Me

Dipping her head, Brenna allowed the letter to rest against the bed, its weight too much for her to hold any longer. Dr. McGovern moved his hand, and both Brenna and Pierce looked at his father's pale face, the pallor now nearly matching that of his white pillowcase. But he was smiling, and Brenna remembered what Dottie had said to her in the waiting room. *He's going to see her soon, so it won't matter now.* She studied his serene face again. It was almost as if he had finally come to peace with the warrior battling within him. It would be his last fight as a soldier, and one he would win.

The rhythm of the heart monitor slowed as Dr. McGovern drifted into sleep. But with a slurred, soft voice he spoke one more time. "She found her new passion, Brenna. It was you. And your sisters. That's why she waited more than ten years before she had Kathleen. She surrendered her love for me and threw herself into motherhood. She loved being a mother. She loved her babies, and she loved the people they grew into. You were all her passion." He opened his eyes wider, looking for Pierce, and Pierce took his hand. "I tried to love your mother, and I never blamed her for leaving me. Forgive her; let it go. She never meant to punish you." He smiled softly to himself. "And she allowed me to find my other passions—medicine and you, Pierce. You were my life, and I have never regretted anything because it all led to you."

He stopped breathing then, while Pierce and Brenna each held a hand until a team of doctors and nurses rushed in and moved them away from the bed as they tried to revive him. Pierce held Brenna close as they watched the activity at the hospital bed slowly cease, and then the time of death was called. They watched as the machines were turned off and the sheet pulled over Dr. McGovern, declaring the death of a soldier of the Second World War, a warrior with a poet's heart whose heartache was finally over.

CHAPTER 25

Dooley was in the waiting room when Brenna and Pierce returned with the news that Dr. McGovern had died. She held the letter with the lock of hair and the photograph close to her chest, and saying the words made her seek comfort in Pierce's arms again. It wasn't until she saw Dooley's jaw stiffen that she realized what she'd done.

He waited to approach her until a doctor came in to speak with Pierce, and Brenna found herself reluctantly facing her best friend. *My fiancé,* she reminded herself. His brown eyes had lost some of their brightness, and he seemed pale and drawn under the harsh fluorescent lighting of the waiting room.

"You're exhausted," he said. "I'm going to take you home."

"I can't go yet. There's so much I need to tell my sisters."

Kathleen stepped forward. "No, Brenn. Dooley's right. Not here. You need to go home and collect your thoughts. We'll meet you there later."

Reluctantly Brenna nodded, and in the midst of hugging and saying good-bye to her sisters, she missed Pierce leaving the room.

Fortunately somebody had had the forethought to remove the JUST MARRIED signs and the bobbing beer cans from the rear of Dooley's truck. He held the truck door open and helped Brenna into the seat.

A sense of panic enveloped Brenna at the thought of returning home as if everything were normal. She turned to Dooley. "Do you mind if we just drive around for a while? I'm not in the mood to talk to anybody right now—too much to sort through, I guess. Just drive."

Dooley nodded, then climbed in behind the wheel and pulled out onto the road, heading away from town. They drove in silence until the houses became sparser and the blacktop road divided into four lanes of traffic.

He glanced over at Brenna, his eyes sad. "I'm sorry about Dr. Mc-

Govern. He was a nice man." He reached into his jacket pocket and pulled out the starched handkerchief Brenna imagined his mother tucking into his pocket that morning in preparation for his wedding.

She took it with a brief smile of thanks and dabbed at her eyes. "Yes, he was. A true gentleman. And he taught me more about life than I ever thought I'd know."

Brenna spotted signs for the interstate, recognizing where Dooley was headed, and began looking for the little dirt road that would take them to the old fishing pond she and Dooley used to go to every Saturday morning.

"Like what?" he asked, as the truck slowed into the turn, then bumped along the unpaved road that was more dirt than gravel. She didn't answer right away as Dooley pulled the truck into a spot in front of the pond, the surface thick with fallen leaves, and she was glad he'd come here. It fit her mood somehow. Maybe it was the symbol of approaching winter, the waiting time. Waiting for spring, and the hope it always seemed to bring.

Brenna thought for a moment, staring at the floating leaves and contemplating Dr. McGovern's sacrifices and the full life he had led despite years of heartache and grief. "That life is what you make of it if you put your whole heart into it." She held the handkerchief to her eyes, remembering the words from her mother's last letter. "That life is more than existence." She pressed her head against the back of the seat and closed her eyes, trying to feel the serenity of the place Dooley had known to bring her. "He and my mother were lovers—before the war. They were supposed to get married." She smoothed her hands over the skirt of her gown. "This was her dress, although she ended up wearing another one, because when she got married she was pregnant and this one must not have fit her anymore."

Dooley's head whipped around to look at her. "You mean your mother had a baby before Kathleen?"

Brenna nodded. "A baby boy—stillborn. Dr. McGovern didn't know about the baby, because all the letters they wrote to each other were intercepted by my father, so that they were forced apart. Remember, my father worked at the post office even then. When Dr. McGovern returned home after the war, my mother was already married to my father. She wanted to run away with Dr. McGovern, and wrote him a letter saying that she would wait for his response, but he never opened it." A sob escaped from her throat. "He never opened it, Dooley. He never knew until right before he died that she still loved him and wanted to go away with him and end her marriage to my father. She waited ten year before having children, hoping he'd change his mind. I suppose that in her mind, once she had children, she'd be stuck with my father forever. And she was."

He turned away. "That's real sad, Brenn. Real sad—especially since I knew your mother and father and could never see why they were together. But how did this teach you anything about life? It sounds like they both made a huge mistake and suffered for the rest of their lives." Something throbbed in his jaw, and for the first time since she could remember, she couldn't guess what thoughts were running through his head.

She looked at him, not caring if her mascara tracked black streaks down her cheeks. He was Dooley, after all: the boy who'd known her since she was running around in diapers and had seen her look a lot worse. "They didn't give up on life, Doo. They kept trying. They made mistakes, but refused to look backward. Even though Dr. McGovern lost my mother, he still found love and happiness in his profession and with his son. He said . . ." A sob broke loose again, and she placed her hand on her throat, above her mother's gold necklace, to calm herself. "He said that my mother renewed her passion for life in me and my sisters." She smiled. "I guess what I'm trying to say is that life isn't over after the first big disappointment. We keep breathing. If only because we don't know how to stop."

He didn't say anything, but put the truck in drive and drove slowly around the pond to the road that would bring them back to Indianola. They rode in silence the whole way home as Brenna pretended to watch the scenery slipping by and tried to ignore the slight tingling under her skin. Tingling that reminded her of the time it had snowed one winter when she was a child and she'd caught snow in her bare hands until Kathleen had made her come inside and run her hands under warm water. She'd cried, wanting the feel of the cold snow to last, but thankful, too, for the healing thaw of the warm water and the way it made her skin vibrate.

Dooley pulled to a stop, and Brenna looked up to see that they were in front of Mrs. Grodin's boardinghouse. Brenna's sisters were parked out on the front porch, on the steps and the porch swing, and they were all trying to pretend that they hadn't noticed Dooley and Brenna yet.

Dooley put the truck in park but didn't turn off the engine. Without looking at her, he said, "I need to ask you something."

She looked at him expectantly, wondering at the tight tone of his voice, almost as if something were strangling him from within.

He swallowed and set his jaw. "I've been thinking about what you said—about Dr. McGovern and what he told you—about finding the one thing you want in life and giving it your whole heart. So, Brenn, what is the one thing that you want more than anything right now?"

She faced him and stared at his beloved face and wanted to lie for him. But ever since Dr. McGovern had died, his words had been flinging themselves around her head, almost as if a huge hand were shaking her awake after having been in a deep sleep for years. Her fingers crept up to her mother's necklace and stilled. She recognized the truth before the words formed in her head. Slowly she said, "I want to restore the Majestic; I want to make it more than just an old theater. I want it to be a place of entertainment and fun that people talk about for miles around."

The truck was silent for a moment before Dooley spoke again. "And what about Pierce? You still love him, don't you?"

When she didn't answer, he continued: "Do you remember the night we decided to get married and I asked you why you wanted to marry me? You told me it was because I'd never break your heart. And you're right—I wouldn't. But that's only because you'd never give it to me in the first place."

She looked down at the white lace and satin of the old wedding dress. She wanted to lie, to deny what she'd been feeling ever since Pierce had returned to Indianola. Maybe it was Dr. McGovern's words, or maybe it was the touch of her mother's necklace against her skin, but somehow she found the strength to tell the truth not only to Dooley, but to herself as well. "Yes, I do—I still love him. I don't think I ever stopped."

Finally he looked at her and cupped her face in his hands. "Then go for it, Brenna. Whether it's restoring the Majestic or giving love a chance, do what I think your mother and Dr. McGovern would tell you to do. Give it your whole heart. You'll never find happiness with your gears stuck in neutral." He gave her a sad grin. "I'm probably not as well-spoken as the old doctor, but I'd tell you to put the pedal to the metal and go for it. Sure, you might hit some bumps, or even crash, but man, what a ride."

"But what about us, Dooley? We're supposed to be getting married."

He kissed her softly on the forehead, then let her go. "Yeah, but that was mostly foolish dreaming on my part. You were just going along for the ride. I'm thinking it would be best for both of us if you finally took the wheel."

She looked closely at him. "I'm not sure if I should laugh or cry."

"Neither. Just give me a hug and let me leave quickly, before your sisters get ahold of me."

Brenna threw her arms around his neck, feeling the wool of his tuxedo under her cheek. "I love you, Dooley. I really do. You're my best friend and you always will be. And I know that one day you'll find an incredible woman who might come close to deserving you."

"Yep. Maybe." He clenched his lips together tightly and nodded, staring out the windshield again. "Do you need me to help you get out of the truck?"

She could tell he was keeping a tight rein on his emotions. She kissed his cheek as she pulled away. "I'll take care of it." She opened the door and swung her legs toward the opening. "Dooley?"

"Yeah?"

"You remember a while back when you were talking about maybe applying to LSU and finishing your degree? Well, I think you should go for it."

He grinned. "You think?"

"Definitely." She hopped to the ground, hugging her skirts around her, and shut the door. She called through the open window, "Good-bye, Doo."

Dooley nodded, put the truck in drive, and drove away, leaving her standing in the middle of the road in her mother's wedding dress and facing her sisters' curious stares. The warm afternoon sun beat down on her, and she tipped her face toward it, feeling the last of the numbness melt, the last fissure of ice shattering into a million little pieces.

Kathleen came down the porch steps toward her and put her hand on Brenna's arm. "What's wrong, Brenna? Where's Dooley going?"

She stepped away from her sister's grasp and walked toward the porch. "Dooley and I have decided not to get married."

Brenna heard Kathleen's quick footsteps following after her. "But why, Brenna? What happened? I thought you two were so happy together."

Brenna stopped at the front door and turned around to face her sisters. "Because marrying him was the easiest thing to do. I think I've come to discover that doing the easiest thing is not necessarily always the right thing. And I'm definitely not ready to marry anybody right now."

Claire put her foot down on the porch floor to stop the swing. "I'm sorry, Brenn. I guess this means we're going to need to renew our efforts to find you a husband."

Brenna looked at her sister with sudden clarity, her gaze shifting from sister to sister until it rested again on Claire. "Did you not understand what I just said? I'm not marrying Dooley or anybody else right now. I learned something about Mama today that's made me think differently for the first time in my life. I don't think I can go back to that girl who allowed all of y'all to run her life."

Her sisters began talking at once except for Mary Margaret, who sat on the top step with a quiet smile on her lips. Finally Kathleen shushed the others and asked, "What did you learn about Mama?"

Brenna rubbed her hands over her eyes. "I'm too tired to go into the details again, so I'll just give you bare facts for now. Mama and Dr. McGovern were supposed to get married, but then he went away to fight in the war. Our father decided to intercept their letters so that each thought themselves forgotten by the other. She was . . . she was pregnant. So when he asked her to marry him she said yes, knowing it was her only way out. And even though the baby was stillborn, she stayed with Daddy all those years." She felt the tears at the back of her throat. "And, until Kathleen was born, she was willing to go away with Dr.

McGovern. But he never knew it because he never opened the final let-ter she wrote to him asking him to come away with her."

Colleen rubbed her hands over her arms despite the warmth of the afternoon. "So what does this have to do with you and Dooley?"

Brenna wanted to groan in frustration. This wasn't the first time she'd ever been misunderstood by her sisters, but it seemed to be the first time that she actually cared.

"Don't you see? Both of them didn't fight hard enough. They al-lowed other people to manipulate their lives so that they could never have the one thing they really wanted. But they didn't give up on liv-ing, either. Instead, they found new directions in their lives. But what a huge, horrible loss. I don't want to live that way. I don't want to live a life filled with regret."

Kathleen approached her and placed an arm around her shoulders. "Come on home with me. I'll run you a nice warm bath and we can talk. Maybe after you've calmed down and had time to think, you'll re-alize your sisters and I have only your best interests at heart."

Brenna pushed away. "You're not listening to me. Have you not heard a word I said? Do you not care what *I* want?" She swept her arm to encompass all of her sisters. "Don't you have enough problems in your own lives that you can stay out of mine for a while?" She looked at Claire. "In case you haven't noticed, Mary Sanford doesn't want to do any more beauty pageants. If you'd actually ask her, like I did, she would tell you that she hates them and that she'd rather just stay home and hang out with her family. And PC would like that, too, because maybe then you'd pay him some attention. Just look at your scrap-book—it tells the whole story right there."

She held up her hand, indicating she wasn't finished, because she wasn't. She could hear her voice, and she wasn't going to silence it after all the trouble she'd gone through to bring it to the surface. "And, Colleen, you're spending too much time on eBay. Notice I didn't say *money,* because I don't think that's the issue here. When was the last time you sat down with Bill in the evening without your damned lap-top on and waiting for your bid? Your scrapbook is empty because you're too busy waiting on bids to put anything in it."

The sound of the squeaking porch swing chain interrupted the silence. Brenna turned around and pressed her forehead against the hard wood of the door. "And, Mary Margaret . . . my problems can't be solved by all the creams and vitamins you keep giving me. Let me try this on my own, okay? I know you want everybody's lives to be perfect like yours, but you've got to let us try on our own."

She heard the smile in Mary Margaret's voice. "You're right, Brenna. You're absolutely right. I just think that we've been in the habit for over thirty years of treating you as our baby sister. Maybe we do all need to take a step back and let you grow up."

Kathleen's voice sounded strained. "What about me, Brenn? What would you like me to do?"

Slowly Brenna turned around to face her oldest sister. "I want you to tell me the truth." She watched as Kathleen flinched, and she knew with a sinking heart that she'd been right. "Remember that time when I found you in the church and you were saying prayers for the dead? Long after I left, I kept hearing the words 'For those who have suffered disadvantage of harm through me.' You've always been the perfect mother, Kathleen. To your own children and to me. A wonderful wife to John, and a leader in the community for all of your charity works. I couldn't figure out why you of all people would be saying that prayer."

Brenna leaned back against the door, needing the support because for the first time in her life she felt as if she had only her own two legs to hold her up. "Then I thought of your scrapbook, where you have all those beautiful borders and page layouts, but you never seem to be able to tell where you should start." She pressed the heels of her hands into her eyes, wanting to stop but needing to continue. "And then when I was in the hospital room with Dr. McGovern and I realized that all those letters I've been reading over the last months had been from Mama, and that Daddy had been responsible for their being lost, it occurred to me that not only had he manipulated my life and Pierce's as well, but that he hadn't done it alone."

Mary Margaret stood, and Brenna felt even weaker when she realized that not one of her sisters registered surprise. "So Kathleen, what did you have against Pierce, or me, that you would help Daddy to break us apart?"

Kathleen's eyes didn't drop from Brenna's face, but her voice was quiet. "I didn't want to. I knew how happy you were. But Daddy knew something about me. Something that I didn't want anybody else to know. And he used that to bully me into helping him."

"What did he know? What could have been so bad that you would jeopardize my happiness to keep it a secret?"

Kathleen closed her eyes and dipped her chin. "That boy Paul—the one who used to hang out with us on Dauphin Island—he came to Indianola about a year after I was married. He'd searched for me, and when he'd finally found me I was already married. And I loved John; I didn't want to hurt him. But there's something about your first love, something that you can't really let go of or forget. Maybe because I knew it was forbidden. I . . . I had an affair. It only lasted a week before I realized that what I was doing was incredibly stupid and foolish and that I was jeopardizing a marriage to a man I loved very much. But Daddy found out about it—I'm not sure how. And he waited years until he could use the information."

"What about everybody else? You all knew. And you didn't do anything."

Mary Margaret spoke, her voice quiet and calm. "We didn't know about it until afterward—when it was too late. Pierce was gone and you were home pretending that you didn't love him anymore, and nothing any of us could say or do would make you try to find him. That was when Kathleen told us what had happened and made us all promise to take care of you, to make sure you were happy. To protect you from Daddy as much as we could." She glanced around at their three older sisters. "It doesn't seem that we did such a good job, does it?"

Kathleen took a step forward. "Oh, Brenna—I'm sorry. And I know that's a stupid word to cover all I did. But I truly am sorry. I wish I could go back and do it all over again, but I can't. I do daily penance and it's still not enough. I won't ask for your forgiveness—because what I did was unforgivable. I've tried to make it up to you every day, and I will continue—if you'll let me. But let me say one thing: Life isn't perfect. It's not supposed to be. We all make mistakes. You bash your head against the wall and you get hurt, but you walk away and make the best of it. And that's what makes it life, Brenna, not perfection. You'll never find happiness if you only expect to find it in a perfect life. Happiness is something we reach for while we try to learn from the disappoint-ments."

Brenna stood facing her sisters for a long moment, while feelings of betrayal, confusion, forgiveness, and exhaustion battled inside her head. She studied their beloved faces, seeing them, perhaps for the first time, as women in their own right instead of simply her older sisters. Women who made mistakes but managed to survive anyway.

Quietly Mary Margaret asked, "What are you going to do now?"

"I don't know," Brenna said, slowly turning the doorknob. She felt like a helium balloon that had lost all its air and sunk to the ground in its empty skin. "I really don't know." She walked through the doorway and let the door snap shut behind her.

CHAPTER 26

Brenna sat in her coat and scarf in the deck chair behind her rented beach house, the closed scrapbook in her lap. She didn't remember packing her car, then heading out to Dauphin Island. She only remembered a need to return to the place of her childhood before her mother died and she and her sisters had not yet become burdened by the passage of time.

She turned her face to the cool autumn breeze and stretched her legs. She wasn't sure how long she'd sat there, only that she'd been there since dawn and had witnessed the sun rise over the gulf, its bright, yellowy light chasing away the shadows that lay in the dark corners of the shore and in her own heart.

As she'd watched the sun slowly climb over the edge of the earth, she'd been rewarded with a long-lost memory of sitting on her mother's lap watching another sunrise. Her sisters had still been sleeping, but she and her mother were early risers, and her mother had bundled her in a blanket and sat with her outside, neither one of them saying a word until the first edges of dawn began to crack the blackened sky.

"Who makes the sun come up, Mama?"

"God does, Brenna. And He makes the moon rise and the stars shine every night."

"Why can't He make the sun shine all the time? I don't like the dark."

Brenna had felt the soft press of her mother's kiss against the back of her head. "I know, peanut. Not many of us do. But we wouldn't appreciate the brightness of the sun as much if we didn't have to go through the night first." Her mother had been silent for a long time, and Brenna knew that this was one of the times when it was best to be absolutely quiet. "You see, Brenn, sometimes we have to go through the darkness first before we can find the light. But the light is always there, just like the sun will always be there on the other side of the night. Will you remember that for me? If I'm not here to remind you, I want you to remember that no matter how dark the night, the sun will always greet you in the morning."

Brenna looked back down at her scrapbook, her fingers gently brushing across the cover as if it were an old friend in need of reassurance. Tilting her face toward the sun, she closed her eyes and felt for her mother's necklace under the scarf around her neck. She could almost believe that if she turned her head and opened her eyes, she would see her mother as she remembered her—looking beautiful in her bathing suit as she sat braiding Kathleen's hair, their soft laughter like another wave from the ocean to Brenna's young ears.

Brenna opened her eyes and then slowly opened the cover of the scrapbook, where the first page of antique envelopes rested inside their plastic sleeves. Her scrawling penmanship covered all the available space on the page, telling Brenna's story of what she'd hoped was found inside the letter. As her gaze skipped over the flowing words, she was surprised to find that she didn't want to read it. She thought of her mother's last unread letter to Dr. McGovern and the wondering that she'd clung to all these years finally lost its shine, leaving her with the prodding need simply to know.

With steady fingers she pulled the first envelope out of the sleeve and, without pausing, slid her fingernail into the corner, gently tearing the yellowed paper until it had been sliced from end to end. Holding tightly to her resolve, Brenna took the letter from the envelope, opened it against the flat page of the album, and began to read.

Brenna sat in the chair for several hours, reading letter after letter. At first she'd been awed by the fact that she was the only person besides the sender who had ever read them, but then the thought saddened her. Some of the stories contained within the fading envelopes were mundane events and simple endearments. Some were notices of births and weddings and new addresses. But there were also a few that contained only good-byes, departures to parts unknown as well as from this world. Brenna wept and used her scarf to wipe her eyes, unsure if she was crying for the sender of the letters whose words were never read, or for the recipient who had never read them.

When she'd reached the last letter she finally looked up and saw the water of the gulf again, its color darkened by the now gunmetal sky. She felt hollow somehow, as if someone had reached in and carved out her insides to make room for something else. She breathed in deeply, allowing the smell of rain and the taste of the ocean to fill her lungs like a memory, as if for the first time in a long while there was room for something inside of her besides the fear of disappointment.

A movement caught the corner of her eye and she turned her head. Pierce stood on a grassy dune not twenty feet away from her. He looked tired, as if he'd driven a long way without any sleep. She became aware of how the air around her had become static from the oncoming storm, and how her skin crackled with her old fear. But when she saw Pierce, her fear evaporated, becoming part of the electrified air.

The wind whipped her hair across her face. "How long have you been standing there?"

"Long enough." His gaze flickered to the opened letter in her hand that was now shaking in the wind, then back to her face.

"How did you find me?"

"Kathleen. Mrs. Grodin wouldn't let me into your apartment, so I went and got Kathleen. She, um, convinced Mrs. Grodin to let us in. Let me tell you, your oldest sister is not one to be messed with if one of her own is in trouble. Anyway, when Kathleen and I discovered that your suitcase and scrapbook were missing, she figured this is where you'd gone."

"Yeah, I guess she'd be the one to figure it out." The sky rumbled overhead as Brenna slowly folded the last letter and put it back inside the book. "She's always known me better than anybody else."

She stood and put the book on the chair and faced him in the wild wind that tasted of salt. He walked toward her, his shoes sinking into the soft sand, then stood facing her. "She told me about your dad, and how she helped him. About what she did to us. She's going to tell John everything now."

Brenna nodded. "I'm glad. It's hard to accept forgiveness if you never ask for it."

He raised an eyebrow, and she thought he was going to touch her, but his hands remained at his sides. "I never thought I'd hear you say something like that. The Brenna I knew would pretend that forgiveness wasn't necessary because nothing had happened."

"People change, Pierce. It just takes some people longer than others."

"You forgive her then?"

Brenna looked down at her feet, at the swirling sand around sun-whitened shells. "Yes. I do. I'm still angry, but I've suddenly found room inside of me for all sorts of new emotions."

He brushed his hand across the stubble on his cheek. "I know what you mean. I think I've finally forgiven my mother. Nathan told me that her last words were for him to find me and tell me that she loved me, and that she left only to save herself. Not to punish me or my father."

"Nathan?"

He smiled and nodded. "Yeah. He's my brother. My mother had him after she left here. She was trying to start over and was in a relationship with his father when he was born. They were still together when she died."

She tilted her head, looking up into his familiar face, where all the similarities between him and Nathan were now readily apparent. "Well, that certainly explains a lot. And I'm glad for you. You always wore your mother's absence like a bruise. I knew to avoid it because of how much it hurt you. I hope knowing that she didn't abandon you will give you peace."

"Me, too," he said softly. "When I told my dad about Nathan, we both decided to give Nathan my mother's piano, if that's all right. If Nathan decides to stay in Indianola, he might decide to leave it at the Majestic."

"Well, at least until the theater's sold or torn down. Just as long as he has a plan B. I certainly don't have much use for a piano at the moment."

Gently he lifted her hair and moved the scarf away from her neck. "Who are you wearing today?"

"Nobody. Just my mother's necklace. I felt that was the only thing I needed right now, so I'm giving the saints a rest." She looked tentatively up at him. "So why are you here?"

He fished inside his jacket pocket and pulled out a business card.

"I've been in New Orleans. Nathan gave me pictures of the old grand-father clock that stands in the Majestic's foyer. I have a contact at a nice antique store on Royal Street—I've sold quite a few of my dad's things to him—and I asked him about the clock."

For a moment she couldn't remember the clock. She had not revis-ited since the dark night of the grand reopening, and the images of the old clock against the windswept beach seemed to elude her.

Pierce continued. "I don't know a lot about antiques, but I knew that the clock was old and in good condition and might be worth some-thing."

A needle of lightning across the bruised sky punctuated the fissure of hope Brenna began to feel. "And was it?"

He didn't smile, but his eyes told her everything before he uttered a word. "Mr. Mercier thinks it could go at auction for anywhere between eighty and one hundred grand."

The sky cracked again with light as soft rolls of thunder swelled across the gulf. Neither of them moved. "One hundred thousand dollars?"

He did smile now. "It was apparently a lot older than I thought, and it also happens to be made by an old German clockmaker, and only two other examples of his work still exist. It's considered a masterpiece in craftsmanship. The other clock, by the way, was owned by the kaiser himself, and if it can be proved that your clock was, too, then it might fetch even more."

Her excitement was quickly replaced by the old doubt. Pierce seemed to sense this and closed the distance between them with a sin-gle step and gently grabbed her shoulders. "Do you know what this could mean?"

She didn't say anything, afraid that if she stared too closely at the sliver of hope, she'd be blinded as if she'd been looking into the sun.

Pierce continued: "You'll have the money to begin the repairs and restoration. You'll be able to make the Royal Majestic—what was it that you had on the sign?—'Indianola's premier entertainment venue' again. Nathan told me some of the plans you had—about doing a dinner the-ater, and date night with child care, and all the special entertainments people can't find in a cinemaplex. Something special and boutique-like.

You wouldn't need to compete with the big multiplexes because you'd have your own special market. It could work. It could really work. And now you have the money to at least start making it happen." He tilted his face down toward hers. "I could stay and help. I'll quit my job and become an investor in the Majestic. Maybe in exchange for being a business partner." His blue eyes flickered, and she leaned into him as his body sheltered her from the wind.

"But you always wanted to travel the world, to get as far from Indianola as you could."

"So did you, remember? And you still can. I'm not making you promise to live in Indianola for the rest of your life. The theater is your passion now—so save it. And once you're done and you get restless, then do something else. You once told me that life was full of possibilities. Prove it."

He seemed to sense her hesitation. "Brenna—this is your chance. Do you want your theater to survive? Then do it—take a leap of faith. But do it with both feet. Even if we fail, there won't be any regret, because we will at least have tried."

A cold drop of rain hit her cheek, reminding her of the approaching storm. She closed her eyes, imagining she could hear the voices of her mother and Pierce's father. *Find your passion. Take a leap of faith.* The wind pushed her closer to Pierce, and she reached her arms around his neck. The feel of his skin under her fingers warmed her, seeming to still the wind and her thoughts so that she could suddenly see everything clearly.

She threw back her head, wanting to yell up to the sky and to the gulls swirling around in the wind. Instead she held tightly to Pierce and said, "Three things. First"—she brought her lips up to his and kissed him—"I love you. I never stopped. Second, yes. Yes, we will restore the Majestic to its former glory and make it one heck of a fun place to be." She kissed him again as the raindrops fell heavier and his arms tightened around her.

He pulled back. "What's the third thing?"

"That if I fail, I won't regret having tried." She bit her lip.

He kissed her hard as the sky seemed to open up, deluging them with rain like a baptism of forgiveness and new hope. With his arm around her he began to run with her up the dunes toward the house, but then stopped. "Your book. Your book is getting wet."

She started to return to the sodden chair but held back. "No. I don't need it anymore."

"But the letters—they'll be ruined."

Brenna kissed him again, tasting rain and gray sky and open water. "It doesn't matter. None of that matters."

He grabbed her hand and pulled her with him, and she glanced back only once at her old scrapbook, where the ink from the letters of the dead smeared and ran across faded pages, dripping off the edges of the album into the sand, then swirled out into the gulf.

PHOTO BY PICTURE PERFECT PHOTOGRAPHY

KAREN WHITE is the author of six previous books. She lives with her family near Atlanta, Georgia. Visit her Web site at www.karen-white.com.

LEARNING

to

BREATHE

KAREN WHITE

This Conversation Guide is intended to enrich the
individual reading experience, as well as encourage us
to explore these topics together—because books,
and life, are meant for sharing.

A CONVERSATION WITH KAREN WHITE

Q. What was your inspiration for Learning to Breathe?

A. As is the case with all of my books, the inspiration comes from several sources, usually appearing years apart, that somehow come together in my mind to inspire a story. The setting came from the small town in Mississippi where my mother and her four sisters and brother grew up. The idea of the unopened letters came inadvertently from my dad, who collects all sorts of things, including old stamps that sometimes come still attached to the envelope. He gave me one such envelope, and I was amazed to see that it had never been opened. I was intrigued, wondering why this letter had never been opened although it had been sent nearly one hundred years before.

The idea of never taking a risk for fear of disappointment came from my daughter. When she was very young, she was obsessed with balloons. Loved them, could never get enough of them. And then, all of a sudden, she stopped wanting them. When waiters at restaurants offered to get her one to tie on her chair, she'd refuse. When I asked her why, she told me, "Because it will lose its air and I won't have it anymore." I don't think she was more than five, but it had a profound effect on me, and I've wondered ever since where an otherwise happy child could have figured out in a small way that it's not necessarily better to love and lose than to have never loved at all.

Q. Brenna and Pierce share a very tumultuous past, full of pain as well as love. Did you know how their relationship would turn out when you began their story?

A. I wasn't really sure how they would end up in terms of a relationship with each other. They both had so much growing to do, and so much pain to work through, I wasn't totally convinced that by the end of the book they could figure out their relationship, too. I knew I would give my readers a satisfactory ending, though—just not necessarily a "ride-off-into-the-sunset-happily-ever-after" ending. As long as there is light and hope at the end of my book, I feel as if I've done my job.

Q. Is there a particular message you try to send readers with each of your books? If so, what is the message from this book?

A. Since my school days and my struggles in English classes to understand the underlying theme of all the literature I read, I've always looked for whatever message the author was trying to send. In my books, too, I try to do more than tell a story with interesting characters. A lot of times, I'm not initially aware of what message I'm trying to get across. Sometimes it's something I'm struggling with personally and writing the book helps me to explore all the facets of life.

In *Learning to Breathe,* I found the recurrent themes of the importance of family—however you define it to be; forgiveness—both of others and oneself; and healing. In all of my books, the protagonist finds herself at a crossroads in her life, unable to move on because of the chains of her past. My books explore finding one's inner strength to forgive the past and move on.

Q. Brenna and her sisters get together for a weekly scrapbooking session. Is scrapbooking something you have always been interested in? Do you have your own scrapbooking group?

A. In my last two books, my protagonists did all sorts of interesting things: cooking, baking, quilting, swimming—all things that I'm quite ignorant of. Finally I was able to use something that I'm completely familiar with! I have been an avid scrapbooker for about ten years and find it an excellent outlet for any latent "Martha Stewartesque" tendencies I might have. I do belong to a scrapbooking group, and we meet once a month, so it's a great social outlet, too.

A large part of scrapbooking deals with preserving pictures and your family's history. Although I do a relatively good job of placing the pictures and designing my pages in a fairly attractive way, I'm horrible at what we scrapbookers call "journaling"—which is basically writing descriptive boxes of text to describe in detail what is going on in the lives of the people captured in the photos. It's funny that although I spend my life writing, in my scrapbooks, I have pretty much just written the basics: time, date, event and the names of the people in the pictures. I guess it's a bit like the shoemaker's children going barefoot!

Q. Each of your books deals with relationships, not only those we have with other people, but our relationship with ourselves. Which of your characters would you say is most reflective of you as a person?

A. I get asked this question a lot, and I have to say that each of my protagonists really exhibits characteristics of my alter ego; in other words, they're who I would like to be in terms of being stronger, smarter, more patient and more heroic in difficult situations. I don't think I could write a book with a fictional me—it would be much too boring!

Q. The theater you describe, the Royal Majestic, sounds like a wonderful place. Is it based on a real place?

A. I'm a card-carrying member of the National Trust, an organization that seeks to protect the buildings, sites, and other structures that form our collective history. This stems from a fascination with old buildings that I have had and cultivated since I was a young girl.

In most of my books, an historical home takes center stage, almost as if it were another major character. In *Learning to Breathe*, I decided to try something different and showcase another type of structure—the old movie theater. In *Preservation* magazine, the official publication of the National Trust, they've featured in the past the fragile nature of these glorious buildings that once were the centerpiece of Main Street America and are being demolished one by one. I guess this was my soapbox stand to show what beautiful treasures these old buildings are and how there are ways to make them profitable again without tearing them down.

Q. There are several different stories woven together throughout Brenna's story. Do you find it difficult to write such complex stories? What is the hardest part for you?

A. My memory not being what it once was, I find that I'm the note-writing queen. I'm not a big planner when it comes to my writing, but for this book—not only with all the different stories going on at one time, but also the sheer number of characters—I had to write a lot of "notes to self" to keep everything straight. And I still got things wrong! Thank goodness for a really great copy editor, who caught a lot of the little mistakes that I somehow missed.

But I enjoy reading complex stories where seemingly unrelated stories converge at the end and everything makes sense. It takes a lot of trust on the reader's part to keep going when things seem to be so unrelated. It's the author's job to make sure she pulls through to give a satisfying (and logical) conclusion to the story. I love stories that come full circle, where mistakes of the past are somehow redeemed in the future, so that lessons learned can make a big impact on the lives of the people remaining. I think I've done that with *Learning to Breathe*.

Q. Classic movies are a recurring element in the novel, and they play an important role in the relationship between Brenna and Pierce. Are you a fan of classic movies as well? What is your favorite?

A. Back in 1975, my parents bought me a little black-and-white television set for my bedroom. This was against everything they believed in, but it was a trade-off for a deal we made about my taking their old bedroom furniture for my room while they bought a new bedroom set. Anyway, being the night owl that I still am, I would flip on the TV long after I was supposed to be asleep and watch old movies. To this day, I remember being riveted to *Jezebel* (with Henry Fonda and Bette Davis) and *Casablanca* (with Humphrey Bogart and Ingrid Bergman). I think it was back then that I figured out that they really don't make things like they used to—especially movies. The stories were just so much larger than life, with bigger scope and drama than you see today. They were an escape from real life, and going to the movies back in the days of the Royal Majestic really was an event.

As far as my favorite classic movie is concerned, *Gone With the Wind* will always be my number one regardless of how many times I watch it. It's one of those rare movies based on a book that was actually as good as the book. And I still cry when Melanie dies and when Rhett walks out on Scarlett for the last time.

Q. Brenna's nephew Timmy, is a fascinating little boy. What or who was your inspiration for him?

A. Probably my daughter. That whole balloon incident when she was a child really made an impression on me. She's not really like that so much anymore (although every once in a while, I'll see evidence of her aversion to disappointment), but I thought it would be interesting to create a fictional child who exhibited this behavior, and then see how he or she "solved" it and became a catalyst to Brenna, who, despite her years, had not been able to work through it for herself.

QUESTIONS FOR DISCUSSION

1. How does scrapbooking affect these women? What do their individual scrapbooks tell us about them?

2. At several points in the novel, Brenna remarks to herself how alike she and Timothy are. In what ways is this true? How are they different?

3. Why does Brenna agree to marry Dooley even though she doesn't love him? What does Dooley say his reasons are for wanting to marry Brenna?

4. Why does Brenna's sister Kathleen keep Pierce and Brenna apart? How does this relate to her relationship with her husband?

5. What is the significance of the book of poems that Kathleen has?

6. Why does Nathan express animosity toward Pierce? What makes Nathan change his assessment of Pierce later?

7. What does the author mean when she refers to "learning to breathe"?

CONVERSATION GUIDE

8. Discuss the ways motherhood is represented in the novel. Are they positive or negative?

9. What is the symbolism of Brenna's collection of unopened letters?

10. When does Brenna learn that Kathleen helped her father keep her from Pierce? How does she come to forgive her?

11. Explain Brenna's outlook on life. How is this related to her relationship with her father?

12. Why does Brenna's father keep Dr. McGovern's letters hidden? How does this come to affect the present?

13. Why does Pierce come back to Indianola in the first place?

READ ON FOR A PREVIEW OF
KAREN WHITE'S NEXT WONDERFUL NOVEL

A YEAR OF RAIN

COMING IN 2008 FROM NAL ACCENT

For thousands of years the Atlantic Ocean has beaten against the beach of my childhood, its watery fingers stealing more and more of the soft silted sand, grabbing at the estuaries and creeks of the South Carolina lowcountry, leaving us with the detritus of old forests, battered dunes, and bleeding loss.

But the shore remains, the sand itself testament to survival; the remnants of large rocks crushed into grains of sand. Just as our family has dared to claim ownership of a parcel of shoreline and ocean for generations, our house defying the elements of nature. Strong winds buffet the sea oats and tall dune grasses, tossing sand and seabirds where they will, winding my sister's golden hair into sunlit spirals of silk until it becomes the only good memory I have of her; the only memory I allowed myself to keep. But the wind pushes on; pushes at the shoreline, at our old house, and at me. Yet somehow, we remain.

I hadn't been back for over eight years; eight years while I tried to forget the sting of salt water in my eyes, the slippery feel of the tide pulling the sand out from under my feet. Of being underwater and not able to breathe as water rolled over me, cascaded around me in a watery rug, sucking the air from my lungs. And the feel of my mother's hands slowly letting me go.

I parked my car on the driveway of crushed rock and shell, and left the radio on, not yet ready to hear the ocean again. The white clapboard house, owned by my mother's family ever since the Revolution, had changed little. Only on closer inspection did I begin to see my sister's artistic hand. The once solid green porch swing now sported leopard spots, and the front walk and porch were covered with brightly hued flowers, their garish blooms radiant and mocking, as if they knew they had once been outlawed by our grandfather. Blatant beauty and bright colors were a sin to him, regardless of the fact that the Creator he worshiped had also created them.

A tire swing hung from the ancient oak tree in the front yard, its frantic movements evidence of recent occupation. Reluctantly I turned off the radio and took my key from the ignition before exiting the car. I glanced around, hoping to catch sight of Gil, the eight-year-old nephew I had never seen, but only the empty yard and the distant sound of the ocean greeted me. I glanced up at the windows on the right side above the porch roof as a shadow seemed to move behind the glass. I stared at them for a long time, wondering if it had been the passing of a cloud reflected in the glass and remembering my sister sneaking out of her window onto the roof, then shimmying down the drainpipe that ran from the roof to the front porch.

I'd never tattled on her. Looking back, I suppose that even then I'd known that her self-destructive behavior would simply find a more dangerous outlet. Watching her run off the first time into the darkened yard with a shadow boy, I had felt the final snap of the invisible cord that had attached us since my birth. It had first started to fray on the day our mother died and we'd been sent to live with her father. We were given separate rooms, and my sister had become a beautiful stranger who regarded me with silent eyes and weeping shoulders. My grief for my mother and my sister found no succor with our grandfather; according to him, we Maitlands were meant to suffer. It's what happens, he explained, when a man curses God. His children, his children's children, and their children would be cursed. From what I have seen of this family, I would have to agree that he's right.

Slowly I walked to the back of the house, a swarm of gnats following like persistent memories, down to the gravel path that led to the dunes, and finally beyond them, the Atlantic Ocean. I stopped on the old railroad tie that marked the end of the path and turned my face to the wind, stilling the first panic at the smell of salt water. I clenched my eyes, and when I opened them again, I saw Diana. She sat on an old Adirondack chair with her feet in the surf, swaddled in a quilt despite the pressing heat of the midafternoon sun. She wore her hair loose, its color not diminished by time or the miles of asphalt that had separated us for so long. Miles and years become suddenly invisible when you find yourself back where you started from, as if you've learned nothing and you are once again the person you once were.

She was watching a sailboat as it headed out into deeper water, its wind indicator on the mast pointing northwesterly in a stiff breeze. Two sailors, a man and a woman in bright yellow Windbreakers, stood in the cockpit, their faces turned into the wind. I moved through the cloying sand so that I stood behind her, not speaking.

"Do you remember how it feels?" She spoke without looking at me, her words deceptively soft.

I watched the sailboat bobbing on the waves as if nodding, the woman moving to adjust a sail. I could almost feel the sleek teak beneath my feet, the damp crispness of the white sails through my fingers. Hear the rushing water beneath the bow and feel the wind blessing my face. "No," I said. "I don't remember at all."

She faced me for the first time, the old familiar sneer darkening her once beautiful face. I had never been able to lie to her; although she was three years older, we had been as twins, inseparable as if we had shared our mother's womb, felt the rhythm of our mother's heart at the same time. Maybe we had known, in that dark corner of heaven our preacher grandfather said babies came from, that being born into our family would require an ally.

Diana reached up with paint-stained fingers and pushed her hair away from skin that appeared too sallow, too tightly aligned over jutting bones for a woman just thirty-one. I swallowed a gasp; her resemblance to our mother was unmistakable now. Long ago, when we were a normal family of mother, father, and two daughters, we had taken delight in the fact that I looked just like our father and Diana had been a reflection of our mother. But now, that reflection included all the demons of memory, and I took a step away from her as the old fears reached out and grabbed me like grasping seaweed in the darkest part of the ocean.

"Is that why you moved to Arizona? It's the goddamn desert, Marnie. I thought you, of all people, would be a little more creative than that." She fished a cigarette pack and a lighter out from under the quilt. With shaking hands she put a cigarette in her mouth and lit it, then took a deep drag. "It didn't make you forget, though, did it? You still remember how it feels."

A large wave broke near the shoreline, sending its frothing edge with bubbling fingers toward me. I jumped back and Diana laughed. "You've been living in the desert too long. Welcome back." She blew out a puff of smoke into the air between us, like the ghost of unspoken words.

"I came because of Gil."

She looked at me again, her eyes flat, her cigarette stilled in her hand. "I know." She turned from me, examining the tall mast of the fading sailboat again, as if hoping to see something new. "I wouldn't expect you to come back for me." She took another drag from her cigarette, her hand shaking so badly she could barely make it to her mouth.

"Quinn called me," I said, feeling embarrassed that I hadn't seen the need to lie. "Is he up at the house with Gil?"

Pale green eyes studied me, and it was as if I were looking into my mother's face. "There's nothing you can do for us here, Marnie. Go back to your desert, to your months without rain, and leave us alone. We don't need you here, and I don't want you here. So go home."

"I am home," I said, surprising myself with the words. It had been eight years since I'd called this place by the ocean home.

She stood suddenly, the quilt falling into the sand and water. I stared in horror at her legs, merely bones with flesh clinging to them, a large white bandage bisecting the upper quadrant of her thigh. *It's been over a month since the accident. Why is it still bandaged?* I looked up into my sister's eyes, hoping to see anything but the defiance I found there. Without a word, Diana turned and walked away from me down the beach, leaving only a trail of cigarette smoke and more hurt than could be contained in the mere vastness of the ocean.

I closed my eyes, wanting to see nothing but endless miles of sand and asphalt, the outstretched arms of the saguaro cactus and the rough-hewn crags of the distant mountains of my adopted home. Instead I heard the crash of the waves against the ancient shore as I turned my back on the unforgiving ocean and headed up over the dunes and back to my grandfather's house to face whatever curse God had decided to visit upon the latest generation of Maitlands.